THE FLAG CAPTAIN

In the spring of 1797, Captain Richard Bolitho brings the 100-gun *Euryalus* home to Falmouth to be flagship of the hastily-formed squadron which has been chosen to make the first British re-entry to the Mediterranean for nearly a year. As flag captain, Bolitho is made to contend with the unyielding attitudes of his new admiral, as well as the devious requirements of the civilian adviser to the squadron. England is still stunned by the naval mutiny at Spithead, in which Bolitho's admiral was personally involved, and as the squadron sets sail the air is already alive with rumour of an even greater uprising in the ships at the Nore. Only when the squadron is drawn into a bloody embrace with the enemy does the admiral see the strength in Bolitho's trust and care for his men—but by then it is almost too late for any of them.

*   *   *

The author, Alexander Kent, has always had a great interest in naval affairs, particularly in the ships and men of the eighteenth century. As a boy he was often to be found exploring Nelson's old flagship, *Victory*, at Portsmouth. At the outbreak of war he joined the navy and served in the Battle of the Atlantic as well as in the Mediterranean and Normandy campaigns. He is an acknowledged master of the sea story, and his hero, Captain Richard Bolitho, has been acclaimed as a strong character and the only true successor to Hornblower.

Also by
ALEXANDER KENT

★

TO GLORY WE STEER
FORM LINE OF BATTLE!
ENEMY IN SIGHT!

THE
FLAG CAPTAIN

★

ALEXANDER KENT

THE
COMPANION BOOK CLUB
LONDON

This edition, published in 1972 by
The Hamlyn Publishing Group Ltd,
is issued by arrangement with
Hutchinson & Co. (Publishers) Ltd.

THE COMPANION BOOK CLUB

The Club is not a library; all books are the
property of members. There is no entrance fee
or any payment beyond the low Club price of
each book. Details of membership will gladly
be sent on request.

Write to:
    The Companion Book Club,
    Borough Green, Sevenoaks, Kent

Made and printed in Great Britain
for the Companion Book Club
by Odhams (Watford) Ltd.
600871509
250-8.72

For the Captain's Lady,
with love

The spirits of your fathers
Shall start from every wave;
For the deck it was their field of fame,
And ocean was their grave.

CAMPBELL

1. Landfall

AS SIX BELLS of the morning watch chimed out from the forecastle belfry, Captain Richard Bolitho walked from beneath the poop and paused momentarily beside the compass. A master's mate who was standing close to the great double wheel said quickly, 'Nor' west by north, sir,' and then dropped his eyes as Bolitho glanced at him.

It was as if they could all sense his tension, he thought briefly, and although they might not understand its cause, wanted to break him from it.

He strode out on to the broad quarterdeck and crossed to the weather side. Around him, without looking, he could see his officers watching him, gauging his mood, waiting to begin this new day.

But the ship had been in continuous commission for eighteen months, and most of her company, excluding those killed by combat or injury at sea, were the same men who had sailed with him from Plymouth on an October morning in 1795. It was more than enough time for them to realize that he needed to be left alone for these first precious moments of each successive day.

The wet sea mist which had dogged them for most of the night while they had edged slowly up the Channel was still with them, thicker than ever. It swirled around the black criss-cross of shrouds and rigging and seemed to cling to the hull like dew. Beyond the nettings with their neatly stowed hammocks the sea was heaving in a deep offshore swell, but was quite unbroken in the low breeze. It was dull. The colour of lead.

Bolitho shivered slightly and clasped his hands behind him beneath his coat-tails and looked up, beyond the great braced yards to where a rear-admiral's flag flapped wetly from the mizzen masthead. It was hard to believe that up there somewhere the sky would be bright blue, warm and comforting, and on this May morning the sun should already be touching the approaching land.

His land. Cornwall.

7

He turned and saw Keverne, the first lieutenant, watching him, waiting for the right moment.

Bolitho forced a smile. 'Good morning, Mr Keverne. Not much of a welcome, it appears.'

Keverne relaxed slightly. 'Good morning, sir. The wind remains sou' west, but there is little of it.' He fidgeted with his coat buttons and added, 'The master thinks we might anchor awhile. The mist should clear shortly.'

Bolitho glanced towards the short, rotund shape of the ship's sailing master. His worn, heavy coat was buttoned up to his several chins, so that in the strange light he looked like a round blue ball. He was prematurely grey, even white haired, and had it tied at the nape of his neck in an old fashioned queue, giving it the appearance of a quaint powdered wig of a country squire.

'Well, Mr Partridge.' Bolitho tried again to put some warmth into his tone. 'It is not like you to show such reluctance for the shore?'

Partridge shuffled his feet. 'Never sailed into Falmouth afore, Cap'n. Not in a three-decker, that is.'

Bolitho shifted his gaze to the master's mate. 'Go forrard and see there are two good leadsmen in the chains. Make sure the leads are well armed with tallow. I want no false reports from them.'

The man hurried away without a word. Bolitho knew that like the others he would know what to do without being told, just as he was aware he was only giving himself more time to think and consider his motives.

Why should he not take the master's advice and anchor? Was it recklessness or conceit which made him continue closer and closer towards the invisible shore?

Mournfully a leadsman's voice echoed from forward. 'By th' mark seven!'

Above the deck the sails stirred restlessly and shone in the mist like oiled silk. Like everything else they were dripping with moisture, and hardly moved by the sluggish breeze from across the larboard quarter.

Falmouth. Perhaps that was the answer to his uncertainty and apprehension. For eighteen months they had been employed on blockade and later the watch over the southern approaches of Ireland. A French attempt to invade Ireland and start an uprising had been expected weekly, yet when it

8

had come just five months ago the British blockade had been caught unready. The invasion attempt had failed more because of bad weather and the French fleet being scattered than any real pressure from the overworked patrols.

Feet clattered in the passageway beneath the poop and he knew it was the admiral's servant going to attend his master in the great cabin.

It was strange how after all that had gone before they were coming here, to Falmouth, Bolitho's home. It was as if fate had overrun everything which both duty and the Admiralty could muster.

'. . . an' a quarter less seven!' The leadsman's call was like a chant.

Bolitho began to pace slowly up and down the weather side, his chin lowered into his neckcloth.

Rear-Admiral Sir Charles Thelwall, whose flag flapped so limply from the masthead, had been aboard for over a year. Even when he had first hoisted his flag he had been a sick man. Old for his rank, and weighed down with the responsibility of an overworked squadron, his health had deteriorated rapidly in the fog and piercing cold of the last winter months. As his flag captain Bolitho had done what he could to ease the pressures on the tired, wizened little admiral, and it had been painful to watch as day by day he fought to overcome the illness which was destroying him.

At last the ship was returning to England to replenish stores and make good other shortages. Sir Charles Thelwall had already despatched a sloop with his reports and needs, and also made known the state of his own illness.

'By th' mark six!'

So when the ship dropped anchor the admiral would go ashore for the last time. It was unlikely he would live long enough to enjoy it.

And then there was the other twist of fate. Two days earlier, as the ship had tacked ponderously clear of the Wolf Rock in readiness for her passage up the Channel, they had been met by a fast moving brig with new orders for the admiral.

He had been in his cot at the time, racked by his dry, deadly cough which left his handkerchief spotted with blood after each convulsion, and had asked Bolitho to read the despatch which had been passed across in the brig's jolly-boat.

The orders stated in the briefest of terms that His Britannic

9

Majesty's Ship *Euryalus* would proceed with all despatch to Falmouth Bay and not to Plymouth as previously arranged. There to receive the flag of Sir Lucius Broughton, Knight of the Bath, Vice-Admiral of the White, and await further instructions.

Once the receipt of the orders had been acknowledged the brig had gone about with undue haste and sped away again. That was also strange. Two vessels meeting for the first time, and with the country in the grip of a war growing in fury and intensity, made even the smallest item of news valuable to the men who kept constant sea watch in all weathers and against any odds.

Even the brig's approach had been cautious, but Bolitho had grown used to such treatment. For the *Euryalus* was a prize ship, and as French in appearance as would be expected from a vessel only four years old.

All the same, it was one more thing to put a finer edge on his sense of uncertainty.

'By th' mark six!'

He turned and said sharply, 'Bring that lead aft, Mr Keverne, and set the other to work at once.'

A barefooted seaman padded on to the quarterdeck and knuckled his forehead. Then he held out the great, dripping lead and watched as Bolitho dug his fingers into the bottom of it, where the inserted plug of tallow gleamed dully with what looked like pink coral.

Bolitho rubbed the small fragments on his palm and said absently, 'The Six Hogs.'

Behind him he heard Partridge murmur admiringly, 'If I'd not seen it I'd never 'ave believed it.'

Bolitho said, 'Alter course a point to larboard, if you please, and pipe the hands to the braces.'

Keverne coughed and then asked quietly, 'What are the Six Hogs, sir?'

'Sandbars, Mr Keverne. We are now about two miles due south of St Anthony Head.' He smiled, suddenly ashamed for allowing the apparent miracle to continue. 'They call the sandbars by that name, although I do not know why. But they are covered with these small stones, and have been so since I can remember.'

He swung round and watched as a sliver of sunlight pierced the swirling mist and touched the quarterdeck with pale gold.

Partridge and the others would have been less in awe of his navigation had he been wrong in his calculations. Or perhaps it was more instinct than calculations. Even before he had been bundled off to sea as a gawky twelve-year-old midshipman he had learned every cove and inlet around Falmouth and several miles in either direction as well.

Even so, memory could play tricks, and it would have been small comfort to the admiral or his own prospects if the coming day had found *Euryalus* aground and dismasted in sight of his home town.

The big topsails flapped loudly and the deck tilted to a sudden pressure of wind, and like an army of departing ghosts the mist seeped through the shrouds and clear of the ship.

Bolitho paused in his pacing and stared fixedly at the widening panorama of green coastline which reached away on either bow, growing and coming alive in the sunlight.

There, almost balanced on the jib-boom, or so it appeared, was St Anthony's beacon, usually the first sight of home to a returning sailor. Slightly to larboard, hunched on the headland, its grey bulk defying the sun and its warmth, was Pendennis Castle, guarding the harbour entrance and Carrick Road as it had down the centuries.

Bolitho licked his lips. They were dry, and not merely from salt air.

'Lay a course to the anchorage, Mr Partridge. I am going to pay my respects to the admiral.'

Partridge stared at him and then touched his battered hat. 'Aye, aye, sir.'

Below the poop it was cool and dark after the quarterdeck, and as he strode aft towards the companion which led to the admiral's day cabin Bolitho was still pondering over what might lie in store for him and his command.

As he ran lightly down the companion to the middle deck and past two small ship's boys who were busily polishing brass hinges on some of the cabin doors, he recalled with sudden clarity how mixed his feelings had once been about assuming command of the *Euryalus*. It was common enough to take prize ships and put them to work against their old masters, it was more common still to let them keep their original names. Sailors often said it was bad luck to change a ship's title, but then seafaring people said a lot of things more from habit than known fact.

She had once been named *Tornade*, flagship of the French admiral Lequiller who had broken the British blockade to cross the Atlantic as far west as the Caribbean, there to cause havoc and destruction until finally run to earth by an inferior British squadron in the Bay of Biscay. She had struck her colours to Bolitho's own ship, the old *Hyperion*, but not before she had pounded the worn two-decker almost into a floating wreck.

The Lords of the Admiralty had decided to rename Bolitho's great prize, mostly it seemed because Lequiller had outwitted them on more than one occasion. It was strange, Bolitho had thought, that those who controlled His Majesty's Navy from the heights of Admiralty seemed to know so little of ships and men that such changes were thought necessary.

Only the *Euryalus*'s new figurehead was English. It had been carved with great care by Jethro Miller at St Austell in Cornwall, as a gift from the people of Falmouth to one of their most popular sons. Miller had been *Hyperion*'s carpenter and had lost a leg in that last terrible battle. But he still retained his skill, and the figurehead which stared with cold blue eyes from the bows with shield and upraised sword had somehow given the *Euryalus* a small change of personality. It bore little resemblance perhaps to the hero of the Siege of Troy, but it was enough to strike fear into the heart of any enemy who might see it and know what was about to follow.

For the great three-decker was a force to be reckoned with. Built at Brest by one of the best French yards, she had all the modern refinements and improvements to hull design and sail plan that any captain could wish.

From figurehead to taffrail she measured two hundred and twenty-five feet, and within her two thousand ton bulk she carried not only a hundred guns, including a lower battery of massive thirty-two pounders, but a company of some eight hundred officers, seamen and marines. She could, when handled properly, act and speak with authority and devastating effect.

When she had commissioned, Bolitho had been made to take every man he could get to crew her constant demands and requirements. Pale-skinned debtors and petty thieves from the jails, a few trained men from other ships laid up for repairs, as well as the usual mixture of characters brought in by the dreaded pressgangs. For they had been hard times, and an ever-demanding fleet had already sifted and poached through every port and village in search of men, and with growing fears of a French invasion no captain could allow himself the luxury of choice when it came to gathering hands to fight his ship.

There had been volunteers too, mostly Cornishmen, who knew Bolitho's name and reputation even although many of them had never laid eyes on him in their lives.

It should have been a great step forward for Bolitho, as he had told himself often enough. The *Euryalus* was a fine ship, and a new one. Not only that, she represented an open acknowledgement of his past record as well as the obvious stepping stone to advancement. It was something dreamed about by every ambitious sea officer, and in a Service where promotion often depended on the death of an officer's superior, the *Euryalus* must have been watched with both admiration and envy by those less fortunate.

But to Bolitho she meant something more, something very personal. While he had been searching the Caribbean and then driving back again to the last embrace in the Bay of Biscay he had been tortured by the memory of his wife, Cheney, who had died in Cornwall, without him, when she most needed him. In his heart he knew he could have done nothing. The coach had overturned and she had been killed, and their unborn child also. His being there would have made no difference. And yet it still haunted him, had made him withdraw from his officers and seamen to a point when he had been tormented by loneliness and loss.

And now he was back again in Falmouth. The big grey stone house would be there waiting for him as always. As it had for all the others before him, and yet it would now seem even more empty than ever.

A marine sentry stamped to attention outside the cabin door, his eyes fixed on some point above Bolitho's shoulder. Like a toy soldier with his blank expression and scarlet coat.

Sunlight lanced through the great stern windows, throwing countless reflections across the deckhead and dark furniture, and he saw the admiral's grey-haired secretary checking papers and documents before stowing them in a long metal box. He made to rise from his seat but Bolitho shook his head and walked slowly to the opposite side of the cabin. He could hear the admiral moving about his sleeping cabin, and imagined him contemplating these last hours of his presence aboard his own flagship.

A mirror hung on the bulkhead and Bolitho paused to study

himself, tugging his coat into position as if under the critical stare of a senior officer at an inspection.

He still could not get used to the new-style uniform, the additional encumbrance of gold epaulettes to denote his rank of post-captain. It seemed wrong that in a country struggling in the worst war of her history men could create and design new forms of personal adornment when their minds would have been better used in thinking up ideas for fighting and winning battles.

He reached up and touched the rebellious lock of hair which hung down above his right eye. Beneath it, and running up into his hairline, was the familiar cruel scar, the constant reminder of his closest meeting with death. But the hair was still black, without even a strand of grey to mark his forty years, twenty-eight of which had been spent at sea. He smiled slightly, his mouth softening and giving his tanned features a youthful recklessness once again as he turned away, dismissing what he saw as he would a satisfactory subordinate.

The door of the sleeping cabin opened and the little admiral walked unsteadily into a swaying patch of sunlight.

Bolitho said, 'We will be anchoring within the hour, Sir Charles. I have made arrangements for you to go ashore whenever is convenient.' He thought suddenly of the many miles of rutted roads, the pain and discomfort, before the admiral could reach his home in Norfolk. 'My own house is of course at your disposal for as long as you wish.'

'Thank you.' The admiral eased his shoulders inside the heavy dress coat. 'To die in battle against your country's enemies is one thing.' He sighed and left the rest unsaid.

Bolitho watched him gravely. He had grown very fond of him, and had come to admire his controlled dedication to others, his humanity towards the men of their small squadron.

He said, 'We will miss you, sir.' He was sincere, yet very aware of the inadequacy of his words. 'I, above all, owe you a great deal, as I think you know.'

The admiral rose to his feet and walked round the desk. Against Bolitho's tall slim figure he seemed suddenly older and defenceless against what lay ahead of him.

After a pause he said, 'You owe me nothing. But for your mind and your integrity I would have been discarded within weeks of hoisting my flag.' He held up one hand. 'No, hear what I have to say. Many flag captains would have used my

14

weakness to enhance their own reputations, to show their indispensability before their commanders-in-chief in higher places. If you had spent less time in fighting your country's enemies and giving your utmost to your subordinates, you would almost certainly have been given the promotion you so richly deserve. It is no shame that you have turned your back on personal advancement, but it *is* England's loss. Perhaps your new admiral will appreciate as I do what sort of a man you are, and be more able to ensure . . .' He broke off in a fit of coughing, the soiled handkerchief balled against his mouth until the convulsion had passed.

He said thickly, 'See that my servant and secretary are sent ashore in good time. I will come on deck in a moment.' He looked away. 'But just for a while I wish to be left alone.'

Bolitho walked back to the quarterdeck in thoughtful silence. Overhead the sky had cleared and was bright blue, while the sea below the nearest headland was agleam with countless dazzling reflections. It would make the admiral's departure all the harder to bear, he decided.

He looked along the length of the upper deck, at the assembled seamen at the braces and at the topmen already strung out along the yards, dark against the clear sky. With all but her topsails and jib clewed up the *Euryalus* was barely making headway, her broad hull tipping easily as if to test the depth of water beneath her keel. Those not immediately employed were watching the shore, the neat houses and green hills. The latter were dotted with minute cows, and there were sheep moving aimlessly beneath the castle walls.

A great silence seemed to hang over the ship, broken only by the slap of water against the weather side, the regular creak of rigging and murmur of canvas aloft. Most of the men would not be allowed ashore, and they knew it. Nevertheless, it was a homecoming, something which every sailor knew, even if he could not explain it.

Bolitho took a glass from a midshipman and studied the shoreline, feeling the familiar drag to his heart. He wondered if his housekeeper and his steward, Ferguson, knew of his coming, if they were there now watching the three-decker's slow approach.

'Very well, Mr Keverne. You may wear ship.'

The first lieutenant who had been watching him intently lifted his speaking trumpet and the moment of peace was past.

'Lee braces there! Hands wear ship!'

Feet scurried across the planking and the air became alive with squealing blocks and the rattle of halliards.

It was difficult to remember these well drilled men as the motley and ragged collection he had first taken aboard. Even the petty officers seemed to find little to grumble about as the men dashed to their stations, yet when the ship had first commissioned there had been more blows and curses than any sort of order. It was a good ship's company. As good as any captain could wish for, Bolitho thought vaguely.

'Tops'l sheets!'

Men leapt like monkeys along the yards and he watched them with something like envy. Working up there, sometimes as much as two hundred feet above the deck, had never failed to sicken him, to his embarrassment and anger.

'Tops'l clew lines!' Keverne's voice was hoarse, as if he too felt the tension under the eyes of the distant town.

Very slowly the *Euryalus* glided purposefully to her anchorage, her shadow preceding her on the calm water.

'Helm a'lee!'

As the spokes squeaked over and the ship swung reluctantly into the wind the canvas was already vanishing along her yards, as if each sail was being controlled by a single force.

'Let go!'

There was a loud splash as the anchor dropped beneath the bow, and something like a sigh transmitted itself through the hull and shrouds as the massive cable took the strain and then steadied itself for the first time in months.

'Very well, Mr Keverne. You may call away the barge and then have the cutter and jolly-boat swayed out.'

Bolitho turned away, knowing he could rely completely on Keverne. He was a good first lieutenant, although Bolitho knew less of him than he had of any previous officer. It was partly his own fault and because of the mounting work laid at his door due to the admiral's illness. Perhaps it had been a good thing for them both, Bolitho thought. The added responsibility, his growing awareness of strategy and tactics, involving not just one but several vessels in company, had given him less time to brood over his own personal loss. His involvement with the admiral's affairs had on the other hand given Keverne more responsibility and would stand him in good stead when he had a chance of his own command.

Keverne was extremely competent, but for one failing. On several occasions during the commission he had shown himself given to short but violent fits of temper over which he appeared to have little control.

In his late twenties, tall and straight, he had a swarthy almost gipsy, good looks. With dark flashing eyes and extremely white teeth, he was a man ladies would be quick to appreciate, Bolitho thought.

Bolitho dismissed him from his mind as the admiral appeared beneath the poop, carrying his hat and blinking his pale eyes in the sunlight.

He stood for several moments watching as the barge was hoisted up and outboard, the tackles squeaking while Tebbutt, the thick-armed boatswain, barked his orders from the starboard gangway.

Bolitho watched him narrowly. The admiral was making every last moment count. Hoarding these small shipboard pictures in his mind.

He heard a familiar voice at his elbow and turned to see Allday, his coxswain, studying him impassively.

Allday showed his teeth. 'Good, Captain.' He glanced at the admiral. 'Will I take Sir Charles across now?'

Bolitho did not reply at once. How often he had taken Allday for granted. Familiar, loyal and completely invaluable, it was hard to imagine life without him. He was broader now than the lithe topman he had once seen brought aboard his beloved frigate *Phalarope* as a pressed man so many years back. There were streaks of grey in his thick hair, and his homely, tanned face was more seasoned, like a ship's timber. But he was really the same as ever, and Bolitho was suddenly grateful for it.

'I will ask him directly, Allday.'

He turned sharply as Keverne said, 'Guardboat approaching, sir.'

Bolitho looked across the glittering water and saw an armed cutter moving purposefully towards the anchored three-decker. It was then that he noticed that not a single craft of any kind had made an attempt to leave harbour and follow the guardboat's example. He felt a twinge of anxiety. What could be wrong? Some sort of terrible fever abroad in the port? It was certainly not the sight of the *Euryalus* this time. Otherwise the guns in the castle would have announced their own displeasure.

He took a glass from its rack and trained it on the cutter. The tan sails and intent faces of several seamen swam across the lens, and then he saw a naval captain, an empty sleeve pinned across his coat, sitting squarely in the sternsheets, his eyes fixed on the *Euryalus*. The sight of the uniform and empty sleeve brought a fresh pang to Bolitho's thoughts. It could have been his dead father returned to the living.

The admiral asked testily, 'What is the trouble?'

'Just some formality, Sir Charles.' Bolitho looked at Keverne. 'Man the side, if you please.'

Captain Giffard of the marines drew his sword and marched importantly to the entry port, and watched as his men mustered in a tight scarlet squad to receive the ship's first visitor. Boatswain's mates and sideboys completed the party, and Bolitho walked down the quarterdeck ladder to join Keverne and the officer of the watch.

The cutter's sails vanished, and as the bowman hooked on to the chains, and the calls trilled in salute, the one-armed captain clambered awkwardly through the port and doffed his cocked hat to the quarterdeck, where the admiral watched the scene with neither emotion nor visible interest. Perhaps he already felt excluded, Bolitho thought.

'Captain James Rook, sir.' The newcomer replaced his hat and glanced rapidly around him. He was well past middle age, and must have been brought back to the Service to replace a younger man. 'I am in charge of harbour patrols and impressment, sir.' He faltered, some of the sureness leaving him under Bolitho's impassive grey eyes. 'Do I have the honour of addressing Sir Charles Thelwall's flag captain?'

'You do.'

Bolitho glanced past him and down into the cutter. There was a mounted swivel gun aboard, and several armed men beside the normal crew.

He added calmly, 'Are you expecting an attack?'

The man did not reply directly. 'I have brought a despatch for your admiral.' He cleared his throat, as if very aware of the watching faces all around him. 'Perhaps if we might go aft, sir?'

'Of course.'

Bolitho was getting unreasonably irritated by the man's ponderous and evasive manner. They had their orders, and nothing this captain could tell him would not keep until later.

He stopped at the top of the ladder and turned sharply. 'Sir Charles has been unwell. Can this matter not wait?'

Captain Rook took a deep breath, and Bolitho caught the heavy smell of brandy before he replied softly, 'Then you do not know? You have not been in contact with the fleet?'

Bolitho snapped, 'For God's sake stop beating around the bush, man! I have a ship to provision, sick men to be got ashore, and two hundred other things to do today. Surely you cannot have forgotten what it is like to command a ship?' He reached out and touched his arm. 'Forgive me. That was unfair.' He had seen the sudden hurt in the man's eyes and was ashamed at his own impatience. His nerves must be more damaged than he had imagined, he thought bitterly.

Captain Rook dropped his eyes. '*Mutiny*, sir.' His single hand moved up his coat and unbuttoned it carefully to reveal a heavy, red-sealed envelope.

Bolitho stared at the busy hand, his mind still ringing with that one terrible word. Mutiny, he had said, but where? The castle looked as usual, the flag shining like coloured metal at the top of its lofty staff. The garrison would have little cause to mutiny anyway. They were mostly local volunteers or militia and knew they were far better off defending their own homes than plodding through mud or desert in some far-off campaign.

Rook said slowly, 'The fleet at Spithead. It broke out last month and the ships were seized by their people until certain demands were met.' He shrugged awkwardly. 'It is finished now. Lord Howe confronted the ringleaders and the Channel Fleet is at sea again.' He looked hard at Bolitho. 'It is well your squadron was in ignorance. It might have gone badly with you otherwise.'

Bolitho looked past him and saw Keverne and several of his officers watching from the opposite side of the deck. They would sense something was wrong. But when they really knew. . . . He deliberately turned away from them.

'I have often expected some isolated outbreak.' He could not hide the anger in his voice. 'Some politicians and sea officers imagine that common sailors are little better than vermin and have treated them accordingly.' He stared hard at Rook. 'But for the fleet to mutiny as one man! That is a terrible thing!'

Rook seemed vaguely relieved that he had at last unburdened himself. Or maybe he had been half expecting to find the *Euryalus* in the hands of mutineers demanding heaven knew what.

He said, 'Many fear that the worst is yet to come. There has been trouble at the Nore too, though we do not hear the full truth down here. I have patrols everywhere in case other troublemakers come this way. Some of the ringleaders are said to be Irish, and the Admiralty may expect this to be a diversion for another attempt to invade there.' He sighed worriedly. 'To live and see this thing is beyond me, and that's a fact!'

Mutiny. Bolitho looked over to where the admiral was in close conversation with his secretary. This was a bad ending to his career. Bolitho had known the full meaning, the hot, unreasoning fury which mutiny could bring in its wake. But that was in isolated ships, where conditions or climate, privation or downright brutality of an individual captain were normally the root causes. For a whole fleet to explode against the discipline and authority of its officers, and therefore King and Parliament as well, was another matter entirely. It took organization and extreme skill as well as some driving force at the head of it to have any hope of success. And it had succeeded, there was no doubt of that.

He said, 'I will speak with Sir Charles at once.' He took the envelope from Rook's hand. 'This is a bitter home-coming.'

Rook made as if to join Keverne and the others, but halted as Bolitho added sharply, 'You will favour me by remaining silent until I tell you otherwise.'

The admiral did not look up or speak until Bolitho had finished telling him of Rook's news. Then he said, 'If the French come out again, England will be done for.' He looked at his hands and let them fall to his sides. 'Where is Vice-Admiral Broughton? Is he not here after all?'

Bolitho held out the envelope and said gently, 'Perhaps this will explain what we are to do, sir.'

He could see the emotions crossing and re-crossing the admiral's wizened face. He had been hating the thought of striking his flag for the last time. But he had accepted it. It was like his illness, unbeatable. But now that there was a real possibility of continuing he was probably torn between two paths.

He said, 'Show our visitor aft.' He made an effort to square his shoulders. 'Then set the hands to work. It would be unwise for them to see their leaders in despair.'

Then followed by his secretary he walked slowly and painfully into the poop's shadow.

When Bolitho joined him again in the great cabin the admiral was sitting at the desk, as if he had never left it.

'This despatch is from Sir Lucius Broughton.' He waved to a chair. '*Euryalus* will remain at Falmouth to receive his flag, but at present he is in London. It seems that a new squadron is to be formed here, although to what purpose is not explained.' He sounded very tired. 'You are to ensure that our people have no contact with the shore, and those sent there because of illness or injury will not be returned.' His mouth twisted angrily. 'Afraid of spreading the *disease* on board, no doubt.'

Bolitho was still standing, his mind grappling with all that the words entailed.

The admiral continued in the same flat voice, 'You will of course tell your officers what you think fit, but under no circumstances must the people be informed of the unrest at the Nore. It is worse than I feared.' He looked at Bolitho's grim face and added: 'Captain Rook is required to assist you with all your supplies, and has instructions to bring any further stores or new spars and cordage direct to the ship.'

Bolitho said slowly, 'Sir Lucius Broughton, I know little of him. It is difficult to anticipate his wishes.'

The admiral smiled briefly. 'His flag was flying in one of the ships which mutinied at Spithead. I imagine his main requirement will be that it does not happen again.'

He groped for his handkerchief and gripped the edge of the desk. 'I must rest awhile and think of what has to be done. It would be better if you went ashore in my place. You may find that things are less dangerous than we imagine.' He met Bolitho's eyes. 'But I would inform Captain Giffard first, so that his marines may be in readiness for trouble.' He looked away and added, 'I have seen the way our people look up to you, Bolitho. Sailors are simple folk who ask little more than justice in exchange for their lot afloat. But . . .' the word hung in the air, 'they are only human. And our first duty is to retain control, no matter at what cost.'

Bolitho picked up his hat. 'I know, sir.'

He thought suddenly of the crowded world beyond the panelled bulkhead. At sea or in battle they would fight and die without question. The constant demands of harsh discipline and danger left little room for outside ideals and hopes. But once the spark touched off the latent power of these same men anything might happen, and it would be no use pleading ignorance or isolation then.

On the quarterdeck again he was conscious of the change around him. How could you expect something like this to remain a secret? News travelled like wildfire in an overcrowded ship, though none could explain how it happened.

He beckoned to Keverne and said flatly, 'You will please go aft and report to Captain Rook. He saw Keverne's dark features settle into a mask of anticipation. 'You will then inform the ship's lieutenants and senior warrant officers of the general position. I will hold you responsible until my return. You will arrange to have the sick and injured taken ashore, but not in our boats, understood?'

Keverne opened his mouth and then closed it again. He nodded firmly.

Bolitho said, 'I will tell you now. There has been rumour of mutiny at the Nore. If any stranger attempts to approach or board this ship he will be deterred at once. If that cannot be done then he will be arrested and put in isolation immediately.'

Keverne rested one hand on his sword. 'If I catch a damned sea-lawyer I'll teach him a thing or two, sir!' His eyes blazed dangerously.

Bolitho faced him impassively. 'You will obey my orders, Mr Keverne. Nothing more or less.' He turned and sought out Allday's thickset figure by the nettings. 'Call away my barge crew immediately.'

Keverne said, 'You are taking your own boat, sir?'

Bolitho replied coldly, 'If I cannot trust them, after what we have borne and suffered together, then I can find no hope or solution for anything!'

Without another word he strode down the ladder where the side party still waited above the swaying cutter at the entry port.

Just a moment longer he stood and looked back at his ship and at the seamen who were already busy rigging awnings and assisting the sick men through the hatchways. As was his custom he had seen that every man aboard was issued with new clothing from the slop chest. Unlike some miserly captains who allowed their men to stay in the rags worn when they were pressed in town or village alike. But right now he could find no comfort at the sight of the wide trousers and checked shirts, the healthy faces and busy preparations. Clothing, and proper food when it was at all possible to obtain it, should be their right, not the privilege handed out by some godlike commander. It was little enough for what these same men gave in return.

He shut the thought from his mind and touched his hat to the quarterdeck and side party before lowering himself down into the barge which Allday had steered purposefully between the cutter and the ship's towering side.

'Shove off forrard!' Allday squinted into the sunlight and watched as the barge edged clear of the other boat. 'Out oars, give way together!'

Then as the barge gathered speed, the oars dipping and rising as one, he looked down at Bolitho's back and pursed his lips. He knew most of Bolitho's moods better than his own, and could well imagine what he must be thinking now. Mutiny in the Service he loved, and to which he had given everything. Allday had discovered all about it from the coxswain of the guardboat, a man he had served with many years back. How could a secret like that be kept for more than minutes?

He ran his eye across Bolitho's squared shoulders with their new and strangely alien gold epaulettes and at the jet black hair beneath his cocked hat. He had hardly changed, he thought. Even though he carried them all through one hazard after another.

He glared at the bow oarsman who had let his eye wander to watch a gull diving for fish close abeam and then thought of what should have been waiting for Bolitho at Falmouth. That lovely girl and a child to welcome him home. Instead he had nothing but trouble, and once more was expected to do another's work as well as his own.

Allday saw Bolitho's fingers playing a little tattoo on the worn hilt of his sword and relaxed slightly. Between them they had seen and done much together. The sword seemed to sum it all up better than words or actual thought.

The barge swung round and glided into the shadow of the jetty, and as the bowman hooked on and Allday removed his hat Bolitho rose and climbed over the gunwale and on to the worn, familiar steps.

He would have liked Allday with him just now, but it would not be right to leave the barge unattended.

'You may return to the ship, Allday.' He saw the flash of

23

anxiety in the big coxswain's eyes and added quietly, 'I will know where you are when I need you.'

Allday remained standing and watched Bolitho stride between two saluting militiamen at the top of the jetty.

Under his breath he muttered, 'By God, Captain, we are going to need *you*!'

Then he looked down at the lolling bargemen and growled, 'Now, you idle buggers, let me see you make this boat *move*!'

The stroke oar, a grizzled seaman with thick red hair, said between his teeth, 'Do yewm reckon the word o' the troubles will reach us 'ere?'

Allday eyed him bleakly. So they all knew already.

He grinned. 'Word is like dung, matey, it must be spread about to be any use!' He dropped his voice. 'So it's up to us to make sure it doesn't happen, eh?'

When he looked astern again Bolitho had already vanished, and he wondered what would be waiting for him on his return home.

2. The Visitor

BOLITHO made himself stand quite still for several minutes as he stared towards the house. He had avoided the road through the town and had used instead the narrow twisting lane with its green hedgerows and sweet smells of the countryside. As he stood in the bright sunlight he was conscious of stillness, the hard pressure of the land through his shoes. It was all so different from the constant movement and sounds of shipboard life, and the realization was one which never failed to surprise and please him. Except that this time it was not the same. He half-listened to the gentle murmur of bees, the distant bark of some farm dog as it scurried around the sheep, while his eyes rested on the house, square and uncompromising against the sky and the sloping hill around which led towards the headland.

With a sigh he strode forward again, his shoes disturbing the dust, his eyes squinting against the glare. Once through the broad gates in the grey stone wall he paused, unsure of himself and wishing that he had not come.

Then as the double doors at the top of the steps opened he

saw Ferguson, his one-armed steward, backed by two servant girls, waiting to greet him, their smiles so genuine that he was momentarily drawn from his own thoughts, and not a little moved.

Ferguson took his hand and murmured, 'God bless you, sir. It is a *fine* thing to have you back home again.'

Bolitho smiled. 'Not for long this time. But thank you.'

He saw Ferguson's wife, plump and rosy cheeked in her white cap and spotless apron, scurrying to greet him, her face torn between pleasure and tears as she curtsied and said, 'Never a warning, sir! But for Jack, the exciseman, we'd not have known you were back! He saw your topsails when the mist lifted, and rode here to tell us.'

'Things have changed, Ferguson.' Bolitho removed his hat and walked through the high entrance, aware of the cool stone, the ageless textures of oak panelling which shone dully in the filtered sunlight. 'There was a time when the young men of Falmouth could smell a King's ship before it topped the horizon.'

Ferguson looked away. 'Not many young men left now, sir. Those not in safe jobs have all been taken or volunteered.' He followed him into the broad room with its empty fireplace and tall leather-backed chairs.

It was very quiet here too, as if the whole house was holding its breath.

Ferguson said, 'I will fetch you a glass, sir.' He gestured to his wife and the two servant girls behind Bolitho's back. 'You'll be wanting some time alone on your first hour. . . .'

Bolitho did not turn. 'Thank you.' He heard the door close behind him and then moved to the foot of the staircase, the wall of which was lined with the paintings of all the others who had lived here before him. So familiar. Nothing had changed, and yet . . .

The stairs creaked as he climbed slowly past the watching portraits. Captain Daniel Bolitho, his great-great-grandfather, who had fought the French at Bantry Bay. Captain David Bolitho, his great-grandfather, depicted here on the deck of a blazing ship, who had died fighting pirates off the African coast. Where the stairs turned to the right old Denziel Bolitho, his grandfather, the only member of the family to reach the rank of rear-admiral, waited to greet him like a friend. Bolitho could still remember him, or thought he could, from the days when he had sat on his knee as a small child. But maybe it was his father's stories about him and the familiar picture which he really recalled. He paused and looked directly at the last portrait.

His father had been younger when the portrait had been finished. Straight-backed, level-eyed, with the empty sleeve pinned across his coat, an afterthought of the painter after he had lost an arm in India. Captain James Bolitho. It was difficult to remember him as he had looked on their last meeting so many years back when he had told Bolitho of his other son's disgrace. Hugh, the apple of his eye, who had killed a brother officer in a duel before fleeing to America to fight against his own country in the Revolution.

Bolitho sighed deeply. They were all dead. Even Hugh, whose deceptions had finally ended in death before his own eyes. A death which was still a secret he could share with no one. Hugh's record of failure and deception would stay a secret, and his memory rest in peace if he had anything to do with it.

Ferguson called from the foot of the stairs, 'I have put the glass by the window, sir. Some claret.' He paused uncertainly before adding, 'In your bedroom, sir.' He sounded ill at ease. 'They were to have been a surprise, but had not been finished at the time of your last visit. . . .' His voice trailed away as Bolitho walked quickly to the door at the end of the landing and pushed it open.

For a moment longer he could see no change. The fourposter bed held in a shaft of dappled sunlight from the windows. The tall mirror where she must have sat to comb her hair when he had been away . . . he felt his throat go dry as he turned to see the two new pictures on the far wall. It was just as if she was alive again, here in this room where she had waited in vain for his return. He wanted to move closer but was afraid, afraid the spell might break. The artist had even caught the sea-green in her eyes, the rich chestnut of her long hair. And the smile. He took a slow step towards it. The smile was perfect. Gentle, amused, the way she had looked at him whenever she had been near.

A step sounded in the doorway and Ferguson said quietly, 'She wanted them together, sir.'

Bolitho looked at the other portrait for the first time. He was depicted wearing his old dress coat, the one with the broad white lapels which Cheney had liked so much.

He said huskily, 'Thank you. It was good of you to remember her wishes.'

Then he walked quickly to the window and leaned over the warm sill. There, just round the hill, he could see the glittering horizon line. What she would have seen from this same window. Once he might have been saddened, even angry, that Ferguson had put the pictures here. To remind him of her, and his loss. He would have been wrong, and now as he stood with his palms resting on the sill he felt strangely at peace. For the first time that he could recall for a long while.

Below in the yard an old gardener peered up and waved his battered hat but he did not see him.

He stepped back into the room and turned once more towards the portraits. They were reunited here. Cheney had seen to that, and nothing could take them apart any more. When he was back at sea again, perhaps on the other side of the world, he would be able to think of this room. The portraits side by side, watching the horizon together.

He said, 'That claret will be warm by now. I'll come down directly.'

Later as he sat at the big desk, writing several letters to be carried to the port officials and chandlers, he thought about all that had happened here in this house. What would become of it when he died? There was only his young nephew, Adam Pascoe, Hugh's illegitimate son, left to claim the Bolitho inheritance. He was away serving with Captain Thomas Herrick at the moment, but Bolitho decided he would soon do something for the boy to make sure of his rightful ownership of this house. His mouth hardened. Much as he loved his sister Nancy, he would never allow her husband, a Falmouth magistrate and one of the biggest landowners in the county, to get *his* hands on it.

Ferguson appeared again, his face set in a frown.

'Beg pardon, sir, but there's a man to see you. He is most insistent.'

'Who is he?'

'I have never laid eyes on him before. A seafaring fellow, there's no doubt of that, but no officer or gentleman, I'm equally sure!'

Bolitho smiled. It was hard to recall Ferguson as the man who had once been brought aboard his ship *Phalarope* by the pressgang, he and Allday together, poles apart it had appeared at the time. Yet they had become firm friends, and even when Ferguson had lost an arm at the Saintes he had continued to serve Bolitho here as his steward. Like Allday, he seemed to have that same protective attitude when anything uncertain or unusual was about to occur.

He said, 'Show him in. He'll not be too dangerous, I think.'

Ferguson ushered the visitor through the doors and closed them with obvious reluctance. He would be waiting within a foot of the entrance, Bolitho guessed, just in case.

'What can I do for you?'

The man was thickset and muscular, well tanned and with hair fashioned into a pigtail. He was wearing a coat which was far too small for him, and Bolitho imagined it had been borrowed to cover up his true identity. For there was no mistaking his broad white trousers and buckled shoes. Even if he had been stark naked he would have known him to be a sailor.

'I begs yer pardon for the liberty, sir.' He knuckled his forehead while his eyes moved quickly round the room. 'Me name's Taylor, master's mate o' th' *Auriga*, sir.'

Bolitho watched him calmly. He had a faint North Country burr, and was obviously nervous. A deserter hoping for mercy, or a place to hide in another ship? It was not unknown for such men to run back to the one and only world where they might be safe with any sort of luck. Yet there was something vaguely familiar about him.

Taylor added quickly, 'I was with you in th' *Sparrow*, sir. Back in seventy-nine in th' West Indies.' He watched Bolitho anxiously. 'I was maintopman then, sir.'

Bolitho nodded slowly. 'Of course, I remember you now.' In the little sloop *Sparrow*, his first-ever command, when he had been just twenty-three, and the world had seemed a place for reckless enjoyment and unbounded ambition.

'We 'eard you was back, sir.' Taylor was speaking rapidly. 'An' because o' me knowin' you like, I was chosen to come.' He smiled bitterly. 'I thought as I'd 'ave to borrow a boat or swim to yer ship. You comin' ashore so soon made things easier like.' He dropped his eyes under Bolitho's gaze.

'Are you in trouble, Taylor?'

He looked up, his eyes suddenly defensive. 'That will depend on you, sir. I was chosen to speak with you, an', an', knowin' you as a fair an' just captain, sir, I thought maybe you'd listen to . . .'

Bolitho stood up and studied him calmly. 'Your ship, where is she lying?'

Taylor jerked his thumb over his shoulder. ' 'Long the coast to th' east'rd, sir.' Something like pride crossed his tanned face. 'Frigate, thirty-six, sir.'

'I see.' Bolitho walked slowly to the empty fireplace and back again. 'And you, and men like you, have seized control, is that it? A *mutineer*?' He saw the man flinch and added harshly, 'If you knew me, really knew me, you'd realize I'd not parley with those who betray their trust!'

Taylor said thickly, 'If you'd 'ear me out, sir, that's all I ask. After that you can 'ave me seized an' 'anged if you so wish it, an' well I knows that fact.'

Bolitho bit his lip. It had taken courage to come here like this. Courage and something more. This Taylor was no freshly pressed man, no lower deck sea-lawyer. He was a professional seaman. It could not have been easy for him. At any moment during his journey to Falmouth he might have been seen anyway by someone wishing to ingratiate himself with the authorities, and a patrol might even now be marching to the gates.

He said, 'Very well. I cannot promise to agree with your views, but I will listen. That is *all* I can say.'

Taylor relaxed slightly. 'We 'ave bin attached to the Channel Fleet, sir, an' in regular commission for two years. We've 'ad little rest, for the fleet is always short o' frigates, as you well knows. We was at Spit'ead when the trouble started last month, but our cap'n put to sea afore we could show our support with the others.' He bunched his hands tightly and continued bitterly, 'I must say it, sir, so's you'll understand. Our cap'n's a 'ard man, an' th' first lieutenant's so taken with abusin' the people there's 'ardly one aboard whose back 'as not bin ripped open by th' cat!'

Bolitho gripped his hands behind him. Stop him now, before he says any more. By listening so far you have implicated yourself in God knows what.

Instead he said coldly, 'We are at war, Taylor. Times are hard for officers as well as seamen.'

Taylor eyed him stubbornly. 'When the trouble broke at Spit'ead it was agreed by th' delegates of the Fleet that we would go to sea an' fight if th' Frogs came out. There's not a single Jack who'd be disloyal, sir. But some o' the ships 'ave bad officers, sir, there's none can say otherwise. There's some where no pay or bounty 'as bin paid for months an' the 'ands near starvin' on foul food! When Black Dick,' he flushed, 'beg pardon, sir, I mean Lord 'Owe, spoke to our delegates it was all settled. 'E agreed to our requests as best 'e could.' He frowned. 'But we was at sea by then an' 'ad no part in the settlement. In fact, our cap'n 'as bin worse instead o' better! An' that's God's truth, on my oath!'

'So you've taken the ship?'

'Aye, sir. Until justice is agreed on.' He looked at the floor. 'We 'eard of the orders to join this new squadron under Vice-Admiral Broughton. It'll maybe mean years away from England. It's not fair that our wrongs should stay unrighted. We knew Admiral Broughton at Spit'ead, sir. 'E's said to be a good officer, but would go 'ard with any more trouble.'

'And if I say nothing can be done, what then?'

Taylor looked him in the eyes. 'There's many aboard who swear we'll 'ang anyway. They want to sail the ship to France an' trade 'er for their freedom.' He hardened his jaw. 'But those like me say otherwise, sir. We just want our rights like the boys at Spit'ead got.'

Bolitho eyed him narrowly. How much did Taylor know of the other unrest at the Nore? He might be genuine, or could be the tool of someone more experienced in revolt. There was little doubt that what he had said of his ship was true.

He said, 'Have you harmed anyone aboard?'

'None, sir, you've my word.' Taylor spread his hands pleadingly. 'If you could tell 'em that you'd put our case to the admiral, sir, it'd make a world o' difference.' Something like a sad smile showed on his rough features. 'I think some of the lieutenants an' th' master are a mite glad it's 'appened, sir. It's bin a terrible un'appy ship.'

Bolitho's mind moved rapidly. Vice-Admiral Broughton might be in London. He could be anywhere. Until he hoisted his flag Rear-Admiral Thelwall was still in command, and he was too sick to be involved in anything like this.

There was Captain Rook, and the officer commanding the local garrison. There were probably dragoons still at Truro, and the port admiral thirty miles away in Plymouth. And all were equally useless at this moment of time.

If a frigate were indeed handed over to the enemy it might act as a general signal to the men at the Nore, who were still hovering on the brink of mutiny. It might even be seen as the thing to do when all else had failed. A chill ran down his spine. If the French got to hear of it they would act without delay to put an invasion into force. The thought of a confused demoralized fleet being destroyed because he alone had failed to act was unthinkable, no matter what the consequences might be later.

He asked shortly, 'What else were you told to explain?'

'The *Auriga*'s anchored in Veryan Bay. Some eight miles from 'ere. Do you know of it, sir?'

Bolitho smiled grimly. 'I am a Cornishman, Taylor. Yes, I know it well.'

Taylor licked his lips. Maybe he had been expecting instant arrest. Now that Bolitho was listening to him he seemed unable to get the words out fast enough.

'If I'm not back afore sunset they'll make sail, sir. We bin approached by an armed cutter more'n once an' we've told 'em to stand off, that we're anchored to carry out some repairs.'

Bolitho nodded. It was not unusual for smaller ships to take refuge in that particular bay. It was quiet and fairly well sheltered in anything but severe weather. Whoever had steered this mutiny to its present state certainly knew what he was doing.

Taylor continued, 'There's a little inn on the west side o' th' bay, sir.'

Bolitho said, 'The Drake's Head. A smugglers' haunt, to all accounts.'

'Maybe, sir.' Taylor watched him uncertainly. 'But if you'll come there tonight an' meet our delegates, we can settle matters there an' then like.'

Bolitho turned away. How easy it all sounded. And what was the *Auriga*'s captain supposed to think about it? Merely pack his chest and leave? The simple reasoning probably seemed sound enough between decks, but it would cut little cloth when it reached higher authority.

But the most important and urgent thing was to stop the ship being taken and given to the enemy. Bolitho had no doubt that her captain was all and more than Taylor had described. There were enough of such petty tyrants throughout the Service, and he had even assumed an earlier command himself because of the previous captain's callousness.

Anyway, he could not hide his head and ignore it.

He said, 'Very well.'

'Thank you, sir.' Taylor nodded vehemently. 'You must come alone, but for a servant. They says they'll kill the cap'n if there's any sort o' treachery.' He hung his head. 'I'm sorry, sir, it was none o' my wantin'. All I wished was to end me days in one piece, with a pot o' prize money at th' end o' it to open a little inn maybe, or a chandler's.'

Bolitho looked at him gravely. Instead, you'll probably end on a yard-arm, he thought.

Taylor said suddenly, 'They'll listen to you, sir. I just know it. With a new cap'n the ship'd be ready to live again.'

'I will promise nothing. Lord Howe's pardon should certainly have applied to your ship, however. . . .' He faced the other man steadily. 'It could go hard with you, as I expect you know.'

'Aye, sir. But when you've lived with misery for so long it is a chance we must face up to.'

Bolitho walked to the door. 'I will ride to the inn at dusk. If what you have told me is true, I will do what I can to bring the matter to a rightful conclusion.'

The relief on Taylor's face faded as Bolitho added flatly, 'If on the other hand this is some delaying tactic to give your people more time to dispose of the ship, be in no doubt of the consequences. It has been done before, and the culprits have always been run to ground.' He paused. 'Eventually.'

The man knuckled his forehead and hurried out into the passage.

Ferguson watched him go with obvious distaste.

'Is it all well, sir?'

'At present, thank you.' He pulled his watch from his pocket. 'Send someone to signal for my barge.' He saw the disappointment on Ferguson's face and added, 'I will be back ashore later today, but there are things to attend to.'

An hour later Bolitho climbed up through the *Euryalus*'s gilded entry port and removed his hat to the pipes' shrill greeting and the stamp and slap of muskets.

Keverne looked unusually preoccupied. When they reached the quarterdeck he said shortly, 'The surgeon is worried about the admiral, sir. He is very low, and I am afraid for him.'

Bolitho glanced at Allday whose face had been screwed up with burning curiosity ever since the barge had reached the jetty.

'Keep the bargemen standing by. I may require them soon.

Then he strode aft and down to the admiral's quarters.

Lying quietly in his cot the admiral seemed even smaller and more fragile. His eyes were shut, and there was blood on his shirtfront as well as the handkerchief.

Bolitho glanced at the surgeon, a thin, wiry man with unusually large and hairy hands.

'Well, Mr Spargo?'

He shrugged. 'I cannot be sure, sir. He ought to be on shore. I am only a ship's surgeon.' He shrugged again. 'But the effort of moving him now might be fatal.'

Bolitho nodded, his mind made up.

'Then leave him here and watch him well.' To Keverne he said, 'Come up to my cabin.'

Keverne followed him in silence until they had reached the wide cabin which ran the whole breadth of the poop. Through the open stern windows was a perfect view of St Anthony Head, moving slightly as the ship swung ponderously on the current.

'I have to go ashore again, Mr Keverne.' He must be careful not to involve his first lieutenant, yet at the same time he had to be primed enough to know what to do if the scheme misfired.

Keverne's face was a mask. 'Sir?'

Bolitho unclipped his sword and laid it on the table.

'There is no news of Vice-Admiral Broughton yet. Nor is there any hint of unrest ashore. Captain Rook's boats will be alongside after our people have had their meal, and you can carry on with loading stores all afternoon and into the dog watches if the sea remains calm.'

Keverne waited, knowing there was more to come.

'Sir Charles is very sick, as you have seen.' Bolitho wished Keverne would show some curiosity, like Herrick would have done when he had been his first lieutenant. 'So you will be in command until my return.'

'When will that be, sir?'

'I am not sure. Later tonight perhaps.'

He had Keverne's interest roused at last.

'Is there something I can do to help, sir?' He paused. 'Will there be trouble?'

'Not if I can prevent it. I will leave written orders for you to act upon if I am delayed for more than the night. You will open them and take whatever . . .' he held up his hand, 'no, *every necessary step* to see that they are carried out without delay.'

His mind grappled with the picture of the chart within his brain. It would take *Euryalus* more than two hours to up anchor and reach Veryan Bay, where the sight of her terrible armament would soon quell even the stoutest heart into submission. But by then it might be far too late.

Why not put to sea now, without further delay? No one would blame him, probably quite the reverse. He frowned and dismissed the idea immediately. This was to be a new squadron. And with the war entering its most dangerous stage so far, it would be a bad beginning for the flagship to pound an anchored consort into a bloody shambles because he had not the nerve or the will to do otherwise.

Surprisingly, Keverne smiled, showing his even teeth.

'I have not been with you for eighteen months and learned nothing of your methods, sir.' The smile vanished. 'And I hope I have your confidence.'

Bolitho smiled. 'A captain can only go so far to share his thoughts, Mr Keverne. His responsibility he must hold to himself, as you will one day discover.' If it goes badly tonight you may be promoted earlier than you imagine, he thought bleakly.

Trute, the cabin servant, stepped gingerly through the door and asked, 'Permission to lay th' table for your lunch, sir?'

Keverne said, 'I will go and attend to the hands, sir.' He watched distantly as Trute busied himself with plates and cutlery at the long table. 'I'll not be sorry to get to sea again.' He left the cabin without another word.

As Bolitho sat moodily at his lonely table toying with the cold rabbit pie which must have been sent directly from the shore by Rook, he thought back over what Taylor had told him. The fact that he had been able to reach Falmouth and find the house so quickly spoke volumes, and suggested there were other watchful eyes already close by, ready to pass the word back to the *Auriga*. Any sort of deception, marines landed at the jetty or some such precaution other than normal port practice, would soon arouse suspicion, and the *Auriga*'s captain would be in grave danger, the consequences terrible.

He stood up angrily. How long would it take before such men were pruned from the Navy once and for all? A new breed of officer was growing up, and finding the scope to attack the enemy as well as better the living conditions of their own seamen. But here and there was the bully and tyrant, often men with influence in high places who could not be broken or removed until moments like these, when it was too late.

Trute returned and eyed him worriedly. 'Did yew not like the pie, sir?' He was a Devon man and viewed Bolitho, like all Cornishmen, with both apprehension and a little awe.

'Later perhaps.' Bolitho glanced at the sword. Old and so worn, the one which appeared in many of those family portraits. 'I will leave this in your care.' He tried to keep his voice normal. 'I shall take a hanger.' He paused. 'And pistols.'

Trute gaped at the sword. '*Leave* it, sir?'

Bolitho ignored him. 'Now pass the word for my cox'n.'

Allday was equally surprised. 'Won't seem the same without the sword, Captain.' He shook his head. 'Whatever next!'

Bolitho snapped, 'I have told you before that one of these days you will open your mouth too wide. You are not so old and wise that you can avoid my displeasure!'

Allday smiled. 'Aye, *aye*, Captain.'

It was hopeless. 'We will be going ashore together. Do you know the Drake's Head?'

Allday became serious. 'Aye. Veryan Bay. 'Tis owned by an old yaw-sighted villain. One eye points forrard, t'other almost abeam, but his wits are as sharp as a midshipman's hunger.'

'Good. That is where we are going.'

Allday frowned as Trute re-entered and laid a brace of pistols on the table beside a curved hanger.

He asked mildly. 'A duel, Captain?'

'Call away the barge. Then give my compliments to Mr Keverne and tell him I am ready to leave, as soon as I have written his orders.'

Bolitho made a further visit to see the admiral, but there was little change. He appeared to be resting quietly, his wizened face more relaxed in sleep.

On deck he found Keverne waiting for him.

'Barge alongside, sir.' Keverne looked aloft at the listless flag. 'The wind has died for some while, I think.'

Bolitho grunted. It was just as if Keverne was trying to warn him. That once he left the ship he was alone and without much hope of assistance. He cursed his own uncertainty. Keverne did *not* know, and anyway, what else could be done? To wait until the new admiral arrived was merely hiding from the responsibility he had accepted as his own. He said abruptly, 'Look after her.' Then he lowered himself down to the waiting boat.

When they reached the jetty he climbed the steps, pausing to look back. Framed against the blue water and clear sky the ship seemed indestructible, permanent. An illusion, he thought grimly. No vessel was stronger than those who served her.

Allday watched critically as the acting coxswain manœuvred the barge clear of the stones for the return journey. Then he asked, 'What now, Captain?'

'To the house. I have things to do, and we will require two horses.'

He reached up and felt the locket beneath his shirt. The one she had given him containing a lock of that perfect chestnut hair. He would leave it at the house. Whatever happened this night, he was not going to have someone else pawing over the locket.

He added slowly, 'A fine day. It is hard to think of war, and other things.'

Allday said, 'Aye, Captain. A tankard and a woman's voice would not come amiss right at present.'

Bolitho was suddenly impatient. 'Well, come along, Allday. When the oven's hot it is time to bake. No sense in wasting time in dreams.'

Allday followed him readily, his mouth set in a smile. Like the wind across the sea, all the signs were there. Whatever the captain was planning, that which was troubling him enough to make him provoke his own anger, would go hard with someone before another dawn.

He thought suddenly of Bolitho's words and grimaced. A topsail yard or a rough backstay, he could manage either. Even a reluctant woman was not too much trouble. But a horse! He rubbed his buttocks. By the time they reached the Drake's Head he would have need for more than a tankard, he thought gloomily.

They left the house before dusk, but by the time they had crossed the river at a small ford, well clear of Falmouth, it was getting dark rapidly. But Bolitho knew the countryside like the back of his hand, and with Allday trotting uncomfortably behind him kept up a good pace until he had found the narrow twisting lane which led to Veryan. In places it was very steep, with the trees almost touching overhead, the thick brush alive with squeaks and startled rustlings as they passed by.

Then a sharp curve and for a few more minutes he saw the

36

edge of the headland itself, with a writhing pattern of surf far below where the rocks lay like black teeth at the foot of the high cliffs.

Allday gasped, 'My God, Captain, this horse has no respect for my rump!'

'Hold your noise, damn you!' Bolitho reined his horse at the top of yet another steep slope and strained his eyes towards a darker line of tangled bushes.

The cliff edge had moved inwards again and probably came to within yards of the bushes. Beyond he could see the sea shining dully in the gloom, flat and unruffled, like pewter. But the bay was in deeper shadow, there might not be a ship there at all. Equally there could be half a dozen.

He shivered slightly and was glad he had allowed Mrs Ferguson to have her way over the boat-cloak. It was cold up here, and the air felt damp. There would be another sea mist in before dawn.

He heard Allday breathing heavily beside him and said, 'Not much farther now. The inn is about half a mile from here.'

Allday grunted. 'I don't like it, Captain.'

'You do not have to *like* it.' Bolitho looked at him. He had told Allday the bones of what was happening and nothing more. Just enough to clear himself if anything went wrong. 'Surely you've not forgotten . . .' He broke off and gripped his arm. 'What was that?'

Allday stood up on his stirrups. 'A hare maybe?'

The shout, when it came, was with the suddenness of a shot. 'Keep still and raise yer 'ands in the air where we can see 'em!'

Allday groped for his cutlass. 'By God, it's a bloody ambush!'

'Belay that, Allday!' Bolitho wheeled his horse against him and knocked his hand away from the weapon. 'It is what I expected, man.'

The voice said, 'Easy, Cap'n! We don't want to cut you down but . . .'

Another voice, more insistent and hard with tension, snapped, 'We can do without wasting time, just you go an' disarm 'em, and lively with it!'

There seemed to be about three men, Bolitho thought. He watched as a shadowy figure reached up to relieve Allday of his cutlass, and heard the clatter of steel as it fell in the lane.

Another man materialized out of the darkness right beside

37

him and said, 'An' you, sir. You'll have pistols with you?'

Bolitho handed them down with the hanger and said coldly, 'I was told that some sort of trust was needed. I did not know it was to be one-sided.'

The man faltered. 'We're takin' a great risk, Cap'n. You might have brung the militia with you.' He sounded frightened.

The man who had not shown himself shouted, 'Take the horses and lead 'em.' A pause and then, 'I'll be astern. One wrong tack and I will fire, no matter the rights an' wrongs of the argument.'

Allday said between his teeth, 'I'll split him, the bugger, for talking like that!'

Bolitho remained silent, allowing the horse to jog along with the man walking at its head. It was no more than he had anticipated. Nobody but a fool would arrange a meeting without taking these elementary precautions. They had probably been followed for the last few miles, the horses' hoofbeats would have drowned most of the noise.

A single light appeared round the bend in the lane and he saw the pale outline of the inn. A small, untidy building, added to and altered over the years without much idea of beauty, he thought vaguely.

There was no moon and the stars looked very small. It was colder too, and he knew that the sea was not far away now, perhaps half a mile to the foot of the cliffs by way of a rugged and dangerous path. No wonder the inn was considered safe for smugglers.

'Dismount.'

Two more figures moved from the building and he saw the glint of metal as he swung himself from the saddle.

'Follow me.'

It was only a lantern burning inside the low-beamed parlour, but after the dark lane it seemed like a beacon. The room smelt of ale and tobacco, bacon and dirt.

The innkeeper stepped into the lamplight, wiping his hands on a long, filthy apron. He was exactly as Allday had described, with one eye veering away as if trying to burst out of its socket.

He said in a thin, wheedling tone, 'None o' my doin', sir. I wants you to remember that I had no part in all this.' He trained his good eye on Bolitho and added, 'I knew your father, sir, a fine man. . . .'

The voice barked, 'Hold your damn noise! I'll leave you hanging on your bloody rafters if you don't stow your whining!'

Bolitho turned slowly as the innkeeper cringed into the shadows. The speaker was about thirty, ruddy-faced, but lacking the toughness expected of a seaman. His clothes were quite good. A plain blue coat and a shirt which had been recently washed. His face was intelligent but hard. A man who became angry very easily, Bolitho decided.

'I do not see Taylor here.'

The man, obviously the leader, said coldly, 'He is with the boat.'

Bolitho looked at the others. There were four of them, and probably two more outside. All seamen, they were ill at ease and watching their spokesman with a mixture of anxiety and resignation.

'You will be seated, Captain. I have sent for some ale.' He lifted his lip in a sneer. 'But perhaps someone of your standing would prefer brandy, eh?'

Bolitho eyed him calmly. The man was trying to provoke him.

'The ale will be very welcome.' He opened his cloak and dropped it on a chair. 'You must be the chosen *delegate*?'

'I am.' He watched with mounting irritation as the innkeeper shuffled to the table with some tankards and a brimming earthenware jug of ale. 'You wait in your kitchen!'

In a more level tone he continued, 'Now, Captain, have you decided to accept our terms?'

'I was not aware that any had been agreed upon.' Bolitho lifted a tankard and noticed with relief that his hand was still steady. 'You have taken a King's ship. This is an act of mutiny as well as one of treason if you persist with the rest of your plan.'

Strangely, the man seemed more satisfied than angry. He looked at the others and said, 'You see, lads! There's no bargaining with the likes of him. You should have listened to me in the first place instead of wasting time.'

A grizzled petty officer replied quickly, 'Easy! Mebbe if you was to tell 'im the other things like we agreed?'

'You're a fool!' He turned back to Bolitho. 'I knew this would happen. The lads at Spithead won their cause because they stood together. Next time there'll be no damn promises strong enough to break us!'

The petty officer said gruffly, 'Would you look at this book, sir.' He pushed it over the table, his eyes on Bolitho's face. 'I bin at sea man an' boy for thirty years. I've never bin in anything like this afore, an' that's God's truth, sir.'

'You'll hang just the same, you fool!' The spokesman eyed him with contempt. 'But show him if it makes you feel better.'

Bolitho opened the canvas-covered book and leafed past the first few pages. It was the frigate's punishment book, and as he ran his eyes down the neatly written records he felt the revulsion twisting his stomach like fever.

None of these men could have known the effect it would have on him. They were merely trying to show him what they had suffered. But in the past Bolitho had always inspected the punishment book of any ship of which he had just taken command. He believed it gave a better picture of her previous commander than any other testimony.

He could feel them watching him, sense the tension surrounding him like a physical thing.

Most of the offences listed were trivial and fairly typical. Disorderly behaviour, disobedience, carelessness and insolence. Many of them he knew from experience would mean little more than ignorance on the part of the man involved.

But the punishments were savage. In one week alone, while the *Auriga* had been patrolling off Le Havre, her captain had awarded a total of one thousand lashes. Two men had been flogged twice in the same period, one of whom had died under the lash.

He shut the book and looked up. There were so many questions he wanted to ask. Why the first lieutenant had done nothing to prevent such brutality? He checked the thought instantly. What would Keverne have done in the past if his own captain had ordered such punishment? The realization made him suddenly angry. He had seen often enough the way men looked at him when things went wrong, as they often did in the complex matters of working a ship-of-the-line. Sometimes it amounted to real terror, and it never failed to sicken him. A captain, any captain, was second only to God as far as his men were concerned. A superior being who could encourage advancement with one hand and order the most vicious punishment with the other. To think that some captains, the *Auriga*'s amongst them, could abuse such power was nothing but abhorrent to him.

He said slowly, 'I would like to come aboard and speak with

your captain.' As several of them started to speak at once he added, 'Otherwise I can do nothing.'

The chief delegate said, 'You may have fooled the others, but I can see through your deception well enough.' He gestured angrily. 'First a show of sympathy, and the next thing we'll know is the gibbet on some sea wall where every passing sailor can see what value there is in trusting the word of an officer!'

Allday gave a savage oath and half rose to his feet, but looked helplessly at Bolitho as he said, 'Rest easy, Allday. When a man thinks that righting a wrong is a waste of time, there is little point in argument.'

One of the seamen said thickly, 'Aye, what's wrong in the cap'n comin' aboard? If 'e breaks 'is faith with us we can take 'im along as 'ostage.'

There was a murmur of agreement, and for an instant Bolitho saw the leader caught off guard.

He decided to make another move. 'If on the other hand you had no intention of seeking justice, and merely wanted an excuse to hand your ship to the *enemy*,' he let his voice drag over the word, 'then I should warn you that I have already made certain arrangements to forestall you.'

'He's bluffing!' But the man's voice was less assured now. 'There's no ship within miles of us here!'

'There will be another mist at dawn.' He thrust his hands under the table knowing they were quivering with excitement or worse. 'You will be unable to make sail before the forenoon. I know this bay well and it is too dangerous.' He hardened his tone. 'Especially without the help of your officers.'

The petty officer muttered, ' 'E's right, Tom.' He craned forward. 'Why not do like 'e says? We got nowt to lose by listenin'.'

Bolitho studied the leader thoughtfully. His name was Tom. It was a beginning.

'Damn your eyes, the lot of you!' The man was flushed with sudden anger. 'A batch of delegates, are you? More like a pack of old women!'

The anger calmed as suddenly as before, and Bolitho was reminded of Keverne.

He said harshly, 'Right then, so be it.' He gestured to the old petty officer. 'You will remain here with one lookout.' He glanced at Allday, his eyes hostile. 'And you can keep this

41

lackey as hostage. If we make the signal I want him dead. If there's some sort of attack we will kill the pair of them and hang them beside our own precious lord and bloody master, right?'

The petty officer flinched but nodded in agreement.

Bolitho looked at Allday's grim features and forced a smile. 'You wanted a rest and a tankard. You have both.' Then he rested his hand briefly on his shoulder. He could almost feel the man's tension and anger beneath it. 'It will be all right.' He tried to give value to his words. 'We are not fighting the enemy.'

'We shall see!' The man named Tom opened the door and made a mock bow. 'Now walk in front of me and mind your manners. I'll not pipe my eye if I have to cut you down here and now!'

Bolitho strode into the darkness without answering. The night was still before them, but there was a lot to do before dawn if there was to be any hope of success. As he hurried down the steep track his mind returned to the punishment book. It was surprising that men driven and provoked by such inhumanity had bothered to try to seek justice by channels they only barely understood. It was more surprising still that the mutiny had not broken out months earlier. The realization helped to encourage him, although he knew it was little enough to sustain anything.

3. Salute the Flag

'BOAT AHOY!' The challenge seemed to come from nowhere.

A man in the bows cupped his hands and replied, 'The delegates!'

Bolitho tensed on the thwart as the anchored frigate suddenly grew out of the darkness, the crossed yards and gently spiralling masts black against the stars. While the jolly-boat manœuvred alongside he noted the carefully spread boarding nets above the ship's gangway, the dark clusters of figures crowding around the entry port. He could feel his heart racing, and wondered if his own apprehension was matched by the waiting mutineers'.

A hand thrust at his shoulder. 'Up you go.'

As he swung himself up through the port a lantern was

unshuttered, the yellow beam playing across his epaulettes while the press of seamen pushed closer to see him.

A man said, ' 'E came then.'

Then Taylor's voice, brittle and urgent. 'Stand aside, mates. There's work to be done.'

Bolitho stood in silence as the head delegate whispered further instructions to the watch on deck. The ship seemed under control, with no sign of argument or drunkenness as might be expected. Two of the guns were run out, and he guessed they were loaded with grape, just in case some suspicious patrol boat came too close for safety.

A petty officer stood watch on the quarterdeck, but there was no officer in view. Nor were there any marines.

The man named Tom said sharply, 'We'll go aft and you can meet the cap'n.' It was impossible to see his expression. 'But no tricks.'

Bolitho walked aft and ducked beneath the poop. In spite of his serving in two ships-of-the-line in succession he had never got used to their spacious headroom. Perhaps, after all, he still yearned for the independence and dash of a frigate.

Two armed seamen watched his approach, and after a further hesitation shuffled their feet to attention.

'That's right, lads, show some respect, eh?' The delegate was enjoying himself.

He threw open the cabin door and followed Bolitho inside. It was well lit by three swaying lanterns, but the stern windows were shuttered, and the air was moist, even humid. A seaman, armed with a musket, was leaning against the bulkhead, and seated on the bench seat beneath the stern windows was the *Auriga*'s captain.

He was fairly young, about twenty-six, Bolitho imagined, with the single epaulette on his right shoulder to indicate he held less than three years' seniority as captain. He had sharp, finely defined features, but his eyes were set close together so that his nose seemed out of proportion. He stared at Bolitho for several seconds and then jumped to his feet.

The delegate said quickly, 'This is Captain Bolitho.' He waited as the emotions changed on the other man's face. 'He is alone. No grand force of bullocks to save you, I'm afraid.'

Bolitho removed his hat and placed it on the table. 'You are Captain Brice? Then I shall tell you at once that I am here without authority other than my own.'

43

Briefly he saw something like shock in the other man's eyes before a shutter fell and he became composed again. Composed yet watchful, like a wary animal.

Brice replied, 'My officers are under guard. The marines have not yet joined the ship. They were due to be sent direct from Plymouth.' He darted a look at the delegate. 'Otherwise *Mr* Gates here would be singing a different tune, damn his eyes!'

The delegate said quietly, 'Now, *sir*, none of that, please. I'd have you dancing at the gratings right now if I had my way! But there'll be time enough for that later, eh?'

Bolitho said, 'I should like to talk with Captain Brice alone.'

He waited, expecting an argument, but the delegate replied calmly, 'Suit yourself. It'll do no good, and you know it.' He left the cabin with the armed seaman, slamming the door and whistling indifferently as he went.

Brice opened his mouth to speak but Bolitho said shortly, 'There is little time, so I will be as brief as I can. This is a very serious matter, and if your ship is handed to the enemy there is no saying what repercussions may result. I have nothing to bargain with, and little to offer to ensure these men are brought back under command.'

The other man stared at him. 'But, sir, are you not the flag captain? One show of force, a full-scale attack, and these scum would soon lose the heart for mutiny!'

Bolitho shook his head. 'The new squadron has not been formed as yet. Every ship is elsewhere, or too far to be any use. My own is at Falmouth. She could be on the moon for all the help she can be to you.' He hardened his voice. 'I have heard some of the grievances and I can find little if any sympathy for your personal position.'

If he had struck Brice the effect could not have been more startling. He jumped up, his thin mouth working with anger.

'That is a *damnable* thing to say! I have worked this ship to the best of my ability, and I have a record of prizes to prove it. I have been plagued with the scum of the gutters, and officers either too young or too lazy to enforce anything like the standard I expect.'

Bolitho kept his face impassive. 'Except for your senior, I understand?'

Before Brice could reply he rapped, 'And kindly sit down! When you address me you will keep a civil tongue in your

44

head!' He was shouting and the fact surprised him. It must be infectious, he thought. But his sudden display of anger seemed to have had the right effect.

Brice sank on to the seat and said heavily, 'My first lieutenant is a good officer, sir. A firm man, but that . . .'

Bolitho finished it for him. 'That is what you *expect*, eh?'

Beyond the bulkhead some voices were raised in argument and then died away just as quickly.

He added, 'Your behaviour, were you now in port, would make you eligible for court-martial.' He saw the shot go home. The sudden clenching of Brice's fingers. 'Surely after the affair at Spithead you should have taken some heed of their requirements? Good God, man, they deserve justice if nothing else.'

Brice regarded him angrily. 'They got what they deserved.'

Bolitho recalled Taylor's words. *An unhappy ship.* It was not difficult to imagine the hell this man must have made her.

'Then I cannot help you.'

Brice's eyes gleamed with sudden malice. 'They'll never allow you to leave the ship now!'

'Perhaps not.' Bolitho stood up and walked to the opposite side. 'But there will be a mist in the bay at dawn. When it clears your ship will be facing something more than words and threats. I have no doubt that your people will fight, no matter what the odds, for by then it will be too late for second thoughts, too late for compromise.'

Brice said, 'I hope I see them die!'

'I doubt that, Captain. In afterlife maybe. For you and I will be dangling high enough for the best view of all.'

'They wouldn't *dare*!' But Brice sounded less sure now.

'Would they not?' Bolitho leaned across the table until they were only two feet apart. 'You have tormented them beyond all reason, have acted more like a demented fiend than a King's officer.' He reached out and tore the epaulette from Brice's shoulder and threw it on the table, his face stiff with anger. 'How *dare* you talk of what they can or cannot do under such handling? Were you one of my officers I would have had you broken long before you could bring disgrace to the commission entrusted to you!' He stood back, his heart pumping against his ribs. 'Make no mistake, Captain Brice, if your ship does escape to be given to the enemy, you were better dead anyway. The shame will otherwise grip you tighter than any damned halter, believe me!'

Brice stared round the cabin and then let his eyes rest on the discarded epaulette. He seemed shocked, even stunned, by Bolitho's attack.

Bolitho added in a calmer tone, 'You cannot kill a man's need to be free, don't you understand that? Freedom is hard to win, harder still to hold, but these men of yours, confused and ignorant perhaps, they all *understand* what liberty means.' He had no idea if his words were having any effect. The voices on deck were getting louder again and he felt a growing sense of despair. He continued, 'All seamen realize that once in the King's service their lot is as good or as bad as their commanders will allow. But you cannot ask or expect them to fight or give of their best when their own treatment is unnecessarily wretched.'

Brice looked at his hands. They were trembling badly. He said thickly, 'They mutinied. Against me, and my authority.'

'Your authority is nearly done.' Bolitho watched him gravely. 'Because of you I have put my coxswain in jeopardy. But you have sacrificed far more than our lives, and I am only sad that you will not live long enough to see what you have done.'

The door banged open and the man Gates stepped into the cabin, his hands on his hips.

'All done, gentlemen?' He was smiling.

Bolitho faced him, aware of the dryness in his throat, the sudden silence in the airless cabin.

'Thank you, yes.' He did not look at Brice as he continued evenly, 'Your captain has agreed to place himself under open arrest and await my orders. If you release the ship's officers immediately . . .'

Gates stared at him. 'What did you say?'

Bolitho tensed, expecting Brice to shout abuse or demand the immediate withdrawal of his promise. But he said nothing, and when he turned his head he saw that Brice was staring at the deck, as if in a state of collapse.

The master's mate, Taylor, pushed through the other men and shouted wildly, 'D'you see, lads? What did I tell you?' He stared at Bolitho, his eyes misty with relief. 'God, Cap'n, you'll never regret this!'

Gates interrupted hoarsely, 'You fools! You blind, ignorant madmen!' Then he looked at Bolitho. 'Tell 'em the rest!'

Bolitho met his stare. 'The rest? There has been an unlawful disobedience of orders. Under the given circumstances I

46

believe that justice will be reasonable. However,' he looked at the watching seamen by the door, 'it will not be entirely overlooked.'

Gates said, 'The rope never overlooks anyone, does it?'

Taylor was the first to break the sudden stillness. 'What chance do we 'ave, Cap'n?' He squared his shoulders. 'We're not as blind as some think. We know what we done was wrong, but if there's some 'ope for us, then . . .' His voice trailed away into silence again.

Bolitho replied quietly, 'I will speak with Sir Charles Thelwall. He is a humane and generous officer, that I will vouch for. He will no doubt think, as I do, that what has happened is bad. But what might have occurred, far worse.' He shrugged. 'I can say no more than that.'

Gates glared around him. 'Well, lads, are you still with me?'

Taylor looked at the others. 'We'll 'ave a parley. But I'm for takin' Cap'n Bolitho's word as it stands.' He rubbed his mouth. 'I've worked all me life to get as far as I 'ave, an' no doubt I'll lose what I've gained. I'll most likely taste the cat, but it won't be the first time. Rather all that than live in misery. An' I don't fancy spendin' the rest o' me days in some Frog town or 'idin' whenever I sees a uniform.' He turned. 'A parley, lads.'

Gates watched them file out and then said quietly, 'If they agree to your empty promises, Captain Bolitho, then I'll first take *his* confession down in writing.'

Bolitho shook his head. 'You can give your evidence at the court-martial.'

'*Me?*' Gates laughed. 'I'll not be aboard when these fools are taken!' He twisted round to listen to the babble of voices. 'I will be back.' Then he left the cabin.

Brice breathed out slowly. 'That was a terrible risk. They might still not believe you.'

'We can only hope.' Bolitho sat down. 'And I trust that you believe it also. That was no mere threat to deceive either them or you.'

He glanced at the door, trying not to show his uncertainty. 'That man Gates seems to know a great deal.'

'He was my clerk.' Brice sounded lost in thought. 'I caught him stealing spirits and had him flogged. By God, if I ever get my hands on him . . .' He did not continue.

The cabin lanterns swayed in unison and settled at a steeper angle. Bolitho cocked his head to listen. There was more breeze, so the mist might not come after all. Perverse as ever, the Cornish weather was always ready to make a man a liar.

The door banged open and Taylor entered the cabin. 'We've decided, sir.' He ignored Brice. 'We agree.'

Bolitho stood up and tried to hide his relief. 'Thank you.' A boat thudded against the hull and he heard orders being shouted to the oarsmen.

Taylor added, 'They've gone for the others, sir, an' yer cox'n.' He dropped his eyes. 'Gates 'as run.'

More voices, and three lieutenants, dishevelled and apprehensive, stepped into the cabin. Two were very young, the third, tall and tight-lipped, was obviously the first lieutenant, the one Taylor had described as *taken with abusing the people*, having them flogged at the slightest pretext. He thought of Keverne and was suddenly grateful.

The lieutenant said harshly, 'I am Massie, sir, the senior.'

He glanced enquiringly at Brice but stiffened as Bolitho said, 'You will place yourself under open arrest.' He added sharply, 'For your own good at present.'

He looked at the other officers. 'How is the wind?'

'Freshening, sir. From the sou' west.' The young lieutenant sounded dazed.

'Very well. Inform the master that we will be raising the anchor as soon as the boat returns. If we are to reach Falmouth before morning we must beat well clear of the bay.' He forced a smile. 'I'd not wish to have the *Auriga* piled on Gull Rock for all to see!'

On deck it seemed cleaner, the air less threatening. An illusion again, but with good reason, Bolitho thought.

He found the frigate's sailing master listening to the lieutenant with silent disbelief.

Bolitho said calmly, 'I will take the responsibility.' In a quieter tone he added, 'Far better to take a small risk than to leave your people with too much time on their hands.' Inwardly he thought, also it is better to make sail in darkness than to confront the *Euryalus*'s broadsides at first light.

When the boat came alongside again he saw Allday scrambling through the entry port, his head turning in all directions as if to take on the whole ship single-handed.

He found Bolitho and said thickly, 'By the Lord, Captain, I never expected this!' The admiration was only overshadowed by his obvious concern.

Bolitho looked at him and grinned. 'I am sorry to have placed you in danger.'

The big coxswain waited until some scurrying seamen had run past. 'I was just about to leave the inn, Captain, and try my luck again on that damned horse. I might have been able to reach Falmouth in time to raise the alarm.'

Bolitho frowned. 'What of your guards?'

Allday shrugged and then pulled up the leg of his trousers. Even in the gloom it was possible to see the small double-barrelled pistol protruding from his stocking.

'I reckon I could have laid those two beauties to rest without too much sweat!'

'You will never fail to amaze me, Allday.' Bolitho stared at him. 'So you had a plan all of your own, eh?'

'Not *all* my own. Bryan Ferguson gave me the pistol before we left. He bought it off one of the Falmouth Packet officers.' He breathed out noisily. 'I'd not be wanting to leave it *all* to you, Captain.' He peered around the quarterdeck. 'Not amongst bloody hounds like these!'

Bolitho turned away, his mind dwelling on Allday's simple loyalty. He wanted to find the right words, something which might convey just how much it meant to him at this moment of time.

'Thank you, Allday. That was reckless but extremely far-sighted of you.'

Why could he never find the words when he needed them? And why was Allday grinning almost enough to split his face in two?

Allday said, 'Strike me blind, Captain, you are a cool one, and there's no mistake. We might both be dead, an' instead here we are as safe as the Tower of London.' He rubbed his buttocks. 'Also, we return to Falmouth as sailors should, and not on some bony, misbegotten animal.'

Bolitho gripped his thick forearm. 'I am glad you are satisfied.'

A lieutenant crossed the deck and touched his hat. 'Capstan manned and boat hoisted, sir.'

'Very good.' He felt suddenly light-headed. Perhaps he had not, after all, realized just how close he had been to disaster. Allday had understood and had been prepared in his own way. But suppose Brice had refused to submit, or Gates had held his grip on the other men? He dismissed it from his thoughts. That

49

part was over, and he could thank God no one had been injured, let alone killed, in the uprising.

'Tell the master to lay a course to clear the foreland, if you please. We will run to the sou' east until we have the sea room to go about.'

The young officer stood quite still, his eyes filling his face in the darkness.

Bolitho added gently, 'Your name is Laker, am I right?' He saw him nod. 'Well, Mr Laker, just imagine that both of your seniors had been killed in action.' Another nod. 'It is your quarterdeck for the moment, and it would be well for your people to see you taking control right away. Trust is like gold, it must be earned to be of any true value.'

The youngster said quietly, 'Thank you, sir.' Then he walked away, and seconds later the capstan began to clank round to the accompaniment of a half-hearted shanty.

Bolitho walked slowly aft and stood near the wheel. He would be ready, in case the frigate drove too close inshore. But if the *Auriga* had any hope of regaining her place in affairs, she had to begin here and now, with her own hands in command.

It was as if Allday was reading his mind.

He said softly, 'Reminds me of when we were in the old *Phalarope*, Captain.' He glanced up as the sails cracked and stirred in readiness for the next order. 'It took a long, long time before we got *our* good name back!'

Bolitho nodded. 'I remember.'

'Loose the heads'ls!'

Feet scampered across the tilting decks, and from forward came the steady clank, clank of the capstan.

'Anchors aweigh there!'

The dark land mass swam slowly across the quarter as the frigate tore free of the ground and paid off into the gentle wind.

Bolitho thought momentarily of Brice down there in his cabin, feeling his ship come alive, with voices other than his own calling the commands. *How would I feel under such circumstances?* He shuddered and then pushed Brice from his mind.

If the same circumstances ever did arise, then, like Brice, he would deserve it, he thought firmly.

'Steady as you go!'

'Nor' west by west, sir!' The big wheel squeaked as the *Auriga* glided slowly towards the land.

Bolitho stayed by the weather rail watching the town in the brittle morning sunlight. The *Euryalus* was swinging almost bows on towards the approaching frigate, her topgallant yards gold in the pale glare, the fierce-eyed figurehead bright against the spray-dappled hull.

He looked around the busy activity on the frigate's main deck, the first time he had seen her in daylight. Brice must have been mean as well as a tyrant. The paintwork was faded and flaking, and the seamen were dressed mostly in ragged scraps of clothing and appeared for the most part half starved. Several of them, without shirts as they worked about the deck, had backs so scarred that they looked as if they had been mauled by some crazed beast.

Forward, the anchor party stood watching the outspreading arms of the bay, the town of Falmouth beyond, still in the morning shadow. A guardboat idled above her own reflection, a blue flag at the masthead to indicate where the incoming frigate was to drop anchor. Both the young lieutenants and the ship's master were concentrating on the last two cables, and Bolitho said quietly, 'You had better pass the word to your gunner to prepare a salute, Mr Laker. With all else on your mind it would be a shame to forget that a rear-admiral demands a salute of thirteen guns.'

The lieutenant looked startled and then gave a shy grin. 'I had not forgotten, sir, although I was not expecting you to test me.' He pointed across the nettings. 'But as you well know, sir, it will require *fifteen* guns.' He was still smiling as he hurried back to join the master by the wheel.

Bolitho walked to the nettings and climbed up on to a bollard. It could not be. The lieutenant had to be deceived by a trick of the light, or the fact that *Euryalus* was swinging her bows towards them.

He jumped back to the deck and saw Allday watching him. There was no error. The flag which now lifted in the sunlight flew from the three-decker's foremast.

Allday said quietly, 'So he's arrived, Captain?'

While the *Auriga* moved slowly towards the anchorage, the salute banging out at regular five-second intervals, Bolitho made himself walk back and forth along the weather side of the quarterdeck. Glasses would be trained on the frigate, he must be seen to be both safe and in control. It seemed to take an age for those last moments to drag by. Moments in which he wondered what had happened to Rear-Admiral Thelwall, and what Broughton would think of his actions. When he looked again he saw the *Euryalus* swinging across the bowsprit as the frigate went about, and with canvas cracking and slapping against the yards turned easily into the wind. The anchor had barely dropped into the water when Bolitho heard another sound, growing in the clear air like a roll of great drums. As he swung round and ran to the side he saw, with something like sick horror, the three rows of gun ports along the *Euryalus*'s side opening together, and as if guided by a single hand, the triple array of black muzzles running out into the sunlight.

The lieutenant murmured, 'My God!'

Taylor ran aft, pointing dazedly. 'Boats comin', sir!'

There were nearly a dozen of them. Cutters and launches, all crammed with marines, their coats shining like blood as they sat motionless between the busy oars.

Some of the seamen seemed unable to drag their eyes from the *Euryalus*'s massive armament, as if they expected every gun to open fire. A few remained staring at the quarterdeck, watching Bolitho, perhaps hoping to read their own fate on his face.

The leading boat rounded the frigate's quarter, shielded from the flagship's guns, and headed towards the entry port. Captain Rook was in the sternsheets, and as he drew alongside he looked up and shouted, 'Are you safe, sir?'

Allday muttered, 'Bloody fool!' But Bolitho did not hear.

He looked down at Rook's red face and replied, 'Of course.' He hoped the seamen nearby would hear him. They would need all their trust in the next few moments.

Rook clambered up to the deck and touched his hat.

'We were worried, sir, very worried indeed.' He saw the two lieutenants watching him and shouted, 'Hand your swords to the lieutenant of marines immediately!'

Bolitho snapped, 'By whose order?'

'I beg pardon, sir.' Rook looked uncomfortable. 'By order of Vice-Admiral Sir Lucius Broughton.' He turned as more boats grappled alongside and the gangway suddenly came alive with grimfaced marines, their muskets and fixed bayonets trained on the crowded main deck.

Bolitho crossed over to the lieutenants. 'Rest assured, I will see that you are not abused.' He looked at Rook. 'I am making *you* responsible.'

The one-armed officer wiped his forehead worriedly. 'As you say, sir.'

Bolitho walked back to the quarterdeck rail and looked along the crowded mass of silent seamen.

'I gave you my word. Keep your peace and obey orders. I shall go across and meet the admiral without delay.'

He saw Taylor make as if to come aft and then stop when a marine jerked a bayonet in his direction.

Bolitho called, 'I have not forgotten, Taylor.'

Then he turned and made his way to the port. A boat was coming from the *Euryalus*. No doubt for him, and an explanation.

He glanced back at the silent, watching men. They were dreading what would happen next. No, they were terrified, he could almost smell their fear, and wanted to reassure them.

He thought suddenly of Brice who had caused it all, and of the clerk Gates who had used the captain's cruelty for his own ends. Now Gates was free somewhere, and Brice might just as easily escape without dishonour. He tightened his jaw and waited impatiently for the boat to get alongside.

We shall see, he thought coldly.

Bolitho raised his hat to the quarterdeck and asked quietly, 'Well, Mr Keverne? I think I need an explanation, and quickly.'

Keverne replied just as quietly, 'I could not help it, sir. Vice-Admiral Broughton arrived during the last dog watch yesterday. He came overland by way of Truro.' He shrugged helplessly, his face worried. 'I had to tell him of your sealed orders, and he required me to open them.'

Bolitho paused by the poop and looked down at the larboard battery of twelve-pounders, still run out and pointing at the *Auriga*. Most of their crews, however, were looking aft at him, their expressions torn between surprise and anxiety. As well they might, he thought bitterly.

But it was not Keverne's fault, and that was something. For a while he had been tortured with the idea that Keverne might have given his secret orders willingly, to ingratiate himself with the new admiral.

He asked, 'How is Sir Charles?'

Keverne shook his head. 'No better, sir.'

The second lieutenant crossed the deck and touched his

53

hat. 'The vice-admiral is waiting to see you, sir.' He fidgeted with his sword hilt. 'With respect, sir, he seems somewhat impatient.'

Bolitho forced a slow smile. 'Very well, Mr Meheux, it is a day for urgency.'

But he did not feel like smiling. He could not blame the admiral for demanding to know of his whereabouts. After all, flag officers were not accustomed to making excuses for their own lateness, or explaining their reasons to subordinates. But to have the frigate put under the guns of his own flagship was unthinkable.

He made himself walk the last few steps to the admiral's quarters at a slower pace. To give his mind time to clear for the confrontation.

A marine corporal opened the door, his eyes blank. Even he seemed like a stranger.

Vice-Admiral Sir Lucius Broughton was standing right aft by the tall windows, a telescope trained towards the shore. He was wearing his undress blue coat and gold epaulettes, and appeared thoroughly engrossed. When he turned Bolitho saw that he was much younger than he had anticipated, about forty, the same age as himself. He was not tall, but his body was slim and upright, giving an impression of height. That again was fairly unusual. Once they had attained the coveted flag rank, admirals often tended to run to portliness. Spared the constant demands of watchkeeping, or appearing on deck at all times of day and night, they reaped rewards other than those of high command.

Broughton's face was neither angry nor impatient. In fact, it was relaxed to a point of complete calm. He had light brown hair, quite short, and tied in a small queue above his collar.

'Ah, Bolitho, so we meet at last.' He was not being sarcastic, merely matter-of-fact. As if Bolitho had just returned from some vague journey.

His voice was easy and aristocratic, and when he walked across a patch of sunlight from the stern windows Bolitho saw that his clothes were of the finest materials, his sword-hilt hand-worked in gold facings.

He replied, 'I am sorry I was not here to greet you, sir. There was some doubt as to your time of arrival.'

'Quite.' Broughton sat down at the desk and regarded him calmly. 'I expect to be receiving news of my other ships very shortly. After that, the sooner we are at sea and working in company the better.'

Bolitho cleared his throat. 'The *Auriga*, sir. With respect, I would like to explain what has happened.'

Broughton pressed his fingertips together and smiled gently. For a few moments he looked almost boyish, his eyes shining with something like amusement.

'By all means, Bolitho, although I would have thought that explanations are hardly needed. Your action to prevent the ship falling in French hands was, to say the least, unorthodox, and at no little personal risk. Your loss to me would have been a hard one, although some might say the loss of the frigate would have been even more serious.' He shifted in the chair, the smile gone. 'But the frigate is here in Falmouth, and all such vessels are too short in numbers for us to be over-particular about their past records.'

'I believe her captain should be removed at once, sir. Also her first lieutenant.' Bolitho tried to relax, but for once he felt uneasy, even out of his depth with the new admiral. He added, 'It took some courage for the ship's company to act as they did. But for the Spithead trouble, and the promises made to our people there, it might never have happened.'

Broughton looked at him thoughtfully. 'You obviously do not believe that. You think that this Brice caused it himself, and possibly you're right.' He shrugged. 'Sir Charles Thelwall told me of his great trust in your reasoning. I will of course be guided by that.'

Bolitho said, 'I gave my word to them, sir. That their complaints would be properly investigated.'

'Did you? Well, of course that would be expected. No blame will attach to you now that you have retrieved the ship intact.' Again the brief smile. 'To lie skilfully and in a good cause is always forgivable.'

'It was no lie, sir.' Bolitho could feel his apprehension giving way to anger. 'They were brutally used—worse, they were driven beyond reason.'

He waited, watching for some sign, but Broughton's face was empty of expression.

He continued slowly, 'I am sure Sir Charles would have acted with humanity, sir. Especially in view of the circumstances elsewhere.'

'Sir Charles has gone ashore.' He could have been speaking

55

of an unwanted piece of baggage. 'I will decide what is to be done. When I have examined all the facts.' He paused. 'Facts, Bolitho, not supposition, then I will tell you what I desire to be done. In the meantime, Captain Brice and his officers will be quartered ashore with the garrison. You will supply a guard watch aboard *Auriga* in company with the marines.'

He stood up and walked round the desk, his movements easy, almost graceful.

'I hate any sort of unnecessary recriminations, Bolitho.' His mouth tightened. 'But I have already had my fill of deputations and degradation at Spithead. I'll suffer none of it under my flag here.'

Bolitho watched him despairingly. 'If I could be given permission to deal with the matter, sir? It will be a bad beginning to take severe action. . . .'

The admiral sighed. 'You are persistent. I hope that characteristic is not confined merely to domestic matters. But if you will write a full report I will see what must be done.' He looked Bolitho steadily in the eyes. 'You must know that being efficient is not the easiest way to popularity.' He seemed to become impatient. 'But enough of that for the present. I will be giving dinner in my cabin tonight. I find it the best way of meeting my officers.' The smile reappeared. 'No objections to that, I trust?'

Bolitho tried to hide his anger. He was more disturbed with his own inability to convince Broughton than he was with the admiral's wishes over dinner. He had managed the interview badly, and blamed himself accordingly. The admiral only knew what he was told, could only act on facts, as he had just explained.

He replied, 'I am sorry, sir. I did not mean to . . .'

Broughton raised one hand. 'Do not apologize. I like a man with fire in his belly. If I had wanted a flag captain who merely said yes all the time, I could have got one of a hundred.' He nodded. 'And you have been up all night. That cannot have helped. Now be so good as to send for the purser. I will tell him what I require from the town. I have just been looking at it. Small, but not too rustic, I hope.'

Bolitho smiled for the first time. 'I was born here, sir.'

The admiral eyed him calmly. 'Now *there* is an admission.'

Bolitho made to leave the cabin but paused and said, 'May I order the guns to be secured, sir?'

'You are her captain, Bolitho, as well as mine.' He lifted an eyebrow. 'You do not approve of my action?'

'It is not that exactly, sir.' It was starting again, but he could not halt the words. 'I have been with this ship for eighteen months. This matter of the frigate is bad enough, without their having to fire on their own kind into the bargain.'

'Very well.' Broughton yawned. 'You really do care, do you not?'

Bolitho nodded firmly. 'About trust, sir? Aye, I do.'

'I really must take you to London with me, Bolitho.' Broughton walked back to the windows, his face in shadow. 'You would be something of a novelty there. Unique in fact.'

Bolitho reached the sunlit quarterdeck without seeing a foot of the journey.

Keverne touched his hat and asked anxiously, 'Any orders, sir?'

'Yes, Mr Keverne. Pass the word for the purser and then . . .' He paused, still thinking of the *Auriga* and Broughton's quiet amusement.

'Then, sir?'

'Then keep out of my way, Mr Keverne, until I say otherwise!'

The master watched him stride to the side and begin to pace back and forth, his brows set in a frown of concentration.

To the baffled Keverne he said quietly, 'More squalls, I'm thinkin'. An' not for the better.'

Keverne glared at him. 'When I need your opinion, Mr Partridge, I'll damn well ask for it!' Then he too hurried away towards the quarterdeck ladder.

Partridge glanced up at the new flag at the fore. Young puppy, he chuckled unfeelingly. Wrath went with rank. Things never changed in the Navy. He turned, realizing that the captain had stopped his pacing and was studying him gravely.

'Sir?'

'I was just thinking, Mr Partridge, how nice it must be to have nothing to do in the whole world but stand in the sun grinning like some village idiot.'

The master swallowed hard. 'Sorry, sir.'

Surprisingly, Bolitho smiled. 'Continue to stand if you wish. I have a feeling that this peace is to be shortlived.' He turned on his heel and walked briskly beneath the poop towards his cabin.

Partridge sighed and mopped his chins with a red handker-chief. A flagship could often make life hard on a sailing master. Then he looked across at the anchored frigate and shook his head sadly. Still, he thought, others were worse off. A whole lot worse.

4. An Example to All

THE SMART, maroon-painted berlin rattled busily over a hump-backed bridge and swung left on to the main coach road for Falmouth.

Richard Bolitho put out one hand to steady himself against the swaying motion as the wheels bounced into the steep ruts and watched the dust pouring back from the horses' hoofs and from beneath the carriage itself. He was only half aware of the passing countryside, the different shades of green and occasional clumps of sheep in the fields adjoining the narrow, twisting road. In his best dress uniform and cocked hat he was hot and uncomfortable, and the berlin's violent motion was worse than any small boat in a choppy harbour, yet he hardly noticed any of these things.

The previous day Rear-Admiral Thelwall had died in his sleep at Bolitho's house, at peace for the first time in many months.

When Captain Rook had conveyed the news to the anchored *Euryalus* Vice-Admiral Broughton had said, 'I understand it was his wish to return to Norfolk. You had better make the necessary arrangements, Bolitho.' He had given one of his relaxed smiles. 'Anyway, I think Sir Charles would have wished to know you were seen with him on the last journey.'

And so with unseemly haste, a small procession of carriages had set out for Truro, where the little admiral's body would await collection for the long ride to the other side of England.

It was difficult to know if Broughton was being sincere about his regrets. It was true he had much to do in his new com-mand, and yet Bolitho got the distinct impression that Broughton was a man who had little time for anything which did not work at full efficiency. Or anyone who was beyond help or further use.

The berlin swerved and he heard the coachman yelling

curses at a small carrier's cart drawn by one sleepy-looking pony. The cart was laden with chickens and farm produce, and the red-faced driver returned the barrage with equal vigour and vulgarity.

Bolitho smiled. It was probably one of his brother-in-law's farm workers, and he realized with a start that in the four busy days since his bringing the *Auriga* into Falmouth he had not laid an eye either on him or any of his relatives.

The coach settled down on a firmer piece of road for the last three-mile run to the sea, and he found himself thinking back over the hectic and demanding days following on his arrival and that of his new admiral.

He could not recall anyone quite like Broughton. He usually seemed so relaxed, yet he had a mind like quicksilver and never seemed to tire.

Bolitho could remember him at his dinner party in the great cabin the way he kept the conversation moving amongst the assembled ship's officers, never monopolizing it, yet making everyone present very aware of his overall control.

He was still not sure he really understood the man behind the charm and the easy refinement which Broughton displayed on most occasions.

Broughton seemed to be unreachable, yet Bolitho knew he was only excusing his own dislike and mistrust for many of the things which the admiral represented. Privilege and an undisputed pattern of power, another world which Bolitho had had little part of, and wanted still less.

When Broughton spoke of his house in London, the constant comings and goings of names and personalities, it was no mere boasting. It was his natural way of life. Something he took as his right.

Listening to him as the wine was passed and the three-decker rolled easily at her anchor, it was excusable to think that all important decisions in the war against France and her growing allies were made not in Admiralty but around the coffee tables of London, or at receptions in houses such as his own. In spite of this, however, Bolitho had no doubt as to Broughton's understanding of wider affairs and the internal politics of the Navy. Broughton had fought at the battle of Cape St Vincent some three months earlier, and his grasp of the tactics, his ability to paint a visual picture for Bolitho's benefit, were impressive.

Bolitho could recall his own envy and bitterness when news of Jervis's great victory had reached him as he had carried out the wretched routine of blockade off southern Ireland. Had the enemy made a real attempt to invade Ireland and the *Euryalus* and her few consorts had managed to call them to battle, he might have felt differently. As he had eagerly scanned the reports of Jervis's victory he had been aware yet again how much luck there seemed to be in drawing two forces together for a convulsive action.

Old Admiral Jervis had been made Earl St Vincent because of it, and another name, that of Commodore Nelson, had brought a ring of new hope for the future. Bolitho could recall seeing the young Nelson briefly during the ill-fated venture at Toulon. He was two years younger than himself, yet already a commodore, and provided he could stay alive would soon reach further heights in the chain of command.

Bolitho did not grudge such a sea officer his just rewards, but at the same time was fully aware of his own backwater, or that was how it appeared.

Euryalus had been joined by three more ships-of-the-line, all seventy-fours, two frigates, including *Auriga*, and a small sloop. Anchored in fine array in Falmouth Bay they made an impressive sight, but he knew from bitter experience that once at sea and spread out in an empty tossing desert they would appear not so vast or invincible. It was unlikely that Broughton's small squadron was to be entrusted with anything but the fringe of more important affairs.

The one bright light in the busy four days of Broughton's command has been his final acceptance of Bolitho's suggestions and pleas on behalf of the *Auriga*'s ship's company.

The master's mate, Taylor, was in custody and would no doubt be disrated. Captain Brice and his first lieutenant were still ashore with the garrison, and the frigate's daily life had shown an amazing improvement. Apart from her own newly arrived marines there were no additional guards aboard, and Bolitho had sent Lieutenant Keverne to take temporary command until a new captain was appointed. The fact that Broughton had agreed to all this, and Keverne was seen to be the chosen officer aboard, made the lieutenant's chance of promotion and permanent command very likely. Bolitho would be sorry to lose him, but glad to see him get such an unexpected chance.

The horses slowed and topped the last rise, so that he could see the harbour and the sea beyond spread like a colourful map below him. The anchored squadron, the busy comings and goings of Captain Rook's shore boats, showed both purpose and readiness. Once at sea, it should not take too long to get each captain used to the other's ways, for the ships to work as one through the mind of their admiral.

But where they would eventually sail, or what their final role entailed, was still a mystery. Broughton knew a lot more than he confided and had said several times, 'You prepare my ships, Bolitho. I will settle the rest once I hear from London.'

Broughton certainly appeared confident that everything was working out to his satisfaction. As the ships laboured from sunrise to sunset, restoring and watering, replenishing cordage and sharing out whatever human harvest collected by Rook's pressgangs, he spent most of his time in his cabin or dining ashore with the local officials who might help speed the refitting of his command.

All the gloom and most of the apprehension which the *Auriga*'s arrival had brought to Falmouth had disappeared, and Bolitho was grateful that Broughton had shown humanity and such leniency over the matter. What had occurred at Spithead must never occur again, and he would have to watch not only the *Auriga* but each ship of the squadron to make doubly certain of it.

He picked up his sword from the seat and watched while the berlin rolled across the worn cobbles and squeaked to a halt outside the familiar coaching inn by the jetty, the horses steaming and tossing their heads, impatient for rest and food.

A few townspeople moved around the square, but he was instantly aware of the redcoated soldiers and an air of tension which had been lacking when he had left with Thelwall's body for Truro.

He saw Rook hurrying towards him, his face working with relief and concern.

'What is it?' Bolitho took his arm and led him into the inn's long shadow.

Rook glanced around him. 'The Nore. The mutiny has not only spread, but the whole of the fleet there is in the hands of mutineers and under arms!' He dropped his voice. 'A brig from Plymouth brought the news today. Your admiral is in a savage mood because of it.'

Bolitho fell in step beside him, keeping his face calm although his mind was racing at this latest news.

'But how can it be that we have only just heard?'

Rook tugged at his neckcloth as if it was choking him.

'A patrol found the London courier dead in a hedgerow. His throat cut and his pouch empty. Someone knew he was riding here and made sure Admiral Broughton would stay in ignorance for as long as possible.' He signalled towards a seaman by the jetty. 'Call a boat alongside, man!'

Bolitho walked to the edge of the warm stonework and looked towards the ships. *Euryalus* shimmered in a heat haze and there seemed to be plenty of work going on both aloft and around her decks. Was it possible that things could change so quickly? That order and training would give way to mutiny and distrust?

Rook added haltingly, 'I do not know if it is my place to say it, but I believe Sir Lucius Broughton was deeply scarred by his experience at Spithead. It will go hard with anyone who tries to disobey him in the future.'

The boat jarred against the jetty and Bolitho followed him into it. Rook remained standing until Bolitho had settled himself in the sternsheets and then gestured to the coxswain to head for the flagship.

Bolitho said slowly, 'Let us hope we can get to sea without any more delay. There is room to think and plan once the land is well astern.' He was thinking aloud and Rook said nothing.

It seemed to take an age to reach the three-decker's side, and as the boat drew closer he saw that the boarding nets had been rigged and there were marines pacing the gangways and standing at both poop and forecastle.

He climbed quickly up the side and through the entry port, removing his hat as the salutes shrilled once more and the guard presented arms.

Weigall, the third lieutenant, said quickly, 'The admiral is expecting you, sir.' He looked uneasy. 'I am sorry your barge was not waiting at the jetty, but all boats are recalled, sir.'

Bolitho nodded. 'Thank you.' He masked his sudden apprehension and walked aft into the poop's shadow. He had to appear calm and normal even though he felt very much the reverse.

At the cabin bulkhead he saw there were three armed

marines instead of the usual solitary guard and that their bayonets were fixed.

He tightened his jaw and opened the door, conscious o Rook's heavy breathing behind him, of his own dry throat as he saw the other officers already assembled there.

A table had been arranged athwartships, backed by chairs, so that the cabin had taken on the appearance of a court of enquiry. He saw too that the officers who were standing watching him in silence were the other captains from the squadron, even the young commander from the sloop *Restless*.

A lieutenant, quite unknown to Bolitho, hurried towards him, his face set in a tight smile which could be either welcome or sheer relief at his arrival.

'Welcome back, sir.' He gestured towards the closed door of Broughton's small chart cabin. 'Sir Lucius is expecting you, sir.'

He seemed to realize that Bolitho was still unmoving and added apologetically, 'I'm Calvert, sir. The admiral's new flag-lieutenant.'

He spoke in the same refined drawl as Broughton, but there was no other similarity. He looked harassed and confused, and Bolitho felt a note of warning in his mind. In the short while he had been at Truro, shaking hands with officials, listening to sonorous condolences, all this had happened. He heard himself say curtly, 'Then lead the way, Mr Calvert, we will no doubt get acquainted in due course.'

It was very hot in the small cabin, and Bolitho saw that the deckhead skylight was shut, so that there was hardly any air left to breathe.

Broughton was standing beside the table, his arms folded, and staring at the door, as if he had been frozen in the same attitude for some time. His dress coat lay on a chair, and in the filtered sunlight his gleaming white shirt showed darker patches of sweat.

He was very calm, his face quite devoid of expression as he nodded to Bolitho and then snapped to the lieutenant, 'Wait outside, Calvert.'

The lieutenant fidgeted with his coat and muttered, 'The letters, sir, I thought . . .'

'God, man, are you deaf as well as stupid?' He leaned on the table and shouted, 'I said *get out*!'

As the door banged shut behind the wretched Calvert,

63

Bolitho waited for Broughton's rage to expand. It was just as if he had kept it contained to the last possible second. Until his return on board to receive the full brunt of it.

Surprisingly, his voice was almost normal as he continued, 'By God, I'm glad you got back aboard punctually.' He gestured to an open envelope on the table. 'Sailing orders at last. That donkey Calvert brought them from London.'

Bolitho waited, allowing Broughton time to calm down. He said quietly, 'Had you wished it, sir, I could have obtained a flag-lieutenant from the squadron . . .'

Broughton eyed him coldly. 'Oh, to damnation with *him*! Some favour I received years ago has to be repaid. I promised to take that fool off his father's hands and away from London.' He broke off and peered up at the skylight, his head on one side as if listening.

Then he said, 'You have heard the news, no doubt.' His chest was moving with sudden anger again. 'These miserable, treacherous scum have the impudence to mutiny, eh? The whole fleet at the Nore aflame with, with . . .' he groped for the word and then added harshly, 'so much for your damned humanity. Conceit is what I call it, if you believe for one single moment that their sort respect leniency!'

Bolitho said, 'With all deference, sir, I think there is no connection between the *Auriga* and the trouble at the Nore.'

'Do you not?' His voice was steady again. Too steady. 'I can assure you, *Captain* Bolitho, I have already had my fill of treachery at Spithead. To have my own flagship taken over by a lot of crawling sanctimonious, lying bastards. The humiliation, the very shame of it clings to me like the stench of a sewer.'

There was a discreet tap at the door and Captain Giffard of the ship's marines peered in and reported, 'All ready, sir.' He withdrew hurriedly under Broughton's stare.

Bolitho said, 'May I ask what is happening, sir?'

'You may.' Broughton dragged his coat from the chair, his face shining damply with sweat. 'Because of you I went against my better judgement. Because of you I allowed the *Auriga*'s mutineers to stay free and untried.' He swung round, his eyes blazing. 'Because of *you* and your damned promises, promises which you had neither the authority nor the right to offer, I must leave them untouched, if only to uphold your authority as flag captain!' He was shouting now, and Bolitho could picture the other captains beyond the closed door sympathizing with him, or grateful that a superior was being cut down to their level. Bolitho did not know any of them enough to decide which. He only knew he was both angry and bitter at the admiral's sudden attack.

He said harshly, 'It was my decision, sir. There was no one else here at the time . . .'

Broughton yelled, 'Do not interrupt me, Bolitho! By God, it might have been better if you had attacked the *Auriga* and blown her to pieces. If they have officers like you at the Nore, then heaven help England!'

He snatched his sword and clipped it into his belt, adding, 'Well, we shall see about mutiny in *this* squadron.'

Bolitho controlled his voice with an effort. 'I am sorry you cannot accept my judgement, sir.'

'Judgement?' Broughton looked at him. 'I call it surrender.' He shrugged and reached for his hat. 'I cannot right a wrong, but by heaven I'll show them I'll have no insubordination in my ships!'

He threw open the door and strode into the great cabin.

'Be seated, gentlemen.' He took his place in the centre chair and gestured to Bolitho to sit beside him. 'Now, gentlemen, I have called this summary court by the authority invested in me which has been given special powers until such time as the present emergency has been curtailed.'

Bolitho looked quickly at the others. Their faces were like masks. They were probably dazed by the swift change of events and wondering how it would affect them personally.

Broughton seemed to be speaking to the opposite bulkhead, his voice even and under control once again. 'The ringleader of the *Auriga*'s insurrection was one Thomas Gates, captain's clerk. He was, er, allowed to escape, and will no doubt be responsible with others for the death of the courier and seizure of my sealed despatches.'

The air in the cabin was stiff with tension, so that shipboard noises seemed suddenly loud and unreal.

Broughton continued calmly, 'The master's mate,' he glanced at a paper before him, 'one John Taylor, at present under guard for conspiracy, is thereby the senior culprit available to this court.'

'May I speak, sir?' Bolitho's voice made every head turn towards him. For just those few seconds he saw the others as individuals, the differing expressions mirrored in their eyes. Sympathy, understanding, from one even amusement.

He shut them out of his thoughts as he continued quietly, 'Taylor was one of many, sir. He came to me because he trusted me.'

Broughton turned to study him, his eyes distant. 'Two of his companions have already laid evidence against him as the ringleader, next to Gates.' For an instant his gaze softened with something like compassion. 'They could be getting even with Taylor for deposing their leader. They might equally be just and loyal seamen.' His mouth hardened. 'That is no longer my concern. This squadron *is*, and I intend to see it fulfils whatever duty laid upon it without interference.' He let his gaze lock with Bolitho's. 'From anyone.'

Then he rapped the table with his knuckles. 'Bring in the prisoner.'

Bolitho sat quite still as Taylor entered between two marines with Captain Giffard marching stiffly at his back. He looked pale but composed, and as he saw Bolitho his face lit up with sudden recognition.

Broughton eyed him coolly. 'John Taylor, you are charged with mutinous conspiracy and seizure of His Britannic Majesty's Ship *Auriga*. You were accused with one other, not yet in custody, of this same act, and are called here to receive sentence.' He tapped his fingertips together and added quietly, 'Your treachery, at a time when England is fighting for her very life, singles you out as a man without either pride or conscience. You, a master's mate, trained and trusted by your superiors, have betrayed the very Service which has given you your means to live.'

Taylor seemed stunned. He replied in a small voice, 'Not true, sir.' He shook his head. 'Not true.'

'However,' Broughton leaned back in his chair and looked at the deckhead beams, 'in view of your past record, and all that my flag captain has done and said on your behalf . . .' He broke off as Taylor took half a step forward, his eyes shining with sudden hope. As a marine pulled him back again Broughton added, 'I have decided not to impose the maximum penalty, as your case, in my personal view, demands.'

Taylor turned his head dazedly and peered at Bolitho. In the same small voice he whispered, 'Thankee, sir. God bless you.'

Broughton sounded irritated. 'Instead, the punishment awarded will be that of two dozen lashes and disrating.'

Taylor nodded, his eyes swimming with emotion. 'Thankee, sir!'

Broughton's voice was like a knife. 'Two dozen lashes *from each ship* assembled here at Falmouth.' He nodded. 'Remove the prisoner.'

Taylor said nothing as the marines wheeled him round and marched him out.

Bolitho stared at the closed doors, the empty space where Taylor had stood, and felt as if the cabin was closing in on him. As if he and not Taylor had received the sentence.

Broughton rose and said briefly, 'Return to your ships, gentlemen, and read my new standing orders which Mr Calvert will make available. Punishment will be carried out at eight bells tomorrow forenoon, Normal procedure.'

As they filed out past Calvert, Bolitho said quietly, 'Why, sir? In the name of God, *why*?'

Broughton looked past him, his eyes bleak, 'Because *I* say so.'

Bolitho picked up his hat, his mind dulled by the sudden savagery of Broughton's justice.

'Any more orders for the present, sir?' He did not know how he was managing to keep his tone formal and devoid of feeling.

'Yes. Pass the word to Captain Brice to resume command of *Auriga*.' He regarded Bolitho for several seconds. 'Mine is the responsibility. So too is the privilege.'

Bolitho met his gaze and replied, 'If Taylor had been given a court-martial, sir . . .' He stopped, realizing how he had stepped into the trap.

Broughton smiled gently. 'A proper court-martial would have hanged him, and well you know it. The sentence would have been carried out too late to make an example, and time and indulgence would have been wasted. As it is now, Taylor's punishment will act as a warning, if not a deterrent to his squadron where we need it most. And he may live to make capital from his one moment of personal insurrection, and will have you to thank for it.'

As Bolitho turned to leave he added, 'There will be a conference here immediately the punishment is completed. Make a signal for all captains to repair on board,' he took out his watch, 'but I can leave that for you to arrange, I think. I

67

have been invited to join a local magistrate for dinner. A man called Roxby, know him?'

'My brother-in-law, sir.' His voice was like stone.

'Really?' Broughton walked towards his sleeping cabin. 'You people seem to be everywhere.' The door slammed behind him.

Bolitho reached the quarterdeck without seeing a foot of the journey. The shadows were more angled and the sun already dipping towards the headland. A few seamen lounged on the gangways, and from forward came the plaintive notes of a violin. The officer of the watch crossed to the opposite side to allow Bolitho his usual seclusion, and beside the boat tier two midshipmen were shrilling with laughter as they chased each other towards the main shrouds.

Bolitho leaned his hands on the bulwark and stared unblinkingly at the orange sun. He did not feel like pacing this evening, and wherever he turned he seemed to see Taylor's face, the pathetic gratitude at receiving two dozen lashes, changing to horror at the final sentence. He would be down below now, hearing the midshipmen laughing and the fiddler's sad lament. Maybe it was for him. If so, Broughton's cruel example had already misfired, he thought bitterly.

He shifted his gaze to the *Auriga* as she swung gently at her cable. Some would say that Taylor's punishment was a worthwhile sacrifice of one man against so many. But for Bolitho's action every man aboard might have been flogged or worse, or the ship could indeed have been lost to the enemy.

But there were others who would say that whatever the outcome, the course of naval justice would never be found by flogging scapegoats. And Bolitho knew Taylor was one of these, and was ashamed because of it.

Bolitho was staring emptily through the great stern windows of his cabin when Allday entered and said, 'All ready, Captain.'

Without waiting for a reply he took down the old sword from its rack on the panelled bulkhead and turned it over in his hands, pausing to rub the tarnished hilt across the sleeve of his jacket.

Then he said quietly, 'You did your best, Captain. There's no value in blaming yourself.'

Bolitho held up his arms to allow the big coxswain to buckle the sword around his waist and then let them fall to his sides. Through the thick glass windows he could see the distant town swinging gently as wind and tide took the *Euryalus* under control. He was again aware of the silence which had fallen over the whole ship since Keverne had come down to report that the lower decks were cleared and that it was close on eight bells.

He picked up his hat and glanced briefly around the cabin. It should have been a good day for quitting the land. A fair breeze had sprung up from the south-west overnight and the air was clean and crisp.

He sighed and walked from the cabin, past the table and its untouched breakfast, through the door with the rigid sentry and towards the bright rectangle of sunlight and the open quarterdeck beyond.

Keverne was waiting, his dark features inscrutable as he touched his hat and said formally, 'Two minutes, sir.'

Bolitho studied the lieutenant gravely. If Keverne was brooding about his sudden removal from possible command he did not show it. If he was thinking about his captain's feelings he concealed that too.

Bolitho nodded and walked slowly to the weather side of the deck where the ship's lieutenants were already mustered. Slightly to leeward the senior warrant officers and midshipmen stood in neat lines, their bodies swaying easily to the ship's motion.

A glance aft told him that Giffard's marines were fallen in across the poop, their tunics very bright in the fresh sunlight, the white cross-belts and polished boots making their usual impeccable array.

He turned and walked to the quarterdeck rail, letting his eyes move over the great press of seamen who were crowded along the gangways, in the tiered boats and clinging to the shrouds, as if eager to watch the coming drama. But he could tell from the silence, the air of grim expectancy, that hardened to discipline and swift punishment though they were, there was no acceptance there.

Eight bells chimed from the forecastle and he saw the officers stiffen as Broughton, accompanied by Lieutenant Calvert, walked briskly on to the quarterdeck.

Bolitho touched his hat but said nothing.

Across the anchorage the air shivered as a solitary gun

boomed out, and then came the doleful sound of drumming. He saw the surgeon below the break in the poop whispering to Tebbutt, the boatswain, and his two mates, one of whom carried the familiar red baize bag. The latter dropped his eyes as he realized his captain was looking at him.

Broughton's fingers were tapping the hilt of his beautiful sword, seemingly in time with the distant drum. He appeared relaxed, and as fresh as ever.

Bolitho tensed as one of the young midshipmen wiped his mouth with the back of his hand, a quick nervous gesture which brought back a sudden memory like the feel of an old wound.

He had been only fourteen himself when he had witnessed his first flogging through the fleet. He had seen most of it in a mist of tears and nausea, and the nightmare had never completely left him. In a service where flogging was common-place and an accepted punishment, and in many cases more than justified, this final spectacle was still the worst, where onlookers felt degraded almost as much as the victim.

Broughton remarked, 'We will be weighing this afternoon, Bolitho. Our destination is Gibraltar, where I will receive further orders and news of developments.' He looked up at his flag at the fore and added, 'A fine day for it.'

Bolitho looked away, trying to shut the persistent drumming from his ears.

'All the ships are fully provisioned, sir.' He stopped. Broughton knew that as well as he did. It was just something to say. Why should this one event mar everything? He should have realized by now that the days when he had been a young frigate captain were gone for good. Then, faces and people were real individuals. When one suffered it was felt throughout the cramped confines of the ship. Now he had to realize that men were no longer individuals. They were necessities, like the artillery and the rigging, the fresh water supply and the very planking upon which he now stood.

He felt Broughton watching and deliberately turned away. But it *did* matter, and he *did* care, and he knew he could not change. Not for Broughton, or to further his own chances of promotion in the Service he loved and now needed more than ever before.

He heard Keverne clear his throat and then something like a sigh from the watching seamen on the gangways.

Around the bows of the *Zeus*, the nearest seventy-four, came a slow procession of longboats, one from each ship in the squadron, the oars rising and falling with the 'Rogue's March' of the drum. He could see *Euryalus*'s boat second in the line, dark green like those now lashed in their tier and crowded with silent men. Each one in the procession carried marines, the lethal glitter of their bayonets and gleam of scarlet bringing colour to the grim spectacle as the boats turned slightly and headed for the flagship.

Broughton said softly, 'This should not take too long, I think.'

'Way 'nough!'

The *Auriga*'s longboat glided alongside and hooked on to the main chains, while the others swayed above their reflections to witness punishment.

Bolitho took the Articles of War from Keverne and walked quickly to the entry port. Spargo, the surgeon, was already down in the boat accompanied by the boatswain's mates, and he glanced up as Bolitho's shadow fell across the rigid oarsmen.

He said, 'Fit for punishment, sir.'

Bolitho made himself look at the figure in the forepart of the frigate's longboat. Bent almost double, his arms lashed out on a capstan bar as if crucified, it was hard to believe it was Taylor. The man who had come to ask for help. For forgiveness and . . . He removed his hat, opened the book and began to read the Articles, the sentence and punishment.

Below in the boat, Taylor stirred slightly, and Bolitho paused to look once again.

The thwarts and planking of the boat were covered with blood. Not the blood of battle, but black. Like the remnants of torn skin which hung from his mangled back. Black and ripped, so that the exposed bones shone in the sunlight like polished marble.

The boatswain's mate glanced up and asked thickly, 'Two dozen, zur?'

'Do your duty.'

Bolitho replaced his hat and kept his eyes on the nearest two-decker as the man drew back his arm and then brought the lash down with terrible force.

A step sounded beside him and Broughton said quietly, 'He seems to be taking it well enough.' No concern or real interest. Just a casual comment.

Just as suddenly it was over, and as the boat cast off again to continue its way to the next ship Bolitho saw Taylor trying to turn his head to look up at him. But he did not have the strength.

Bolitho turned away, sickened by the sight of the contorted face, the broken lips, the thing which had once been John Taylor.

He said harshly, 'Dismiss the hands, Mr Keverne.' He glanced involuntarily back again at the re-formed procession. Two more ships to go. He would never live through it. A younger man possibly, but not Taylor.

He heard Broughton's voice again, very near. 'If he had not been one of your old ship's company—er, the *Sparrow* was it?'—he sighed—'you would not have felt so involved, so vulnerable.'

When Bolitho did not reply he added curtly, 'An example had to be made. They'll not forget it, I think.'

Bolitho straightened his back and faced him, his voice steady as he replied, 'Neither will I, sir.'

For just a few more seconds their eyes held, and then the shutter seemed to fall as Broughton said, 'I am going below. Make the signal for all captains as soon as possible.' Then he was gone.

Bolitho took a grip of his thoughts, his anger and disgust.

'Mr Keverne, you will instruct the midshipmen of the watch to bend the signal for all captains to repair on board.'

Keverne watched him curiously. 'When shall it be hoisted, sir?'

A voice called, 'Signal from *Valorous*, sir. Prisoner has died under punishment.'

Bolitho kept his eyes on Keverne. 'You may hoist it now.' Then he turned on his heel and strode aft to his cabin.

5. A Bad Beginning

SHARP AT TWO BELLS of the forenoon watch Vice-Admiral Sir Lucius Broughton strode on to the *Euryalus*'s quarterdeck. After nodding briskly to Bolitho he took a glass from a midshipman and proceeded to study each ship of his squadron in turn.

Bolitho ran his eye quickly along the upper deck where gun crews were going through their drill, watched with extra attention, now that the admiral had arrived, by Meheux, his round-faced second lieutenant.

It had been three days since they had sailed from Falmouth, a long, slow three days during which they had logged a mere four hundred miles. Bolitho gripped the quarterdeck rail, his body angled against the steep tilt, as with her consorts *Euryalus* plunged ponderously on a slow starboard tack, her great yards braced round, the straining topsails hard-bellied like metal in the wind.

Not that it had been bad sailing weather, quite the reverse. Skirting the Bay of Biscay, for instance, Partridge, the master, had remarked that he had rarely seen it so favourable. Now, with a freshening north-westerly ruffling the sea into an endless panorama of crisp white-caps it seemed likely the opportunity was going. It would soon be time to reef, rather than make more sail.

Once clear of the land Broughton had decided to start putting his ships through their paces, to check the flaws and draw out the varied qualities or otherwise of his new command.

Bolitho darted another glance towards him, wondering what new complaints or suggestions would come out of his inspection.

In any flagship a captain was constantly aware of his admiral's presence, must allow for every mood or whim and somehow work it into his own scheme for running a routine without confusion. And yet he was surprised to find that he still knew Broughton hardly at all. He seemed to run his daily life by the clock with very little deviation. Breakfast at eight, dinner at half past two and supper at nine. Exactly at nine o'clock each forenoon he would come on deck and behave just as he was doing now. If anything, he appeared too rigid, and not merely in his habits.

The first day at sea, for instance, he had put his battle tactics into immediate operation. But unlike usual practice, he had retained the *Euryalus* at third place in the line, with only the one remaining seventy-four, the *Valorous*, stationed astern.

While the ships had tacked and floundered in a quarter sea to obey his curt signals Broughton had remarked, 'One must study the captains just as much as the ships they command.'

Bolitho grasped immediately what he meant and had appreciated the sense of it.

It was pointless in some actions to have the most powerful

ship, the one flying the admiral's flag in particular, crashing headlong into the enemy's line. She could be disabled and rendered useless when she was most needed, when the admiral had the time and information of the enemy's intentions.

Without using a glass he could see the leading ships quite easily, keeping the same positions that Broughton had ordered from the outset. Leading the line, and almost hidden by the straining topsails and forecourse of the next astern, was the two-decker *Zeus*. She was an elderly seventy-four, a veteran of the Glorious First of June, St Vincent and several smaller actions. Her captain, Robert Rattray, had been in command for three years and was known for his aggressive behaviour in battle, a bulldog tenacity which showed clearly on his square, weathered face. Exactly the kind of captain to take the first searing crash of a broadside when testing the enemy's line. A seasoned, professional seaman, but with little else in his head but a strong sense of duty and a desire to do battle.

Captain Falcon of the *Tanais*, the second seventy-four, was quite the opposite. A mournful, untidy-looking man, with hooded, thoughtful eyes, he would be one to follow without question, but would use his imagination as well as his training to explore Rattray's first approach.

About a mile astern of the *Euryalus* was the last in the line, the *Valorous*. Commanded by Captain Rodney Furneaux, a tight-lipped and haughty autocrat, she had proved to be a fast and manœuvrable vessel under nearly all circumstances, and provided she could maintain her station would be well placed to protect the flagship or run down to assist any of her consorts if they got into difficulties.

Bolitho heard the glass close with its customary snap and turned to touch his hat as Broughton walked towards him.

He said formally, 'Wind still from the nor' west, sir, but freshening.' He saw Broughton's eyes move slowly along the sweating lines of seamen at the guns. 'The new course is sou' west by west.'

Broughton gave a grunt. 'Good. Your gun crews appear to be adequate.'

That was one thing Bolitho had learned. Broughton usually opened the day with some such comment. Like a spur, or a calculated insult.

He replied calmly, 'Clear for action in ten minutes or less, sir, and then three broadsides every two minutes.'

Broughton studied him thoughtfully. 'That is your standard, is it?'

'Yes, sir.'

'I have heard of some of your *standards*.' Broughton placed his hands on his hips and peered up at the maintop where some marines were exercising with a swivel gun. 'I hope our people will remember when the time comes.'

Bolitho waited. There would be more.

The admiral said absently, 'When I dined with your brother-in-law at Falmouth he was telling me something of your family background.' He turned and looked hard at Bolitho. 'I knew of your brother's, er, misfortune, of course.' He let it sink in before adding, 'How he deserted from the Navy.'

He paused, his head slightly on one side.

Bolitho faced him coldly. 'He died in America, sir.' It was strange how easily the lie came now. But the resentment was as strong as ever, and he had a sudden mad desire to say something to shock Broughton from his safe, all-powerful pillar. What would he say, for instance, if he knew that Hugh had been killed in action, right there, where he was now standing? At least Broughton's probing remarks had allowed him to think of Hugh's death without so much remorse and despair. As his eye moved briefly across Broughton's shoulder to the broad, orderly quarterdeck, the great double wheel with its attentive helmsman and master's mate, it was hard to see it as the bloody shambles on that day Hugh had died. Using his own body as a shield to save his son Adam, who was still completely ignorant of his father's presence, as men had screamed and died in the din of battle.

Broughton said, 'And all over a duel, I believe? Could never understand the stupid attitude of people who made duelling a crime. Do you pride yourself as a swordsman, by any chance?'

Bolitho forced a smile. 'My sword has often been a comfort in battle, sir.' He could not see where this line of talk was leading.

The admiral showed his teeth. They were very small and even. 'A duel is for gentlemen.' He shook his head. 'But as there seem to be so many in Parliament today who are neither swordsmen nor gentlemen, I suppose we must expect this sort of obstruction.' He glanced towards the poop. 'I will take a walk for half an hour.'

75

Bolitho watched him go up the poop ladder. The admiral's daily walk. It never varied either.

He let his mind return to Broughton's plan of battle. Perhaps the answer lay with him rather than the plan. Too much rigidity. But surely he would have learned from experience that in many cases ships were called to give battle when scattered and without any set order at all? At St Vincent where Broughton had actually fought, Commodore Nelson had once again confounded the critics by dashing into the attack without regard for any set stratagem. Bolitho had mentioned it to Broughton and had gained one further clue to his unwavering attitude.

He had snapped, 'Nelson, Nelson, that's all I hear! I saw him in his damned *Captain*, although I was busy myself at the time. More luck on his side than any sense of timing.' He had become very cool with equal suddenness. 'Give your people a plan, something to learn and learn until they can act as one in total darkness or the middle of a typhoon. Keep at them without rest until they can think of nothing else. You can keep your damned heroics for my part. Give me a plan, one that is well tried, and I'll give you a victory!'

Bolitho thought back over that one brief insight. Broughton was actually jealous. Senior to Nelson, an officer he did not even know except by reputation, with influence and breeding to support his every move, and yet he was jealous for all that.

It did not add much to Bolitho's knowledge of his superior, but it did make him seem more human.

Broughton had never mentioned Taylor's death or the savage flogging since weighing anchor. Even at the hasty conference after the punishment he had made little comment, but for one about maintaining discipline at all times.

In fact, as the wine had been passed around the assembled captains in the same cabin where Taylor had heard his terrible fate, Broughton had been completely at ease, even jocular as he had told the others of the sailing orders for Gibraltar.

Bolitho could recall seeing the *Auriga*'s longboat grounding on a sandbar, the marines digging a hasty grave for Taylor's corpse, working fast in the sunlight to beat a rising tide. Taylor would rot in an unmarked grave. A martyr, or a victim of circumstances, it was hard to know which.

Once at sea again Bolitho had watched his own ship's company for any sign of unrest, but the daily routine had kept them too busy perhaps for recriminations or argument. The squadron had sailed without further incident and with no fresh news of the troubles at the Nore.

He shaded his eyes to peer at the glittering horizon line. Somewhere out there, far to windward and visible only to the masthead lookouts, was the ship in question, the *Auriga*, once again under the command of her original captain, Brice. Bolitho had made it his business to summon him aboard just prior to sailing and had given him a warning as to his behaviour. He had known it to be useless even as he was speaking to him.

Brice had stood quite still in his cabin, his hat beneath his arm, his pale eyes avoiding Bolitho's until he had finished.

Then he had said softly, 'Vice-Admiral Broughton does not accept that there was a mutiny. Neither, sir, did you when you came aboard my ship. The fact that I am being returned to my rightful command surely proves that whatever wrongs were committed were by others.' He had smiled slightly. 'One who escaped, and the other who was treated with more leniency than might be expected in these dangerous times.'

Bolitho had walked around the table, feeling the other man's hate behind the mask of quiet amusement, knowing his own feelings were little better.

'Now hear my words, Brice, and remember them. We are going on a special mission, maybe an important one for England. You will do well to change your ways if you wish to see your homeland again.'

Brice had stiffened. 'There'll be no more uprisings in my ship, sir!'

Bolitho had forced a smile. 'I was not referring to your own people. If you betray your trust once more, I will personally see that you are brought to a court-martial, and that *you* receive the justice you so obviously enjoy imposing on others!'

Bolitho walked to the nettings and glanced down at the water leaping against the tall side. The squadron was about one hundred miles north-west of Cape Ortegal, the very corner of Spain. If ships had minds of their own, would *Euryalus* be remembering it too? he wondered. It was here that she fought under the French flag against Bolitho's old *Hyperion*. Where her decks ran scarlet and the battle raged without let-up until its grisly conclusion. But maybe ships did not care after all. Men died, crying for half-remembered wives and children, for mothers, or for their comrades in hell. Others lived on in a maimed existence ashore, forgotten by the sea and avoided by many of those who could have helped them.

But the ships sailed on, impatient perhaps with the fools who manned them.

'Sir! *Zeus* is signalling!' The midshipman of the watch was suddenly galvanized into action. He jumped into the shrouds, his big telescope already to his eye. '*Zeus* to Flag. Strange sail bearing nor' west.' He looked down at Bolitho, his face shining with excitement.

Bolitho nodded. 'Excellent, Mr Tothill. That was quickly done.' He glanced round and saw Keverne hurrying towards him. The signal probably meant nothing, but after drills and dragging uncertainty any sort of change was welcome. It had swept his other thoughts away like cobwebs.

'Sir?' Keverne eyed him intently.

'Dismiss the hands from drills and prepare to set the t'gallants on her.' He looked aloft, his eyes watering in the crisp breeze. 'The royals too if the wind gets no worse.'

As he hurried away Broughton reappeared on the quarter-deck, his face very calm.

Bolitho said, 'Sail to the nor' west, sir.' He saw the brightness in the admiral's eyes and guessed how hard it was for him to appear so controlled.

Broughton pursed his lips. 'Signal the *Auriga* to intercept.'

'Aye, sir.'

Bolitho beckoned to the signal midshipman and could almost feel Broughton's impatience at his back. Only the previous day he had sent the other frigate, *Coquette*, on ahead at full speed to reach Gibraltar with his despatches, and to make sure there was no change in plans for his squadron. With *Auriga* to windward and the little sloop *Restless* sweeping down-wind in the hopes of snatching a French or Spanish fisherman for information, it had left his resources very strained.

The boy reported, '*Auriga* has acknowledged, sir.'

Bolitho could picture the scene on the frigate's deck as the distant flags had been studied, probably from some swaying yard far above the sea, by another midshipman like Tothill.

He could well imagine Brice's feelings at this moment too. A chance to further his position with the admiral and before the whole squadron would not be taken lightly. And heaven help any poor wretch who displeased him at such a time.

He took the big glass and climbed up beside the midshipman in the weather shrouds, and trained it towards the horizon. The frigate leapt into view, her topsails already filling as she went about and dashed towards the newcomer. He could imagine the sounds of spray cascading over her bowsprit, the scream of blocks and rigging as more and more canvas thundered out from her yards to contain and hold the wind for her own power.

It was easy to forget men like Brice at such times, he thought vaguely. *Auriga* was a beautiful little ship, a living, vital thing as she heeled to the wind and buried her lee gunports in foam.

He returned to the deck and said, 'Permission to give chase, sir?' For another small moment he shared a common understanding and excitement with Broughton. Saw his jaw tighten, the gleam in his eyes.

'Yes.' He stood aside as Bolitho raised his hand to Keverne. Then he added, 'All ships will, however, retain their stations. See to it.'

As the signal soared up the yards and broke to the wind Bolitho saw the other ships hoist their acknowledgements as one. Every captain must have been waiting for this, praying for something to break the monotony and the uncertain watchfulness which had dogged them since Falmouth.

Overhead the growing spread of canvas cracked and boomed, the great yards bending like bows until they looked as if they would tear free from the masts. The hull tilted still further, so that men hastening about the upper deck seemed to be leaning at strange and unreal angles, while more, and still more, canvas bellied out to the wind.

On the lower gundeck the ports would be completely submerged, and Bolitho could hear the pumps already clanking as the hull took the strain and accepted it.

But they were overhauling the nearest seventy-four, and through the straining criss-cross of rigging and shrouds he could see the officers on the *Tanais*'s quarterdeck peering astern at the flagship as she began to creep up on them.

Broughton said testily, 'Signal *Tanais* to make more sail, dammit!'

As he walked away to the opposite side Bolitho heard Partridge mutter, 'Her'll 'ave the sticks out of 'er if she does, by God!'

Bolitho snapped, 'Mr Tothill, get to the masthead and double quick! I need some good eyes up there today.'

He made himself walk slowly back and forth on the weather side, hating the slow pace of the squadron as he tried to picture what the other ship was doing.

'Deck there! *Zeus* is signalling, sir! *Enemy in sight!*' His voice was shrill with excitement. 'A frigate, steering due east!'

Keverne rubbed his hands. 'Running for Vigo, I shouldn't wonder.'

He looked unusually tense, and Bolitho guessed he was probably picturing what might have been with himself commanding *Auriga* instead of Brice.

He replied, 'There's a good chance we can head her off, Mr Keverne.'

Brice had the wind almost under his coat-tails and was fairly flying across the path of his slow and ponderous consorts. The Frenchman could either try to outpace him or go about and lose valuable time trying to beat out to sea again. If he chose the latter course, one of the ships in the line might even get an opportunity . . .

He jerked round as Broughton rapped, 'God damn the *Valorous*!' He threw his telescope to a seaman. 'Now *she's* falling back.'

The signal soared aloft immediately to *Euraylus*'s yards. *Make more sail*. But even as the acknowledgement broke from the two-decker Bolitho saw her fore topgallant sail disintegrate like ashes as it tore itself to fragments in the wind.

Bolitho said, 'Shall I signal *Zeus* to chase independently, sir? She's got a good lead.' He knew the answer already, saw Broughton's mouth tightening as he added, 'The Frenchman might still slip away from *Auriga*.'

'No.' One word, with nothing to show disappointment or anger.

Bolitho looked away. The Frenchman would be surprised that there was no change in the squadron's line of advance. He was somewhere right ahead of the column, hidden by *Zeus*'s tall pyramid of sails, and moving very fast. But *Auriga* had crossed over now, and he could see her speeding downwind, every sail set and drawing its full as she tore towards the enemy. As she lifted and smashed down across the serried lines of whitecaps he could see the sunlight playing on her bared copper, and her sleek hull which shone in the glare like glass.

Zeus edged slightly out of line and Bolitho held his breath as he watched the French frigate sway momentarily into view.

80

About five miles away. It did not seem possible that they had converged on her so quickly.

Auriga would be about three miles distant, and she had already overreached the other frigate. Bolitho tried to clear his mind, to think what he would do in the enemy's place. Go about, or try to continue towards the land hidden below that mocking horizon? There was certainly no chance of beating the *Auriga* on her present course. Yet, if he made a dash for it he was almost sure to run into the arms of a British patrol along the Portuguese coast. Vigo was the last safe refuge, unless he was prepared to turn and fight.

Broughton said, 'Make a general signal. Shorten sail and re-form correct stations.' He eyed Bolitho bleakly. '*Auriga* can handle the Frog now.'

As the signal was passed and repeated up and down the line Bolitho could almost sense the frustration around him. Four powerful ships, yet because of Broughton's inflexible rules as impotent as merchantmen.

A dull bang echoed across the water and Bolitho saw a puff of brown smoke drifting towards the French ship. Brice had fired a ranging shot, but they could not see where it fell.

Every glass came up as Keverne said hoarsely, 'The Frog's wearing ship! By God, look at him!'

The French captain had mistimed it badly. Bolitho could almost pity him as he put his ship round in an effort to cross the *Auriga*'s bows. He could see her bared bilge, the sun dancing on her straining sails as the yards swung still further until she was heeling right over in her own spray. A solid thunder of gunfire echoed and re-echoed across the tossing water, and Bolitho imagined Brice's first broadside smashing into the exposed bilge as he used his advantage of wind and position to follow her round.

Somebody in the *Euryalus*'s foretop raised a cheer, but otherwise there was complete silence as seamen and marines watched the frigates overlapping, clawing closer and closer to each other, the smoke already whipped free in the wind.

Another ripple of flashes, this time from the Frenchman, but the *Auriga*'s masts and yards remained intact, whereas the enemy's canvas was pitted with holes, her main topsail tearing itself to ribbons after the first barrage.

Keverne whispered, 'A good prize, I'm thinking. We can do with another frigate anyway.'

81

It was hard to distinguish what was happening now. The two ships could only be half a cable apart, and getting nearer each minute. More cannon fire, and then the enemy's mizzen topgallant pitched down into the rolling smoke, the ripped canvas and rigging following it into the bedlam below.

Broughton said, 'She'll strike soon.'

'The wind's droppin', sir.' Partridge kept his voice hushed, as if fearful of breaking the concentration.

Broughton replied. 'It does not matter now.'

He was smiling.

A new silence had fallen, and across the last three miles which separated the *Zeus* from the two frigates they could see that the gunfire had ceased and both ships lay locked together. It was over.

Broughton said softly, 'Well, well, Bolitho. What do you have to say about *that*?'

Some marines on the forecastle removed their shakos and began to cheer, the cry taken up aboard the *Tanais* directly ahead.

Bolitho brushed past the admiral and snatched a telescope from its rack as the cheering began to falter and die almost as soon as it was begun. He felt his skin chill as he watched the flag fluttering down from the *Auriga's* peak like a wounded bird, to be replaced instantly by another. The same flag which still lifted jauntily above the tattered sails of her adversary. The tricolour of France.

Keverne gasped, 'By God, those bastards have struck to the Frogs! They never even tried to fight 'em!' He sounded stunned with disbelief.

The *Auriga* was already drifting clear of the Frenchman, and there was fresh activity on her deck and yards as she swung slowly downwind and away from the helpless squadron. Through the glass Bolitho could see her marines, their red coats making a patch of colour as they were disarmed and herded below by a French boarding party. Not that a boarding party was necessary, he thought bitterly. The whole of the ship's company, which seconds before had been fighting so well, had surrendered. Gone over to the enemy. He replaced the glass, unable to hold it because his hand was shaking with both anger and despair.

Without effort he could see the delegates gathered in the little inn at Veryan Bay. Allday and his hidden pistol. The man called Gates. And John Taylor, crucified and maimed because he had tried to help.

Partridge said in a small voice, 'No chance of catchin' 'em now. They'll be in Vigo afore dusk.' He looked away, his shoulders slumped. 'To see it 'appen like that!'

Broughton was still staring at the two frigates, which were already pulling away and spreading more sail.

'You may signal *Restless* to take station to windward.' He sounded remote, like a stranger. 'Then make a general signal to resume original course.' He looked at Bolitho. 'So there's an end to your talk of loyalty.' His tone was like a whip.

Bolitho shook his head. 'You told me you must understand a captain as much as the ship he commands. I believe you, sir.' He moved his gaze towards the distant *Auriga*. She seemed to have grown smaller under the alien flag. 'Just as I believe that while men like Brice are permitted their authority, such things as we have witnessed today may continue.'

Broughton stepped back, as if Bolitho had uttered some terrible obscenity. Then he said, 'Captain Brice may have fallen in battle.' He walked aft. 'For his sake, I trust that is the case.' Then he vanished into the gloom below the poop.

Lieutenant Meheux said loudly, 'Well, there was nothing *we* could do to stop it. Now, if I could have got my battery to bear we could have given them a lesson in manners.'

Several unemployed officers joined in the discussion, and Allday, who had been standing below the poop in case he was needed, glared at them with disgust.

He saw Bolitho pacing slowly back and forth on the weather side, his head lowered in thought. All the rest of them were pretending to console him and themselves, but really they wanted to be reassured and had no idea what the captain was thinking.

But Allday knew, had seen the pain in his grey eyes at the first sight of that hated tricolour. He would be recalling the time he had been made to fight another British ship under an enemy flag, with his own brother in command.

He was feeling *Auriga*'s shame like his own, and all these empty-headed puppies could talk about was their own blameless part in it.

Allday strode towards Bolitho, hardly realizing that his feet had started to move. He saw Bolitho halt, the swift anger in his eyes at being disturbed.

'What is it?' The voice was cold, but Allday was undeterred.

'I was just thinking, Captain.' He paused, gauging the moment. 'The Frogs have just got a British frigate, but not by force of arms.'

'Well?' He sounded dangerously calm.

Allday grinned. 'I was just looking around while all that was going on.' The grin got wider. 'Now this three-decker, for instance. I seem to remember we took her together without too much difficulty in the face of some *very* angry Frogs.'

Bolitho glared at him. 'That is a damn stupid comparison to make! If you can think of nothing more useful to say then be good enough to get out of my sight!' His voice was loud enough to make several heads turn in their direction.

Allday walked slowly away, hopeful and at the same time afraid that he had for once mistimed his attempt to help.

Bolitho's voice halted him.

'Now that you mention it, Allday.' Bolitho dropped his eyes as the other man turned towards him. 'It was a fine prize. And still is. Thank you for reminding me. It was wrong I should forget what British seamen can do.'

Allday glanced at the silent lieutenants and smiled gently before sauntering back to his place by the poop ladder.

Bolitho's voice broke the silence again.

'Very well, Mr Keverne, you may pipe the lower battery to quarters and exercise the crews now that the ports are no longer awash.'

He paused and looked over the nettings so that Keverne had to hurry forward to hear the rest of his words. Even then he was not sure if he was meant to listen.

Bolitho said quietly, 'We will meet again, my friend. And things may be a little different.'

Eighteen days after seeing the *Auriga* strike her colours to the enemy, Broughton's squadron dropped anchor at Gibraltar. Due to the loss of time incurred at the start of the voyage while the admiral had exercised the ships in his plan of battle, the arrival beneath the Rock's great shadow was even later than Bolitho had anticipated. They had been beset by constantly shifting winds, and once when some ninety miles west of Lisbon had been forced to ride out a storm of such swift and savage intensity that the *Zeus* had lost six men overboard. And yet the very next day had found all the ships floating helplessly in a dead calm, their sails flat and devoid of any movement while the sun made the daily routine almost unbearable.

Now, with awnings rigged and gunports open to a lazy offshore breeze, the squadron rested beneath the afternoon glare, their boats plying back and forth to the land like busy water-beetles.

Bolitho entered his cabin where all the other captains had been summoned within an hour of anchoring. They looked tired and strained after the voyage, and the swift pattern of events which had followed their arrival at Gibraltar had left none of them much time for rest.

Needless to say, it was Rattray of the *Zeus* who was the first to speak.

'Who is this fellow with the admiral? Does anyone know him, eh?'

Captain Furneaux of the *Valorous* took a glass of wine from the cabin servant and eyed it critically.

'Don't look much of a diplomat, if you ask me.' He turned his haughty face towards Bolitho. 'In war we seem to attract the *oddest* sort of advisers, what?'

Bolitho smiled and nodded to the others and then walked to the open stern windows. On the far side of the bay, quivering and misty in haze, was Algeciras, where already many telescopes would be trained on the British squadron, and messengers riding to carry the news inland to the garrisons.

The visitor aboard the flagship, the man whose sudden and unheralded appearance was causing such speculation, was certainly unusual. He had come offshore in the Governor's launch and had swarmed up through the entry port almost before the side party had got into position to receive him.

Dressed in well cut and expensive coat and breeches, he had snapped, 'No need for all this sort of thing. No damn time to waste!'

His name was Sir Hugo Draffen, and in spite of his dress and title he looked like a man who was more accustomed to hard activity and physical effort rather than one of more leisurely pursuits. Thickset, even squat, his face was very tanned, his eyes surrounded with tiny wrinkles as if well used to the sun and more severe climates than Whitehall.

Broughton, called hastily from his quarters where he had spent most of the remainder of the voyage, had been strangely quiet, even subservient towards his guest, and Bolitho imagined there was far more to Draffen than any one of them yet realized.

Captain Gillmor of the frigate *Coquette*, sent on ahead of the squadron in search of fresh information, said gloomily, 'He came aboard my ship when I anchored.' He was a lanky, even ungainly young man, and his long face was frowning as he relived the meeting with Draffen. 'When I suggested I should return and contact the squadron he told me not to bother.' He shuddered. 'And when I asked him why, he told me to mind my own damn business!'

Falcon of the *Tanais* put down his glass and said grimly, 'At least you were spared seeing *Auriga*'s disgrace.'

The others looked at him and at each other. It was the first time it had been mentioned.

Bolitho said, 'I doubt that we will be in suspense much longer.' He wondered briefly if the others had noticed his exclusion from the talk now going on in Broughton's cabin. It was unusual, but then, so it appeared, was Draffen.

Gillmor said sharply, 'Had I been there, I'd have sunk both of 'em rather than let such a thing occur.'

Furneaux drawled, 'But you were *not* there, young fellow, so you are conveniently spared any of the blame, eh?'

'That will do, gentlemen.' Bolitho stepped between them, aware of the sudden tension. 'What happened, happened. Recriminations will help no one, unless they are used to act as a guard and a warning.' He looked at each of them in turn. 'We will have plenty of work to do before long, so save your energy for that.'

The doors opened and Broughton, followed by Draffen and the flag-lieutenant, entered the cabin.

Broughton nodded curtly. 'Be seated, gentlemen.' He shook his head as the servant offered him a glass. 'Wait outside until I have finished.'

Bolitho noticed that Draffen had gone to the stern windows, either disinterested in what was happening or placing himself where he could see their faces without being observed himself.

Broughton cleared his throat and glanced at Draffen's squat figure, almost black against the sunlit windows.

'As you are well aware, our fleet has been excluded from the Mediterranean since the close of last year. Bonaparte's advances and conquests in Italy and Genoa closed all harbours against us, and it was found necessary to withdraw.'

Draffen crossed from the window. It was a quick, agile movement, and his words matched his obvious impatience.

'If I may interrupt, Sir Lucius?' He turned his back on Broughton without awaiting a reply. 'We will cut this short. I have little use for the Navy's indulgence in its own affairs.' He smiled, the wrinkles around his eyes pulling together like crow's-feet. 'England is alone in a war against a dedicated and, if you will pardon the expression, a *professional* adversary. With the fleets of France and Spain combining at Brest for one great attack, and then invasion of England, the withdrawal of ships to reinforce the Channel and Atlantic fleets seemed not only prudent but greatly urgent.'

Bolitho eyed Broughton narrowly, expecting some sign of anger or resentment, but his face was like stone.

Draffen continued briskly, 'Jervis's victory over that combined fleet at St Vincent has postponed, maybe smashed altogether, any chance of a military invasion across the English Channel, and has also proved the poorness of co-operation between the Franco/Spanish Alliance at sea. So it would seem sensible to assume that Bonaparte will spread his influence elsewhere, and soon.'

Broughton said suddenly, 'Shall I continue?'

'If you wish.' Draffen took out a watch. 'But please be quick.'

Broughton swallowed hard. 'This squadron will be the first force of any size to re-enter the Mediterranean.' He got no further.

'Look at this chart, gentlemen.' Draffen snatched it from Lieutenant Calvert's hand and opened it on the table.

As the others crowded closer Bolitho darted another glance at Broughton. He looked pale, and for a few seconds he saw his eyes gleaming with anger across Draffen's broad back.

'Here, two hundred and fifty miles along the Spanish coast is Cartagena, where many of their ships were based prior to sailing for Brest.' Bolitho followed the man's spatulate finger as it crossed southward over the Mediterranean to the craggy outline of the Algerian coast. 'South-east from Spain, a mere one hundred and fifty miles, lies Djafou.'

Bolitho realized with a start that Draffen was looking up at him, his eyes very still and intent.

'Do you know it, Captain?'

'By reputation, sir. Once the lair of Barbary pirates, I believe. A good natural harbour, and little else.'

Draffen smiled, but his eyes were still unblinking. 'The Dons seized it some years ago to protect their own coast trade. Now that they are allied to the French its harbour may be seen in another light entirely.'

Rattray asked gruffly, 'As a base, sir?'

'Maybe.' Draffen straightened his back. 'But my agents have reported some comings and goings from Cartagena. It would be well if our re-entry to the Mediterranean was given a purpose, something positive.' He tapped the chart again. 'Your admiral knows what is expected of him, but I will tell you now that I intend to see *our* flag over Djafou, and without too much delay.'

In the sudden silence Broughton said stiffly, 'My squadron is under strength, sir.' He glanced away and added, 'However, if you think . . .'

Draffen nodded firmly. 'Indeed I *do* think, Sir Lucius. I have made arrangements for bomb vessels from Lisbon. They will be here within a day or so.' His tone hardened. 'If the fleet at Spithead and the Nore had been less concerned with their own domestic affairs I daresay your squadron would be fifteen or even twenty sail-of-the-line instead of four.' He shrugged. 'And having only *one* frigate now. . . .' He shrugged again, dismissing it. 'But that remains your own concern.' He snapped his fingers. 'Now, I suggest a toast, so get that servant in here.' He grinned at their mixed expressions. 'After that, there will be plenty to do.'

He looked again at Bolitho. 'You say very little, Captain.'

Broughton snapped, 'I will instruct my flag captain in my own way, if you please, Sir Hugo.'

'As it should be.' Draffen remained smiling. 'However, I will be joining the squadron for some of the time.' He took a glass from the servant, adding, 'Just to ensure that your way is also mine, eh?'

Bolitho turned away, his mind already busy with Draffen's brisk but extremely sparse information.

It was good news indeed to know that British ships would be attacking the southern approaches of Bonaparte's growing empire once again. To take and hold a new and strategically placed base for the fleet was a plan of both skill and imagination.

But if on the other hand Broughton's squadron was being used merely as a cat's-paw, a means to make the enemy withdraw forces back to the Mediterranean on a large scale, things might go badly for all of them.

There was no doubting Draffen's authority, although what his exact status was remained a mystery. Maybe the news had already reached him of a worsening situation at the Nore. The sacrifice of this small squadron to ease enemy pressure around the Channel ports would seem no worse than Taylor's death had measured with Broughton himself.

Whatever had been already decided, Bolitho knew that he would be directly involved in each part of it. The outlook should have cheered him, but the thought of having Broughton *and* Draffen in overall control was another prospect entirely.

Broughton had moved away to talk with Furneaux, and Draffen crossed to Bolitho's side, obviously about to take his leave.

He said, 'Glad to have met you, Captain. I think we are going to get on very well together.' He signalled to Calvert and then added calmly, 'As a matter of fact, I used to know your brother.' Then he swung on his heel and made his way to Broughton and the others.

6. Ships in Company

BOLITHO did not see Sir Hugo Draffen again for three days. But he was kept too busy with affairs aboard the *Euryalus* and the other ships of the squadron to find much time for speculation over his parting remarks.

The fact that he had known Hugh implied that Draffen had lived or worked in the West Indies or even America during the Revolution there. Otherwise there seemed little point in being so secretive about the meeting. Draffen had the mark of a trader, one of the sort who helped create colonies merely by finding a personal reason for making money. He was shrewd and, Bolitho imagined, not a little ruthless when it suited him.

Bolitho knew there might be nothing more in Draffen's remarks than a first move in making contact between them. If they were going to work in harmony over the next weeks or months, it was a natural thing to expect of him. But the caution built up in Bolitho over the years since his brother's change of allegiance had made him sensitive to a point of being over-cautious whenever Hugh's name was mentioned.

There was much to do. Taking on extra stocks of food and water for the coming voyage and gathering any additional equipment which could be begged, borrowed or bribed from the Rock. Once abroad in the Mediterranean they would be without base or supplies, other than that which they might seize for themselves.

And there was now an additional, more pressing need for self-dependence. Two days after anchoring Bolitho had seen a sloop of war tack busily into the bay carrying, it was said, despatches and news from England.

Eventually Broughton had sent for him, his features grim as he had said, 'The mutiny at the Nore is worse. Nearly every ship is in the hands of the *delegates*.' He had spat out the word like poison. 'They're blockading the river and holding the government to ransom until their demands are met.'

Broughton had jumped to his feet and moved restlessly about his cabin like a caged animal.

'Admiral Duncan was blockading the Dutch coast. What can he do with most of his ships at anchor and under the flag of revolution?'

'I will inform the other captains, sir.'

'Yes, at once. That sloop is returning to England at once with despatches, so there is little fear of our people being inflamed.' He added slowly, 'I have included in my report the details of the *Auriga*'s loss. It might suit the French to use her for spying, so the sooner our ships are aware of her new identity the better. We do not know yet that she *did* strike her colours in mutiny.' He had not looked at Bolitho. 'All her officers may have been killed or disabled as she closed for boarding. In the confusion she could have been overwhelmed.' He had obviously not believed it any more than Bolitho.

Nevertheless, there was sufficient doubt to allow Broughton to make the evasive comments in his report. The news of a British ship changing sides for any reason at a moment like this might spark off even worse troubles in the fleet, if that were possible.

Broughton had been content to give more and more work to Bolitho while the squadron completed its preparations for sailing. The news from the Nore, coupled with the *Auriga*'s loss, had made a deep and noticeable impression on him. He seemed withdrawn, and, when alone with Bolitho, less composed than ever before. His experiences at Spithead aboard his own flagship had obviously scarred him deeply, as Rook had once suggested.

He spent a good deal of his time ashore, conferring with Draffen or the Governor, but always went alone, keeping his thoughts to himself.

Lieutenant Calvert seemed unable to do anything right for his admiral, and his life was fast becoming a nightmare. Highbred he might be, but he seemed completely incapable of grasping the daily affairs of signals and directives which passed through his hands for the captains of the squadron.

Bolitho suspected that Broughton used his flag-lieutenant to work off some of his own nagging uncertainties. If it was his idea to make Calvert's existence a misery he was certainly succeeding.

It was pitiful to hear Midshipman Tothill explaining respectfully but firmly the rights and wrongs of signal procedure to him, and, almost worse, Calvert's obvious gratitude. Not that it helped him very much. Any sudden burst of anger from Broughton and Calvert's latest hoard of knowledge seemed to dissipate to the wind for ever.

On the afternoon of the third day, as Bolitho was discussing the preparations with Keverne, the officer of the watch reported that the two bomb vessels were arriving and already dropping anchor close inshore.

Shortly afterwards a launch grappled alongside and her coxswain passed a sealed letter aboard for Bolitho's attention. It was from Draffen, and typically brief. Bolitho was to meet him aboard the *Hekla*, one of the bombs, immediately. He would come by way of the launch which had brought the letter.

Broughton was ashore, so after giving Keverne his instructions Bolitho clambered into the boat to be rowed to the *Hekla* for the meeting.

Allday watched him leave with ill-disguised annoyance. For Bolitho to use anything but his own barge was unthinkable, and as the launch pulled away from the *Euryalus*'s side he felt a sudden pang of anxiety. If anything ever happened to Bolitho, and he was suddenly like this, alone. . . . What would he do? He was still staring after the boat as it vanished around the *Zeus*'s stern, his eyes unusually troubled.

In all his service Bolitho had never before laid eyes on a bomb vessel, although he had heard of them often enough.

The one towards which the launch was moving with such haste was much as he had expected. Two-masted and about a hundred feet in length, with a very sturdy hull and low bulwarks. Her oddest characteristic was the uneven placing of her foremast. It was stepped well back from the stemhead, leaving the ship with an unbalanced appearance, as if her real foremast had been shot away level with the deck.

Almost as large as a sloop, yet with neither the grace nor the agility, a bomb was said to be the devil to handle in anything but perfect conditions.

As the boat hooked on to the chains he saw Draffen standing alone in the centre of the tiny quarterdeck shading his eyes to watch him climb aboard.

Bolitho raised his hat as the small side party shrilled a salute, and nodded to a young lieutenant who was watching him with a kind of fascination.

Draffen called, 'Come up here, Bolitho. You'll get a better view.'

Bolitho took Draffen's proffered hand. Like the man, it was tough and hard. He said, 'That lieutenant. Is he the captain?'

'No. I sent him below just before you came aboard.' He shrugged. 'Sorry if I disturbed your traditional ceremonial, but I wanted my chart from his cabin.' He grinned. 'Cabin indeed. My watchdog has better quarters.'

He gestured forward. 'No wonder they build these bombs the way they do. Every timber is twice as thick as that in any other vessel. The recoil and downward shock of those beauties would tear the guts out of a lesser hull.'

Bolitho followed his hand and saw the two massive mortars mounted in the centre of the foredeck. Short, black and incredibly ugly, they nevertheless had a muzzle diameter of over a foot each. He could imagine without effort the great strain they would put on the timbers, to say nothing of those at the receiving end of their bombardment.

The other vessel anchored close abeam was very similar, and aptly named *Devastation*.

Draffen added half to himself, 'The bombs will sail at night. No sense in letting those jackals at Algeciras know too much too early, eh?'

Bolitho nodded. It made good sense. He looked sideways at the other man as Draffen turned to watch some seamen flaking down a rope with the ease of spiders constructing a web.

Draffen was older than he had imagined. Nearer sixty than fifty, his grey hair contrasting sharply with his tanned features and brisk, muscular figure.

He said, 'The news from England was bad, sir. I heard it from Sir Lucius.'

Draffen sounded indifferent. 'Some people never learn.' He did not explain what he meant but instead turned and said, 'About your brother. I met him when he commanded that privateer. I understand you destroyed his ship eventually.' His eyes softened slightly. 'I have been learning quite a lot about you lately, and that piece of information makes me especially envious. I hope I could do what you did if called.' The mood changed again as he added, 'Of course, I cannot possibly believe *all* I've heard about you. No man can be that good.' He grinned at Bolitho's uncertainty and pointed over his shoulder. 'Now take what the *Hekla*'s commander has told me, for instance. Never heard the like!'

Bolitho swung round and then stared with astonishment. The man facing him, his long, horse-face changing from confusion to something like wild delight, was Francis Inch, no longer a mere lieutenant, but wearing the single epaulette on his left shoulder. Commander Inch, *Hyperion*'s first lieutenant at that final, bloody embrace with Lequiller's ships in the Bay of Biscay.

Inch stepped forward, bobbing awkwardly. 'It's me, sir! Inch!'

Bolitho took his hands in his, not realizing until now just how much he had missed him, and the past he represented.

'I always told you that I should see you get a command of your own.' He did not know what to say, and was very conscious of Draffen's grinning face, and Inch peering at him that familiar, eager way which had once nearly driven him mad with exasperation.

Inch beamed. 'It was either a bomb or first lieutenant of a seventy-four again, sir.' He looked suddenly sad. 'After the old *Hyperion* I didn't want another. . . .' He allowed his grin to break through. 'Now I have this.' He looked around his small command. 'And this.' He touched the epaulette.

'And you have a wife now?' Bolitho guessed that Inch would have refrained from mentioning her. He would not wish to remind him of his own loss.

Inch nodded. 'Aye, sir. With some of the prize money you

got for us I have purchased a modest house at Weymouth. I hope you will do us the honour. . . .' He became his old self again, unsure and bumbling. 'But then, I am sure you will be too busy for that, sir. . . .'

Bolitho gripped his arm. 'I will be delighted, Inch. It is good to see you again.'

Draffen remarked dryly, 'So there is warm blood in a sea officer after all.'

Inch shuffled his feet. 'I shall write to Hannah tonight. She will be pleased to hear about our meeting.'

Bolitho eyed Draffen thoughtfully. 'You certainly kept this as a surprise, sir.'

'The Navy has its ways of doing things.' He looked at the towering Rock. 'And I have mine.'

He turned to Inch. 'Now, Commander, if you will leave us alone, I have some matters to discuss.'

Bolitho said, 'Dine with me tonight, Inch, aboard the flagship.' He grinned to cover the sudden emotion brought on by Inch's appearance. 'Your next promotion may be speeded that way.'

He saw Inch's pleasure as he scurried over to his lieutenant, and guessed he would soon be retelling some of the old stories for his benefit.

Draffen remarked, 'Not much of an officer, I suspect, 'til you got your hands on him.'

Bolitho replied quietly, 'He had to learn the hard way. I never met a man more loyal nor one so lucky in many ways. If we meet the enemy, I suggest you stay close by Commander Inch, sir. He has the knack of remaining alive when all about him are falling and the ship herself is in pieces.'

Draffen nodded. 'I will bear it in mind.' He changed to a brisker tone. 'All being well, your squadron is sailing tomorrow evening. The bombs will follow later, but your admiral can give you fuller details than I.' He seemed to come to a decision. 'I have made it my business to study your record, Bolitho. This venture we are undertaking will call for much resource and initiative. You may have to twist the Admiralty rules to suit the occasion. I happen to know that such methods are not unknown to you.' He smiled dryly. 'In my experience I have found that war needs special men with their own ideas. Hard and fast rules are not for this game.'

Bolitho had a sudden mental picture of Broughton's face

when he had requested him to give *Zeus* permission to chase the Frenchman. Of his plan of battle, his apparent mistrust of anything untried or smelling of unorthodox methods.

He said, 'I only hope we are not too late and that the French have not enlarged the defences at Djafou.'

Draffen looked round quickly and then said, 'I have certain influence, connections if you like, and I do not intend you should have to rely entirely on luck and personal bravery. I know the Algerian coast well, and its people, who for the most part are both murderous and completely untrustworthy.' The smile returned. 'But we will use what we can, and make the best of it. As John Paul Jones said under very similar circumstances, "If we cannot have what we like, we must learn to like what we have!"'

He thrust out his hand. 'I must go and see some people ashore now. No doubt we will be meeting again very shortly.'

Bolitho watched him climb down into his boat and then joined Inch by the bulwark.

Inch said, 'A strange man, sir. Very deep.'

'I believe so. He wields a good deal of power, nevertheless.'

Inch sighed. 'He was telling me earlier about the place where we are going. He seems well versed in details.' He shook his head. 'Yet I can find hardly anything about it.'

Bolitho nodded thoughtfully. Trade, but what sort of trade would anyone find in a place like Djafou? And where was the connection with the Caribbean and his meeting with Hugh?'

He said, 'I must return to my ship. We will talk more at dinner, although there are no familiar faces for you to see, I am afraid.'

Inch grinned, 'Except Allday, sir. I cannot imagine you without *him*!'

Bolitho clapped his bony shoulder. 'And neither can I!'

Later, as he stood alone in his cabin, Bolitho opened his shirt and toyed with the small locket, his eyes unseeing as he stared through the stern windows. Inch would never guess how much his arrival had meant to him. Like the locket, something to hold on to, something familiar. One of his old Hyperions.

There was a tap at the door and Calvert entered nervously, holding some papers before him as if for protection.

Bolitho smiled. 'Be seated. I will sign them, and you may distribute them to the squadron before dusk.'

Calvert did not hide his relief as Bolitho sat at the desk and reached for a pen. Bolitho's action saved him from having to face Broughton when he came offshore. His eyes fell on Bolitho's sword lying on the bench seat where he had put it when he returned from seeing the *Hekla*.

In spite of all his caution he said, 'Oh I say, sir, may I look at it?'

Bolitho stared at him. It was unlike Calvert to say much, other than mutter excuses for his mistakes. His eyes were positively shining with sudden interest.

'Certainly, Mr Calvert.' He sat back to watch as the lieutenant drew the old blade from the scabbard and held it in line with his chin. 'Are you a swordsman like Sir Lucius?'

Calvert did not reply directly. He ran his fingers around the old and tarnished hilt and then said, 'A beautiful balance, sir. Beautiful.' He looked at Bolitho guardedly. 'I have an eye for it, sir.'

'Then see that you restrain your *eye*, Mr Calvert. It can cause you much trouble.'

Calvert replaced the blade and became his old self again. 'Thank you, sir. For allowing me to hold it.'

Bolitho pushed the papers towards him and added slowly, 'And try to be more definite in your affairs. Many officers would give their arms for your appointment, so make good use of it.'

Calvert withdrew, stammering and smiling.

Bolitho sighed and stood up as Allday entered the cabin, his eyes immediately falling on the sword, which he replaced on its rack against the bulkhead.

He said, 'Mr Calvert was here then, Captain?'

Bolitho smiled at Allday's curiosity. 'He was. He seemed very interested in the sword.'

Allday eyed it thoughtfully. 'And so he might. Yesterday I saw him showing off to some of the midshipmen. They lit a candle, and Drury, the youngest of 'em, held it in the air for Mr Calvert to strike at.'

Bolitho snapped, 'That was a damned stupid thing to do.'

Allday shrugged. 'Need have no worry, Captain. The flag-lieutenant's blade parted the wick and flame without even touching the candle.' He cleared his throat noisily. 'You'll have to watch that one, Captain.'

Bolitho looked at him. 'As you say, Allday. I will.'

*   *   *

Jed Partridge, the master, tugged at his battered hat as Bolitho strode from beneath the poop and reported, 'Steady, sir. Sou' east by east.'

'Very well.'

Bolitho nodded to the officer of the watch and then crossed to the weather side of the quarterdeck, filling his lungs with the cool evening air.

The squadron had weighed in the remorseless heat of a noon sun, but with an encouraging north-westerly breeze had soon formed into a tight column, each ship taking her prescribed station and keeping their interchange of signals to a minimum.

Many telescopes must have followed them from the Spanish coast, and there would be plenty of speculation as to their destination. It was unlikely that the enemy would give much weight to so small a force, but there was no sense in taking chances. Once clear of the land each captain would know that almost any ship he might meet would be an enemy. Even neutrals, and there were precious few of those, must be treated with suspicion and as possible informers of the squadron's course and whereabouts.

But now it was evening, and in the Mediterranean it was a time which Bolitho always found full of fresh fascination. While the four ships-of-the-line rolled and plunged easily in a deep swell, with a steady and unwavering wind sweeping down across the larboard quarter, he could see the shadows lengthening on the gangways, the sea beyond the bows already vague in deeper purple. Yet astern the sky was salmon pink, the dying sunlight trailing down from the horizon and making the *Valorous*'s topsails shine like giant sea shells.

If this wind and sea held, it would be possible for all of them to keep good station during the night, which should please Broughton, he thought.

Keverne crossed the deck and said, 'The visibility will not endure much longer, sir.'

Bolitho glanced towards the master's rotund shape by the helmsmen. 'We will alter course two points directly, Mr Partridge.' He sought out Midshipman Tothill by the lee shrouds and added, 'You will bend on the signal for the squadron. Tack in succession. Steer east by south.'

He did not have to bother further with the midshipman. Tothill and his signal party had already proved themselves more than capable. He would make a good officer, Bolitho thought vaguely.

He said to Keverne, 'Each ship will show a stern light, in case we get scattered. It may help the *Coquette* if she comes searching for us.'

The frigate in question was sweeping some fifteen miles astern of the column, a wise precaution to ensure they were not already being shadowed by some curious enemy patrol.

The little sloop *Restless* was only just visible to windward of the *Zeus*, and Bolitho imagined that her young and newly appointed commander would be considering the sudden importance of his role. The sloop was the only vessel present and fast enough should a suspicious sail need investigating.

It was always the same. Never enough frigates, and now that the *Auriga* was denied them they must be even more sparing in long-range operations.

Tothill called, 'Signal bent on, sir.'

'Good.' Bolitho nodded to Keverne. 'Carry on. I must inform the admiral.'

He found Broughton and Draffen sitting at opposite ends of the long table in the admiral's dining cabin, and sensed the complete silence stretching between them.

'Well?' Broughton leaned back in his chair, his fingers tapping slowly against an untouched glass of claret.

'Ready to alter course, Sir Lucius.' He saw Draffen watching him, his eyes gleaming in the light from the overhead lanterns and the pink glow through the windows.

'Very good.' Broughton tugged out his watch. 'No sign of pursuit?'

'None, sir.'

Broughton grunted. 'Carry on then, if you please. I may come up later.'

Draffen rose to his feet and steadied himself against the table as *Euryalus* tilted her massive bilge into another lazy trough.

'I would like to join you if I may, Captain.' He nodded equably to Broughton. 'Never get weary of watching ships under command, y'know.'

Broughton snapped, 'Er, just a moment!' But when Bolitho turned back from the door he shook his head. 'Nothing. Attend to your duties.'

On the quarterdeck Draffen remarked calmly, 'Sharing the admiral's quarters is not the easiest way of travelling.'

Bolitho smiled. 'You can have my own quarters with pleasure, sir. I spend more time in my chartroom than I do in a cot.'

The other man shook his head, his eyes already seeking out the various parties of seamen mustered at their stations in readiness for the next order from aft.

'Sir Lucius and I come from different poles, Bolitho. But it would be well to forget social differences for the present at least.'

Bolitho forgot Draffen and the tensions in the great cabin and turned towards Keverne.

'Make the signal.' And as the flags darted up the halliards and broke impatiently to the wind he added sharply, 'Be ready, Mr Partridge.'

'*Zeus* has acknowledged, sir!'

The leading ship was in fact already swinging importantly on her new course, her topsails and driver flapping for a few more moments until brought under control. *Tanais* followed, one curved side glowing in the dying sunlight as she laboured too readily in response to canvas and rudder.

Keverne raised his speaking trumpet, his lithe figure poised against the rail as if to test the agility of the great ship beneath him.

'Braces there!' He pointed into the purple shadows below the mainmast trunk. 'Mr Collins, take that man's name! He's stumbling about like a whore at a wedding!'

Unknown voices mumbled out of the gloom, while from aft the wheel creaked obediently, Partridge's white hair changing to yellow as he squinted at the lighted compass bowl.

'Heave! Lively with it!'

The men leaned back, angling their bodies to take the strain of the ship's massive yards, while the marines clumped noisily and in perfect time on the mizzen brace. The hull tilted still further, the sails shivering and booming to the change of pressure.

Bolitho leaned over the rail, searching along the length of his command, his ears interpreting the varying groans from shrouds and rigging, the action automatic yet ever watchful.

'Lay her on the larboard tack, Mr Partridge.' He looked aloft, watching as Broughton's flag and the masthead pendant licked out lazily and then pointed almost directly across the starboard bow.

'East by south, sir!' Partridge rolled to the other side of the compass as Bolitho came aft to stare down at the swaying card.

'Steady as you go.' He felt the ship responding, saw the huge, dark rectangles of canvas stiffening to the wind as she settled obediently on her new tack.

The light was going fast now. As it always did hereabouts. One minute a bright and seemingly everlasting sunset, and then nothing but the cream of spray beneath the counter, an occasional whitecap as the wind explored the edge of a deep trough in the sea's face.

He heard Keverne bark, 'The weather forebrace! In God's name take in that slack, man! Mr Weigall, your people must do better than this!'

Voices echoed above the thrumming din of rigging and canvas, and he imagined the third lieutenant cursing Keverne's uncanny eyesight, or shrewd guesswork, as the case may be.

Draffen had been watching in silence, and as the hands mustered once again at their various divisions he murmured, 'I hope I will be aboard when you get a chance to show her real paces under sail.' He sounded as if he was enjoying himself.

Bolitho smiled. 'There'll be no such opportunity at night, sir. We may well have to reef tops'ls as it is. There is always a risk of collision when moving in close company.'

Keverne came aft again and touched his hat. 'Permission to dismiss the watch below, sir.'

'Yes. That was well done, Mr Keverne.'

A voice called, 'The *Valorous* is on station, sir!'

'Very well.' Bolitho moved to the weather side as the parties of seamen and marines hurried across the planking and vanished to their messdecks below. A cramped, teeming world where they lived between the guns they would serve in battle, with little more than a shoulder's breadth to swing a hammock. He wondered what some of them were thinking of their new destination.

Draffen's face glowed momentarily as he peered at the compass. Then he moved back to Bolitho's side and fell in step with him as he began to pace slowly up and down below the empty nettings.

'It must be a strange feeling for you, Bolitho.'

'How so, sir?' Bolitho had almost forgotten that he was not alone in his usual restless pacing.

'To command a ship like this. One which you yourself took in battle.' He hurried on, exploring a theme which had obviously given him some thought. 'In your shoes I would be wondering if I could *defend* a vessel when I had in fact seized her in the face of great odds.'

Bolitho frowned. 'Circumstances must always play a great part, sir.'

'But tell me, as I am greatly interested. What do you think of her as a ship?'

Bolitho paused by the quarterdeck rail, resting his palms on it, feeling the wood shaking under his touch as if the whole complex mass of timber and rigging was a living being.

'She is fast for her size, sir, and only four years old. She handles well, and the hull has some fine factors, too.' He gestured forward. 'Unlike our own ships-of-the-line, her planking is continued right around the bow, so there is no weak bulkhead to receive an enemy's fire.'

Draffen showed his teeth. 'I like your enthusiasm. It is some comfort. But I imagined you would say otherwise. A born sea officer, a man from a long line of sailing men, I'd have laid odds on your despising the work of an enemy shipyard.' He laughed softly. 'I was wrong, it appears.'

Bolitho eyed him calmly. 'The French are fine builders. Line for line their hulls are faster and better than our own.'

Draffen spread his hands in mock alarm. 'Then how can we win? How have we been victorious against greater numbers of the enemy?'

Bolitho shook his head. 'The enemy's weakness does not lie in his ships, or in his courage either. It is leadership. Two-thirds of their trained and experienced officers were butchered in the Terror. And they'll not regain their confidence while they are bottled up in harbour by our blockade.' He knew Draffen was deliberately drawing him out but continued, 'Each time they break out and engage our squadrons they learn a little more, grow steadily more confident, even if a sea victory is denied them. Blockade is no longer the answer, in my opinion. It hurts the innocent as much as those for whom it is intended. Clearcut, decisive action is the solution. Hit the enemy whenever and wherever you can, the size of the actions is almost immaterial.'

The officer of the watch was admonishing a defaulter who had been brought aft, his voice grating in a fierce whisper.

Bolitho moved away with Draffen falling in step beside him.

Draffen asked, 'But there will be a final confrontation between the two major fleets, eventually?'

'I have no doubts, sir. But I still believe the more attacks we can make on the enemy's communications, his bases and trade, the more likely we are of a lasting victory on land.' He smiled awkwardly. 'As a sailor it hurts me to say it. But no victory can be complete until your own soldiers have hoisted a flag on the enemy's battlements!'

Draffen smiled gravely. 'Maybe you will have a chance to put your theory into action very shortly. It will largely depend on our meeting with one of my agents. I arranged for him to make a regular rendezvous. It is to be hoped he has found it possible.'

Bolitho pricked up his ears. That was the first he had heard of anything about a rendezvous. Broughton had given him the briefest of detail so far. The squadron was to patrol off Djafou, out of sight of land, while the *Coquette* explored inshore for further information. Normal tactics. Normal and frustratingly dull, he had thought. Now with the prospect of gaining other, more secret news of the enemy's deployment, the whole face of the operation had changed.

Draffen said, 'I find it slightly unnerving when I think of tomorrow. We might meet with an entire enemy fleet. Does that not upset you?'

Bolitho looked at him, but his face was in deep shadow. It was hard to tell if he was testing him again or merely making light of what was a very real possibility.

'I have lived with that prospect in fear, excitement or mere bewilderment on and off since I was twelve, sir.' Bolitho kept his voice equally grave. Then he grinned. 'But so far I have never had any of my reactions taken into consideration, least of all by the enemy!'

Draffen chuckled. 'I will go below and sleep easily now. I have taxed you too much as it is. But please keep me informed if anything unusual occurs.'

Bolitho stood aside. 'I will, sir. You *and* my admiral.'

Draffen walked away laughing to himself. 'We will talk further.' Then he was gone.

The midshipman of the watch hurried across the deck and reported to his lieutenant that the stern light had been lit. Through the mass of rigging Bolitho could see the *Tanais*'s own lantern shining like a firefly and playing across the ruffled water of her wake.

He heard the lieutenant say sharply, 'It took you long enough, Mr Drury!' And then the boy's mumbled reply.

It was not difficult to see Adam Pascoe's shape standing there in the shadows instead of the luckless Drury.

Bolitho had tried not to worry about his young nephew, but meeting with Inch had again made the boy's absence seem suddenly real and beyond his reach. There had been letters, of course, both from him and his captain, Bolitho's best friend, Herrick. But, like the *Euryalus*, his ship, the old sixty-four *Impulsive*, had little concern for the warmth and hope brought by the mail boats, or hoarded in some harbour office on the offchance the ships might one day drop anchor.

Bolitho began to walk again, trying to picture Adam as he had last seen him. But he would be different now. Perhaps a stranger? He quickened his pace, suddenly aware of his concern.

It was two years since they had parted. The boy to join Herrick's ship and he to take command and tend to the refitting of his prize, the *Euryalus*. He would be seventeen, perhaps already awaiting his chance to try for promotion to lieutenant. Would two more years have changed him much? he wondered. Would he still be forming his own mould, or taking after Hugh?

He realized with a start that the midshipman was blocking his path, his eyes gleaming white in the shadows.

'Beg pardon, sir, but the officer of the watch sends his respects, and, and,' he faltered under his captain's gaze, 'and could we take in a reef. The wind appears to be getting up, sir.'

Bolitho studied him impassively. He had not even noticed the change in the wind's sound through the shrouds. He had been more worried by his own thoughts than he had realized.

He asked sharply, 'How old are you, Mr Drury?'

The boy gulped. 'Thirteen, sir.'

'I see. Well, Mr Drury, you have a long and very stormy passage ahead of you before you attain your own command.'

'Yessir.' He sounded fearful of what was coming next.

'And a young officer without fingers can find the handicap a real problem. So in future I do not wish to learn of your agility with a candle as a target for sword-play, do you understand?'

'No, sir, I—I mean, yes, sir!' He almost fell as he ran back to the officer of the watch, his mind no doubt buzzing with the captain's unfaltering source of private information.

Keverne appeared on deck, dabbing his mouth with his handkerchief and already peering aloft at the booming canvas.

'Trouble, sir?'

'We will reef tops'ls directly, Mr Keverne.' He kept his tone formal. Whatever he felt or feared, it was right that he should display none of it, share none of it with those who depended on his judgement. He watched Keverne hurrying away, buttoning his coat and bellowing for a bosun's mate.

But sometimes, like tonight, it was harder than he would have imagined.

7. 'Broadside!'

NOON THE FOLLOWING DAY found the ships clawing slowly on a larboard tack with the wind almost abeam, their yards braced hard round to take maximum advantage of it. Shortly after first light they had altered course again and were now heading east-north-east, pinned down on their broken reflections by a sun which made any physical effort a torture. It was like a furnace, and even the wind, steady as ever from the north-west, seemed without any kind of freshness or relief, and stung the faces and bodies of the seamen like hot sand.

Bolitho plucked his shirt away from his chest and moved into the shadow of the hammock nettings as Keverne and Partridge lowered their sextants and began to compare notes. This usual procedure was watched and copied by several of the midshipmen, although unlike their superiors they were not involved in the importance of the situation.

Up on the poop, shaded by a small awning, he could see Draffen's stocky figure pacing back and forth, up and down, his shoes clumping noisily on the sun-dried planking.

Keverne crossed to Bolitho and said wearily, 'It matches your own calculation, sir.' Like the other officers he had discarded coat and hat, and his shirt was clinging to his body like another skin. He sounded too tired for either admiration or surprise at his findings.

It had been an uneventful night, with the squadron sailing

well and keeping their allotted stations. At dawn Broughton had come on deck, something so unusual as to give Bolitho a warning of the day's importance.

As the signals had soared aloft for the new course, and preparations for cleaning ship and preparing breakfast had begun, Broughton had remarked sourly, 'We are supposed to be contacted by one of Sir Hugo's *friends* this forenoon. By God, I hate to have to rely on some damned amateur!'

He did not say if he was describing Draffen or his agent, and the look on his face decided Bolitho against even tactful questioning.

Draffen's earlier confidence had visibly faded as the searing morning had dragged on. Any sudden shout from one of the ship's company made him pause in his walk and stand stock-still until he had found the cry to be meaningless.

Bolitho said, 'Well, Mr Keverne, there is nothing we can do at present.'

Two hours earlier the masthead lookout had hailed the deck, and as every eye had been raised to his tiny, swaying perch some two hundred feet above their heads, he had reported sighting land.

In spite of his hatred for any sort of height, Bolitho had made himself climb up the dizzy, vibrating ratlines, past the maintop, on and up until he had joined the pigtailed seaman who had made the report.

With his legs wrapped tightly around the crosstrees he had forced himself to ignore the deck far below him and had concentrated on opening his telescope, aware the whole time that the lookout was whistling between his teeth and not even bothering to hold on.

The sight was almost worth the anguish and embarrassment of the climb. There, far to the south, was a long, uneven ridge of mountains, ice blue in the harsh sunlight, disconnected from the land by sea mist, and strangely beautiful. The African coast. The mountains, he had estimated, were nearly thirty miles distant, but seemed unreachable and without reality.

Now, once again there was no sight of land, and away on either beam the sea danced and glittered in millions of blinding reflections, so that seamen working aloft and along the braced yards fumbled and groped with each precarious movement, their eyes too dulled by glare to be trusted.

The other ships had become more separated, so that the

line was well stretched, the *Tanais* being some two miles ahead of *Euryalus*.

Broughton had conceded that if they were to be sighted by some small sailing vessel carrying Draffen's agent it was prudent to extend the formation. And if seen by less friendly eyes it would be well to make the squadron appear as large as possible. Far away to leeward the sloop's topsails shone like burnished steel as she pushed busily downwind like a terrier sniffing out a rabbit.

There was still no sign of the *Coquette*, nor might there be for some time yet. She could be investigating some strange sail well astern of the squadron. Equally she might be in serious trouble with an enemy.

Calvert appeared on the quarterdeck, his face screwed up with both worry and strain in the sun's brightness.

He said, 'Sir Lucius sends his compliments, sir. Will you join him in his day cabin.'

Bolitho glanced at Keverne, who turned his mouth down and said, 'Perhaps there is a change of plan, sir?'

Bolitho strode after Calvert's hurrying shape, wondering if Keverne was implying resentment at knowing so little. Like himself. When he entered the cabin it took his eyes several seconds to get accustomed to the gloom, the comparative coolness after the unprotected quarterdeck.

Draffen was seated beside the desk, although Bolitho had not even seen him leave the poop.

'Sir?' He saw Broughton standing by an open stern window, his light brown hair glossy in the reflected glare. Far astern, the *Valorous* held rigidly to her tack, so that she appeared like some elaborate model, balanced on the admiral's epaulette.

Broughton snapped, 'I have asked you down here to explain further to Sir Hugo the necessity of keeping the *Restless* in company and within signalling distance.' He breathed out hard. '*Well?*'

Bolitho thrust his hands behind him. In the presence of the admiral and Draffen, both of whom were impeccably dressed as before, he felt suddenly unkempt and dirty. He could feel the tension between the two men, and guessed they had been arguing before his arrival.

Draffen interrupted evenly, 'I must find my agent, Captain. The sloop is fast and small enough for the purpose.' He shrugged. 'I can say no fairer than that, now can I?'

Bolitho tensed. They were both drawing on him, each using his opinion to make him an ally. Never before had Broughton asked for his opinion on matters of strategy. And although Draffen had displayed an easy confidence after their first meeting, he had given away little of his intentions.

Bolitho said, 'May I ask, Sir Hugo, what manner of ship we are expecting to meet?'

Draffen shifted in his chair. 'Oh, something small. Probably an Arab trader or suchlike.' He sounded vague. Or evasive.

Bolitho persisted. 'And if we miss meeting her, what then?'

The admiral swung away from the window, his tone sharp. 'I am expected to keep this squadron beating back and forth for another week!' He glared at Draffen. 'A week of avoiding open battle, of countless alterations of course.'

'I know all that, Sir Lucius.' Draffen remained unmoved. 'But this business demands great tact and caution.' His tone hardened. 'As well as the efficient running of your ships.'

Bolitho stepped forward. 'I can understand your concern, Sir Hugo.' He was very conscious of being in between these two powerful and unyielding men. Outside of the Navy he had had little contact with such people, and blamed himself for failing to understand them, to appreciate their worlds, each so different from his own.

'In this small squadron we have some three thousand officers and men to provision every day we are at sea. And that does not include the two bombs. Fresh water will become a real problem in this climate. And unless we can foresee some contact with a new source of supply it will be necessary to withdraw to Gibraltar before we have completed our mission.'

Draffen nodded. 'I am sorry, Captain. You make good sense. A landsman tends to see ships as ships and not as people, mouths to be fed like luckier souls ashore.'

Broughton stared at him. 'But that is exactly what I have just been telling you!'

'It was not what you told me, Sir Lucius, but the *way* you told it!'

He stood up and eyed each of them in turn. 'However, I must ask you to signal the *Restless* to close with the flagship. Your master assures me this wind will hold for a while.' He looked at Bolitho. 'That is also your opinion, I believe?'

Bolitho nodded. 'It seems likely, sir. But you cannot be certain.'

'It will have to suffice. I will transfer to the sloop and go with her to sweep closer inshore. If I cannot make contact with my agent before dusk I will rejoin the squadron.'

Broughton rubbed the back of his neck with his hand. 'In which case we will carry on to Djafou as arranged?'

Draffen hesitated and then said, 'It would seem so.'

The admiral gave a thin smile. 'So be it.' He snapped his fingers at Calvert who had been hovering on the far side of the cabin. 'Make a signal to *Restless* to close the flagship immediately.' He moved briskly up and down across the black and white squared deck covering. 'You will then make a further signal to *Valorous*.'

Bolitho darted a glance at the flag-lieutenant as he wrote hurriedly in his book. It was to be hoped he was getting it all down correctly.

'Er, *Valorous* will take over command of the squadron and continue on present course. *Euryalus* will head down and make contact with *Restless*.' He shot Draffen a brief smile. 'That will save time and allow you some extra hours for your, er, search.'

He swung round towards Calvert again. 'Well, what in hell's name are you gaping at? Go and attend to those signals *at once!*'

As the door closed behind Calvert's back he added, 'Young fool! He may be a fine jack-a-dandy in St James's, but he is as much use as a blind seamstress to me!'

Draffen stood up and walked towards the adjoining cabin which stood opposite the larger one used by the admiral.

'I will change out of these clothes before I leave.' He eyed Broughton calmly. 'I would not wish to be placed in Calvert's category by the sloop's commander.'

Broughton waited until he had gone and then said vehemently, 'My God, my patience is wearing thin.'

'I will go and attend to the new course, sir.'

'Yes.' Broughton watched him distantly. 'I shall be glad when we are at Djafou. I am heartily sick of interference.'

Bolitho hurried back to the quarterdeck, feeling the heat striking his shoulders like embers from a fire.

As he glanced quickly aloft at the masthead pendant and then at the compass he said sharply, 'Call all hands, Mr Keverne. We will wear ship directly. Then you may get the t'gallants on her.'

He heard the squeal of pipes, the immediate rush of feet as

the seamen poured up into the sunlight, pausing only to peer aft to see the cause for the sudden excitement.

Astern, the *Valorous* was already making more sail, her acknowledgement to Broughton's signal vanishing from her yard as her forecourse billowed free and then filled to the wind. The signal would please her captain, Bolitho thought. Furneaux had never really appreciated his station astern of the line. This sudden order would show the others exactly where he stood in Broughton's eyes.

He forgot them as Midshipman Tothill called, '*Restless* has acknowledged, sir.' He glanced despairingly at Calvert's back, who was peering at the signal book as if it was in Arabic.

Bolitho smiled. 'Very well. Mr Partridge, we will see how she likes the feel of the wind again.'

He looked at the men below the gangways and mustered at the foot of each mast. 'Carry on, Mr Keverne.'

'Hands aloft! Loose t'gallants!'

Keverne waited until the rush of barebacked seamen had reached the upper yards, their bodies black against the sky, like monkeys.

'Man the braces!'

He glanced round as Partridge dropped his hand and the helmsmen threw themselves on their spokes and began to heave the wheel over.

'Let go and haul!' Keverne's voice was metallic and unreal through his trumpet. 'Heave, you idle lot of old women!'

Creaking and groaning the great yards began to swing round, the hull plunging deeply in the swell as it swayed ponderously out of the line. Overhead the sails flapped about in momentary confusion, whilst above the noise Bolitho could hear the captains of the tops urging their men on with threats and curses. The topgallant sails were already whipping out from their yards, hardening into firm, tanned rectangles as the canvas took the strain, tugging at blocks and rigging alike and trying always to pluck an unwary topman from his perch and hurl him to the deck far below.

'Steer sou' east by south.'

Bolitho braced his legs, feeling the deck vibrate through his shoes as the sails pushed the ship forward and down across the lip of another deep trough. Spray burst jubilantly above the figurehead and pattered across the men working busily at headsail sheets. He watched the topmen racing each other to the deck, their bare feet thudding on the planking as once more they awaited orders.

Standing almost before the wind, the ship was already gathering way, the deck swaying easily from side to side instead of fixed at one set angle when close hauled.

Bolitho looked aloft, thinking of how she would appear to the *Restless*. The sloop was being made to beat into the teeth of the wind, and Broughton's change of heart would save her and everyone else a good deal of time. Bolitho knew that Broughton's reasons were probably different, that he really wished to get rid of Draffen, if only for a short while.

But for a few moments he could feel content. The *Euryalus* was behaving magnificently, and he toyed with the idea of having Keverne set the royals as well. But that one extra layer of canvas might just be visible to some hostile craft as yet unseen below the horizon.

He turned as Draffen came on deck and said, 'You wished to see her sail, sir.' He watched Draffen's eyes hurrying about the taut, drumming shrouds, the hard-bellied sails, appreciating everything he saw, if not understanding all of it.

He said, 'She's a lady, Bolitho. It makes all this trouble worth while.'

Bolitho noticed he was wearing a plain green coat and loose breeches. Under his coat he also saw the glint of metal. Draffen was obviously used to carrying a pistol, and seemed the sort of man who would be well able to take care of himself.

He was shading his eyes as he tried to understand what the *Restless* was trying to do as she reeled once again across the wind, her sails flapping and almost aback before she swung away on her new tack.

Bolitho crossed to the starboard side and looked for the squadron. *Euryalus*'s sudden increase of speed had left them bunched together and seemingly entangled, their silhouettes overlapping so that they looked like a single, ill-designed monster.

He called, 'Mr Keverne, we'll shorten sail in thirty minutes. *Restless* can lie under our lee until Sir Hugo is aboard.'

Later, while the *Euryalus* lay hove to, her hull rolling sickeningly in a beam swell and her sails banging and useless in noisy torment, Broughton came on deck to watch as Draffen was rowed across in the sloop's jolly-boat.

He said, 'Well, that is that.' He sounded satisfied.

Bolitho saw Draffen pause in his climb up the sloop's side and turn to wave his hand.

He said, 'I would like to tack to the nor' east, sir. It will save time later when we run down and rejoin the squadron.'

Broughton turned his back on the sloop as her topsails filled to the wind and she started to pay off away from her massive consort. 'Very well.' Broughton eyed him searchingly. 'I suppose you cannot bear the thought of resuming your place in the line so soon after this brief freedom?' He smiled. 'Well, it will do Furneaux no harm to exercise his power a little longer.'

Bolitho walked over to Keverne who was still watching the sloop. 'We will steer nor' east, Mr Keverne, and lay her on the larboard tack. So call all hands again, and then they can have their meal. I imagine the activity might have given them a new appetite.' He saw the villainous-looking chief cook, a bearded giant with one eye, peering up from the main hatchway. 'Although I hate to think what *he* puts into it sometimes.'

He crossed to the weather side as once again the seamen swarmed up the ratlines and out along the yards. Broughton understood him better than he realized. Independence and initiative, his father had once told him, were the two most precious things to every captain. Now, commanding a flagship, and tied to the squadron's apron strings, he knew well enough what he had meant.

He thought suddenly of the house at Falmouth. The two portraits opposite the window. He was strangely moved to find he could think of them without grief or bitterness. It was almost like having someone there. Waiting for his return home.

Keverne was back again, his face expressionless. 'This afternoon there will be two hands for punishment, sir.'

'What?' Bolitho stared at him and then nodded. 'Very well.'

The moment of peace had passed. But as he walked to the quarterdeck rail he found himself praying that it might return.

At six o'clock that same day, Bolitho sat behind his desk looking through the stern windows, his mind busy with the affairs of his command. Trute, the cabin servant, placed a pot of fresh coffee by his elbow and padded away without a word. He had grown to accept the captain's strange moods, his apparent need to be alone, even to pour his own coffee. Like his desire to have the desk facing aft, and whenever possible to dine off it instead of his beautiful table in the adjoining cabin. Trute had served three captains, and never met his sort before. The others had all expected to be waited on hand and foot, and at all times of day or night. Equally they had been swift and harsh when showing their displeasure. He had decided that although he liked Bolitho as a considerate and fair master, he had felt more comfortable with his previous captains. At least it had been possible to know exactly what they were thinking for most of the time.

Bolitho sipped the scalding black coffee and wondered when it, like many other items, would become a luxury. It was never possible to feel confident, to know that a ship was not over-reaching her margin of safety when it came to food and water.

He heard four bells chime out, the clatter of feet somewhere below as a warrant officer, probably caught dozing, dashed to perform his duties for the last dog watch.

It had been a busy afternoon for Bolitho, mainly because he had been trying to catch up with matters concerning his own ship rather than attending to those of the whole squadron. There had seemed an endless procession waiting to catch his ear.

Grubb, the carpenter, grey haired and always pessimistic about the enemy of all ships—rot. Not that he had found any in his daily molelike excursions in the bowels of the hull, places which had never seen, would never see, any light but that of a lantern. It was as if he wanted Bolitho to know of his tireless efforts on his behalf. And it all took time.

He had given several minutes to Clode, the cooper, concerning the purser's earlier complaint about the state of some of the water casks. But then Nathan Buddle, the purser, quite often voiced complaints, provided they did not directly concern his own department. He was a thin, furtive-looking man, with skin like parchment, who wore an almost permanent hunted expression which Bolitho suspected hid things which did *not* concern rotten casks. In fairness, he had found nothing wrong with Buddle's daily accounts, but like all his trade, the purser had to be constantly watched.

And as Keverne had reported earlier, two men were brought aft for punishment, watched as usual on such occasions by all unemployed members of the ship's company.

Bolitho hated such spectacles, just as he knew them to be inevitable. It always seemed to take such a long time. The gratings to be rigged, the culprits to be stripped and seized up, and his own voice reading the Articles of War above the din of wind and canvas.

The actual punishment excited little interest amongst the spectators.

The first man, awarded twelve lashes, had been caught stealing from one of his messmates. The opinion was probably that he was getting off lightly, compared with what his fellow seamen had intended and would certainly have carried out but for the timely intervention of the ship's corporal. Bolitho had heard of cases where men who stole from their messmates had been thrown overboard at night, while one had actually been found minus the hand used for his crime. In the teeming, defenceless world of shipboard life few had much sympathy for a thief.

The second seaman had received twenty-four lashes for neglect of duty and insolence. Both latter charges had been laid by Sawle, the ship's junior lieutenant. Bolitho blamed himself for this particular case. He had promoted Sawle to lieutenant some six months earlier, but had he not been so involved with the squadron's affairs under the ailing Admiral Thelwall, he knew now he would have thought twice about it. Sawle had shown the makings of a good officer, but it had been mostly on the surface. He was a sulky-looking youth of eighteen, and Bolitho had told Keverne to ensure his tendency to bully subordinates did not get out of hand. Maybe Keverne had done his best, or perhaps he considered Sawle's attitudes unimportant provided he carried out his other duties to his satisfaction.

Either way, the seaman's bloodied back was a grim reminder to Bolitho of the constant need to supervise Sawle in the future. He was one of his officers and therefore his authority had to be upheld. Nevertheless, if Meheux, the cheerful, round-faced second lieutenant, or Weigall, the third, had been in Sawle's place the incident would have got no further. Meheux was popular because of his raw, north country humour. His well-founded boast that he could reef or splice as efficiently as any seaman would have prevented anything worse than a contest, man to man. Weigall, who had the build, and unfortunately the intelligence also, of a prize-fighter, would have laid the culprit low with one of his massive fists and forgotten the incident completely. Weigall was not unpopular with the men of his division, but for the most part they avoided him. He was in charge of the middle gundeck, and had unfortunately been rendered very deaf during an engagement with a blockade runner. Sometimes he imagined his men were talking about him behind his back, and would have them doing extra drills in the twinkling of an eye.

Bolitho leaned back in his chair and watched the *Euryalus*'s wake bubbling astern as the wind pushed her over, holding her steady while she thrust onward to the north-east.

He poured some more coffee and grimaced. It would soon be time to wear ship and spread more sail for the uncomplicated run before the wind to find the squadron again. This one afternoon and evening of comparative freedom had given him time to think and reconsider, to examine those closest to him, yet as ever separated by rank and station. Broughton had left him entirely alone, and Calvert had implied that he was for the most part going over his charts and re-reading his sealed orders as if to find something previously missed.

There was a tap at the door and the marine sentry bawled, 'Midshipman o' the watch, sir!'

It was Drury. Doing an extra watch because of his earlier troubles with his lieutenant over the lantern.

'Mr Bickford's respects, sir, and would you come up, please.'

Bolitho smiled as he saw the boy's eyes exploring the cabin, noting everything for future description in the more meagre quarters of the gunroom.

'And why, Mr Drury? You seem to have forgotten the best part.'

Drury looked confused. 'A sail, sir. To the nor' west.'

Bolitho jumped up. 'Thank you.' He hurried for the door. 'I might arrange for Trute to show you over my cabin later, Mr Drury, but for now we have work to do.'

Drury blushed and dashed after him, so that they arrived on the tilting quarterdeck together.

Bickford was the fourth lieutenant, one who took his duties very seriously, but appeared totally lacking in humour.

He said, 'Masthead has just reported a sail, sir. To the nor' west.'

Bolitho walked up the deck to the weather side and peered towards the horizon. It was hard and silver bright, like the edge of a sword. But the wind was steady, and that was something. But it might rise to a squall before another dawn. It would then take time to rejoin the squadron, to contact Draffen in the *Restless*.

Bickford took his silence for uncertainty.

'It is my belief, sir, that she is the *Coquette*.' He raised his voice slightly to impress Drury and another midshipman nearby. 'It would be the most likely explanation.'

Bolitho lifted his head and stared up at the bulging topsails, the cracking vehemence of the masthead pendant. Like a giant whip. He thought of the dizzy climb, the dreadful shaking in those shrouds.

'I see, Mr Bickford, thank you.'

The lieutenant nodded firmly. 'That is why she comes alone and with such confidence, sir.'

Keverne climbed the companion ladder to the quarter-deck and hurried towards him.

Bolitho was still looking up at the straining yards. 'Mr Keverne, get aloft with a glass. As fast as you can climb. There is a ship to larboard. Maybe alone.' He glanced at Bickford. 'Maybe not.'

He saw Bickford and the others stiffen and draw back and knew that Broughton had arrived on deck.

'Ah, Bolitho, what is all this scampering and excitement?'

'A sail, sir.' He gestured above the nettings towards the horizon.

'Hmm.' Broughton turned to watch as Keverne swarmed easily up the weather shrouds. 'What is she, I wonder?'

Bickford said quickly, 'I think her to be the *Coquette*, sir.'

Broughton's eyes did not blink as he said to Bolitho, 'Would you remind that officer that if I am in such dire distress as to require an opinion of no value, he will be the first to be told.'

Bolitho smiled as Bickford melted into the others by the rail. 'I believe he understands, sir.'

It was strange how they could stay outwardly calm, he thought. In spite of Broughton's mild show of interest, he knew his mind was alive with questions and calculations. It would be interesting to see if he would ask for an opinion of his flag captain this time.

Keverne arrived, thudding to the deck by means of a back-stay, and hurried across, his dark features working with excitement.

'Merchantman, sir. But well armed, fifty guns, I'd say.

Standing right before the wind, but carrying no royal yards.'
He realized Broughton was glaring at him and added,
'Spaniard, sir. No doubt of it.'

Broughton bit his lip. 'Damn his eyes.'

'Even without royals she could still give us a merry chase,
sir.' Bolitho was thinking aloud. 'But if we can take her we
might get information.' He paused, studying the set of
Broughton's tense shoulders. 'Information which would be
yours to share as you thought fit.'

He had not misjudged the moment. Broughton swung round,
his eyes shining.

'By God, I can see Sir Hugo's face when he arrives back
empty handed and we tell him of our news.' He sighed. 'But
what is the use? By the time you put this great elephant about
that Don'll be flying for home. I cannot afford a long chase,
one to take me away from the squadron.'

Bolitho said, 'I think we have all missed the one important
detail, sir.' He slapped one fist into his palm. 'In a way
Mr Bickford made some sense.' He looked at the others, his
mouth lifting in a grin. Bickford was hanging back, as if afraid
of receiving another rebuff.

Bolitho continued, 'That Don thinks the *Euryalus* is French!'
He looked at Broughton, at the doubts and disappointment
giving way to cautious hope. 'And why not, sir? After all this
time they'll not be expecting one solitary British ship in the
Mediterranean. And there's been no time for news to reach
them of our leaving the Rock.'

Broughton walked to the nettings and climbed lightly on to
a bollard. He stared fixedly at the horizon as if willing the ship
to show herself to him.

The masthead lookout called, 'Ship still runnin' afore the
wind, sir!'

Broughton returned to the deck, rubbing his chin. 'She *must*
have seen us. Even the Dons are not that blind.'

Bolitho replied, 'But the moment we shorten sail or begin
to tack he'll know well enough what we are about.'

'Hell, Bolitho! You raise my hopes and then dash 'em again!'

'I can see her, sir! Two points before the beam!' Drury was
clinging to the quivering shrouds, a telescope jammed to
one eye.

Bolitho took a glass from the rack and steadied it against the
deck's plunging movements. Then he saw it, a pale wedge on

the horizon. Running free with all sails set, her master was making the most of the fresh wind.

'She's coming up fast, sir.'

Again he considered the idea of climbing to the masthead. Instead he asked, 'Fifty guns, you think, Mr Keverne?'

'Aye, sir. I've seen her sort before. Well armed to fight off pirates and the like. Mile for mile we could outpace her, but I doubt match her agility.'

Broughton snapped, 'I can see this getting us nowhere.'

'We must draw her to close quarters, sir.' Bolitho walked quickly to the wheel and back without even being aware of it. 'But keep the advantage. Without holding the wind gage we'll soon be left astern.'

Partridge suggested, ''Oist a Frog flag, sir?'

The admiral banged his hips with impatience. 'Too bloody obvious!'

He saw Captain Giffard and his marine lieutenant at the poop rail training telescopes on the newcomer. 'Get those officers out of my sight! Red coats in a French man-o'-war, what are you doing, Giffard?'

The two marines vanished like magic.

Bolitho said slowly, 'Man overboard, sir.'

'What was that?' Broughton stared at him as if he had taken leave of his sanity. '*Man overboard?*'

'The one thing at sea to make a ship heave to without warning.'

Broughton opened his mouth and shut it again. He could hardly contain his sudden flood of uncertainty and doubts.

Bolitho persisted gently, 'We'll need a good swimmer. A crew standing by for the quarterboat. We can pick 'em up later.' He nodded. 'It's worth it, sir.'

Broughton considered in silence. 'It might just work. Give us the time to . . .' He stamped one foot on the deck. 'By God, yes! We *will* try it!'

Bolitho took a deep breath. 'Mr Keverne, take in the fore-course. We will remain under tops'ls and jib. It is common enough on this tack and should excite little attention.' He watched Keverne dashing away and sought out Partridge. 'Taking in the forecourse will cut her speed a little. We do not want to cross her bows too much.'

Partridge smiled and bobbed his head, his chins wobbling against his neckcloth. He had been wounded at Broughton's scathing attack on his earlier suggestion, but seemed in good spirits again. The forecourse was already flapping and curling inwards as seamen scampered to sheets and halliards, urged on by Keverne's speaking trumpet.

When the first lieutenant came to report it had been brailed up and secured against its yard, Bolitho said, 'Send an experienced petty officer aloft to watch the Spaniard and report any sign of alarm. Then you may pipe the hands to quarters. We will not be able to clear for action on the upper deck, so this will have to be done quickly, and well. We do not want our people injured by boat splinters and falling spars to no good purpose.'

As Keverne dashed away again Broughton asked sharply, 'How long?'

'An hour at the most, sir. I'll bring her up a point to the wind. That should help.'

'It will be too dark to see in three hours.' Broughton nodded grimly. 'So be it then.'

The admiral was about to walk to the poop and then stopped to add softly, 'But you disable my flagship, Bolitho, and I cannot promise any hope for you.'

Bolitho looked at the master. 'Bring her round a point to wind'rd.'

Then he made himself walk slowly along the weather side, his hands clasped behind him. If the *Euryalus* was disabled, there would be little hope for any of them, he decided.

Bolitho trained his glass on the other ship. Since she had first appeared above the horizon and the *Euryalus* had cleared for action, he had expected some sign of alarm or recognition, but the oncoming vessel maintained her set course and now lay less than two miles distant. If *Euryalus* continued on her present tack the Spaniard would cross her stern with about a mile between them.

She was exactly as Keverne had described. Two-decked and carrying every available sail, she was making a fair display of speed, the spray bursting above her scarlet and blue figure-head as high as the bellying forecourse. He could just distinguish the old-fashioned, triangular mizzen sail above her ornately carved poop, the flash of sunlight on trained telescopes as her officers examined the *Euryalus*, no doubt wondering at her purpose and destination.

Keverne said grimly, 'Getting close, sir.'

Bolitho walked to the quarterdeck rail and saw a burly seaman standing amongst a chattering group of onlookers.

'Ready, Williams?'

The man squinted up at him and grinned awkwardly. 'Aye, sir.'

Bolitho nodded. The man had no doubt been well primed with rum by well-wishers. Not too much, he hoped, or the ruse might develop into a sudden sea burial.

He said, 'Pass the word to the middle and lower gundecks, Mr Keverne.' He walked back to the weather side again and trained his glass on the other ship. 'Starboard side to load with double shot. Make sure they do not run out until the order. One sight of a gun muzzle sniffing the wind and our friends will be off and away.'

As Keverne beckoned to a midshipman Bolitho called to Lieutenant Meheux who commanded the upper gundeck. He was staring at his own batteries, his round face unusually glum.

'Never fear, Mr Meheux, your crews will have work enough soon. But a view of them loading and casting off the lashings and our trick will misfire.'

Meheux touched his hat and then resumed his stance of gloomy disappointment.

Allday hurried across the quarterdeck and held out Bolitho's sword. As Bolitho raised his hands and he swiftly buckled it around his waist, he said, 'I've told the coxswain of the quarter boat what you want, Captain.' He grinned. 'And what he'll get if he makes a mess of it!'

Bolitho frowned. The Spaniard was going to pass farther astern than he had gauged. He would have to act now, or never.

'Right, Williams, over you go!'

The big seaman clambered on to the larboard gangway, and with his face set in a mask of determination began to lean over the rail.

Keverne muttered harshly, 'God, he is making the most of his performance.'

'There 'e goes!' Partridge hurried back to his place near the wheel as with a violent thrashing of arms Williams pitched over the rail and vanished.

Bolitho ran to the nettings as the cry 'Man overboard!' brought the crew of the quarterboat dashing from their various attitudes of unlikely concentration. He breathed out more easily as the seaman's head appeared bobbing and spluttering close to the side, and snapped, 'Back the mizzen tops'l, Mr Keverne! Get that boat away!' He had feared that Williams's enthusiasm would make him mistime his fall. The steep tumblehome of the three-decker's side could easily have broken an arm or skull had he been careless.

He tore his eyes from the orderly confusion as the boat's crew swarmed down into the tethered craft below the quarter, while overhead the mizzen topsail banged and flapped against the mast and yard, acting like a brake on some runaway juggernaut, just long enough to peer towards the Spanish ship. She was about two cables from the point where she would cross *Euryalus*'s wake, and he could see figures scampering along her forecastle, as if to get a better view of the drama.

Bolitho raised his hand. 'Now! Stand by to go about!'

Already the mizzen yard was squeaking back to its original position, while from their hiding-places beneath the gangways the seamen ran to their stations, encouraged by derisive cheers from the unemployed gun crews.

Partridge called, 'Ready, sir!'

'Put the helm down!' Bolitho trained his glass on the Spaniard. There was still no sign of alarm as far as he could see.

'Helm a'lee, sir!'

Up forward the headsail sheets had already been let go, and as the wheel went over and the great hull began to swing very slowly into the wind, Keverne urged the men at the braces to even greater efforts as they strained back, panting and cursing, their eyes on the yards above them.

Sails boomed and swelled, and as the ship continued to swing Bolitho saw sudden activity on the other vessel's poop, an officer waving wildly and pointing to his men who were still grouped around the bows.

'Off tacks and sheets!'

Bolitho shaded his eyes to peer aloft through the tangle of flapping sails and jerking shrouds to where the topmen were already fighting their way to the topgallant yards in readiness for the next part of the attack. For a moment longer he hardly dared to draw breath. The wind was still quite strong, and at worst might bring down the topmasts, or leave the heavy ship thrashing helplessly and all aback.

But the pendant was swinging, the ship was still responding, wheeling across the eye of the wind like a well-disciplined mammoth.

'Let go and haul!' Keverne had not raised his eyes from the men on deck. '*Heave* there!'

Slowly but steadily the great yards began to respond to the braces, until with a sound of hill thunder the sails billowed out, full and bulging to the wind, while the deck heeled over to the opposite tack.

Bolitho watched fixedly as the other ship appeared to swim backwards through the mass of rigging around the foremast, until she lay not safely across the larboard quarter, but there, fine on the starboard bow.

There was no sign of the boat or the swimmer, and he found time to hope someone was watching out for them.

'Pass the word, Mr Keverne! Lower batteries run out!'

As the port lids lifted and he heard the familiar squeak and groan of gun tracks, he could imagine the cursing men far below his feet as they hauled their massive charges up the tilting decks towards the sunlight.

'Run up the colours, Mr Tothill!'

Broughton's voice made him turn. 'That was a fierce turn, Bolitho. I thought you would have the sticks out of her.' He had appeared on deck in his gold-laced coat, wearing the beautiful sword, as if for another of his inspections.

There was a dull bang and a puff of smoke drifted across the Spaniard's poop. A gun must have been kept loaded and ready, Bolitho thought, although he did not see where the ball went.

'Get the t'gallants on her, Mr Keverne! This one intends to run for it!'

The two ships were on parallel courses, with the *Euryalus* now some two cables' length astern.

There was another bang, and someone gasped with alarm as a ball smacked through the fore topsail and splashed down far to windward.

The Spanish ship had a very curved stern, and Bolitho guessed she had some powerful guns mounted there to protect herself from a pursuer.

Broughton snapped, 'No sense in delaying things.'

Bolitho nodded. Any minute now and a ball might bring down a vital spar. 'Middle battery, Mr Keverne. Fire in succession!'

To Partridge he snapped, 'Bring her up a point to wind'rd!'

While the *Euryalus* swung slightly away from her intended victim the middle gundeck erupted in a cloud of brown smoke. From forward to aft, cannon after cannon crashed out at regular two-second intervals, each massive twenty-four-pounder hurling itself inboard as the savage orange tongue left its muzzle.

Bolitho watched the leaping waterspouts bursting near and beyond the Spaniard's quarter, saw splintered woodwork fly from her bulwark as some of the balls smashed home.

From below he could hear the gunners cheering, the squeak of trucks as they raced each other up the canting deck towards the ports.

Keverne was watching him, his eyes dark with tension. 'They have not struck, sir.'

Bolitho bit his lip. The red and orange flag of Spain still floated above the poop, and even as he watched another gun banged across the water and a ball screamed close overhead like a tortured spirit in hell.

He had expected the Spaniard to strike at the first sight of the flag. There was about a cable between them, and with her topgallant sails drawing well the *Euryalus* was beginning to pare the range away with each minute.

Something caught his eye, and he saw the quarterboat, black against the glittering water, while its crew, and presumably Williams, stood to cheer the one-sided battle.

The Spaniard's quarter battery belched orange tongues again; this time three, perhaps four, had fired, and before the smoke had blown clear Bolitho felt the deck jump as a ball slammed into the *Euryalus*'s hull like a hammer.

'Bring her up a point again, Mr Partridge.' What was that fool of a Spaniard doing? It was sheer madness to risk any more fighting. If he continued to run before the wind *Euryalus* would overhaul him. If he stood away, she would rake his stern and dismast him in seconds.

More flashes, and this time a ball ploughed into the starboard gangway, and two seamen rolled screaming and kicking on the deck below, cut down by the flying splinters.

Bolitho said, 'Lower batteries, Mr Keverne.' He held on, watching the defiant flag. Hoping. Then he snapped, '*Broadside!*'

The two lower gundecks had been given plenty of time. It

had been almost a leisurely business as gun-captains had checked their crews, and the lieutenants had paced up and down, ducking beneath the massive deck beams to peer through the open ports, as with tired dignity the *Euryalus* turned slightly away from her enemy, showing the double line of guns like black teeth. The next instant, as lieutenants blew on their whistles and captains jerked their lanyards, every gun roared out as one, the whole ship quaking as if grinding across a submerged reef.

On the quarterdeck Bolitho watched the smoke billowing down towards the Spaniard, while above it he saw her mizzen tilt forward before plunging down over her poop, the crash audible even above the broadside's echo, which still reverberated across the sea like thunder.

As the smoke drifted beyond the other ship he saw the gaping holes in her exposed bilge and along her quarter, the trail of rigging and broken spars alongside as she swung drunkenly downwind, exposing her tall stern as if for the final, devastating blow.

But a voice yelled, ' 'E's struck!' And the cheer was taken up below where the crews were already sponging out and reloading for the next broadside.

Bolitho said, 'A brave captain.'

'But stupid.' Broughton was peering towards the Spaniard as she continued to drift helplessly with her smoke, so pitiful after her original appearance of vitality and life.

'We will shorten sail at once, Mr Keverne, and keep her under our lee.' He waited until Keverne had passed his orders before adding, 'Now we might discover what was important to him that needed defending so desperately.'

8. The Prize

VICE-ADMIRAL BROUGHTON snatched a telescope from the midshipman of the watch and strode briskly to Bolitho's side. 'What in hell's name are they doing over there?' He trained the glass on the other ship which still drifted about half a cable under the *Euryalus*'s lee.

Bolitho did not answer. He, too, was studying her as she yawed and plunged, the newly hoisted white ensign flapping jauntily from her mainmast to prove that Lieutenant Meheux and his boarding party had at least achieved something.

He glanced up at the flapping sails and rattling shrouds. It was nearly an hour since the boats had been lowered to take Meheux and his men across to the prize, and in that time there had been a distinct and worrying change in the weather. The sky was clouding over very rapidly, so that the sea had lost its colour and warmth, and the fast-moving crests of the steep waves were dirty grey and menacing. Only the horizon appeared clear, cold and steel bright, as if being lit by power other than the setting sun. Without consulting the masthead pendant he knew the wind had backed still further, and now blew almost from the west, its strength mounting with each frustrating minute.

They were in for a blow, and, hampered by the disabled ship and very little information from Meheux, it could not have been at a worse time.

Broughton snapped, 'The jolly-boat's returning. And about damn time!'

Watching the small boat as it dipped and curtsied over crest and trough was visible evidence of the worsening weather.

The other boats had already been recalled and hoisted inboard, this one being Meheux's only link with the flagship.

In the sternsheets Bolitho saw the intent figure of Midshipman Ashton, who with a master's mate and reliable petty officer had been sent with Meheux to take charge of the prize.

While the little boat wallowed sickeningly below the *Euryalus*'s quarter Ashton cupped his hands and yelled, 'She's badly holed, sir! And the rudder lines have been shot away!'

Bolitho craned over the rail, conscious of the men nearby listening to him as he shouted, 'What is she? What is taking so long?'

Ashton replied, 'The *Navarra*, sir. Outward bound from Malaga.' He almost pitched overboard as an angry wave hurled the boat into a trough. 'General cargo and, and . . .' He seemed aware of the admiral's presence for the first time. 'And a lot of passengers, sir.'

'For God's sake, Bolitho! Ask the young idiot about her captain's explanation!'

But in reply Ashton called, 'He was killed in the broadside, sir. And most of his officers.' He peered up at Bolitho, adding miserably, 'The ship is in a terrible state, sir.'

Bolitho beckoned to Keverne. 'I think you had better go across. The sea is getting up, and there seems more to our prize than we thought.'

But Broughton halted Keverne in his stride. 'Belay that order!' He looked at Bolitho, his eyes cold in the strange light. 'And if Keverne cannot cope with the problem, what then? More delay, with us getting caught in a squall in the middle of it. *You* go.' He flinched as overhead the shrouds and rigging began to hum and whine like badly tuned instruments. 'Decide what must be done, and be sharp about it. I do not want to lose her, but rather than waste hours or even days struggling back to the squadron with a lame duck for company, I'll scuttle her, here and now.' He sensed Bolitho's unspoken question and added, 'We can take the crew and passengers aboard if need be.'

Bolitho nodded. 'Very well, sir.'

He saw Keverne watching him, his face trying hard to hide his disappointment. Denied the chance to hold command of the *Auriga*, he was now losing yet one more opportunity to better his position. If the *Navarra* could be saved, but was unfit to accompany the flagship, the prize officer who sailed her back to Gibraltar might well find himself appointed as captain.

Bolitho had obtained his own first real chance of command by the same method, and could feel for Keverne's distress and possible resentment.

He thrust it from his mind as he signalled to the jolly-boat. If the wind mounted any further there might be no prize at all within the hour.

Allday had appeared at his side and helped him into his coat as he murmured, 'You'll be wanting me of course, Captain.'

Bolitho glanced at him. Saw the sudden anxiety, like the time he had gone to the bomb vessel without him.

He smiled. 'As you say, Allday. *Of course.*'

Getting into the boat was as dangerous as it was uncomfortable. One moment it was driving hard against the ship's side, the next plummeting into a trough, the oarsmen fighting and cursing to stop its timbers from being stove in.

Bolitho jumped outwards and down, knowing that if he misjudged it he was likely to be sucked bodily beneath his ship's great bilge, or be ground into the side by the careering jolly-boat.

Breathlessly he crouched in the sternsheets, blinded by spray, and knocked almost senseless by his jump, which had been more like a fall.

Allday grinned into the flying spray as the oarsmen turned the boat away from the ship and started to fight back downwind.

'Nasty blow, Captain!'

Bolitho said, 'These squalls can go in minutes. Or they can drive a ship to despair.' It was amazing how Allday had regained his usual good spirits now he was with him again, he thought.

When he peered astern he saw the *Euryalus* plunging heavily, her close-reefed topsails just giving steerage way as she edged carefully clear of the other vessel. In the steel-grey light she looked huge and formidable, and he was thankful to see Keverne had already ordered the lower gunports to be closed. The ship was rolling badly, and open ports would invite unnecessary work for the pumps, as well as adding to the discomfort of the men who had to live there.

Even in the poor light it was easy to see the Spanish ship's savage scars. The poop and lower hull beneath it had been smashed into gaping holes in several places, the blackened timbers protruding like broken teeth as testimony of that one, reduced broadside.

Midshipman Ashton shouted, 'Mr Meheux has rigged some swivel guns, sir. But the crew appear too dazed to try and retake the ship.'

Allday growled, 'There'll be nothing to retake in a moment!'

After three attempts the boat managed to get under the *Navarra*'s lee and eventually hooked on to her main chains. Bolitho took his dignity in his hands and jumped wildly for the entry port ladder, feeling his hat whisked from his head and his body soaked to the waist as a lazy breaker swirled up and along the hull as if to drag him away.

Hands reached down to haul him unceremoniously to the deck where Meheux and the master's mate were waiting to meet him, their faces showing their surprise at his sudden and undignified arrival.

Allday clambered after him, and Bolitho saw that somehow he had managed to retrieve his hat from the sea, although it was unlikely it would ever be the same again.

He took it from the coxswain's hands, examining it critically

as he gave his breathing time to return to normal, his eyes
giving the swaying deck a brief glance as the extent of the
damage became more apparent.

The severed mizzen mast, the tangle of fallen rigging and
charred canvas, while on the deck nearby lay several gaping
corpses, their blood paling in the blown spray and seeping
away like life itself.

He said, 'Well, Mr Meheux, I would be obliged if you will
give me your observations and conclusions.' He turned as a
block fell from somewhere overhead and crashed amongst a
pile of shattered planks, which had once been some of the
ship's boats. 'But be brief.'

The *Euryalus*'s second lieutenant glanced around the disordered deck and said, 'She is badly holed, sir. There are
several rents close to the waterline also. If this gets any worse
she will take in more than the pumps can manage.' He paused
as if to allow Bolitho to hear the measured clank of pumps.
'The real problem is the great mass of people below, sir. Quite
apart from her ship's company, this ship is carrying about one
hundred passengers. Women, even children, are jammed down
there. If they get out of hand there will be too great a panic to
control.' He gestured to the shattered boat tier. 'And there's no
hope for them there either, sir.'

Bolitho rubbed his chin. All those passengers. So why did
her captain risk their lives by trying to fight a three-decker?
It did not make sense. Nor did it match a Spaniard's normal
attitude when it came to self-preservation.

'You have thirty seamen in your party, Mr Meheux.' He
tried not to think of those terrified people battened down
below. 'Send some to put extra members of the *Navarra*'s crew
on the pumps. By working in relays we can keep it in check.
Then the rudder. Have you done anything there?'

'My petty officer, McEwen, is attending to the lines, sir.'
Meheux shook his head, obviously thinking it all a waste of
time. 'But the tiller head is damaged too, and will come adrift
in anything like a heavy sea.'

Midshipman Ashton had climbed in through the entry port
and was shaking himself like a half-drowned terrier.

Bolitho took a hasty glance at the sky. The fading light made
the scudding clouds appear faster and lower. Either way they
were in for a bad night, he thought grimly.

He saw Meheux watching him worriedly, no doubt wondering how he was going to cope with an impossible task. He slapped the lieutenant on the shoulder and said with a confidence he certainly did not feel, 'Come, Mr Meheux, your face is like a thunderstorm to a bowl of fresh milk! Now get our people to work, and I will let Mr Ashton show me the passengers.'

He followed Ashton beneath the poop where a corpse in a gold-laced coat lay where it had fallen from a fire-scorched ladder. It must be the captain, he thought. The man's face had been almost blown away, yet there was hardly a speck of blood on the immaculate coat.

Two pigtailed seamen were standing by the wheel gingerly moving the spokes in response to a muffled voice from below a companion ladder as the petty officer bawled his instructions. They saw Bolitho and one of them grinned with obvious relief. 'We leavin' 'er, zur? 'Er'll never steer proper with this 'un.'

Perhaps seeing his own captain again after seemingly being abandoned on this shattered, listing vessel had momentarily made him forget his normal respect when addressing his officers. But Bolitho only saw the man's homely face split into a grin. A man he had hardly noticed before amidst the *Euryalus*'s eight hundred souls, yet one who at this moment seemed like an old friend in an alien and despairing place.

He smiled. 'I think we might prefer even this to a raft.'

As he ducked beneath the deck timbers the seaman winked at his mate. 'Wot did Oi tell 'ee? Oi knew our Dick'd not leave us fer long.'

The petty officer, his hands and arms glistening with thick black grease from the rudder, appeared behind them and snarled, 'Probably 'e don't trust yew. Any more'n what I does.' But even he was surprised to learn his captain had arrived on board, and was content to leave it at that.

One deck down, Bolitho followed Ashton along a madly lurching passageway, very aware of the groaning timbers, the creak and clatter of loose gear and discarded belongings which seemed to mark each foot of the journey. He could hear the sea sluicing against the hull, the long shuddering protest as the ship lifted herself through another trough before heeling heavily away from the wind. His feet skidded, and in the swaying lantern light he saw a man's body spreadeagled across a hatch coaming. His trunk was almost cut in half by a ball which must have come through an open port, catching him as he carried a message, or ran for his life before the merciless bombardment.

Two seamen were standing by another companionway, the top of which was sealed with a heavy hatch cover. They were both armed, and stared at Bolitho with surprise and something like guilt. They had probably been rifling some of the cabins, he thought. That could be sorted out later. Just so long as they had not yet broached a spirit store or found some wine in an officer's sea chest. Thirty men, inflamed by drink, would be little use for saving the ship or anything else.

He asked sharply, 'Are they all down there?'

'Aye, sir.' One of them thumped his musket on the hatch. 'Most of 'em had been put there afore the attack, sir.'

'I see.' It was a wise precaution in spite of the terror and the thunder of cannon fire. Otherwise many more would have died with the captain and his officers.

Allday hissed, 'You're not going down there, Captain?'

Bolitho ignored him. 'Open it.'

He cocked his head to listen to Meheux shouting orders, the answering patter of bare feet on the deck above. Another crisis, but Meheux would have to manage on his own. Right now he had to see the passengers, for down there below the waterline he was sure he might find the answer to one of his questions, and there was no time left for delay.

At first Bolitho could see nothing. But when the seamen flung back the hatch cover and Ashton held his lantern directly above the ladder he felt the sudden tension and fear rising to greet him like something physical.

He climbed down two of the steps, and as the lantern light fell across his body he was almost deafened by a violent chorus of cries and shouts, and saw what appeared to be hundreds of eyes shining in the yellow beam, swaying about in the pitching hull as if detached from anything human. But the voices were real enough. Rising together in shock and terror, the shriller cries of women or children making him halt on the ladder, suddenly aware that many of these people were probably quite ignorant of what had happened in the world above them.

He shouted, 'Be silent, all of you! I will see that no harm comes . . .'

It was hopeless. Hands were already reaching from the gloom, clawing at the ladder and his legs, while the mass of glittering eyes swayed forward, pushed on by the press of figures at the rear.

Ashton said breathlessly, 'Let me, sir! I speak a little Spanish.'

Bolitho pulled him down to the ladder and shouted, 'Just tell them to keep quiet!'

As Ashton tried to make himself heard above the clamour Bolitho called to the two seamen, 'Get some more hands down here! Lively, or you'll be trampled to pulp!'

Ashton was tugging at his sleeve and pointing below him. 'Sir! There's someone trying to say something!'

It was in fact a plump, frightened-looking man, whose bald head shone in the lantern like a piece of smooth marble as he cried, 'I speak the English, Captain! I will tell them to obey you if you only get me out of this terrible place!' He was almost weeping with fear and exhaustion, but was managing to keep a grip on something which Bolitho now recognized as a wig.

'I'll have you all out of there in a moment. Stay on the ladder and tell them.' He felt suddenly sorry for the unknown man, who was neither young nor very firm on his feet. But right now he was his most valuable asset, one he could not afford to lose from view.

The bald man had a surprisingly carrying voice, although he had to break off several times to regain his breath. Some of the noises had died, and the crush of figures beneath the ladder eased back in response to his pleas.

The master's mate and three seamen came panting along the passageway and Bolitho shouted, 'Ah, Mr Grindle, you were quick. Now get ready to pass the children aft, though God knows how many there are down there. Then the women . . .' He broke off as a terrified figure tried to push past Ashton on the ladder. He seized him by the coat and said harshly, 'Tell this one that I will have him thrown overboard if he disobeys my orders!'

In a calmer tone he continued, 'You may put all the fit men to work on deck under Mr Meheux.'

Grindle looked at him dubiously. 'They bain't seamen, sir.'

'I don't care. Give 'em axes and have that wreckage hacked away. Cut loose any top hamper you can find. You may cast the poop guns over the side if you can manage it without letting them run wild.' He paused to listen to the wind whipping against the hull, the growing chorus of groans and bangs which seemed to come from every side, above and below.

Grindle nodded. 'Aye, aye, sir. But we'll not save 'er, I'm thinkin'.'

'Just do as I say.' He halted the man before he could move away. 'Look, Mr Grindle, there is something you must face. These people cannot abandon ship, for there are no boats, nor could we build a raft in this sea. Their officers are dead, and they are near giving in to their terror.' Grindle was an experienced man, he deserved an explanation, even at this late stage.

The master's mate nodded. 'Aye, sir. I'll do what I can.' He raised his voice. 'You lads there! Watch the 'atch, while we goes down to get the bairns out!'

Another seaman came staggering down the passageway. 'Captain, sir! Mr Meheux sends his respects, and the *Euryalus* is signalling!' He gaped as Grindle reeled through the hatch carrying two screaming babies as he would a bundle of canvas.

Bolitho snapped, 'Give Mr Grindle a hand.' To Ashton he called, 'On deck and see what is happening.' The boy faltered and then ran as Bolitho shouted, 'Well, move yourself, my lad! I may have need of your Spanish presently.'

The tide of scrambling, gasping figures was growing every minute, with the seamen occasionally reaching into it to haul out some man who was trying to remain hidden with the women.

Bolitho had vague impressions of dark hair and frightened eyes, of tear-stained faces, an atmosphere of despair and near panic.

Ashton was back again, pushing through the throng, his hat awry as he reported, 'The admiral wishes to know when you are returning, sir.'

Bolitho tried to shut out the din, the clawing uncertainty of other people's fear which hemmed him in on every side.

Then he snapped, 'Signal the ship at once. I need more time. It will be pitch dark soon.'

Ashton stared at him. 'It is all but dark now, sir.'

'And the wind?' He must think. Detach his mind from this throng of terrified, unreal figures.

'Strong, sir. Mr Meheux says it is still rising.'

Bolitho looked away. It was settled. Perhaps there had never been any doubt.

'Go and make your signal. But inform the admiral that I will endeavour to get sail on this ship within the hour.' Ashton looked stunned. Maybe he had expected Bolitho to order them from the ship. The jolly-boat could still make the crossing, at least with some of them.

Grindle panted past, his grey hair standing on end like dead grass. Bolitho called, 'How many so far?'

He scratched his head. ' 'Bout twenty kids. Fifty or so women!' He grinned, showing a line of uneven teeth. 'Sailor's dream, annit, sir?'

Grindle's humour seemed to steady Bolitho. He knew he had been about to call back the midshipman before he could signal his ship. To make a last-minute compromise. One which Broughton might overrule with every justification and so recall him to the *Euryalus*.

He dismissed it instantly. Imagining Meheux trying to manage all on his own while he hid behind his proper role was unthinkable.

Ashton returned almost immediately. He was white faced and visibly alarmed.

'Signal from *Euryalus*, sir. If you are sure you can save the prize will you confirm it now?' He swallowed hard as something crashed across the upper deck, followed by shouts and wild curses from the seamen.

'Then confirm it, Mr Ashton.'

The midshipman added, 'In which case you are ordered to proceed independently to the squadron rendezvous. The flagship is making sail.'

Bolitho tried to hide his feelings. No doubt Broughton was more afraid of losing control of his squadron than anything. It was, after all, his first responsibility. If he allowed himself to be caught in a bad storm it might take him days to find his ships, to learn if Draffen had discovered anything useful.

He weighed his own reactions against their true value. Keverne could manage well enough, he had already proved that. Whereas here . . . He broke out of his thoughts and clapped Ashton on the shoulder. 'Now be off with you.' As Ashton ran back along the passageway he called after him, 'Walk. It does no harm to appear calm, no matter what your feelings may be!'

The midshipman glanced back at him and then forced a smile, before continuing on his way. Walking.

Allday called above the noise, 'Can you come on deck, Captain?' He peered at some male passengers who were being herded in the opposite direction by two armed seamen. 'Blow me, Captain, 'tis like the gates of hell opening!'

Grindle asked, 'What'll *I* do, sir?'

'Keep the passengers quiet until I can send the petty officer to relieve you. Then try and find some charts, and together we'll decide what to do next.'

He followed Allday up the ladder and then said, 'Get that corpse cleared away. It is no sight for children at first light.'

Allday watched him and gave a grim smile. Earlier it seemed they must abandon. Now he was speaking of first light. Things might get better after all.

On deck the wind and sea greeted Bolitho like forces gone mad. The light had almost disappeared, except for slivers of grey sky left darting between the clouds. Just enough for him to see the men reeling about the scarred decks, the bare space where the broken mizzen had lain trapped in its attendant rigging.

He rapped out his orders and then said to Meheux, 'You have made a fine start.'

He turned to watch as Meheux raised one arm to point across the rail. The *Euryalus* was a mere shadow already, with the paler patches growing above her as her topsails filled to the wind and she began to go about. For a moment longer he saw her side glistening in spray, the checkered lines of her sealed ports, and pictured Keverne at his place on the quarterdeck, perhaps already imagining this to be yet another chance for him.

'We will have to stand before the wind, Mr Meheux. Any attempt to tack and we would lose the rudder and worse.'

The master's mate came stumbling out of the darkness, a chart clutched against his chest.

'She was 'eadin' for Port Mahon, sir. Most o' the passengers are traders an' their families, as far as I can make out.'

Bolitho frowned. The *Navarra* was much farther south than need be when they had intercepted her. Another mystery, yet still no answers.

He said, 'We will try and set the tops'ls, Mr Meheux. Put two good men on the wheel. Mr Ashton can translate your requirements to the Spanish hands.'

Bolitho looked round for the *Euryalus*, but she had completely vanished. He said, 'I would rather have the *Navarra*'s men aloft for the present, where we can keep our eyes on them.'

Meheux grimaced. 'They'll be unhappy to go up in this wind, sir.'

'If they refuse, tell 'em there's only one other place they can go.' He gestured between his straddled feet. 'About a thousand fathoms straight down hereabouts!'

Another seaman sought him out and shouted, 'There's some fifty wounded in the fo'c'sle, sir! Blood all over the place! 'Tis a fearful sight!'

Bolitho watched the shadowy figures climbing gingerly up the ratlines, urged on by Meheux with angry gestures and his own idea of Spanish.

'Go below and tell McEwen to discover if we have a doctor amongst the passengers. If so, have him brought on deck.'

Meheux was calling again. 'There's a good few severed lines on the main topmast, sir! It could carry away as soon as we get sail on her!'

Bolitho shivered, aware for the first time that he was soaked to the skin.

'Man the braces, Mr Meheux. Put some of the passengers on them too. I want every damned ounce of muscle you can find!' To Grindle he yelled, 'Ready on the helm there!' His voice was almost drowned by the wailing wind, the leaping curtains of spray against the weather side, like spirits trying to drag her over and down.

He looked for a speaking trumpet, but could see nothing but the faces of the helmsmen glowing in the compass light like wax masks.

Was he doing the correct thing? The squall might blow itself out in minutes, in which case he would be better to lie to under a close-reefed main topsail. But if it did not pass as quickly as it had come upon them, he must drive ahead of it. It was their only chance. Even then, the rudder might carry away, or the pumps might be unable to contain the steady intake of water. And until daylight it was impossible to learn the extent of the damage, or their true plight.

Meheux bellowed, 'Ready, sir!'

Bolitho recalled Broughton's comment. *So be it.* How long ago that seemed now. But he knew it could be little more than three hours since their flag had shown itself above the *Navarra*'s deck.

From forward he heard the jib cracking wildly, the impatient rattle of blocks, and imagined the men on the yards, strung out like limpets on driftwood, and just as helpless.

'Loose fore tops'l!' He saw Meheux swing away to relay his order. 'Put the helm up, Mr Grindle!' He waved his arm urgently. '*Easy* there! Take the strain on those new rudder lines!'

Ahead, through the darkness he heard the sudden clamour of billowing canvas, the muffled cries from far above the heeling deck.

'Lee braces!' He slipped on the unfamiliar deck as he strained his eyes forward. 'Loose the main tops'l!'

Grindle yelled excitedly, 'She's answerin', sir!'

Reeling and fighting back against the thrust of rudder and braced topsails the *Navarra* was sliding drunkenly in a steep beam sea, her masts leaning over farther and still farther to the unwavering pressure.

'Hard over, Mr Grindle!' Bolitho ran back to the rail to watch as the main topsail showed faintly in the darkness, holding the ship over.

The wheel continued to turn, while Bolitho shouted to the invisible men below him at the braces until his throat felt like raw flesh.

But she was coming round. Slowly and painfully, her sails thundering and booming like live things, the solitary jib a pale crescent through the black lines of shrouds and stays.

He dashed the spray from his eyes and ran to the weather side. Already the angle of the waves had altered, and the angry, broken crests were now coming straight for the larboard quarter. All about him he could hear the protesting groan of wood and hemp, the clatter of broken gear, and waited for something to come tearing down from aloft to signal his failure.

But nothing fell, nor did the helmsmen lose control of their wheel. Whoever had designed the *Navarra* had known a thing or two, he thought dazedly.

'We will steer due east, Mr Grindle.' He had to repeat it to make himself heard. Or perhaps like him the others were too stunned, too battered by noise and weather, to make sense of anything any more.

'Braces there!' Without light it was like yelling at an empty deck. A ghost ship in which he was alone and without hope.

'Let go and haul!' The strain and gloom were playing tricks with his vision, and he had to count the seconds, gauging the swing of the yards rather than trusting his streaming eyes.

Meheux came reeling aft, his figure rising and falling like a seaport drunk as he slipped, cursing obscenely, against the Spanish captain's corpse at the foot of the ladder.

'She'll need take a second reef, sir.' He paused, seemingly amazed he was still alive. 'Better get the Dons to do it now. You'll not get 'em aloft again in this, no matter what you threaten 'em with!'

Bolitho cracked his lips into a grin. The uncertainty and the fears were giving way to a kind of wild excitement. Like going into a battle. A madness all of its own, and no less gripping than real insanity. Later, it would pass, and leave a man empty. Spent, like a fox before the hounds.

He shouted, 'See to it! Then make fast and belay.' The grin was still there, fixed on his mouth. 'And pray that it holds in one piece!'

Meheux sounded equally wild, his northern accent unusually broad. 'I bin praying since th' minute I came aboard this wreck, sir!' He laughed into the dashing droplets of spray. 'It's bin a mite helpful to my way o' thinking!'

Bolitho swayed aft to the wheel.

'We will reef, Mr Grindle, but the moment you feel she may broach to, then let me know. I dare not tack, so we will have to spread more sail rather than less of it.'

The petty officer appeared at his side. 'No doctor, sir. An' there are some fierce-lookin' rents, starboard side aft.'

'Tell Mr Meheux to get his Dons down there as soon as he has cleared the yards. I want every bucket, anything which will hold water, put into a chain of men. It will save the pumps from being swamped, and will keep the Spaniards busy for a while.'

The man hesitated. 'Some o' the women are willin' to go forrard an' tend the wounded, sir.'

'Good. See they are escorted, McEwen.' He raised his voice. 'And make sure they come to no other hurt, understood?'

He grinned. 'Aye, sir.'

Grindle muttered, 'It'd take a powerful fine Jack to manage a woman in this lot, by the Lord Jesus it would!'

Ashton had appeared again. 'Can you come, sir? I think we need some shoring up to be done in the carpenter's walk by the aft hold. I—I've tried but I cannot . . .' His voice trailed away.

And that was how the night was to continue. Until Bolitho's mind found it hard to distinguish the passing hours as he applied it to one crisis after another. Faces and voices became blurred, and even Allday seemed unable to stem the constant stream of demands for help and guidance as the *Navarra* ploughed wildly into the leaping wave crests.

But somehow the pumps were kept going, the relays of men having to pull their exhausted companions clear before they could take over the fight against the hull's greedy intake. The bucket chain worked without respite, until totally exhausted the men fell like corpses, oblivious to the spurting water across their bruised bodies or the kicks and curses from the British sailors. The rudder lines grew slack and the business of steering more difficult and wearing, but they did not part, nor did the sails tear from the yards, as well they might under the wind's onslaught.

At the first hint of dawn, almost guiltily, like an unsuccessful attacker, the wind eased, the wave crests smoothing and settling, while the battered ship became more steady beneath her new masters.

Bolitho never left the quarterdeck, and as the first warmth of a new day gingerly explored the horizon he saw that they had the sea to themselves.

He rubbed his sore eyes, noting the lolling shapes of his men beneath the bulwarks, Meheux asleep on his feet, his back against the foremast trunk as if tied there.

In one more second he would give way. Would fall asleep himself, totally spent. He could not even find the sense of satisfaction, the feeling of pride, in what he had achieved. There was nothing but an all-consuming desire to sleep.

He shook himself and called, 'Send for McEwen!' He faltered. His voice sounded like the croak of some disgruntled sea bird.

'Turn the hands to, Mr Grindle, and we will see what we have at our disposal.'

Two women appeared at the break of the forecastle and stood staring around them. One had blood on her apron, but saw him watching her and lifted her hand in greeting. Bolitho tried to smile, but nothing came. Instead he waved back to her, his arm feeling like lead.

There was so much to do. In a few more moments the questions and the demands would start all over again.

He breathed in deeply and rested his hands on the rail. A ball had cut out a piece from it like a knife paring soft cheese. He was still staring at it when Allday said firmly, 'I have placed a cot for you below the poop, Captain.' He paused, anticipating a protest, but knowing Bolitho had little strength left to make it. He added, 'I will call Mr Meheux to take over the watch.'

The next thing Bolitho knew was that he was stretched out on a small hanging cot and someone was removing his sodden shoes and torn coat. And the same realization brought sleep. Like a black curtain, instant and complete.

9. A New Enemy

BOLITHO sat at a makeshift table in the *Navarra*'s small stern cabin and stared moodily at a chart. He had slept for three hours, oblivious of everything, until some latent instinct had brought him out of the cot, his eyes and ears groping for an explanation.

In the space of those three hours the wind had completely died, leaving not a hint of its past fury, and as he had hurried on deck he had seen the sails hanging lifeless, the sea breathing gently in a flat calm.

While Meheux had got on with the business of burying the dead, and Grindle had tried to produce some sort of routine for counting and then feeding the passengers and Spanish crew, he had made a slow and methodical search of the dead captain's quarters.

He raised his eyes and looked around the cabin where a man like himself had once planned, rested and hoped. Through a great rent in the side he could see the dazzling blue water lapping against the hull as if to mock him. From the stern windows he could feel the mounting heat, for the *Euryalus*'s broadside had smashed every piece of glass, just as it had turned the cabin into a shattered, blackened ruin. A fire had probably started, and when he had searched for the ship's papers and log he had found only black, sodden ashes. Nothing to give him information, nor even a sextant to help fix their approximate position. The night's storm could have driven them many miles to the east. Land might be thirty or fifty miles distant, Spain or North Africa. He could not be sure.

Meheux entered the cabin, his shoes crunching on broken glass. He looked tired and strained, like the rest of the boarding party.

'We seem to have got some sort of mid-day meal cooking at last, sir.' He gestured to the chart. 'Any hope of fixing our position yet?'

'No.' There was little point in deluding the lieutenant. If anything happened to himself, it would be Meheux's job to get the ship to safety. 'To be becalmed like this is no help at all.' He studied Meheux gravely. 'How are you managing with the passengers?'

He shrugged. 'They are chattering like a lot of gulls. I don't suppose they realize yet what is happening to them.'

Nor I, Bolitho thought. He said, 'After our people have eaten we will put them to work again on the hull. The water intake is still very bad, so make sure the pumps are inspected too.'

Allday appeared in the sagging dorway, his face set in a frown. 'Pardon, Captain, but one of the Dons wishes to speak with you. But if you wish, I'll send him packing so that you can have your meal in peace.'

Meheux nodded and said, 'I am sorry, I forgot to mention it. The little fat Spaniard who has been helping Ashton with the interpreting asked me earlier. With so much on my mind . . .'

Bolitho smiled. 'I doubt that it is of much importance, but have him sent in, Allday.' To Meheux he added, 'I am so desperate for information I have little choice in the matter.'

The Spaniard entered nervously, his head bowed beneath the deck beams although he had a good two feet clearance. He was wearing his wig, but Bolitho realized with surprise that it made him look older rather than more youthful.

Bolitho had already discovered his name was Luis Pareja, on passage to Port Mahon where he apparently intended to end his years.

'Well, señor, what can I do for you?'

Pareja peered round at the shot holes and charred woodwork before saying timidly, 'Your ship did terrible damage, Captain.'

Meheux muttered harshly, 'Had we given you a full broadside you would be down on the sea bed with those others, so mind your manners!'

Pareja flinched. 'I did not mean to imply that you . . .' He shifted his feet and tried again. 'Many of the others are worried. They do not know what is to happen, or if we will reach our homes again.'

Bolitho eyed him thoughtfully. 'This ship is now a British prize. You must understand it is not possible in war to know exactly how such matters will proceed. But there is ample food aboard, and I expect to meet with our ship soon.' He imagined he saw a flash of doubt in the man's eyes and added firmly, 'Very soon now.'

'I shall tell them.' Pareja sounded less sure than ever. 'If I can help in any way, then please tell me, Captain. You saved our lives by staying with the ship, that I do know. We would certainly have perished otherwise.'

'Tell me, Señor Pareja.' Bolitho dropped his eyes. To show extra confidence might be taken by Pareja as uncertainty in his own ability. He continued, 'Do you know of any reason why the captain came so far to the south?'

Pareja pouted. 'There was some talk. But in the haste of departure I did not take so much notice. My wife needed to leave Spain. Since the alliance with France things have become very bad at home. I hoped to take her to my estate in Minorca. It is not vast, but . . .'

Meheux asked, 'Tell us about the talk?'

'Easy, Mr Meheux.' Bolitho shot him a warning glance. 'He has his troubles too, eh?' He turned and asked easily, 'You were saying something, señor?'

Pareja spread his plump hands. 'I heard one of the officers, alas now dead, saying that they were to meet with some vessel. To allow a passenger to be transferred. Something of that nature.'

Bolitho tried to hide his sudden interest. 'You speak good English. A great help.'

Pareja smiled modestly. 'My wife speaks it well. And I have done much business with London—in happier days.'

Bolitho made himself sit very still, conscious of Meheux's impatience, of the ship's sluggish movement beneath him.

He asked calmly, 'Do you remember where this meeting was to take place?'

'I think not.' He screwed up his face so that he looked like a plump child playing make-believe in an old wig.

Bolitho pushed the chart gently towards him. 'Look at this. The names along that coastline.' He watched intently as Pareja's eyes moved emptily over the well-worn chart.

'No.'

Meheux moved away, biting his lip. 'Blast him!'

Bolitho turned in his chair to mask his disappointment. 'If you remember anything, Señor Pareja, be so good as to tell one of my men.'

Pareja bowed gravely and made as if to leave. Then he halted, one hand raised as if demanding silence. He said excitedly, 'But the officer did say something more.' Again the quaint frown. 'That . . . that it felt strange to do business with the French again.' He peered at Bolitho's grim features and added, 'But that is all. I am sorry.'

'Mr Meheux. Are there any Frenchmen aboard?' He held his breath.

Before the lieutenant could reply Pareja said quickly, 'But yes. There is such a man. He is called Witrand and came aboard so late at Malaga that he had no cabin.' He looked startled. 'Yet he was allowed to share these quarters with the captain? Very strange.'

Bolitho stood up slowly, his mind hardly daring to hold any hope. And yet it was just possible. Someone important enough to share with the captain might well be able to arrange an unorthodox transfer at sea. It would only mean a few days more aboard for the rest of the passengers, and power, like wealth, was very insistent. This man Witrand could be a smuggler or a high-born criminal on the run. A traitor or a merchant trying to outwit his competitors. But he might have information, anything which could throw some light on events in these waters.

There was a sudden commotion in the passageway and he heard Allday say angrily, 'It is no use! You cannot go in there!' And then in a strange, heavy accent, '*Eet ees no bloody good, See-nora!*'

But the door rocked back on its broken hinges and a woman stormed into the cabin, her eyes blazing as she said, 'Ah, there you are, Luis! Everyone is waiting to hear what is happening! And you stand here making gossip like some fishwife!'

Bolitho looked at her with surprise. She was tall and had

long hair, as dark as his own, and was wearing what must be a very costly blue gown. But it was smeared with salt stains, and there were darker patches near her waist which he guessed were blood.

Pareja was embarrassed and said, 'This is my wife, Captain. Like yourself, she is English.'

Bolitho moved the remaining chair towards her. 'Please be seated, Señora.'

She was nearly a head taller than her husband, and at a guess some twenty or so years younger. Striking rather than beautiful, her features were dominated by very dark eyes, and a mouth which was now set in a line of stubborn determination and anger.

'I will not be staying.' She looked at him for the first time. 'All the others have been talking of my husband's new importance in your eyes. I merely came to see that he did not make a fool of himself.'

'Now, my dove!' Pareja stepped back as she swung to face him.

She said, 'Do not *dove* me! You promised to take me away from the war, and from fear of war! And as soon as we are at sea what happens?' She gestured with something like contempt towards Bolitho. 'This one seizes our ship, and nearly kills us all in doing it!'

Meheux snapped, 'Hold your tongue, madam! Captain Bolitho is a King's officer and you'll do well to remember it!'

'*Captain*, is he?' She gave a mock curtsy. 'We are honoured indeed.'

Allday made as if to seize her from behind but Bolitho shook his head.

'I am sorry you have been inconvenienced, Señora Pareja. I will do what I can to ensure you are all returned to Malaga just as soon as I can arrange it.'

She had her hands on her hips, and he could see her supple body trembling with her anger.

'You know that is unlikely, Captain. We will more likely be pushed from ship to ship, suffering indignities at the hands of your sailors, until we are left stranded in some port. I have heard of such things before, believe me!'

She had a strong voice, like her limbs, and she appeared to be well able to take care of herself. Yet as she stood in the scarred cabin, her dress still showing the marks left from the storm and from tending the wounded, Bolitho could hear her voice giving away something more. Desperation, but not fear. Disappointment, rather than any horror at her predicament.

He said, 'I will see that you and your husband are moved to an officer's cabin. I understand your own was destroyed?'

'Yes. And all my trunks!' She glared at her husband. 'But his were safe, of course!'

'But, my dove!' Pareja was almost kneeling to her. 'I will take care of you!'

Bolitho looked away. Embarrassed and sickened.

To Meheux he said, 'Have them taken to the cabin now. I must find out . . .' He broke off as a startled shout was followed instantly by a shot.

He snatched up his sword and pushed Pareja aside as he ran through the door, Meheux and Allday pounding behind him.

The sun was so bright and blinding that for a few seconds he could see nothing unusual. Several passengers were still standing by the main hatch where they had been told to wait for the issue of food. Others were caught in various attitudes of surprise or fright as they peered up at the forecastle, where two men stood behind a mounted swivel gun, training it aft, towards the quarterdeck. Beside it, one of Meheux's seamen lay moaning quietly with blood seeping from a pistol ball in his shoulder.

Pareja called nervously, 'That is the man! Witrand!'

Bolitho stood very still. One jerk of the lanyard and a blast of canister would sweep the deck from forward to aft. It would not only cut him down but most of the people in between as well.

He called, 'Stand clear of that gun! You can do nothing!'

'Do not speak so foolishly, Capitaine!' The man's voice was smooth but surprisingly loud. 'Some of your men had the, er, misfortune,' he smiled, 'the misfortune to discover some very fine brandy below. I fear they will be of little help to your cause.' The muzzle moved slightly. 'Throw down your weapons. The Spanish seamen will be resuming their duties. I have no doubt that even they can sail the ship when required.' He was smiling broadly, his teeth very white in his tanned face. 'Your own ship has gone away. There is no point in sacrificing yourself,' his tone hardened, 'or others, for your own pride!'

Bolitho's mind grappled with the problem which he was now facing. Even if he and the others still sober controlled the poop, they could not work the ship. Whereas Witrand's swivel gun would ensure that he remained master of the upper deck, as well as all the food and water. There might be no Spanish officers left alive, but Witrand was right. The crew could manage to set sail, and it would not be long before some enemy ship appeared to investigate their behaviour.

Allday whispered, 'If we cut back to the cabin we can hold 'em off with muskets, Captain.'

The voice called, 'I am waiting, Capitaine! Throw down your weapons *now*!'

Meheux asked, 'Would he fire? He could kill half of those women and children down there.'

Bolitho began to unbuckle his sword. 'We are no good to anyone dead. Do as he says.'

Something like a great sigh came from the motionless passengers as Bolitho and his companions placed their weapons on the deck. Two armed Spaniards ran along the starboard gangway, pistols trained, until they had climbed the poop ladder behind Bolitho, at a distance they could not possibly miss.

Witrand handed over the swivel gun's lanyard to the other man and then walked slowly along the same gangway. Reaching the quarterdeck he gave a short bow.

'Paul Witrand, Capitaine. At your service.'

He was of medium height, square jawed, with the look of a soldier about him. There was recklessness too, something Bolitho recognized, and which he might have discovered in time but for the arrival of Pareja's wife. Maybe she had come aft deliberately.

He said coldly, 'I have submitted to save life. But in due course we will meet with my ship again. Even keeping me as hostage will not help you then.'

'Just *one* ship, Capitaine? Interesting. What could her mission be in waters dominated by France, I wonder?' He shook his head. 'You are a brave officer, and I respect you for that, But you must accept this fate, as I accepted your sudden arrival aboard here. It would have been better for both of us had we never met.' He gave an expressive shrug. 'But war is war.' He studied Bolitho for several seconds, his eyes almost yellow in the glare. 'I do not doubt you would refuse to sail this ship for me.' He smiled gently. 'But you will give me your word, as a King's officer, not to try and retake her.' He picked up Bolitho's sword. 'Then you may keep this. As a token of my trust in that honour, eh?'

Bolitho shook his head. 'I can give no such assurance.'

Meheux said thickly, 'Nor I.'

'Loyalty too?' He seemed quite composed. 'Then you will be taken below and put in irons. I am sorry of course, but I have much to do. Apart from myself there are just three French companions. The rest,' he shrugged with obvious contempt, 'Spanish rubbish. I will be hard put to keep them away from the passengers, I think.'

He beckoned to the armed seamen and then asked, 'Your ship, she is French built, yes?'

'She was the *Tornade*.' Bolitho kept his voice level, but his mind was almost bursting as he tried to think of a scheme, no matter how weak, which might give him back control. But there was nothing.

Witrand's yellow eyes widened. '*Tornade*? Admiral Lequiller's flagship!' He banged his forehead with the palm of his hand. 'I was foolish not to realize it. You with your unpronounceable name. The man who took the *Tornade* in a mere seventy-four!' He nodded, suddenly serious. 'You will be quite a prize yourself, if and when we ever see France again.'

The seamen jabbed them with their pistols and Witrand said sharply, 'Go with them.' He looked at Allday, standing with his fists clenching and unclenching, his face still shocked at what was happening. 'Is he one of your officers?'

Bolitho looked at him. This was a moment when life might end. Also he might never see Allday again if they became separated. He replied quietly, 'He is a *friend*, m'sieu.'

Witrand sighed. 'And that is something rare.' He smiled sadly. 'He may stay with you. But any trick, and you will be killed.' He shot Pareja a scathing glance. 'Like traitors, there is only one true solution.'

Bolitho turned towards the companion ladder, seeing the faces of the nearby passengers, and Pareja's wife by the poop. She was standing very still, only the quick movement of her breast displaying any sort of emotion. Something squeaked, and when he turned his head he saw the white ensign was already fluttering down from the mainmast.

Like the loss of his sword, it seemed to symbolize the completeness of his defeat.

*   *   *

Bolitho rested his back against a massive cask of salt beef, listening to the muffled sounds beyond the door and conscious of his companions' silence. But for a tiny circular port in the door, through which he could see the feeble light of a lantern, the place where he and the others were imprisoned was in total darkness. He was thankful for that. He did not want them to see his face or his despair.

He heard the chain move, felt the irons about his ankles jerk slightly as Meheux or one of the others changed his position. Allday was sitting next to him, sharing the same cask to rest his back, and Grindle was on the opposite side of the tiny storeroom shackled to Ashton. Each wrapped in his own thoughts. Brooding perhaps on the twist of fate which had brought them here.

It was impossible to tell what was happening elsewhere in the ship. The pumps had not stopped, but occasionally they had heard other sounds. Shouts and curses, and a woman sobbing and screaming. Once there had been another pistol shot, and Bolitho imagined that Witrand was having difficulty in controlling the Spanish crew. After the *Euryalus*'s deadly cannon fire, the storm and the humiliation of being seized as a prize, it was easy to picture the scene between decks. Without their own familiar officers and sense of purpose, any discipline might soon give way to a drunken disorganized chaos.

The wind had not returned. Just feeling the ship's slow, uneasy motion, the useless clatter of loose gear, told him that much.

Meheux said savagely, 'If ever I live to get my hands on those drunkards I'll have them flogged to ribbons, the useless buggers!'

Bolitho replied, 'The brandy was a clever ruse on Witrand's part.' He added with sudden bitterness, 'I should have made a thorough search.'

Grindle said worriedly, 'You was too busy savin' their lives for that, sir. No use in blamin' yerself.'

'I'll agree with that.' Allday stirred restlessly. 'Should have left 'em to rot!'

Bolitho called, 'Are you feeling better, Mr Ashton?' He was worried about the midshipman. When he had been dragged into the storeroom he had seen the bloody bandage around his head, and how pale he had appeared. It seemed that Ashton had tried to hold off the attackers on his own, calling for his men, who unknown to him were already too drunk to help even themselves. Someone had clubbed him brutally with a musket, and he had not spoken more than a few words since.

But he answered readily, 'I am all right, sir. It will soon pass.'

'You acted well.'

Bolitho guessed that Ashton was probably thinking too of his future. He was only seventeen, and had already shown promise and no little ability. Now his prospects might seem dark and empty. Prison, or even death by fever in some forgotten enemy garrison. He was too junior and unimportant to be considered for exchange, even if the proper authorities ever gave it a thought.

Bolitho tried to picture his own ship, where she now lay and what Broughton might be doing. The admiral had probably dismissed them all from his thoughts. The storm, the likelihood of the *Navarra*'s foundering, would soon make him look on them as memories and little more.

He stirred against the cask, hating the iron around his ankles. He had been a prisoner before, but could find no solace in the memory. Then there had been a chance, although very slight, of escape and turning the tables on his captors. And always the real possibility of other British ships arriving to assist him. A slight chance could always offer hope. But now there was nothing like that. *Euryalus* would not return to look for him. How could she when the very mission they had come to do still lay untouched?

His stomach contracted, and he realized he had not eaten since yesterday. It seemed like a week ago. The ordered world of his own ship, a sense of being and belonging.

He pictured Pareja's wife, probably retelling Witrand how easy it had been to delay him from seeking him out from amongst the other passengers. Or maybe she was up there weeping, watching her elderly husband kicking out his breath at the mainyard on the end of a rope. Where had she come from? And what would bring a woman like her to this part of the world? A puzzle which would now stay unanswered.

Feet scraped beyond the door and Allday said hotly, 'Come to gloat no doubt! The bastards!'

The bolt was withdrawn and Bolitho saw Witrand squinting into the storeroom, two armed men at his back.

The Frenchman said, 'I would like you to come on deck, Capitaine.'

He sounded calm enough, yet there was something about him which made Bolitho stiffen with interest. Maybe a wind was returning at last and Witrand had less confidence in t‍ crew than he pretended. But the deck felt as sluggish as before, the mournful clank of pumps just as regular.

He asked coldly, 'Why must I come? I am content to stay here.'

Witrand gestured to one of his men, who stepped cautiously inside with a key for the leg irons. He snapped, 'Prisoners have no choice! You will do as I order!'

Bolitho watched the seaman unlocking the irons, his mind grappling with Witrand's sudden change of manner. He *was* worried.

Meheux helped him to his feet and said, 'Take care, sir.' He sounded just that much too bright, Bolitho reflected, and was probably imagining his captain was about to be inter-rogated, or worse.

He followed Witrand along the passageway, aware of the silence all about him. Apart from the pumps and the gentle creak of timbers, he could hear no voices at all. And that in a ship crowded with apprehensive passengers.

It was late afternoon, and on deck the sun was blinding hot, the seams sticking to Bolitho's shoes as he followed Witrand up a ladder and on to the poop. The glare from the glittering blue water was so intense that he almost fell across some of the splintered planking, so that Witrand put out his hand to steady him.

'Well, what is it?' Bolitho shaded his eyes and looked at the other man. 'I have not changed my mind. About anything.'

Witrand did not seem to hear. He took Bolitho by the arm and pulled him round towards the rail, his voice suddenly urgent. 'Look yonder. What do you understand about them?'

Bolitho was suddenly aware that the ship's main deck and forecastle were crammed with silent, watching figures. Some men had climbed into the shrouds, their intent figures dark against the limp sails as they peered towards the horizon.

Witrand held out a telescope. 'Please, Capitaine. Tell me.'

Bolitho steadied the glass on his forearm and trained it across the rail. Most of the people on deck had turned to watch him, and even Witrand was studying his profile with something like anxiety.

Bolitho moved the glass very slowly, catching his breath as

the small brightly coloured lateen sails swam hesitantly into the lens. Three, four, maybe five of them, each making its own gay reflection on the sea's face, like the wings of gaudy moths, he thought.

He lowered the glass and looked at Witrand. 'They are chebecks.' He watched the uncertainty on Witrand's face. 'Perhaps five of them.'

Witrand stared at him and then waved at the *Navarra*'s lifeless sails. 'But they are moving, and approaching fast! How can that be?'

'Like galleys, m'sieu, they can travel speedily under oars as well as sail.' He added very quietly, 'It is my belief that they are Barbary pirates.'

Witrand stepped back. '*Mon Dieu, Le Corsair!*' He snatched the glass from Bolitho and trained it towards the tiny sails for several seconds. Then he said in a more controlled tone, 'This is bad. What do you know of such people?'

Bolitho looked away. 'They are savage, barbarous fighters. If they get aboard this ship they will kill every man before they carry off the cargo.' He paused. 'And the women.'

Witrand sounded short of breath. 'But our guns are good, yes? My God, they answered your ship well enough. Surely we can smash those puny craft before they draw close?'

Bolitho eyed him gravely. 'You do not begin to understand. These chebecks can manœuvre quickly, while we lie becalmed. That is why they have survived so long, and so successfully. Once within range they will use their sweeps to get under our stern. Then they will pound us to submission. Each one will no doubt carry a heavy cannon in her bows. That is their way.' He let it sink in. 'It has proved very effective. I have heard of ships-of-war lying becalmed and helpless, unable to do anything but watch as these galleys cut out one merchantman after another from the very heart of a convoy.'

He looked again towards the horizon. The sails were already much closer, and he could see the shining banks of long oars rising and falling in perfect rhythm. Above them, the bright lateen sails gave a new menace to their appearance, and he could picture their crews' excitement at the prospect of so easy a capture.

Witrand asked, 'What must we do?' He spread his hands. 'They will kill you too, Capitaine, so we must work together.'

Bolitho shrugged. 'Normally I would get the ship's boats

into the water and try to warp her round. We could then present a broadside. But we have no boats, apart from the small one which brought me here.' He rubbed his chin. 'But in any case, it would be asking a lot.'

'In the name of God, man! Are you going to stand there and do nothing?' He waved towards the silent onlookers, who were beginning to realize the new threat as the little hulls glided nearer and nearer. 'And what of them, eh? You will let them die? Suffer torture and rape? Surely you can do *something*?'

Bolitho smiled grimly. 'Your concern for their lives is touching. You have changed in several ways since our first meeting.' Before the Frenchman could reply he snapped, 'Have my officers released at once, and give them their weapons.' He saw the flicker of a challenge in Witrand's eyes fade as he added harshly, 'You have no choice, m'sieu. And if we are to die today I would rather do it with my sword in my hand.'

Witrand nodded and gave a brief smile. 'That is so. I agree.'

'Then have Señor Pareja brought aft. He can interpret my orders for me.'

Witrand was already beckoning to a messenger as he asked, 'The wind? Will it come?'

'In the cool of late evening perhaps.' He eyed him steadily. 'By then it will not concern us if we fail.'

Minutes later, Meheux and the others joined him on the poop, Ashton staggering painfully and supported on the lieutenant's arm.

On the main deck Bolitho saw the released petty officer, McEwen, and six seamen also being allowed to walk aft, the remainder of them presumably still too drunk to be roused. The latter might die in complete ignorance, Bolitho thought absently, and be better for it.

'You need me, Captain?' It was Luis Pareja, looking fearful and timid at the same time.

Bolitho smiled at him. Pareja had been under guard, which showed that he had no private arrangements with the Frenchman.

He said, 'I want you to tell everyone what I need to be done.' He saw him darting a frightened glance over the rail. 'A lot will depend on you, señor. How you sound and the way you look.' He smiled again. 'So let us go down to the quarterdeck together, eh?'

Pareja blinked up at him. 'Together, Captain?' Then he

nodded, the sudden determination pathetic on his round face.

Meheux whispered fiercely, 'How can we fight 'em off, sir?'

'Get our own men and form a single gun crew. I want the best cannon taken to the stern cabin. You will have to work fast to rig tackles for it, but it must be done. These craft will be within range in an hour. Maybe less.' He touched the lieutenant's torn coat and added, 'And run up the colour again, Mr Meheux.' He saw Witrand open his mouth as if to protest and then turn away to the rail. He added, 'If we must fight, then it will be under *our* flag!'

Allday watched the flag jerking up the halliards and observed cheerfully, 'I'll lay a fine wager that those bloody pirates have never seen a King's ship like *this* lady afore.'

Bolitho looked at Pareja. 'And now, señor, come with me. Together we will try and make some naval history today, eh?'

But as he looked down at all the upturned faces, the women pulling their children against their dresses, the air of despondency and growing fear, it was all he could do to conceal his true feelings from them.

10. Survival

'NOT LONG NOW, SIR.' Grindle tucked his thumbs into his belt and watched the oncoming craft without emotion.

In the last thirty minutes they had formed into line, the manœuvre completed without hurry or effort, as if they had all the time in the world.

Now, curving steadily towards the *Navarra*'s larboard quarter, they looked like some historic procession of oared galleys, an impression increased by the dull booming of drums, the latter essential if the men toiling at the long oars were to keep perfect timing.

The leading chebeck was about a mile away, but already Bolitho could see the cluster of dark-skinned figures gathered above her long beak head, and guessed they were preparing the bow gun for the first attack. The sails, as on the other craft, had been furled, and he could see a blue forked burgee flapping from her foremast displaying the emblem of the crescent moon.

He tore his eyes from the slow, purposeful approach and said to Grindle, 'I am going below for a moment. Keep an eye open here until I return.'

As he hurried beneath the poop he tried to concentrate his thoughts on what he had done so far, to find any loophole in his flimsy plan of defence. When Pareja had interpreted his orders he had watched the faces of crew and passengers alike. To them, any plan would seem better than standing like dumb beasts for the slaughter. But now, as they crouched throughout the hull and listened to those steady, confident drumbeats, that first hope might soon disperse in panic.

If only they had had more time. But *Euryalus*'s broadside had left the ship in too sad a state for quick repairs. She was down by the bows, and even if a wind got up she would sail badly without her mizzen. It had been necessary to rid the poop of its guns in order to lighten her aft where the damage had been worst. But the thought of the guns lying on the sea bed at a time when they were really needed did nothing to help ease his mind.

In the stern cabin he found Meheux and his seamen working feverishly to complete their part of the plan. The *Navarra* had mounted two powerful stern chasers, one of which had been smashed by a ball from the *Euryalus*. But the remaining one had been hauled and raised from its restricted port on the starboard side of the transom and now stood in the centre of the cabin, its muzzle pointing towards the windows. Not that there were any windows left now. Meheux had cut them all away, leaving the gun with a wide arc of fire from quarter to quarter. Hastily rigged tackles were being checked by McEwen, while the other seamen were busily stacking powder and shot against the cabin bulkhead.

Meheux wiped his streaming face and forced a grin. 'She should do well, sir.' He patted the fat breech. 'She's an English thirty-two-pounder. I wonder where these thieving buggers got her from?'

Bolitho nodded and strode to the gaping windows. By craning over the sill he could see the leading boat, her oars like gold in the sunlight. Most of the *Navarra*'s cannon were old and little use. They were carried more to deter any would-be pirate than for firing in deadly earnest. She had depended more on her agility than her prowess in combat, as did most merchant vessels the world over.

This cannon was certainly the one true discovery of any

worth. Similar to those which made up *Euryalus*'s lower gun-deck it was recognized as a powerful and devastating weapon when in the right hands. Nicknamed a Long Nine by the seamen, being nine feet in length, it could throw a ball with fair accuracy over one and a half miles, and still be able to penetrate three feet of oak.

And accuracy was more important than anything else at this moment.

Bolitho turned his back on the sea and said, 'We will fire as soon as the leading chebeck is end on to us.'

McEwen, who was a gun-captain aboard his own ship, asked, 'Double-shotted, sir?'

He shook his head. 'No. That is well enough for a ship-to-ship engagement, when there is nothing opposite you but another broadside. But today we cannot afford to be erratic.' He smiled at their shining, grimy faces. 'So watch your charges, and make sure each ball is a good one.'

He took Meheux aside and dropped his voice. 'I believe they will try and attack from ahead and astern simultaneously. It will divide our resources and give the enemy some idea of our ability.'

The lieutenant nodded. 'I am wishing we had not seen this damned ship, sir.' He grinned ruefully. 'Or that we had sunk her with a full broadside.'

Bolitho smiled, remembering Witrand's own words. *Better for both of us had we never met.* Well, it was too late for regrets now.

He paused in the doorway, his eyes passing over the busy seamen and seeing the cabin's air of dejection at being so badly used.

'If I fall today, Mr Meheux,' he saw the sudden alarm in the lieutenant's eyes and added quietly, 'you will carry on with the fight. This enemy will offer no quarter, so bear that well in mind.' He forced a smile. 'You were the one who was pleading for battle yesterday. You should be well satisfied!'

He walked swiftly towards the sunlight again, past the unattended wheel, to where Grindle stood watching the approaching craft as if he had never moved.

Along both bulwarks of the upper deck the Spanish sailors stood or crouched beside their guns, the largest of which were twelve-pounders. Here and there, wherever they could find some sort of cover, he could see some of the passengers, hastily provided with muskets from the arms chest, while others had appeared carrying elaborate sporting guns from their own baggage to add their weight to the defences.

He shut his ears to the distant drums and tried to visualize the ship's firepower as it would display itself within the next few minutes. Several of the larboard guns were useless, up-ended and smashed by the *Euryalus's* brief onslaught. Much depended on what the enemy would do first.

The pumps were still working steadily enough, and he wondered whether Pareja's translation had brought home to those trying to control the intake of water the true value of their work. Or whether at the first crash of gunfire they would run from the pumps and give the sea its own victory.

There had been a good few peasant women amongst the passengers. Tough, sun-dried creatures, who had not shown either resentment or fear when he had suggested they might help by assisting on the pumps. For, as he had wanted to explain, there were no longer any passengers in the *Navarra*. It was a ship's company upon whose determination and strength depended survival and life itself.

Grindle called, 'Them's splittin' up, sir!'

The two rearmost vessels were already swinging steeply from the line and pulling parallel with the drifting *Navarra*, their long stems cutting the water apart like scythes as they glided purposefully towards the bows.

Bolitho looked along the upper deck and saw Witrand standing by the foremast, a pistol in his belt and another laid nearby on a hatch cover. Ashton was with him, his pale face screwed up with determination and pain as he waited for his orders from the poop.

Bolitho called, 'You may run out, Mr Ashton.'

He bit his lip as the guns squeaked protestingly towards the open ports. Now the gaps in the defences were all the more apparent, especially on the larboard side and quarter where the damage was most severe.

He beckoned to Pareja who had been standing as if mesmerized below the poop ladder.

'Tell them to fire on the order. No random shots, nor do I want them to waste time and energy by aiming at empty sea.'

He narrowed his eyes against the glare and watched the two graceful craft turning slowly as if to cross the *Navarra's* bows. They were about two cables clear. Biding their time.

Astern it was much the same, with the three boats moving in perfect unison towards the larboard quarter, and at a similar distance.

He could hear Meheux rapping out orders, and wondered if he had any faith in his ability to hold off the attackers.

He stiffened, realizing that one bank of oars on the leading boat had halted, poised above the sea, so that even as he watched the hull seemed to shorten until it was pointing directly towards him. Only then did the motionless bank of oars begin to move again, but at a slower pace, the water creaming back from her stem in a fine white arrowhead.

There was a sudden puff of dark smoke from her bows, followed instantly by a loud bang. He saw the water quiver as the invisible ball hurled itself just a few feet above the surface to smash hard into the *Navarra*'s side directly below where he was standing. He heard sharp cries of alarm from below, a momentary pause in the pumping, and saw several figures leaping up and down on the enemy's forecastle as if in a frenzy of excitement.

Another bang, from ahead this time, and he saw a tall water-spout leap skyward some three cables abeam. The other chebeck had fired and missed, but the plume of spray gave a good hint of the size of her gun.

Helplessly the Spanish seamen waited by their ports, staring at the mocking squares of empty water and tensing their bodies for the next ball.

They did not have to wait long. The boat closest to the larboard quarter fired, and the ball smashed hard into the poop, hurling wood splinters across the sea alongside and making the deck quiver violently.

Bolitho snapped, 'I am going aft, Mr Grindle.'

He trusted Meheux to obey his orders more than he did his own ability to remain inactive under this searching, merciless bombardment. Yet that was how it must be if they were to have even a shred of hope.

He found Meheux leaning against the gun, his eyes wary as he watched the oared hull gliding easily towards the quarter, now a cable away.

Bolitho tensed as the chebeck's bow gun belched smoke and fire, and felt the ball crash into the transom below him. Probably close to the damage already made worse by the storm.

Meheux said between his teeth, 'By God, she'll come apart with much more of this, sir!'

Bolitho looked along the gun barrel, noting the stiffness in the naked backs and shoulders of the seamen, who like Meheux were expecting the next shot to be amongst them.

Bang. The muffled explosion was followed by the telltale shiver as a heavy ball struck the *Navarra*'s hull right forward. But he could not be up there as well as here. And this was the ship's vital and most sensitive part.

The next shot from astern cleaved through the empty gun-port on the transom, and Bolitho gritted his teeth as he listened to it smashing deep into the hull, the attendant cries and screams which told him it had found more than mere timber this time.

Meheux snarled, 'What is he waiting for, damn him?'

Bolitho realized that the enemy had not fired again, although his previous timing between shots had been regular and extremely quick. He watched, hardly daring to hope, as with sudden determination the chebeck began to edge across the *Navarra*'s stern. For a moment longer he tortured himself that it was just an illusion. That the *Navarra* was really moving slightly in some additional undertow.

Meheux said breathlessly, 'He's coming in for the kill, sir!' He darted Bolitho a quick glance, his eyes wild with admiration. 'By God, he thinks we are undefended here!'

Bolitho nodded grimly. The chebeck's commander had tested their ability to hold him off and was certainly moving closer for a direct shot into the *Navarra*'s stern. Seeing the damage, the two ports left empty in the transom, he might well believe her to be helpless.

Meheux said sharply, 'Right, my boys.' The men seemed to come alive around the gun. 'Now we shall see!' He stooped behind the breech, his eyes glittering above it in the sunlight like two matched stones as he watched the enemy's slender masts edging into direct line astern.

'Right traverse!' He stamped with impatience as the men threw themselves on their handspikes. 'Well!' He was sweating badly, and had to dash it from his eyes with his torn sleeve. 'Point!'

McEwen stepped clear, pulling his trigger lanyard until it was bar taut.

'Ready!' Meheux swore obscenely as the chebeck swung

momentarily out of line before the drum brought the oars back under control.

In the sudden stillness Bolitho's voice was like a pistol-shot. 'Now, Mr Meheux!'

'Aye, sir.' The seconds felt like hours as Meheux stayed crouched behind the gun like a carved figure.

Then with a suddenness that caught Bolitho unprepared even though he had been expecting it, Meheux leapt aside and yelled, '*Fire!*'

In the close confines of the cabin the noise was like a thunderclap, and as the men reeled about coughing and choking in the dense smoke, Bolitho saw the gun hurl itself inboard on its tackles, felt the planking shaking wildly beneath him, and wondered dazedly if it would tear itself free and smash him to pulp against the bulkhead. But the tackles held, and as the billowing smoke funnelled clear of the windows he heard Meheux yelling like a maniac, 'Look at the bastard! Just see him now, lads!'

Bolitho pushed towards the windows and stared with amazement at the leading boat which seconds before had made such a picture of grace and purpose. The massive thirty-two-pound ball must have ploughed right among one bank of oars, for many appeared missing, and beneath the pall of smoke he could see the slim hull broaching to, the remaining bank of oars hacking and slashing at the water in a wild attempt to hold it steady.

Meheux roared, 'Stop your vent! Sponge out!' To Bolitho he shouted, 'Double-shotted this time, sir?'

'If you can be quick, Mr Meheux.' Bolitho's ears were still ringing from the explosion, but he could feel his sudden desperate excitement rising to match the lieutenant's as he added, 'And grape for good measure if you have any!'

To the seamen who worked so eagerly in the shattered cabin the gun was as familiar as those which shared their daily lives.

The strain and tension of waiting helplessly and watching the enemy shoot into the battered hull without being able to hit back was past in an instant. Yelling and whooping they rammed home the charges, watched closely by McEwen, who was too experienced a gun-captain to allow anything to alter his sense of vigilance. He even fondled each ball before allowing it to be rammed into the muzzle, making quite sure it was as perfect as could be hoped for in a Spanish ship.

Bolitho saw the damaged chebeck begin to edge painfully towards the starboard quarter and managed not to watch the seamen frantically trying to reload before she was gone from view. But a Long Nine normally had a crew of fifteen men to attend to its needs. Meheux had half that number.

'Run out!' He had done it in two minutes.

The other two chebecks were reversing their swoops and backing away from the *Navarra*'s sudden challenge. One of them fired, but the shot must have passed well clear for none of them saw where it fell.

Meheux yelled hoarsely, 'Left traverse!' He dashed to the side of the cabin, squinting his eyes as he tried to gauge the enemy's speed.

Bolitho heard more crashes and shouts from the upper deck and said, 'I must leave you.'

Meheux did not even hear him. 'Left, left, *left*!' He snatched up a handspike and threw his own weight to the gun. He was still peering and squinting over the breech as Bolitho tore himself away and ran back to the poop.

He had just reached the sunlight again when Meheux fired. As he ran to the starboard side he saw the double-shot smash into the chebeck's hull, watched with fixed fascination as the narrow deck began to tilt over, the packed mass of figures surging towards the shattered side like sheep stampeding down a steep hill. The two massive balls must have smashed the hull close on the waterline. The strain and impetus of the oars would have done the rest. Even now the hull was settling down, the milling figures of her crew spilling over the gunwale or running in confusion towards the bows. Neither of the other chebecks was making any attempt to draw near to save life or pursue the attack, and he wondered momentarily whether the stricken boat contained their leader.

He felt Grindle tugging his arm. 'One of 'em's turnin', sir! She's comin' straight for the bows!'

Bolitho stared along the deck and saw a chebeck's slim masts bearing down at full speed, her furled sails appearing to be within feet of the *Navarra*'s jib boom. At the last possible moment it changed course and swept purposefully towards the ship's larboard bow, the oars swinging back against her hull like some great seabird folding its wings as it glided in for a closer embrace.

Bolitho yelled, 'Larboard battery! *Fire!*'

As Ashton staggered along the line of guns each one lurched inboard, the smoke billowing across the enemy craft, the balls doing little damage but cut her foremast in two like a young sapling under an axe.

Bolitho felt the grinding shudder, saw grapnels thudding over the gangway, and dragged out his sword.

'Repel boarders!' He saw the Frenchman snatch up his pistols and push some of the dazed seamen towards the side. 'Mr Ashton! The swivel gun!'

He saw Allday charging along the deck towards him, his cutlass already drawn and shining dully in the smoky sunlight.

He snapped, 'I told you to stay with Mr Ashton!' But knew it was useless. Allday would never leave his side in a fight, no matter what he said.

Heads were already coming up and over the bulwark, which having no boarding nets was protected only by its gangway. Bolitho watched the seamen hacking and slashing with pikes and cutlasses alike, heard the yells and cries rising to a deafening crescendo as more and more dark-skinned attackers fought their way up the ship's side. Some were already on the forecastle, only to vanish like blown paper as the swivel gun belched fire and swept them away in a hail of canister.

'Jesus! Watch your back, Captain!' Allday swung his cutlass and hacked a turbanned figure across the face, cutting the jaw away before even a scream could escape.

Bolitho saw a bearded giant wielding an axe cut down two Spanish seamen and then run crazily towards one of the hatchways. He thought of the women and children, the terrified wounded, and what could change any spark of hope into a raging defeat if this giant got amongst them. Before Allday could intervene he was across the hatch, one foot on the coaming, as the onrushing man skidded to a halt, the axe poised above his head, still bloody from its earlier victims.

The axe started to descend and Bolitho leapt to one side, his sword darting under the man's massive forearm, swinging him round above the hatch, his teeth bared in agony as the razor-edged blade grated against and between his ribs. Bellowing and roaring like a wounded beast he still came on, the axe making a silver arc as he slashed at Bolitho, forcing him back and back towards the poop. A seaman charged forward with a boarding pike, but the giant knocked it to one side and brought the axe across the man's neck without even losing its precision, sending the man flailing across the deck, his head almost severed from his body.

Bolitho knew that if he was pinned against the poop the other man would cut him down just as easily.

He braced himself, and as the man raised the axe above his head, seemingly oblivious to the terrible wound left by the sword, he darted forward, the blade pointed straight for his bearded throat. But his shoe slipped on a patch of blood, and before he could recover he felt himself falling hard against one of the guns, the sword clattering from his hand and beyond his reach.

In those split seconds he saw everything like one great painting, the faces and expressions standing out as if fixed in the mind of an artist. Allday, too far away to help, parrying with a red-turbanned pirate. Grindle and some seamen grappling wildly below the larboard gangway, sword-blades flashing and ringing, eyes wide with ferocity and terror.

He saw too the man with the axe, pausing, balancing on his great bared toes as if to measure this final blow. He was actually grinning, savouring the moment.

Bolitho did not hear the shot through all the other awful sounds, but saw his attacker tilt forward, his expression changing to one of complete astonishment and then a mask of agony before he pitched forward at his feet.

Witrand's pistol was still smoking as he lowered it from his forearm and yelled, 'Are you 'urt, Capitaine?'

Bolitho groped for his sword and stood up, shaking his head. 'No, but thank you.' He grinned. 'I think that we are winning this fight.'

It was true. Already the boarders were retreating along the gangway, leaving their dead and wounded to be trampled underfoot as the battle swayed back and forth above the deck.

Bolitho pushed past several yelling Spaniards and stood beside Allday, his sword parrying a scimitar and opening the shoulder of its owner in a long scarlet gash. Allday watched the man reel towards the side and slashed him down with his heavy cutlass, gasping, 'That'll speed him on his way, by God!'

Bolitho wiped his streaming face and peered down into the boat alongside. Already it was being poled clear, and he could see some of the boarders leaping back on to its narrow side deck, beneath which the hidden oarsmen were trying to free their blades from the *Navarra*'s side.

Several muskets were banging from below, and he felt a ball rasp against the rail by his fingers, and saw a red-robed figure pointing him out to some marksmen on the chebeck's slender poop.

But the oars were gaining control, and as the drumbeat rose above the yelling Spanish seamen, the screaming wounded and those of her own crew who were floundering in the water, the chebeck began to move down the ship's side.

Bolitho noticed that her consort was some mile distant, and must have stayed out of range for the whole fight.

He thought of Meheux in the cabin and shouted hoarsely, 'I must tell them to use the gun!'

He turned to run aft and almost fell across a sprawled corpse, its face glaring fixedly at the lifeless sails and one hand still grasping a bloodied sword. It was Grindle, the master's mate, his grey wisps of hair giving the impression that it was somehow managing to stay alive without him.

Bolitho said, 'Take him, Allday.'

Allday sheathed his cutlass and watched Bolitho hurrying away. To the dead master's mate he said wearily, 'You were too old for this kind of thing, my friend.' Then he dragged him carefully into the shade of the bulwark, leaving a smeared trail of blood behind him.

Meheux managed to get one more shot into the enemy before the power of their oars carried them safely out of range. The chebeck which had so daringly boarded the *Navarra* had dropped almost three cables astern when Meheux was satisfied enough to fire. The ball smashed the other vessel on the poop, carrying away the small lateen mizzen and ripping through the carved scrollwork before plunging into the sea in a welter of spray.

The leading chebeck had sunk, leaving only a few pieces of flotsam and corpses as evidence. The rest made off to the south as fast as their oars could drive them, while the *Navarra*'s dazed and bleeding defenders stared after them, still unable to accept their own survival.

Bolitho returned to the poop, his legs heavy, his sword arm throbbing as if from a wound.

The Spanish seamen were already heaving the enemy's corpses overboard, to bob alongside in a macabre dance before they drifted away like so many discarded rag dolls. There were no prisoners, for the Spanish were in no mood to give quarter.

161

Bolitho said to Meheux, 'They'll not attack us again today, I'm thinking. We had best get the wounded below. Then I will inspect the damage to the hull before it gets dark.'

He looked round, trying to free his mind from the dragging aftermath of battle.

'Where's Pareja?'

Allday called, 'He took a musket ball in the chest, Captain. I tried to keep him from showing himself.' He sighed. 'But he said that you would expect him to help. To keep the crew's spirits up.' He gave a sad smile. 'He did, too. Funny little fellow.'

'Is he dead?' Bolitho recalled Pareja's eagerness, his pathetic subservience in his wife's presence.

'If not, Captain, then it will soon be so.' Allday ran his fingers through his thick hair. 'I had him put below with the rest.'

Witrand crossed the blood-spattered deck and asked calmly, 'Those pirates will return, Capitaine?' He glanced round at the limping wounded and the exhausted, lolling survivors. 'And what then?'

'We will fight again, m'sieu.'

Witrand eyed him thoughtfully. 'You saved this hulk, Capitaine. I am pleased I was here to see it.' He pursed his lips. 'And tomorrow, who knows, eh? What ship will come and discover us, I wonder?'

Bolitho swayed and then said tightly, 'If we are met by one of your frigates, m'sieu, I will surrender the ship. There would be no point in letting these people suffer any more.' He added quietly, 'But until that time, m'sieu, this ship, like her flag, is mine.'

Witrand watched him go and shook his head. '*Stupefiant!*' was all he said.

Bolitho ducked his head beneath the low deck beams and looked gravely at the untidy lines of wounded. Most of them lay quite still, but as the ship yawed sluggishly and the lanterns spiralled from the deckhead it seemed as if every shape was writhing in agony, condemning him for their suffering.

The air was foul with a stench of cooking oil and blood, of bilge and vomit, and he had to steel himself before he could continue on his way. Allday was holding a lantern in front of him, so that some of the faces of the injured and wounded leapt into focus as he passed, only to fade into darkness again, their pain and despair mercifully hidden.

Bolitho wondered how many times he had witnessed sights like these. Men crying and weeping for forgiveness. Others demanding assurances that they were not really dying. That by some miracle they would live to see daylight. Here, the language and intonation were different, but all else the same. He could recall the time as a frightened midshipman aboard the *Manxman*, an eighty gun ship-of-the-line, seeing men fall and die for the first time and watching their agony after the fight was finished. He could remember being ashamed, disgusted with himself for feeling nothing but an overwhelming joy and relief at being whole and spared the agonies of the surgeon's saw and knife.

But he had never been able to conquer his feelings completely. As now, compassion and helplessness, something as impossible to control as his fear of heights.

He heard Allday say, 'There he is, Captain. Down by the lamp room.'

He stepped over two inert shapes, their faces already covered by scraps of canvas, and followed closely on Allday's heels. Around and beyond the swaying lantern he could hear voices moaning and gasping and the gentler crooning assurances of women. Once when he turned his head he saw several of the Spanish peasant women resting momentarily from their work on the pumps. They were naked to the waist, their breasts and arms shining with sweat and bilge water, their hair matted in the filth and the effort they had given to their work. They made no attempt to cover their bodies, nor did they drop their eyes as he had passed, and one gave him what might have been a smile.

Bolitho paused and then knelt down beside Luis Pareja's body. He had been stripped of his fine clothes, and lay like a fat child staring at the gently swaying lanterns, his eyes unmoving, dark pools of pain. The great bandage around his chest was sodden with blood, the centre of which gleamed in the dim light like a bright red eye as his life continued to pump steadily away.

Bolitho said softly, 'I came as soon as I could, Señor Pareja.'

The round face turned slowly towards him, and he realized that what he had taken for a pillow was in fact a soiled apron spread across someone's knees to keep his head from the deck.

As the lantern lifted higher he saw it was Pareja's wife, her dark eyes not on her dying husband but staring fixedly away into the darkness. Her hair was hanging loose and disordered about her face and shoulders, and yet her breathing seemed regular, as if she was composed, or perhaps numbed by what had happened.

Pareja said thickly, 'You saved these people, Captain. From those murderous Saracens.' He tried to reach up for his wife's hand but the effort was too much and his fist dropped against the bloodied blanket like a dead bird. 'My Catherine will be safe now. You will make sure.' When Bolitho did not reply he struggled violently on to one elbow, his voice suddenly strong again. 'You *will*, Captain? You give me your word, eh?'

Bolitho nodded slowly. 'You have it, señor.'

He glanced quickly at her face, half hidden in shadow. Catherine was her name, but she seemed as distant and unreal as ever. When Pareja had spoken her name Bolitho had expected her to break, to lose her reserve and aloof poise, but instead she had continued to stare beyond the lanterns, her mouth glistening slightly in the smoky glare.

Ashton stumbled through the gloom and said, 'Beg pardon, sir, but we have managed to rouse the drunken seamen at last. Shall I muster them aft for your attention?'

Bolitho snapped, 'No. Put them on the pumps!' He spoke so harshly the midshipman recoiled. He continued in the same tone, 'If the women see them, so much the better. They were too useless to fight, so they can work at the pumps until they drop as far as I am concerned!'

Behind his back Allday shot the midshipman a quick glance of warning, and without another word the boy hurried away.

Bolitho said to Pareja, 'I could have done nothing without your assistance.'

Then he looked up as she said tonelessly, 'Save your words, Captain.' She reached over and closed her husband's eyes. 'He has left us.'

The candle flame in Allday's lantern flickered and leaned towards the glass, and beneath his knees Bolitho felt the deck's sudden tilt, the attendant clatter of loose gear, as if the ship was awakening from a sleep.

Allday whispered, 'The wind, Captain. It's here at last.'

But Bolitho remained beside the dead man, trying to find the words, and knowing that, as ever, there were none.

Eventually he said quietly, 'Señora Pareja, if there is anything I can do to help, please say. Your husband was brave, very much so.' He paused and heard Meheux's voice shouting orders on the poop. There was much to do. Sail to be set and a course shaped to get the ship to the squadron if at all possible. He looked at her hands resting on her lap beside Pareja's still face. 'I will send someone to assist you as soon as I have been on deck.'

Her voice seemed to come from far away. 'You cannot help me. My man is dead, and I am a stranger to his people once more. I have nothing but the things I am wearing and a few pieces of jewellery. Not much for what I have suffered.' She eased Pareja's head away and let it rest on the deck. 'And it is thanks to you, Captain.' She looked up, her eyes glinting in the lights. 'So get back to your *duties* and leave me in peace!'

Bolitho rose and walked aft towards the companion ladder without a word.

On the open poop again he made himself stand quite still for several minutes, breathing the cool evening air, watching the dull red glow of sunset along the horizon.

Allday said, 'Pay no heed to that one. It was no fault of yours. Many have died, and a good few more'll go afore this war's done.' He grimaced. 'She's lucky to be alive tonight, as we all are.'

Meheux came aft and said, 'Can I put the Dons to work, sir? I thought we might set the tops'ls and forecourse to get the feel of her again. If the strain is too much we can reef or strip down to jib and main tops'l.' He rubbed his hands noisily. 'To be moving again is a miracle!'

'Carry on, Mr Meheux.' Bolitho walked to the rail and stared up at the first pale stars. 'We will lay her on the larboard tack and steer east sou' east.' He glanced towards the helmsman, almost expecting to see Grindle watching him. 'But at the first sign of strain call all hands and shorten sail immediately.'

As the lieutenant hurried away to rouse the weary seamen Allday asked, 'Shall I go and find the cook, Captain? 'Tis my belief that a hot meal can work wonders when all else has failed.' He stiffened as Witrand's figure moved below the poop. 'And him, will I clap him in irons as he deserves?'

Bolitho studied him impassively. 'He'll be no more trouble, Allday. While there is a fear of pirates hereabouts, I think our authority will stand.' He turned away. 'Yes, you may put the cook to work.' As Allday walked to the companion he added, 'And thank you.'

Allday paused with one foot hanging in space. 'Captain?'

But Bolitho did not say any more, and after a further hesitation Allday clattered down the ladder, his mind grappling with this new and strangely disturbing mood.

At midnight, as the *Navarra* sailed slowly into a deepening darkness Bolitho stood by the lee gangway, his hair stirring in the cool wind, while more of the dead were buried. He had no prayer book, and there was no Spanish priest amongst the passengers to read over those who had died in or after the fighting.

In a way, he thought, the silence was more moving and sincere, and he was conscious of the other sounds: of sea and canvas, of shrouds and the creak of the tiller. A more fitting epitaph for men who had once lived off the sea which was now to receive them for ever.

Grindle and Pareja had been buried together, and Bolitho had seen Ashton rubbing his eyes as the master's mate had splashed down alongside.

Meheux called, 'That's the lot, sir.'

His voice was hushed, and Bolitho was thankful to have him here. Meheux understood without being told that the dead were being buried at night to make it as easy as possible for those who remained alive. There was absolutely no sense in adding to their grief, and there would be more dead tomorrow, he was certain of that.

He replied, 'Very well. I suggest you trim the main yard, and then dismiss the watch below. You and I will stand watch and watch, though I doubt anyone will want to usurp our doubtful privilege.'

Meheux said simply, 'I am proud to share it with you, sir.'

Bolitho turned and walked up the tilting deck until he had reached the taffrail. The western horizon was very dark, and even the ship's lively wake was difficult to see.

Below his feet, in the gutted stern cabin he could hear McEwen whistling softly as he fussed over his thirty-two-pounder. It was strange how safe they all seemed to feel. How assured.

He turned his head as the Spanish seamen finished trimming the main yard and noisily secured the braces to their belaying pins. Even they—who because of the stroke of some politician's or monarch's pen were deemed to be enemies—appeared content under his command.

He smiled wearily at his grotesque thoughts, the ramblings of his mind, and began to pace slowly back and forth across the poop. Once, as his eye fell on the nearest hatchway, he recalled the bearded giant with his axe, and wondered what would have happened but for Witrand's quick action. With his second pistol he could just as easily have killed him too. In the grim business of hurling the boarders back over the side no one would have noticed an additional shot. Perhaps even Witrand felt safer with him alive.

Bolitho shook himself with sudden irritation. His fatigue was playing tricks on him. Tomorrow might find their roles changed once more, with himself a prisoner and Witrand going about his mysterious affairs again, and this a mere interlude. Part of the pattern for the whole.

And that was how war must be faced. To give an enemy personality was too dangerous. To allow him to share your own hopes and fears was asking for self-destruction.

He wondered what Broughton would have done under similar circumstances, and was still thinking about it when Meheux came to relieve him.

And so, under a light wind and her sparse sails drawing well, the *Navarra* continued on her journey. The only sounds to mark her passing were those of the pumps, the occasional cry of a wounded man between decks, and to Bolitho as he lay sleepless in his makeshift cot they seemed to sum up completely what together they had achieved.

He was shaving in the stern cabin, a broken mirror propped against a sagging bookshelf, when Meheux hurried in to announce that a sail had been sighted, almost dead astern, and moving very fast.

Bolitho looked at his torn and blackened shirt and then reluctantly pulled it over his head once more. Maybe the shave was a waste of time, but he felt better for it, even if he did still look like a ragged scarecrow in the mirror.

Meheux was watching him with silent fascination. Bolitho could feel his eyes on the razor as he wiped it on a scrap of cloth before dropping it into a bulkhead locker where he had found it.

He said slowly, 'Well, Mr Meheux, there is not much we can do about it this time.'

He picked up his sword and fastened it around his waist before following Meheux on to the poop. It was early morning, and the air still fresh before the heat which would come later. He noticed the shrouds were hung with clothing, mostly women's garments, and Meheux muttered apologetically, 'They asked to be allowed to wash 'em, sir. But I'll have the lot hauled down now you are on deck.'

'No.'

Bolitho took the telescope and raised it to his eye. Then he tossed it to a seaman saying, 'The glass is smashed. We will just have to wait and see.'

He walked to the taffrail and shaded his eyes against the growing glare to search for the other vessel. He saw the telltale pyramid of sails on the fine horizon line almost immediately, shining in the sunlight and very clear. A step on the deck made him turn and he saw Witrand watching him.

'You are an early riser, m'sieu.'

Witrand shrugged. 'And you are very calm, Capitaine.' He looked at the sea. 'Even though your freedom may be short.'

Bolitho smiled. 'Tell me, Witrand, what were you doing in this ship? Where were you bound?'

The Frenchman smiled broadly. 'I have lost my memory!'

The masthead lookout yelled, 'She's a frigate, sir!'

Meheux asked quietly, 'What do you think, sir? Shall we alter course and make a run for it?' Then he smiled sheepishly as Bolitho pointed at the reefed topsail and listing deck. 'I agree, sir. There is little point.'

Bolitho thrust his hands behind him, trying not to show his disappointment. A frigate could mean only one thing. An enemy.

Witrand said quietly, 'I understand your feelings, Capitaine. Can I do something to assist you? A letter per'aps to a loved one? It might take months otherwise. . . .' His eyes fell to the sword as Bolitho's fingers touched the hilt. 'I could send the sword to England.' He added gently, 'Better that than to let some dockside dealer get his claws around it, eh?'

Bolitho turned to watch the other ship which was so rapidly overhauling the crippled *Navarra* it made him feel as if they were on converging courses. He could see her bulging topsails and topgallants, the bright tongue of her masthead pendant as she pushed and plunged across the dancing water in full pursuit.

There was a puff of brown smoke, gone instantly in the wind, and then a bang. Seconds later a tall waterspout shot skywards within fifty feet of the larboard quarter.

Muffled cries floated through the open hatches, and Bolitho said dully, 'Heave to, Mr Meheux.' He glanced up at the mainmast and asked, 'Where is the flag?'

'I am sorry, sir.' Meheux seemed stunned. 'We used it to cover Mr Grindle before he was buried.'

'Yes.' Bolitho twisted round so that they should not see his expression. 'Well, run it up now, if you please.'

Meheux hurried away, calling the seamen from the gang-ways and ratlines where they had been clinging to watch the newcomer.

Minutes later, with her ensign flapping against the clear sky, the *Navarra* rounded into the wind, her loose canvas banging in protest, her decks crowded with figures who had swarmed up from below to see what was happening.

Bolitho steadied himself against the uneven motion and walked slowly to Witrand's side.

'Your offer, m'sieu. Was it genuine?' Bolitho moved his fingers around the buckle of the sword-belt, his eyes hidden as he said, 'There is someone. I . . .'

He broke off and swung round as a great burst of cheering floated across the water.

The frigate was sweeping down to run across their quarter, and as she tacked violently in the wind he saw a flag breaking from her gaff. It was the same as his own, and he had to look away once more, unable to hide his emotion.

Ashton was dancing up and down yelling, 'She's *Coquette*, sir!'

Meheux's face was split in half with a huge grin, and he slapped Allday's shoulder as he shouted wildly, 'Well then!' Another slap. 'Well then, eh?' It was all he could find to say.

Bolitho looked across at the Frenchman. Then he said, 'It will not be necessary, m'sieu.' He saw the understanding in the man's yellow eyes. 'But thank you.'

Witrand moved his gaze to the frigate and said quietly, 'It would seem that the English have returned.'

11. An End to the Waiting

IT TOOK a further two days to find the squadron, and during that time Bolitho often wondered what might have occurred but for *Coquette's* timely arrival. The *Navarra's* chronometer was smashed, and she was without either sextant or reliable compass. Even if she had been spared the additional battering of the storm, Bolitho knew he would have been hard put to it to estimate his position, let alone shape a course to the squadron's area of rendezvous.

Gillmor, the *Coquette's* tall and gangling captain, had called it the devil's luck, and there seemed much to suggest it was so. For had he kept to his original station, scouting and patrolling across the squadron's wake, he would certainly never have found the battered and partly disabled *Navarra*. But instead he had sighted a sail and had altered course to investigate, only to lose it during the night of the storm. The next day he had found it again, to discover it was a British sloop from Gibraltar. Further, the sloop was in fact searching for him. She had arrived at the Rock within twenty-four hours of the squadron's departure with a despatch for Broughton, and having passed it to Gillmor had made off again in great haste, no doubt very aware of her own vulnerability in such hostile waters.

Gillmor knew nothing of the contents of his sealed envelope, and could speak of little but his amazement at sighting the *Navarra* and then her flag flying above so much damage. His astonishment was considerably increased when he found the stained and ragged figure who greeted his arrival on board to be his own flag captain.

With so many women displayed on the ship's decks it was no surprise to Bolitho that the *Coquette's* company offered plenty of volunteers when it came to selecting men for work on the repairs. Even the frigate's first lieutenant, well known it seemed for keeping a cold eye on his ship's supply of spare spars and cordage, allowed a jury-mast to be sent across to replace the broken mizzen.

Several times during working hours Bolitho had heard shrill laughter and discreet giggles from between decks, and guessed that the *Coquette's* seamen were making their presence felt.

And on the morning of the second day, while he stood by the *Navarra*'s weather rail, he felt something like pride as he watched the sun shining on the familiar topsails of the squadron, the speedier shape of the sloop *Restless* as she dashed away from her consorts to investigate the new arrivals.

Meheux said quietly, 'They look fine, sir.' He too seemed touched by the occasion. 'I'll not be sorry to quit this floating ruin.'

Then, while the *Coquette* made more sail and hurried ahead of her battered companion, her yards already alive with signal flags, Bolitho watched his own ship, shining brightly in the glare, her tan sails quivering in haze as she moved slowly on the starboard tack. Like the other three ships-of-the-line, she appeared motionless above her reflection, with only the smallest crust of white around her stem to indicate her steady approach.

Bolitho said, 'She will be sending a boat directly. You will retain command here, Mr Meheux, until the *Navarra*'s future is decided. I doubt you will have long to wait.'

Meheux smiled. 'I am relieved to hear it, sir.' He gestured towards an open hatch whence came the unending groan and clank of pumps. 'What about our men down there? Shall I send 'em over under guard, sir?'

Bolitho shook his head. 'They have worked well enough, and I suspect they'll think twice in future before they take on a free cargo of brandy.'

Ashton called, 'The flagship has signalled the squadron to heave to, sir.' He looked stronger again, although his eyes were squinting as if he was suffering from a headache.

Bolitho heard Allday growl, 'My God, here comes your barge, Captain! I'll kill that cox'n for the way he steers her!'

He said, 'Fetch Witrand up here. We will take him to *Euryalus* with us.'

The next moments were unreal and not a little moving for Bolitho. As the barge came alongside, the tossed oars shining like twin rows of polished bones, and Meheux followed him to the gangway, he realized that most of the *Navarra*'s passengers were crowding the side to see him depart. Some were waving to him, and several of the women were laughing and weeping at the same time.

He thought he saw Pareja's widow watching from the poop, but was not sure, and wondered what he should do to help her.

Witrand stood beside him and shook his head. 'They are sorry to lose you, Capitaine. Our common suffering of the past days has united us, eh?' Then he glanced at the *Euryalus* and added soberly, "Owever, that was yesterday. Tomorrow all is different again.'

Bolitho followed Ashton and the Frenchman down into the barge where Allday was hissing threats at a rigid-faced seaman by the tiller. For a moment longer he glanced up at the rows of faces, the shot holes and the many scars where the dark-skinned attackers had hurled their grapnels to swarm aboard in a yelling horde. As Witrand had said, that was yesterday.

The return to his own command was no less overwhelming. The seamen who clung to the shrouds or swayed precariously on the hards were openly grinning and cheering, and as he clambered through the entry port, his ears almost deafened by the shrill of fifes and drums from the small marine band, he found time to notice that the normally wooden-faced marines in the guard were far from still.

Keverne stepped forward, trying not to let his gaze wander across Bolitho's tattered clothing. 'Welcome back, sir.' Then he smiled. 'I have won my wager with the master.'

Bolitho tried to keep his mouth under control. He saw Partridge craning forward to see him between the swaying lines of marines and called, 'You thought I would never return, eh?'

Keverne said hastily, 'No, sir. He thought you would be here yesterday.'

Bolitho looked around at the massed faces. They had all come a long way together. Once, during the wretched *Auriga* affair, he had imagined he had seen hostility. A sense of disappointment in what he had done or tried to do. The fact that they had known him better than he had perhaps realized stirred him deeply.

He said, 'I must report to the admiral.' He studied Keverne's dark features, but even he appeared genuinely pleased to see him return to the ship. He could not have blamed him for showing opposite feelings, especially after his earlier setbacks.

Keverne said, 'Sir Lucius instructed me to tell you he will be reading the despatches brought by *Coquette*.' He gave a wry smile. 'He intimated, sir, that you might wish to take half an hour to, er, refresh yourself.' He let his eyes move to Bolitho's

172

torn coat. 'He was watching your return from his quarter gallery.'

At that moment Witrand was assisted through the port, and Bolitho said, 'This is M'sieu Paul Witrand. He is a prisoner, but will be treated with all humanity.'

Keverne looked at the Frenchman doubtfully and then said, 'I will attend to it, sir.'

Witrand gave a stiff bow. 'Thank you, Capitaine.' He glanced aloft at the great yards and loosely flapping sails. 'A prisoner per'aps, but to me this ship must still be like a part of France.'

Lieutenant Cox of the marines, a sleek young man whose immaculate uniform fitted so tightly that Bolitho imagined it impossible to stoop in it, marched forward and touched Witrand's arm. Together they walked towards the head of the companion.

Bolitho said, 'Come aft, Mr. Keverne. Tell me all the news while I change.'

Keverne followed him past the watching seamen and marines. 'I would think that you have it all, sir. Sir Hugo Draffen rejoined the squadron, but I have heard little beyond that he met his agent and obtained some information about Djafou's defences.'

Inside the cabin it was cool after the quarterdeck and the day's mounting heat. He stared with surprise at several pieces of furniture which had not been present before.

Keverne said, 'Captain Furneaux was aboard during your absence, sir. He was acting flag captain, but returned to *Valorous* when we received *Coquette*'s signals.'

Bolitho glanced at him, but Keverne's face was devoid of amusement. Furneaux had obviously expected his new and coveted role to be permanent.

He said, 'Have them sent back to him when convenient.'

Keverne leaned against the quarter windows and watched as Bolitho stripped and sluiced his weary body with cold water. Trute, his servant, took the filthy shirt, and after the smallest hesitation dropped it from an open window. Bolitho's appearance as he had entered his cabin had made a deep and obvious impression on Trute, and he could hardly drag his eyes from him.

Bolitho pulled on a clean shirt and then sat in a chair while Trute deftly fashioned his hair into a short queue at the nape of his neck.

'Then there has been no change since my leaving the ship?'

Keverne shrugged. 'We sighted a few sail, sir, but *Restless* was unable to close with them. So it is unlikely they saw us either.' He added, 'I spoke with the sloop's commander, but he saw nothing of Sir Hugo's agent. He was in an Arab fishing boat, and Sir Hugo went across to her alone. He insisted.'

Bolitho waited impatiently for Trute to finish tying his neckcloth and then stood up. The wash and change of clothing had wiped away the dragging tiredness, and the familiar faces and voices around had done much to restore him.

Nevertheless, Keverne's news, or lack of it, was very worrying. Unless something was achieved quickly they would be in serious trouble. Word of their presence would soon reach Spain or France, and even now there might be a powerful force on its way to seek them out.

Allday entered the cabin carrying Bolitho's sword. He shot a glare at Trute and said, 'I've oiled the scabbard, Captain.' He raised the tarnished hilt a few inches and let it snap down again. 'Like new, she is.'

Bolitho smiled as he slipped the belt around his waist. Allday was frowning as he readjusted the clasp, and he knew that but for Keverne's presence he would probably be grumbling that it was the second time he had done so in a month. He would make heavy suggestions that he should eat more, for like most sailors Allday placed much value in eating and drinking to the full whenever possible.

Overhead a bell chimed the hour and Bolitho walked to the door. 'I am sorry I have not been able to assist you in your promotion, Mr Keverne. But I have no doubt as to an opportunity very soon.'

Keverne smiled gravely. 'Thank you, sir. For your concern.'

Bolitho walked quickly down the companion ladder to the middle deck, thinking of Keverne's reserve, the permanent defence against showing his inner feelings. He might make a good captain one day, he thought. Especially if he could keep his temper in hand.

The marine sentries stamped to attention and a corporal opened the double doors for him.

He heard Broughton's voice long before he had reached the stern cabin and braced himself accordingly.

'God damn your eyes, Calvert! This is appalling! You had best go to one of the midshipmen and discover how to spell!'

Bolitho entered the cabin and saw Broughton in black silhouette against the tall windows. He threw a screwed-up ball of paper at the flag-lieutenant who was sitting at the opposite side of the desk to his clerk, shouting violently, 'My clerk can do twice as much in half the time!'

Bolitho looked away, embarrassed for Calvert and with himself for being here to see his humiliation. Calvert was quivering with both nervousness and resentment, while the clerk was smiling at him with obvious relish.

Broughton saw Bolitho and snapped, 'Ah, here you are. Good. I will not be long.' He snatched up another sheet of paper from beneath Calvert's fingers and turned it to the windows, his eyes darting along the scrawling writing at great speed. There were shadows beneath his eyes, and he looked extremely angry.

He glared at Calvert again. 'My God, why were you born such a fool?'

Calvert half rose, his shoes scraping on the deck covering. 'I did not ask to be born, sir!' He sounded almost ready to burst into tears.

Bolitho watched the admiral, expecting him to explode at the lieutenant's rare show of defiance.

But he said indifferently, 'If you had, the request would probably have been denied!' He pointed at the door. 'Now get to work on those orders and see they are ready for signature in one hour.' He swung on his clerk. 'And you can stop grinning like an old woman and help him!' His voice pursued him to the door. 'Or I'll have you flogged for good measure, damn you!'

The door shut and Bolitho felt the cabin closing in on him in the oppressive silence.

But Broughton said wearily, 'Be seated.' He walked to the table and picked up a decanter. 'Some claret, I think.' Almost to himself he added, 'If I see one more snivelling subordinate before I take a drink I feel I must surely go out of my mind.' He walked to Bolitho's chair and held out a glass. 'Your health, Captain. I am surprised to see you again, and from what Gillmor of the *Coquette* has been babbling about, I think you too must feel some relief at being spared.' He walked to the quarter windows and stared towards the *Navarra*. 'And you have a prisoner, they tell me?'

'Yes, sir. I believe him to be a courier. He was carrying no letters, but it seems he was to be transferred to another vessel at sea. The *Navarra* was well off her course, and I think he may have been intended to land in North Africa.'

Broughton grunted. 'He may tell us something. These French officials are well versed in their duties. After watching their predecessors losing their heads in the Terror, they have to be. But a promise of a quick exchange with an English prisoner might help loosen his tongue.'

'My cox'n got to work on his servant, sir. A plentiful cargo of wine was very helpful. Unfortunately, the man knew little of his master's mission or destination, other than that he is a serving officer in the French artillery. But I think we might keep our knowledge a secret until we can make better use of it.'

Broughton watched him bleakly. 'That will be too late anyway.' He crossed to the decanter again, his face set in a frown. 'Draffen has obtained an excellent plan of Djafou and its defences. He must have some very remarkable friends in such a loathsome area.' He added slowly, '*Coquette* brought me bad news. Apparently there has been some extra Spanish activity, especially at Algeciras. It is feared the two bomb vessels cannot sail without an escort. And with the threat of another Franco-Spanish attempt on our blockade, no such frigates can be spared.' He gripped his fingers together and snapped, 'They seem to blame me for *Auriga*'s desertion to the enemy, damn them!'

Bolitho waited, knowing there was more. It was very bad news indeed, for without bomb vessels this particular assault might have to be postponed. But he could appreciate the decision not to send them without escort. They were unwieldy in any sort of a sea and easy prey for a patrolling enemy frigate. The *Auriga* could indeed have been held at Gibraltar for the task, and the Commander-in-Chief probably thought Broughton's inability to hold on to her a good excuse for not releasing any of his own from the blockade of Cadiz and the Strait of Gibraltar.

Or perhaps the fact was there simply were no available vessels left spare or within call. It was strange he had hardly thought of the mutiny since leaving the Rock, although it was obviously on Broughton's mind for much of the time. Even now, as they sat drinking claret, with the bright sunlight throwing a dancing pattern of reflections across the deckhead and furniture, the French might be landing in England, or encamped around Falmouth itself. With the fleet in turmoil it was possible. He dismissed it immediately, cursing his returning drowsiness for allowing his mind to follow Broughton's.

The admiral said, 'We must act soon, or by God we'll be fighting some French squadron before we know where we are. Without a base or anywhere to repair damage, we'll be hard put to reach Gibraltar, let alone take Djafou.'

'May I ask what Sir Hugo advises?'

Broughton eyed him calmly. 'His task is to form an administration in Djafou on our behalf, once it has been taken. He knows the place from past experience, and has been accepted by local leaders.' Some of his anger made his cheeks flush. 'Bandits, the whole bunch, by the sound of 'em!'

Bolitho nodded. So Draffen had laid the foundations of the whole operation, and would manage affairs for the British government once the place had been occupied and perhaps until the fleet returned in real strength to the Mediterranean. Before and after. The piece in between was Broughton's responsibility, and his decision could make or break not only the mission but himself as well.

He said, 'Spain has been too involved in recent years in maintaining her colonies in the Americas to spare much money or help for a place like Djafou, sir. She has been beset with fighting local wars in and around the Caribbean. With privateers and pirates as well as the accepted powers, according to her shift of allegiance.' He leaned forward. 'Suppose the French are also interested in Djafou, sir? Spain might easily change sides against her again in the future. Another sure foothold in the African mainland would be exactly to the French liking. It would give Djafou an additional value.'

He watched Broughton sipping his claret. Gaining time before committing himself to an answer. He could see the small lines of worry about Broughton's eyes, the way his fingers tapped against the arm of his chair.

Throughout the ship and the squadron Broughton's rank and exalted authority must seem like something akin to heaven. Even a lieutenant was so far above a common seaman as to be unreachable, so how could anyone really understand a man like Broughton? But now, to see him pondering and mulling over his own scanty suggestions gave him one of those rare and surprising glimpses of what true authority could mean to the man behind it.

Broughton said, 'This man Witrand. Do you see him as a key?'

'Partly, sir.' Bolitho was thankful for Broughton's quick mind. Thelwall had been old and sickening for all of his time in *Euryalus*. Bolitho's previous superior, a wavering, dilatory commodore, had all but cost him his ship and his life. Broughton at least was young and ready enough to see where a local move by the enemy might point to something far greater in the future.

He added, 'My cox'n did discover from Witrand's servant that he has done some work in the past arranging for quartering of troops, siting artillery and so forth. I believe he is a man of some authority.'

Broughton gave a faint smile. 'Sir Hugo's twin in the enemy camp, eh?

'Yes, sir.'

'In which case time might be shorter than I feared.'

Bolitho nodded. 'We were told of ships gathering at Cartagena. It is only one hundred and twenty miles from Djafou, sir.'

The admiral stood up. 'You are advising me to attack without waiting for the bombs?'

'I cannot see any choice, sir.'

'There is always a choice.' Broughton eyed him distantly. 'In this case I can decide to return to Gibraltar. If so, then I must carry with me an excellent reason. But if I decide to mount an attack, then that attack *must* succeed.'

'I know, sir.'

Broughton walked to the quarter windows again. 'The *Navarra* will accompany the squadron. To release her would be spreading the news of our presence and strength with better efficiency than if I wrote Bonaparte a personal invitation. To sink her and scatter her crew and passengers through the squadron might be equally unsettling at a time when we are about to do battle.' He turned and looked at Bolitho searchingly. 'How *did* you fight off the chebecks?'

'I pressed the passengers and crew into the King's service, sir.'

Broughton pursed his lips. 'Furneaux would never have done that, by God. He would have fought bravely, but his head would now be adorning some mosque, I have no doubt.'

He added brusquely, 'I will call my captains on board for a

conference in one hour. Make a signal accordingly. We will then set sail and use the rest of the day to form the squadron into some order. The wind is nothing to wonder at, but it remains steady from the north-west. It should suffice. You will make it your business to study Draffen's plan and acquaint yourself with every available detail.'

Bolitho smiled gravely.

'You *have* decided, sir.'

'We may both regret it later,' Broughton did not smile. 'Attacking harbours and defended pieces of land is always a chance affair. Show me a set plan of battle, an array of enemy ships, and I will tell you the mind of their commander. But this,' he shrugged disdainfully, 'is like putting a ferret to the hole. You never know how the rabbit is going to run, or in which direction.'

Bolitho picked up his hat. 'I placed Witrand in custody, sir. He is a clever man and would not hesitate to escape and use his knowledge if he saw a chance. He saved my life in the *Navarra*, but I'll not underestimate his other qualities because of that.'

The admiral did not seem to be listening. He was toying with his watch fob and staring absently towards the windows. But as Bolitho walked to the door he said sharply, 'If I should fall in battle . . .' He hesitated while Bolitho stood quite still watching him—'and I think it is not unknown for such things to happen—you will of course be in overall command until otherwise ordered. There are certain papers . . .' He seemed to become angry with himself, even impatient, and added, 'You will continue to assist Sir Hugo.'

Bolitho said, 'I am sure you are being pessimistic, sir.'

'Merely cautious. I do not believe in sentiment. The fact is I do not entirely trust Sir Hugo.' He held up his hand. 'That is all I can say. All I intend to say.'

Bolitho stared at him. 'But, sir, his credentials must surely be in order?'

Broughton replied angrily, 'Naturally. His status with the government is more than clear. His motives trouble me, however, so be warned and remember where your loyalty lies.'

'I think I understand my duty, sir.'

The admiral studied him calmly. 'Don't use that offended tone with me, *Captain*. I thought my last flagship was loyal until the mutiny. I'll have nothing taken for granted in the future. When you are looking into the cannon's mouth duty is a prop for the weak. At such a time it is true loyalty which counts.' He turned away. The brief confidence was over.

The conference was held in Bolitho's day cabin, and everyone present seemed well aware of its importance. It was obvious to Bolitho that the news of the impending attack on Djafou and the lack of support from the bomb vessels had already reached each of the men now facing him. It was the strange, inexplicable way of things in any group of ships. News flashed from one to another almost as soon as the senior officer had decided for himself what was to be done.

As he had struggled through the mass of notes and scribbled plans which Broughton had sent for his examination he had wondered too if the admiral was testing him. It was, after all, their first real action together where the squadron would be used as a combined force. The fact that Broughton had pointedly suggested he should hold the conference in his own quarters added the growing conviction that he was now under his scrutiny no less than any other subordinate.

He had met Draffen only once since his return on board. He had been friendly but withdrawn saying very little about the impending action. Maybe like Broughton he wanted to see the flag captain at work on his own ground, unaided by either of his superiors.

He was sitting now beside Broughton at the cabin table, his eyes moving occasionally from face to face as Bolitho outlined what they had to accept regardless of opposition.

The deck was swaying heavily, and Bolitho could hear the scrape of feet on the poop, the dull mutter of canvas and spars as the ship heeled to a slow larboard tack. Astern he could see the *Valorous*, her topsails drawing well, and knew that the steady north-westerly was already freshening. He had to be brief. Each captain had to return to his ship as soon as possible to explain his own interpretation of the plan to his officers. And their bargemen would face a long hard pull from the flagship without having to fight the growing weight of the wind.

He said, 'As you have seen, gentlemen, the bay at Djafou is like a deep pocket. The eastern side is protected by this headland.' He tapped the chart with his dividers. 'It is like a curved beak and affords good protection to ships at anchor inside the bay.' He watched their faces as they craned forward to see it better. Their expressions were as mixed as their characters. Furneaux, looking down his nose disdainfully, as if he already knew all the answers. Falcon of the *Tanais*, his hooded eyes thoughtful but giving very little away, and Rattray, with his bulldog face set in a grim frown of fierce concentration. He most of all seemed to find it difficult to visualize a plan of battle when set down on paper. Once in action, he would trust to his unyielding stubbornness, facing what he could see with his own eyes until he was a victor or a corpse.

The two younger captains, Gillmor, and Poate of the sloop *Restless*, were less reserved, and Bolitho had seen them jotting down notes from the beginning of the conference. They alone would be unhampered by the line of battle, could patrol or dash in to attack whenever their sense of timing and initiative dictated. They had all the independence which Bolitho so dearly envied, and missed.

'In the centre of the approach is the castle.' He was already seeing it in his mind as he had constructed it from Draffen's memory and newly acquired reports. 'Built many years ago by the Moors, it is nevertheless very strong and well protected with artillery. It was constructed on a small rocky island, but has since been connected to the western side of the bay by a causeway.' Draffen had told him briefly that the work had been done by slaves. Then, as now, he wondered just how many had died in pain and misery before seeing its completion. 'There is said to be a Spanish garrison of about two hundred, also a few native scouts. Not a great force, but one well able to withstand a normal frontal assault.'

Rattray cleared his throat noisily. 'We could surely tack straight into the bay. There would be some damage from the fort's battery, but with this prevailing nor' westerly we'd be through and inside before the Dons could do more'n mark us.'

Bolitho looked at him impassively. 'There is only one deep channel and it lies close to the fort. Well within a cable at one place. If a ship was put down by the battery in the first attack, the rest of us would be unable to enter. If it was the last in the line, none of us would get out again.'

Rattray scowled. 'Seems a damn stupid way to build a fortified harbour, if you ask me, sir.'

Captain Falcon smiled gently. 'I suspect there has not been much cause to welcome large vessels in the past, Rattray.'

Draffen spoke for the first time. 'That is true. Before the

Spaniards seized the port as their own it was constantly changing hands amongst local leaders. It was used by small coastal shipping.' He looked calmly at Bolitho. 'And chebecks.'

Bolitho nodded. 'There is one additional entrance to the fort. By water. Sometimes in the past, when under siege, the defenders received supplies directly by sea. Small vessels can enter beneath the north-east wall. But even then they come under constant watch from inner and outer ramparts.'

There was a momentary silence, and he could almost feel their earlier excitement giving way to gloom. It looked hopeless. Within the two bombs anchored round the beaked headland they could have carried out a steady bombardment of the fort. The upper works would be in no condition for such heavy treatment, and the Spanish gunners would be unable to hit back because of the out-thrust headland. No wonder Draffen seemed withdrawn. He had planned and investigated almost every detail of approach for his venture. But because of the bombs' delay in sailing, and indirectly the loss of the *Auriga*, he was now watching all of it fade into doubt and uncertainty.

He continued. 'The bay is about three miles wide and two deep. The town is small and barely defended. So this must be a landing operation from east and west simultaneously. Half of the squadron's marines will land here, below the headland. The rest will march inland after being ferried ashore here.' The points of the dividers rapped the chart, and he saw Falcon biting his lower lip, no doubt seeing the difficulties which the marines were going to face from both directions. The whole coastal area was grim and unfriendly, to say the least. A few steep beaches backed by massive hills, some of which had crumbled into cliffs and deep gullies, any of which would make excellent places for ambush.

It was not surprising the fort had managed to survive and had fallen to the Spaniards only because of some alliance with a local tribal leader. The latter had since died and his people scattered beyond the forbidding mountains which were often visible from the sea.

But once in the hands of the French, with all their military skill and territorial ambition, Djafou would become an even greater menace. A place of shelter for their ships while they waited to dash out on some intruding British squadron.

It was all he could do to hide his despair from the others. Why was it there never seemed enough of anything when it was most needed? With twenty sail-of-the line and a few transports filled with seasoned soldiers and horse artillery they might have achieved in days what the French must have been planning for many months.

Witrand probably knew the answer to the whole puzzle. That was another surprising thing. When Bolitho had mentioned the Frenchman to Draffen he had merely shrugged and remarked, 'You'll get nothing out of him. His presence here is enough to show as a warning, but little else.'

He glanced through the stern windows. Already the sea was breaking into small fresh white horses, and he could see *Valorous*'s pendant standing out stiffly to the wind as an additional warning.

'That is all for the present, gentlemen. Lieutenant Calvert will give each of you his written orders. We will proceed to Djafou without further delay and cross the bay tomorrow morning.'

Broughton stood up and studied all of them coldly. 'You have heard my intentions, gentlemen. You know my methods. I will expect all signals to be kept to a minimum. The squadron will attack from east to west and take full advantage of the sun being in the enemy's eyes. Bombardment from the sea and a combined land assault from both directions at once should suffice.' He paused and added quietly, 'If not, we will attack again and again until we have succeeded. That is all.' He turned and walked from the cabin without another word.

As the other captains paid their respects and then hurried away to summon their barges, Bolitho saw Draffen peering down at the chart and frowning.

The door closed behind the last captain and Draffen said heavily, 'I hope to God the wind drops. It might at least stop Sir Lucius from carrying out the attack.'

Bolitho stared at him. 'I thought you were as keen as anyone to see Djafou fall, sir?'

Draffen grimaced. 'Things have changed now. We need allies, Bolitho. In war we cannot be too choosy about our bedfellows.'

The door opened and Bolitho saw Keverne watching him. Waiting for orders, or with a fresh list of demands and needs for the ship and the squadron.

He asked slowly, 'Are there such allies?'

Draffen folded his arms and met his gaze. 'I am certain of it.

I still hold some influence out here. But they respect only strength. To see this squadron beaten in its first battle with the Spanish garrison will do nothing to bolster our prestige.' He waved one hand across the chart. 'These people live by the sword. Strength is their only unity, their one true god. Our need of Djafou is a temporary thing, something to sustain our cause until we have re-entered the Mediterranean in real strength. When that happens it will be forgotten, a miserable, barren hole as it was before. But not to those who have to continue an existence there. To them Djafou is the past and the future. It is all they have.'

Then he smiled and walked towards the door. 'I will see you tomorrow. But now I have work to do.'

Bolitho turned away. It was strange how different Djafou had been made to appear by two men. Broughton and Draffen. To the admiral it was an obstacle. One hindrance in his overall strategy of command. To Draffen it seemed to represent something else entirely. Part of his life perhaps. Or of himself.

Keverne said, 'All captains have returned to their ships, sir.' If he was feeling any anxiety he was not showing it. One day perhaps he would be in a position to worry like Broughton. But now he had to do his duty and nothing more. Maybe it was better that way.

He said, 'Thank you, Mr Keverne. I will be up directly. But now you may have Mr Tothill make a signal to the squadrons to take stations as ordered.' He paused, sick of the delays and the constant uncertainties. 'We attack tomorrow if the wind holds.'

Keverne showed his teeth. 'Then there's an end to the waiting, sir.'

Bolitho watched him leave and then returned to the windows. Aye, an end to it, he thought. And with any luck, a beginning, too.

12. The Fortress

'WAKE UP, CAPTAIN!'

Bolitho opened his eyes and realized he must have fallen asleep across his desk. Allday was peering down at him, his face yellow in the glow of the single deckhead lantern. Both candles on the desk were guttered and dead, and his throat felt dry and smoky. Allday placed a pewter cup on the desk and poured some black coffee into it.

'It will be dawn soon now, Captain.'

'Thank you.'

Bolitho sipped the scalding coffee and waited for his mind to repel the last dragging claws of sleep. He had been on deck several times during the night, checking last details before daylight, studying the wind, estimating the squadron's course and speed. He had finally fallen into deep sleep while going over Draffen's notes, but in the sealed cabin he could feel no benefit from it.

He stood up, suddenly angry with himself. They were all committed to the coming day. Nothing could be gained by supposition at this early stage.

'A quick shave, Allday.' He downed the coffee. 'And some more of that.'

He heard something clatter in the cabin below, and knew Broughton's servant was about to call his master. He wondered if he had been sleeping, or just lying in his cot, fretting over the coming battle and its possible consequences.

Allday returned carrying another lantern and a jug of hot water.

'Wind's holding steady from the nor' west, Captain.'

He busied himself with the razor and towel as Bolitho threw his shirt on the bench and slumped back in his chair again.

'Mr Keverne called all hands an hour since.'

Bolitho relaxed slightly as the razor scraped over his chin. He had not even heard a sound as *Euryalus*'s company of several hundred souls had come alive to the pipe's bidding. While he had lain on the desk in an exhausted sleep they had been fed and had set about cleaning down decks in spite of the surrounding darkness. For, no matter what lay ahead, there was no sense in allowing them to brood about it. When they commenced to fight they would expect the ship around them to be as normal as possible. It was not only their way of life, but their home also. Like the faces at the mess tables, the ones which would soon be peering through open gun ports, everything was as familiar as the spread sails and the sluice of water against the hull.

While Allday completed the hasty shave with his usual dexterity, Bolitho let his mind drift back over the previous

185

day's frantic preparations. The whole complement of marines from all the ships had been divided in two equal halves. Half had been transferred to Rattray's *Zeus* at the head of the line. The remainder to *Valorous* astern. Almost all the squadron's large pulling boats had been divided in the same way, and Bolitho could pity the two ships' uneasy night with so many extra people to accommodate.

He stood up and wiped his face, peering as he did so through the stern windows. But outside the cabin it was still too dark to see anything but a brief scattering of spray from around the rudder. The ships were heading almost due east, with the coast some five miles on the starboard beam. Broughton had been right to continue as before, with the wind comfortably across the quarter, instead of trying to complete the final manœuvre for his approach towards the land. The vessels might have become scattered, whereas now, with a favourable wind and the usual discreet stern lanterns, they would be able to halve the time when the admiral made his signal.

In the thick glass he could see his own reflection, with Allday standing behind him like an additional shadow. His own shirt was still open and he saw the locket swinging slowly to the ship's motion, the dark lock of hair hanging rebelliously above his eye. Involuntarily he reached up and touched the deep scar beneath the lock of hair gently with one finger. It was automatic, yet he always expected to feel heat there, or pain, like the actual memory of the time he had been cut down and left for dead.

Behind him Allday smiled and relaxed slightly. The familiar action, the apparent surprise Bolitho always seemed to show when he touched the scar, were always reassuring. He watched as Bolitho tied his neckcloth carelessly around his throat and then stepped forward with coat and sword.

'Ready, Captain?'

Bolitho paused with one hand in a sleeve and turned to study him, his grey eyes calm again.

'As I will ever be.' He smiled. 'I hope God is merciful today.'

Allday grinned and extinguished the lanterns. 'Amen to that, I say.'

Together they went out into the cool darkness.

'Deck there! Land ho!' The masthead lookout's voice sounded very loud in the clear air. 'Fine on the starboard bow!'

Bolitho paused in his pacing and peered through the black lines of rigging. Beyond the gently spiralling bowsprit and flapping jib he could see the first flush of pink dawn spreading down from the horizon. A little to starboard there was what appeared to be a sharp sliver of cloud, but he knew it was the crest of some far-off mountain, tipping itself in colour from the hidden sun.

He tugged out his watch and held it close to his eyes. It was already getting lighter, and with luck *Valorous* would now be hove to while she unloaded her cargo of marines into the boats, casting them adrift to make their own way ashore. *Euryalus*'s Captain Giffard was in command of that landing party, and Bolitho could pity him. It was bad enough to lead some two hundred marines with their heavy boots and weapons across rough, unknown territory, but when the sun found them it would become torture. Marines were disciplined and drilled like soldiers, but there the similarity ended. They were used to their strange shipboard life. But because of it and its cramped lack of space and exercise they were no match for the hard slogging required in a forced march.

Keverne said, 'I can see *Tanais*, sir.'

Bolitho nodded. The pink glow was etched along the seventy-four's main yard like fairy fire in a Cornish wood, he thought. Her stern light already appeared fainter, and when he glanced up at the masthead pendant he saw the main top-sail was shining with moisture and gaining colour with every slow minute.

There was a scrape of feet and Keverne whispered, 'The admiral, sir.'

Broughton strode on to the quarterdeck and stared towards the distant mountain as Bolitho made his formal report.

'Cleared for action, sir. Chain slings rigged to the yards and nets spread.' Broughton could hardly not know of these things with all the noise they made. Screens torn down, guns released from their lashings, and the patter of many feet as the seamen prepared their ship and themselves to do battle. But it had to be said.

Broughton grunted. 'Are we in sight of the squadron yet?'

'*Tanais*, sir. We will be able to signal the rest directly.'

The admiral walked to the lee side and peered towards the land. It was not much more than a darker shadow, above which the crested mountain seemed suspended in space.

He said, 'I'll be pleased when we can put the squadron about. I hate being on a lee shore and unable to see where I am.'

He fell silent again, and Bolitho heard the regular clump of shoes back and forth along the starboard gangway, like someone hitting a tree with a hammer.

Broughton snapped, 'Tell that officer to stay still, damn him!'

Keverne relayed his sudden burst of irritation and Bolitho heard Meheux call, 'I beg your pardon, Sir Lucius!' But he sounded cheerful for all that. Bolitho had recalled him from the *Navarra* to resume charge of his beloved upper battery of twelve-pounders, and Meheux had hardly stopped smiling since his return.

Nevertheless, it did reveal something of Broughton's uneasiness.

Bolitho said, 'I had the prisoner taken below to the orlop, sir.'

The admiral sniffed. 'Damn Witrand! It would do him good to stay up here with us.'

Bolitho smiled. 'One thing seems certain. He knows more of this place than I first suspected. When Mr. Keverne went to escort him below he was dressed and ready. No surprise, sir, not what you would expect at all from a man innocent of military affairs.'

Broughton said, 'That was shrewd of Keverne.' But it was only a passing interest, and Bolitho guessed his mind was still firmly fixed on what lay behind the shadows.

More feet clattered on the deck and Broughton swung round as Calvert stepped awkwardly over a gun-tackle.

'Mind your feet! You make more noise than a blind cripple!'

Calvert mumbled something in the gloom, and Bolitho saw some of the nearby gun crews grinning knowingly at each other. It must be over the whole ship about Calvert's conflict with his admiral.

'Good morning, gentlemen.' Draffen came from beneath the poop, dressed in a frilled white shirt and dark breeches. He had a pistol in his belt, and sounded very refreshed, as if he had just emerged from a dreamless sleep.

Midshipman Tothill called, '*Zeus* in sight, sir!'

Bolitho walked to the quarterdeck rail and stared along the length of his ship. The *Tanais* was growing steadily from the shadows, and beyond her, a little to larboard, he could just make out the leading seventy-four, her upper yards already shining in the reflected glow.

The sun's rim lifted over the horizon, the warm light reaching away on either bow, touching the lively wave crests, spreading still further, until Tothill exclaimed, 'There's the land, sir!'

It was hardly a proper sighting report, but in the sudden excitement no one else seemed to notice. Which was just as well, Bolitho thought, in view of Broughton's edginess.

'Thank you, Mr. Tothill,' he replied coldly. 'That was very prompt.'

The strengthening sunlight made the midshipman's face glow like one enormous blush, but he had the sense to remain silent.

Bolitho turned to watch the land gaining personality as the shadows were pushed aside. Long rolling hills, grey and purple for the moment, but already showing their barren slopes with the deeper patches of darkness where gullies and other steep clefts remained hidden to the watching eyes.

'*Valorous* is in sight, sir.' Lucey, the fifth lieutenant, who was also in charge of the quarterdeck nine-pounders, kept his voice low. 'She has set her t'gallants.'

Bolitho walked up the tilting deck to the weather side and stared across the hammock nettings. The rearmost seventy-four made a fine picture as she forged after her slower-moving consorts, topsails and topgallants shining like polished shells, while her hull remained in shadow as if unwilling to show itself. Soon now a lookout would sight the frigate standing well out to seaward, and then the little *Restless*, creeping closer inshore, and the last to be freed from the night's darkness. The prize, *Navarra*, would remain within visual signalling distance but no nearer. It would do no harm for the defenders of Djafou to think Broughton had at least one other ship-of-war at his disposal. Bolitho had even advised the master's mate sent across to relieve Meheux to make as many signals as he liked to give the impression he was in contact with more ships below the horizon.

So much depended on the first attack. The enemy, especially Spaniards, might feel less willing to fight against a growing force of ships if the early assault went against them.

Bolitho made himself walk slowly up and down the weather

189

side, leaving the admiral standing motionless by the foot of the mainmast.

The poop and nettings seemed strangely bare without the customary reassuring scarlet lines of marines. But for the rest, his ship appeared to be ready. He could see both ranks of guns on the upper deck now, their crews stripped to near nakedness. with coloured neckerchiefs tied around their ears as protection against the cannons' roar. Above, through the spread nets he saw the swivel guns manned in the tops, while more seamen waited at braces and halliards momentarily unemployed and watching the quarterdeck.

Partridge blew his nose violently into a green handkerchief, and then froze as Broughton shot him a savage glance. But the admiral said nothing, and the white-haired master thrust the offending handkerchief into his coat, grinning sheepishly at Tothill.

Bolitho rested one palm on his sword. The ship was alive, a vital, intricate weapon of war. He recalled his last fight aboard the *Navarra*, the stark contrast between this ordered world of discipline and training and the other ship's crude defences. The frightened Spanish seamen as they allowed their terror to change to bloody ferocity, hacking at the retreating boarders until there was none left alive. The half-naked women resting from their efforts at the pumps, shining in their sweat as he had passed. Meheux cursing as he had slipped in the Spanish captain's blood, and Ashton's youthful voice rising above the din as he had urged his gunners to fire and reload in his amateur Spanish.

And little Pareja. Wanting to please him. Feeling really needed, perhaps for the first time in his life. He thought too of his widow, wondering what she was doing at this moment. Hating him for leaving her without a husband? Regretting all the things which had brought her to Spain in the first place? It was hard to tell. A strange woman, he thought. He had never met anyone quite like her before. Wearing the finery of a wealthy lady, yet with the bold and fiery arrogance of one used to a much harder life than Pareja had given her.

Tothill's voice shook him from his thoughts. 'Signal from *Zeus*, sir. Repeated by *Tanais*.' He was scribbling busily on his slate. '*Enemy in sight*, sir.'

Broughton swore silently. 'Hell's teeth!'

Tanais's topsails and rigging had hidden Rattray's signal

from the flagship, so time had been lost in repeating it down the line. Bolitho frowned. It was another argument for having *Euryalus* leading, he thought. He could imagine Rattray passing his order to a midshipman like Tothill. He would be very aware of his position in the van and would want to get his signal hoisted as soon as possible. There was nothing in the signal book which would suffice for a word like Djafou. Wanting to make haste and avoid spelling it out letter by letter, he had made a more familiar signal instead. Captain Falcon would have devised something more imaginative, or said nothing at all. How easy it was to know a ship's ways once you knew her captain.

The land had changed colour as the sun climbed higher above its own image, the purples giving way to scorched green, the grey rocks and gullies becoming sharper defined, as if from an artist's drawing in the *Gazette*.

But the overall appearance had not changed. Treeless and without any sign of life, above which the air was already distorted in haze, or perhaps it was dust swirling around on the steady sea breeze.

There was the western headland, and overlapping it, its nearest side still in deep shadow, the one shaped like a great beak. Exactly abeam was a round hill, the side of which had cracked and fallen into the sea. It was a good four miles distant, but Bolitho could see the sea breaking in white feathers across the crumbled rocks, driven along the cheerless shoreline by the wind, as if searching for an inlet.

Zeus would be level with the nearest headland now, and able to see the fort in this visibility. Rattray might already be in a position to gauge for himself what he was expected to face within the next few hours.

Broughton snapped, 'Tell *Zeus* to make more sail. She can get on with landing her marines.' He glared at Calvert. '*You* see to the signal and try to be of some use.'

To Bolitho he added more calmly, 'Once Rattray has got his boats away, make the signal to wear in succession. We will have seen the outer defences and be able to measure our approach.'

Bolitho nodded. It made sense. To go about and return along this same course was safer than to make the attack now as ship by ship they crossed the bay's entrance. If the first sight of the fort proved different from the plans and scribbled reports, they would still have time to claw away from the shore. Nevertheless, when *Zeus* turned to lead the line back again it was to be hoped Rattray would keep an eye firmly fixed on the closeness of the land and the behaviour of the wind. If the wind got up suddenly, or veered, they would all be hard put to it to work clear of the rocks, let alone find time to give battle.

He watched the flags dashing up the yards and breaking to the wind, and moments later the answering activity above *Zeus*'s decks as more and still more canvas billowed out in response to Broughton's signal.

So far everyone was doing and acting exactly as Broughton had laid down. It might take Rattray an hour to get all his boats away, and by that time the remaining ships would be in position beyond the bay's entrance.

Bolitho glanced up as a voice called, 'Thar's the *Coquette*, sir! Two points abaft the weather beam!'

Bolitho plucked at the front of his shirt. It was already damp with sweat, and he knew that in a short while it would be even hotter. He smiled in spite of his thoughts. Hotter . . . in more ways than one.

Partridge, seeing the small smile, nudged the fifth lieutenant and whispered, 'See that? Cool as a chambermaid's kiss!'

Lieutenant Lucey, who was usually cheerful and easy-going, had been dreading the daylight and what it might mean for him. Now as he saw the captain smiling to himself he felt a little better.

All at once they were level with the first headland. After the long, slow approach it seemed to take everyone by surprise. As the edge of land peeled back Bolitho saw the great fort, blue-grey in the morning sunlight, and felt strangely relieved. It was exactly as he had pictured it in his mind. One massive circular building and a smaller round tower within. A bare flagpole was centred on the smaller tower, gleaming in the sunlight like a white hair. But there was no flag as yet, nor any sign of alarm. It looked so still that he was reminded of a great, lonely tomb.

As the ship moved steadily across a sluggish offshore chop he saw deeper into the bay. One small vessel at anchor, probably a brig, and a few fishing dhows. He wondered how far Giffard and his marines had managed to march, and whether they would be able to cross the causeway.

He saw the *Restless* tacking carefully away from the headland, and was thankful to see that Poate, her young commander, had two leadsmen busy in the chains. The sea bottom shelved very steeply, but it was always possible someone had overlooked a rocky ledge or reef when the charts were last corrected.

Because of its overlap, the second headland passed much closer, and as it crept out to hide the silent fortress from view Keverne exclaimed, 'Look, sir. Someone's awake!'

Bolitho took a telescope and trained it towards the sloping side of the beak. Two horsemen, quite motionless, but for an occasional flick of a tail or the wind ruffling the long white burnous which each rider wore. Looking down on the ships as they tacked slowly into the growing sunlight far below them. Then, as if to a signal, they both wheeled their horses and disappeared below the ridge, not hurriedly, nor with any sign of excitement.

Bolitho heard a voice say, 'The *word* is goin' out about us, lads!'

He glanced at Broughton, but he was staring at the empty skyline, as if the horsemen were still watching him.

And apart from the normal sounds of sea and wind everything was too quiet, the waiting made more obvious and unsettling. Giffard had even taken the marine band with him, and for a moment Bolitho toyed with the idea of getting the fiddler to strike up some familiar shanty for the seamen to sing. But Broughton seemed in no mood for any distraction and he decided against it.

He glanced from Broughton's stiff back to some of the nearby seamen at the nine-pounders. The latter were standing to peer over the nettings at the slow-moving wall of rock and stone. How strange it must seem to most of them. They might not even know where they were, or see the worth of their being maimed or killed for such a dismal place. And Broughton, he was probably just as doubtful of the reasons for bringing him here, yet could share his apprehension with no one.

Bolitho turned to watch Draffen, but he had already gone below, content, it appeared, to leave it all to the professionals. He walked slowly to the weather side again. In war, as he had learned from experience, there was no such creature. You never stopped learning. Unless you were killed.

'*Zeus* is drawing abeam th' headland, sir!'

Bolitho walked to the lee side of the quarterdeck. 'Thank you, Mr Tothill.'

It was all he could do to keep his voice even and unruffled. The final manœuvre of reassembling the squadron and then wearing ship in succession to return along the same stretch of barren coastline had taken far longer than expected. Rattray had got all of his boats away quickly enough, but once inshore it was obvious the oarsmen were having great difficulty in getting their overloaded craft to the proposed landing places. There were half-submerged rocks as well as a hitherto unsuspected current which swung the boats around like leaves on a millrace, their oars flailing in confusion until finally brought under control.

Even Broughton had conceded they should have allowed extra time, and as the *Zeus* made more sail again to resume station at the head of the line he could barely hide his anxiety.

The sloop had anchored as close as she dared to the great beaked headland, her masts spiralling uncomfortably in the swell, the slim hull made to seem puny by the mass of dark rock behind her.

But now they were approaching the bay once more, with *Zeus* passing the anchored *Restless* so close he appeared to be heading straight for disaster on the point of the great beaked headland. All the ships were close hauled on the starboard tack, their yards braced tightly to give them maximum advantage from the fresh wind. The two leading ships had already run out their larboard guns, and as he trained his telescope over the nettings Bolitho saw *Zeus*'s lower battery was lifted to what must be the maximum elevation, the double line of black muzzles appearing to scrape against the headland as she forged past. It was of course yet another illusion brought about by distance. She was a good two cables clear, and he hoped Rattray had some good helmsmen who would be ready to act very smartly when required.

Tothill shouted, 'Signal from *Restless*, sir! The marines have reached the top of the headland!'

Bolitho turned and saw the big blue flag rippling from the sloop's main yard, and as he moved his glass slightly beyond her he saw some of the marines scurrying around the lip of the hillside, shining in the fierce sunlight like a horde of bright red insects.

Broughton snapped, 'Good. If they hold that hill nobody

can shoot down on us from it.' He moved to the quarterdeck rail and watched Meheux walking slowly along the larboard line of guns.

Bolitho looked at Keverne. 'You may run out now. Pass the word to Mr Bickford on the lower gundeck to gauge each shot well. His are the heaviest pieces we have today.'

Keverne touched his hat and beckoned to three midshipmen who were messengers for the gundecks. As he leaned over the rail, speaking in a sharp, urgent whisper, Bolitho watched their faces. Ashton, still pale, with his bandage around his head. Little Drury, the inevitable smudge on his round face, and Lelean of the lower gundeck, whose extreme youth was badly marred by the most pimply skin Bolitho had ever seen.

When they scurried away Keverne yelled, 'Run out!' And as the order was piped from deck to deck the hull shook inwardly to the sudden rumble of trucks, the shouts of gun-captains to their crews to take charge as the massive weapons trundled down the tilting decks and through the open ports.

The air quivered suddenly to a slow and measured bombardment, the sound dragging itself out and rolling back against the headland until it seemed as if every ship had fired. In the van *Zeus* was wreathed in her own smoke, her black muzzles gone from view as her men sponged out frantically for another broadside.

Bolitho watched the smoke rolling inshore and being sucked into the bay by some freak down eddy. If the Spanish garrison were in any doubt earlier, they knew now, he thought grimly.

Another broadside, again perfectly timed, the guns shooting out their long orange tongues, the ship's reefed main topsail jerking violently in the upthrust of heated air.

Every glass was trained on the dancing lines of white-horses around and beyond the leading seventy-four. But there was still no sign of a falling shot, or any intimation that the enemy had returned fire.

Broughton said harshly, 'Fair. Very fair.'

Bolitho glanced at him. Perhaps Broughton was still testing his flag captain. Feeling him out for suggestions which he might accept or scornfully reject. But he could add nothing for Broughton's benefit. It was still too early.

He lifted his glass again as a voice yelled, 'There's a ball! Fine on *Zeus*'s larboard quarter!'

Bolitho watched the ball's progress, counting seconds as the feather of white spray slashed viciously from wave to wave, throwing up a waterspout a good mile beyond the *Zeus* like a sliver of ice.

He heard Lieutenant Lucey whisper to Partridge, 'By God, that was a long shot!'

There was another, almost exactly along the same line as before, and no less powerful.

Broughton remarked, 'One gun, Bolitho. If that is all they have we need not wait much longer.'

'Signal from *Zeus*, sir.' Tothill was clinging to the lee shrouds to watch the leading ship. 'Disengaging.'

Bolitho looked at Partridge. 'How long was that?'

The master examined his slate. 'Ten minutes, sir.'

Ten minutes to cross the fort's arc of fire, during which time they had only got off two balls.

'*Tanais* is closing the range, sir.' Keverne steadied his glass against his forearm. 'She'll be ready to fire in a minute or so.'

Bolitho did not reply, holding his breath until the big red and black flag broke from *Tanais*'s topsail yard to show she was within sight of the enemy.

Falcon did not wait as long as Rattray, and his guns started belching fire and smoke almost immediately. The gunnery was impeccable, with the forward ones firing their second balls almost before the aft sections had run in for reloading.

Broughton rubbed his hands. 'That weight of metal'll give the Dons sore heads, eh?'

But the enemy remained silent as before, and Bolitho said quickly, 'I think the Spaniards are using a fixed battery, sir. They were sighting shots used on *Zeus*, but this time . . .' He broke off as the reverberating crash of gunfire welled out of the bay, followed by a terrible sound of splintering wood.

As he strode to the rail he saw the smoke spurting from the *Tanais*'s poop, and a black tangle of broken rigging pitching overboard as the shots slammed into her. Two, maybe more, he thought, with another which had missed whipping the wave crests apart like an enraged dolphin.

Something like a sigh came from the watching men as more shots hammered into the *Tanais*'s hull and pieces of wood whirled high into the air before splashing into the sea on either side of her.

Falcon's men fired again, but the rhythm was gone, and here and there along her tumblehome Bolitho could see an angled muzzle to show a gun was unmanned, or an empty port which told its own story better than words.

Keverne said, 'Four guns at a time, I'd say, sir.' He sounded cool and detached. An onlooker.

Lucey remarked, 'Quite big too, by the look of them.'

Bolitho glanced at him. Lucey was only twenty and had been terrified. Bolitho knew all the signs, the constant swallowing, the inability to find anything for the hands to occupy themselves with, all the little things which told of a man's mounting terror. Now Lucey was swopping comments with Keverne like an old campaigner. He hoped the pretence would last, for his sake.

Broughton said, 'I can't see for the damn smoke! What is Falcon doing?'

The smoke was funnelling through the *Tanais*'s stern windows, but whether from a fire or the exertions of the guns it was hard to tell. She was still managing to shoot, but she looked in a bad way. Her braced sails were easy targets and were pitted with holes, the latter from her own wood splinters as much as the enemy's gunfire. Long trailers of severed rigging hung over her gangways, and Bolitho could see men already hacking it away with axes, the distance making their efforts all the more frantic.

Partridge cleared his throat. 'She's dipped 'er flag, sir.' He was squinting at his big turnip watch. 'Nigh on fifteen minutes that time.'

Broughton said, 'I hope your thirty-two-pounders earn their keep, eh?' He was smiling, the skin drawn back tightly from his even teeth to make his efforts a lie.

But Bolitho was thinking of other things. Fifteen minutes, during which time his ship would be subjected to another merciless bombardment. The Spanish gun crews did not even have to alter their elevation. They merely waited and fired, as ship after ship the squadron sailed across that strip of open water. Sun in their eyes or not, it was as easy as shooting birds off a branch.

'I suggest you signal the squadron to discontinue the action, sir.' He kept his voice low, but saw the words affecting Broughton as if he had cursed him. He added quickly, 'Independent action in support of the landing parties would . . .' He got no further.

'*Never!* Do you imagine I'll let a few bloody Dons make me

withdraw?' He glared at him with something like contempt. 'By God, I thought you were made of sterner stuff!'

Bolitho looked past him and called, 'Shake out the forecourse, Mr Keverne! Then hands aloft and get the t'gallants on her!' He held the lieutenant's eyes with his own. 'As quick as you can!'

As the men swarmed up the ratlines in response to the order he made himself walk slowly to the quarterdeck rail. He knew Broughton was staring after him but shut him from his mind. Broughton had made his decision, and the order had to be obeyed. But the *Euryalus* was his ship, and he would fight her to his best ability, and Broughton could think what he liked.

The big forecourse billowed out with a clap like thunder, the seamen scampering wildly as the wind momentarily took charge. Bolitho felt the deck tilting still further as the fore top-gallant was released and hardened its belly to the wind, the additional thrust making the spray fly above the figurehead and jib boom.

To Partridge he snapped, 'Steady as you go!'

'Steady she be, sir. West by north.'

The dark headland was slipping past more rapidly as the ship spread her canvas tautly in the sunlight. High above the decks the topmen worked like demons, and when he raised his glass Bolitho saw some marines dancing up and down on the headland and waving their muskets as the flagship plunged level with the out-thrust beak of land.

There was the opposite side of the bay now, misty with haze, or perhaps still foggy from *Tanais*'s own smoke. How blue the water looked below that far headland. Blue and unreachable. He touched his lips with his tongue but they were bone dry.

He heard Lucey whisper shakily, 'My God. My God.' He probably imagined he was speaking to himself, or not at all.

Up forward, with one foot resting casually on a carronade slide, Meheux was peering into the bay. He had drawn his sword, and as Bolitho watched he lifted it very slowly above his head. He stood motionless in the sunlight, and Bolitho was reminded of an old heroic statue he had once seen on a visit to Exeter.

The sword moved slightly and he heard Meheux shout, 'Target in sight, sir!'

Bolitho cupped his hands, aware of the stiff, gripping tension all around him.

'Fire as you bear!' He saw some of the crouching seamen peering up at him, their faces like masks. He twisted his mouth into a grin and yelled, 'A cheer, lads! Show 'em we're coming!'

For an instant longer nothing happened, and while the ship forged steadily past the last piece of cliff Bolitho thought they were too stricken to respond. Then a seaman jumped up beside a twelve-pounder and shouted, 'Huzza for the *Euryalus*! An' another huzza for our Dick!'

Bolitho waved his hat as the wild cheering swept along the upper deck and was taken up by the men in the crowded batteries below. The madness was beginning, nor would it stop until the next time. And the time after that.

Meheux's voice was almost drowned as he bellowed, 'Fire as you bear!'

Bolitho gripped the rail as the first trio of guns roared out from forward. The harsh bark of the upper deck battery swallowed completely by the deafening thunder of the thirty-two-pounders. He wiped his streaming eyes as the smoke lifted above the larboard gangway and swirled and plunged around him, watching the distant fort, the waterspouts below and beyond as the ship's first attack smashed home. What looked like white powder was drifting from the fortress wall, the only sign that they were hitting it also.

He heard Keverne rasp, 'God, 'tis like trying to fell an oak with a toothpick!'

Still the firing continued, three by three, with the guns hurling themselves inboard where they were seized and re-loaded by men already dazed beyond reason. Beyond anything but the need to load and run out. To keep on firing no matter what was happening.

Meheux was walking behind the guns now, his sword tapping a breech or pointing towards the fort for another captain's benefit, his face frowning with concentration.

Broughton asked, 'Where are the other marines? Your Captain Giffard should be at the causeway by now.'

Bolitho did not reply. His mind was rocking to the crash of guns, his eyes almost raw with smoke and strain as he concentrated everything on watching the fort. He could see the dark smudge below its circular wall where the sea entrance was situated. The double line of square windows, like gunports, which appeared to circle the whole building.

Two of them suddenly flashed with fire, and he imagined he

saw the line of the nearest ball streaking across the sea towards him. The thud against the lower hull was muffled, and he saw the other ball throwing up a burst of spray far abeam.

He glanced astern. The ship was almost halfway across the bay, and with all sails drawing well would reach the opposite headland in about five minutes.

Again the telltale tongues of fire, and this time both balls smashed into the *Euryalus*'s side with the force of hammers striking a wooden box.

Three hits, and he did not yet know how serious. Yet the fortress was outwardly unmarked, with just a few patches of fallen chippings to show for their efforts.

Astern he could see the *Valorous*'s topmasts rounding the headland, and knew what Furneaux must be thinking as he watched the flagship under the onslaught of those great guns.

He turned to the admiral, who was standing with his hands on his hips, his eyes fixed on the fort as if mesmerized.

'May I signal *Valorous* to stand off, sir?'

'Stand off?' Broughton's eyes moved slightly to fix him with an unmoving stare. 'Is that what you said?' A muscle jumped in his cheek as the lower battery roared out again, the smoke driven downwind by the darting tongues of flame.

Bolitho studied him for several seconds. Perhaps Broughton was caught off balance by the squadron's inability to hurt the fort, or maybe he was dazed by the continuous crash of cannon fire.

He said bluntly, 'Ships are being damaged to no purpose, sir.' He winced as the planking beneath his shoes gave a violent jerk. Another hit somewhere below the quarterdeck.

All at once, as the wind whipped the smoke clear of the deck, he saw Broughton's face clearly in the sunlight and knew what was wrong. Broughton had not been testing him in the past, or trying to gauge the extent of his capability. The realization was like a dash of icy water on his spine. Broughton did not know what to do next! His plan of battle was too rigid, and, found wanting, had left him with nothing to replace it.

He said, 'It is all we can do at present, sir.'

Partridge called, 'Eight minutes, sir!'

Suddenly Broughton nodded. 'Very well. If you think so.'

Bolitho shouted, 'Cease firing! Mr Tothill, signal *Valorous* to stand off and discontinue action immediately!'

The fortress fell silent as soon as *Euryalus*, and he guessed the garrison had to keep a careful watch on supplies of powder and shot. Not that they need have much fear of being beaten, he thought bitterly. Almost every ball fired from the fortress had hit home.

'*Valorous* has acknowledged, sir.'

Bolitho watched the two-decker's shape lengthening as she began to tack, her sails almost aback as she swung heavily into the wind.

He called, 'Report casualties and damage, Mr Keverne.' To Broughton he said quietly, 'We will have to support the marines, sir. They will be waiting for help.'

The admiral was studying the passing shoreline with something like resignation. Below a man was screaming and whimpering, and Bolitho felt the growing need to tend to his men and his ship. But he persisted, 'What instructions, sir?'

Broughton seemed to shake himself, and when he replied his voice was stronger again, but without conviction.

'Signal the squadron to close around the flagship.' His lips moved as if trying to form an order which would not come.

Bolitho looked at Tothill. 'Make that signal at once.'

'Then I think we might land a second force, of seamen.' Broughton was pouting his lower lip. 'Some guns too, if we can discover a favourable beach.'

Bolitho looked away. 'Very well, sir.' Already he could visualize the tremendous effort and strain of getting even one thirty-two-pounder ashore and hauled up the hillside. And nothing but a gun of that size would do any good against the fortress. It would take a hundred men, maybe more, and others to be near by to ward off any sudden attack by enemy skirmishers. A Long Nine weighed over three tons, and one such weapon would not be enough.

But it was better than having the squadron pounded to fragments in a senseless procession back and forth across the bay's entrance.

He turned, caught off guard as Tothill said, 'Sir!'

'What is it? Have they all acknowledged?'

'Not that, sir.' The midshipman pointed across the starboard nettings. '*Coquette* is off station and making more sail, sir.'

As he raised his telescope Bolitho saw the telltale balls dashing to the frigate's yards and breaking out in bright patches of colour.

Tothill said, 'Signal, sir. *Strange sail bearing north-west.*'

Bolitho lowered the glass and looked at Broughton. 'Shall I order *Coquette* to give chase, sir?'

Tothill's voice cut across Broughton's reply. '*Coquette* is making another signal.' A pause, and Bolitho watched the muscle jerking in sharp, regular intervals in Broughton's cheek. Then, 'Strange sail has gone about, sir.'

Broughton let his arms fall to his sides. 'Probably an enemy frigate. *Coquette* would have been able to close with her had she been anything else.' He looked at Bolitho. 'She'll be screaming our presence to the world now.'

'I suggest we recall the marines, sir.'

Bolitho pushed away his earlier ideas about landing guns and all the tackle and boats it would have required. There was no time for that now, and they might be lucky to regain all their marines if an enemy squadron was near by.

'No.' Broughton's eyes were like stones. '*I will not withdraw. I have my orders. So have you.*' He gestured towards the line of barren hills. 'Djafou must be taken before any enemy ships reach here! *Must* be, do you understand?' He was almost shouting, and several of the seamen by the guns were staring up at him.

Draffen's voice cut through the brief silence like a knife. Where he had been during the action Bolitho did not know, but now he looked very calm, his eyes cold and steady, like a hunter at the kill.

'Let me make a suggestion, Sir Lucius.' As Broughton turned to him he added quietly, 'For I think you will agree we have wasted quite enough time with *conventional* methods.'

For a brief instant Bolitho expected the admiral to show some of his earlier defiance.

But instead he replied, 'I will agree to hear your suggestions, Sir Hugo.' He looked round as if seeking the companion ladder. 'In my quarters, I think.'

Bolitho said, 'I will signal the squadron to steer due west, sir. With *Restless* and *Coquette* remaining on station at present.'

He waited, seeing Broughton's mind wrestling with his words. Then he replied, 'Yes.' He nodded more firmly. 'Yes, attend to it.'

As they left the quarterdeck Keverne said softly, 'We fared better than *Tanais*, sir. She lost twenty killed. We have seven dead and five with splinter wounds.'

Bolitho was still looking towards the poop and wondering what Draffen could suggest at this late stage.

'Damage?'

'Sounded worse than it was, sir. The carpenter is below now.'

'Good. Tell Mr Grubb to get his men to work on it as soon as he can.'

He paused as the first corpse was carried through the main hatch and dropped loosely to await burial. In the space of a few minutes they had lost seven lives. About one a minute.

Bolitho clasped his hands behind him and walked slowly towards the weather side, his face suddenly angry. *Euryalus* was the most modern device known to man's ingenuity at making war. Yet an ancient fort and a few soldiers had made her as impotent as a royal barge.

He snapped, 'I am going to see the admiral, Mr Keverne.'

'Sir?'

'I too have some ideas which I will put to him directly!'

Allday watched him pass and gave a slow smile. Bolitho was angry. It was about time the captain took charge, he thought, for all their sakes.

13. Second Chance

VICE-ADMIRAL BROUGHTON looked up from his desk, his expression a mixture of surprise and annoyance.

'We had not quite finished, Bolitho.' He gestured towards Draffen, who was leaning against the cabin bulkhead. 'Sir Hugo was just explaining something to me.'

Bolitho stood firmly in the centre of the cabin which seemed vaguely empty without its more valuable fittings and furniture. These had been taken below the waterline for safety before the fruitless attack on the fortress. Nevertheless, Broughton was lucky to have been spared the usual disorder which would be found in a British built three-decker. Then, his quarters, like all the rest of the ship, would have been stripped bare, the normally hallowed cabins wreathed and stained in smoke from their own guns. But the nearest cannon were safely beyond the bulkhead, so that after the air of alertness and battle tension on the upper deck this cabin added to Bolitho's sense of frustration and growing anger.

He replied, 'I would suggest we act quickly, sir.'

Broughton raised one hand. 'I am aware of the urgency.' He seemed to sense Bolitho's anger and added coldly, 'But speak your mind if you wish.'

'You have seen the fortress, sir. The futility of trying to beat it into submission from the sea. Using ships against sited shore batteries and defences has never, in my experience, been of any use.'

Broughton eyed him bleakly. 'If you want me to admit that you advised me against such action in the early stages, then I will do so. However, as we have neither the facilities nor the strength for a combined attack, nor the time available to starve the garrison into submission, I do not see we have any alternative.'

Bolitho breathed out slowly. 'The only thing which has made Djafou a thorn in the side of every maritime nation using these waters is the fort, sir.'

Draffen said shortly, 'Well, Bolitho, that is surely rather obvious?'

Bolitho looked at him. 'I would have thought it obvious also to whoever devised this plan in the first place, Sir Hugo.' He turned back to the admiral. 'Without it this bay is value-less, sir.' He waited, watching Broughton's eyes. 'And *with* it, this bay is still quite useless to us.'

'What?' Broughton sat upright as if he had been struck. 'You had better explain!'

'If we succeed in taking the fortress we will still be hard put to hold the bay as a base, sir. Given time, the enemy, particu-larly the French army, would land artillery further along the coast and make the anchorage untenable for our ships. So we would be like the present defenders. Driven back inside that stone pile and able only to stop others from using the bay for shelter or whatever use they might see in it.'

Broughton stood up and walked slowly to the quarter windows. 'You have still made no mention of an alternative.' He sounded less abrupt.

Bolitho said slowly, 'Return to Gibraltar. Inform the Commander-in-Chief of the true facts, and I am sure he will give you the support and the ships for making another attempt to obtain a base.' He expected Broughton to turn on him, but when he said nothing continued firmly, 'A base where we would be better placed to widen the scope of future fleet operations. Further east, where we still have friends who would be prepared to rise against their new oppressors, given enough help and encouragement.'

Broughton said, 'You said that Djafou is useless?' He appeared unable to get it out of his mind.

'Yes, I do. I am certain that if the powers in Admiralty were properly aware of its conditions and facilities they would never have agreed to the first suggestion.'

Draffen said sharply, 'In case you did not know, Bolitho, it was agreed on *my* suggestion.'

Bolitho studied him calmly. At last, after all the uncertainties and missing parts to the puzzle, something was coming out into the open.

He said, 'Then it would be better to admit you were wrong, sir.' He hardened his voice. 'Before any more of our people are killed.'

Broughton snapped, 'Easy, Bolitho! I'll have no petty argument under my flag, dammit!'

'Then let me just say this, sir.' Bolitho kept his voice very even, although inwardly he could feel nothing but anger and despair. 'Unless you put the squadron in such a position where we have more sea room to fight, you may be caught on a lee shore. With the prevailing nor' westerly, and no space to regain an advantage, you will be in real danger should an enemy arrive here. In open sea we can still give the enemy a bloody nose, no matter what the odds prove to be.'

Broughton said, 'Sir Hugo has already suggested a further plan.'

Draffen pushed himself away from the bulkhead. He was smiling, but his eyes were very cold.

'You have been too long on your feet, Bolitho. I am sorry I did not appreciate the fact earlier. This is my idea. It is only a framework, of course, but I am almost sure I can obtain the aid we now desperately need.'

Broughton said in a weary tone, 'Sir Hugo's agent can be contacted somewhere along the coast, it seems.'

'Exactly.' Draffen was relaxing very slowly. 'I have had dealings with a powerful tribal leader. I have even met him on some occasions, Habib Messadi has much influence along these shores, and no love for the Spanish intruders.'

Bolitho replied quietly, 'But *we* will be intruders if the Spanish garrison is made to go. Where is the difference?'

'Oh, in heaven's name, Bolitho!' Broughton sounded angry. 'Will nothing satisfy you?'

Bolitho kept his eyes on Draffen. 'This Messadi is, I presume, an outlaw of some kind, otherwise how could he exert such power on a coastline like this?'

Draffen's smile faded. 'He is not the sort of man you would let loose in Westminster Abbey, I will allow you that.' He shrugged. 'But to make this mission successful I would accept aid from Newgate or Bedlam if I thought it might help.'

'*Well*, Bolitho?' Broughton was looking from one to the other with obvious impatience.

But Draffen spoke first. 'As I said to you earlier, one day Djafou will be discarded by us for something better. Like the proposal you have just made to Sir Lucius. Messadi controlled Djafou for many years and has no love for the French or the Dons. Surely it would be better to keep him as an ally, some additional thorn to prod the enemy's side?'

Broughton snapped, 'I agree.'

Bolitho turned away. Without effort he could see the yelling figures swarming across the *Navarra*'s bloodied decks, the terror on the crew's faces when the chebecks had been sighted. And now Broughton was about to take such people as allies, merely because he could not accept the prospect of returning empty-handed to Gibraltar.

He said, 'I am against it.'

Broughton sat down heavily. 'I have great respect for your past record, Bolitho. I know you to be a loyal officer, but I also realize you are often plagued by too much idealism. There is no officer in the squadron I would rather have as my flag captain.' His tone hardened. 'But I will suffer no insubordination. And if necessary I will have you removed.'

Bolitho felt the sense of helplessness returning, the contest of desires pulling at him like claws. He wanted to throw the words back in Broughton's face, yet could not endure the prospect of Furneaux in control of the squadron's small resources.

He heard himself say tightly, 'It is my duty to advise you, sir, as well as obey orders.'

Draffen beamed. 'There you are, gentlemen! We are agreed at last!'

Bolitho looked at him bitterly. 'What do you intend?'

'With Sir Lucius's permission I will make use of the sloop

again. I have no doubt my agent will be expecting some sort of news from me, so the rest should be made easier for us.' He looked shrewdly at Bolitho's grave features. 'As you have said yourself, the squadron is better fitted for fighting in open waters than exposing itself to unnecessary risk inshore. I will need no more than two days, and by that time we should be ready for a final and conclusive assault.' He smiled, and Bolitho saw a new light in his eyes. For a few seconds his expression was one of complete cruelty. 'A flag of truce to the garrison, an explanation of what will assuredly happen if Messadi's men take the fortress, to the defenders and their womenfolk . . .' He said no more.

Broughton muttered, 'For God's sake, Sir Hugo, it won't come to that surely?'

'Of course not, Sir Lucius.' Draffen was openly cheerful again.

Broughton seemed suddenly eager to finish the conference. 'Signal the *Restless*, Bolitho. *Coquette* can take over watch on the bay.'

As he left the cabin Draffen followed him, his voice almost gentle as he murmured, 'Do not take it so seriously, Captain. I have never doubted your qualities as a sea officer. So you must trust *my* ability in these matters, eh?'

Bolitho paused and looked at him. 'If you mean I am no match for your politics, Sir Hugo, then you are right. I want no part of them, ever!'

Draffen's face hardened. 'Do not overreach yourself, my friend. You may attain high command in the Navy one day, provided . . .' The word hung in the air.

'Provided I hold my tongue?'

Draffen swung towards him angrily. 'You, of all people, can hardly afford the re-telling of your past if you wish to better yourself! Do not forget, I knew your brother. There are some in high places who might reconsider any officer's chances of advancement once they were reminded of some flaw in his family background, so watch your manners, Captain!'

Bolitho felt suddenly very calm. As if his body was suspended in the air. 'Thank you for reminding *me*, Sir Hugo.' He was amazed at the sound of his voice. Like a complete stranger's. 'At least we will be able to dispense with all pretence from this moment onward.' He turned and walked quickly towards the companion ladder.

He found Keverne pacing back and forth on the quarterdeck, his face deep in thought.

'Signal *Valorous* to relay the admiral's order to *Restless*. She is to up anchor and close with the flagship immediately. She will then take Sir Hugo Draffen aboard and act under his instructions.' He ignored Keverne's curious stare. 'You may then secure all guns and have our people fed. Well?'

Keverne asked, 'Shall we withdraw, sir?'

'Attend to the signal, Mr Keverne.' He looked dully at the distant hills. 'While I do some thinking.'

He turned as Lieutenant Sawle appeared below the quarter-deck accompanied by Witrand.

'Where are you taking the prisoner, Mr Sawle?'

The lieutenant stared at him blankly. 'He is to be transferred to the sloop, sir.' He seemed confused. 'Lieutenant Calvert says it is at the admiral's bidding.'

'Come here.' Bolitho watched the Frenchman climbing lightly up the ladder, forgetting for the moment his earlier contempt and anger at Draffen's threat.

'I will say farewell, Capitaine.' Witrand stretched and sniffed the warm sea air. 'I doubt we will meet again.'

'I did not know of this, Witrand.'

'That I will believe, Capitaine.' Witrand eyed him curiously. 'It seems that I may be expected to aid your cause. A joke, eh?'

Bolitho thought of Broughton's growing desperation. He might have agreed with Draffen to allow Witrand's transfer to the sloop in the hopes he would give away some secret about his own mission. He replied quietly, 'A joke. Perhaps.'

He shaded his eyes to watch the *Valorous* as she hoisted Broughton's signal to her yards. Somewhere, hidden around the beaked headland the anchored sloop would see it and come hurrying to do his bidding. Witrand would probably stay aboard her and later be conveyed with despatches to Gibraltar.

Bolitho held out his hand. 'Goodbye, m'sieu. And thank you for what you did on my behalf.'

The Frenchman's grasp was firm. 'I 'ope that one day we will meet again, Capitaine.' He shrugged. 'But . . .' He broke off as Sawle and two armed seamen appeared on the quarter-deck. He added quickly, 'If anything should 'appen to me. There is a letter. For my wife in Bordeaux.' He dropped his voice. 'I would be grateful.'

Bolitho nodded. 'Of course.' He watched Witrand being escorted to the entry port to await a boat. 'Take care.'

Witrand tossed him a casual wave. 'You also, Capitaine!'

An hour later Bolitho was still pacing up and down the weather side oblivious to the searing heat which had turned his shirt into a sodden rag, or the blinding glare thrown back from the sea.

Draffen had been transferred to the sloop and had already disappeared around the out-thrust curve of the coastline, yet he had hardly been aware of anything but Witrand's simple request.

Lieutenant Weigall was officer of the watch and was content to keep well clear of his captain. Alone with his deafness, he stayed on the lee side, his prizefighter's face set in its usual frown as he surveyed the men working along the upper deck.

By the poop, Allday watched Bolitho's anguish and wondered why he could think of nothing to help him. He had refused to leave the deck for a meal, and had turned on him with something like blind anger when he had tried to coax him below for a brief respite from the heat.

'Deck there!' The lookout's voice was like a croak. The seaman was probably parched with thirst. 'Sail on th' weather bow!'

Allday glanced at Bolitho expectantly but he was still pacing, his face grave and expressionless. A quick look towards Weigall told him that he had heard nothing at all.

Already flags were soaring aloft on the *Tanais's* yards, and Allday strode quickly to a dozing midshipman and prodded him sharply in the ribs.

'Stir yourself, Mr Sandoe!' He saw the boy staring at him with fright. 'There's work to be done!'

Then he crossed to the other side and waited until Bolitho had completed another turn along the deck.

'Captain?'

Bolitho paused and swayed wearily on the tilting deck. He saw Allday's face swimming before him, and realized with a start of anger that he was smiling.

Allday said firmly, 'Sail on th' weather bow, Captain.'

'What?'

He looked aloft as the voice pealed down. 'One ship, sir!'

Weigall had at last realized something was happening and was moving about the deck like a caged animal.

Far above the deck the small figure of the midshipman could be seen moving up to join the lookout. Moments later his voice floated down to all the upturned faces.

'She's a bomb vessel, sir!'

When Allday looked at Bolitho again he was stunned to see his eyes were blurred with emotion.

Bolitho said quietly, 'Thank God.' He reached out and seized Allday's thick forearm. 'Then there's still time.' He turned away to hide his face and added, 'Call the master. Tell him to lay off a course for the squadron to intercept and then,' he ran his fingers through his hair, 'then we shall see.'

Later, as the *Euryalus* swung heavily across the wind and started on a new tack towards the small sliver of sail, Bolitho stood very still at the quarterdeck rail, while every other officer stayed at a respectful distance on the opposite side, their voices murmuring with busy speculation.

Broughton came on deck and walked to Bolitho's side. His voice was offhand and remote.

'What is she?'

Bolitho saw Tothill's men with their next hoist of flags and said, 'There is only the one, sir, but she will suffice.'

Broughton stared at him, confused by his vague reply.

Then Tothill shouted, 'Signal, sir. '*Hekla to Flag. Request instructions.*'

Once again Bolitho felt his throat quivering with suppressed strain and emotion. The *Hekla* had arrived. Somehow Inch had managed to join them with neither escort nor another bomb for company.

Without awaiting the admiral's comments he said, 'Signal her captain to repair on board forthwith.'

Then he turned and looked at the admiral, his eyes calm again. 'With your permission, sir, I would like to attempt what we came to do.' He paused, seeing the flush mounting to Broughton's cheeks. 'Unless you would still prefer to ally yourself with pirates?'

Broughton swallowed hard and then replied, 'Report to me when *Hekla*'s captain is come aboard.' Then he turned and walked stiffly towards the poop.

Bolitho looked down at his hands. They were shaking, yet quite normal in appearance. His whole body seemed to be quivering, and for a brief instant he imagined his old fever was returning.

But it was not the fever. It was something ar more powerful.

Keverne crossed the deck and touched his hat. 'Strange-looking craft, sir.' He faltered under Bolitho's gaze. 'The bomb, I meant, sir.'

Bolitho smiled, feeling the tension draining out of him like blood.

'Just now she is the most welcome sight I have seen for a long, long while, Mr Keverne.' He plucked at his shirt and added, 'I will go aft and change. Call me when the *Hekla*'s boat is near. I want to greet her captain myself.' Then he strode away.

Keverne said, 'You know, I think I may never understand our captain.'

Weigall swung round from the rail. 'What? What did you say?'

'Nothing.' Keverne walked to the opposite side. 'Return to your dreams, Mr Weigall.'

He glanced up at Broughton's flag flapping from the fore-mast and found himself wondering at the swift change in Bolitho's mood. But it did appear as if the waiting was done, and that at least was something.

After the furnace heat of the day the night air was almost icy. Bolitho stood up in the sternsheets of his barge and signalled to Allday with his arm.

Allday barked, 'Easy all!' and as one the oars rose dripping from the water and remained still, so that the dying bow wave gurgling around the stem seemed suddenly very loud.

Bolitho turned and strained his eyes into the darkness astern. They were following, and he could see the dancing phosphorescence around the two leading boats like bright clinging weed and occasional white feathers from the muffled oars.

The first boat loomed from the darkness and hands reached out to seize the gunwales to prevent further sound from any sort of collision. It was Lieutenant Bickford, his voice serious and quite normal, as if he were reporting his division for inspection.

'The rest are close astern of me, sir. How much further, do you think?'

Bolitho felt the two hulls rising and falling on the deep inshore swell, and wondered where the squadron had reached when the wind had at last decided to fade to a light breeze. All day, as he and the others had worked to put his plan of attack into motion, he had expected it to drop, a kind of inbuilt instinct which he could never properly explain. If it had done so before he was ready the plan would have had to be postponed, perhaps cancelled altogether.

He replied, 'About three cables, I believe. We will carry on now, Mr Bickford, so keep a good lookout.'

At a further command the boats drifted apart once more, and as the oars started to move Bolitho sat down on the thwart, his eyes trained slightly to starboard where he would first see the bay's western headland. Provided he had not misjudged the drift or the uneasy power of the swell.

He made himself think back over the busy afternoon, trying to discover any flaw in his hazardous plan. Yet each time he seemed to see Inch's face, hear his voice as he had sat in the *Euryalus*'s stern cabin. A voice so weary and drained of life that he had seemed much older than his twenty-six years.

It was hard to recall Inch as he had once been as a junior lieutenant, eager but bumbling, loyal but without experience, more so when Bolitho considered what he had just done on his behalf. Inch had waited fretting at Gibraltar for an escort, knowing how desperately the two bombs were needed, and realizing too that no such escort might ever arrive. He had taken his courage in both hands and had confronted the local admiral for permission to sail unaided. Typically, the admiral had granted permission, on the written understanding that whatever happened as a result would be Inch's own responsibility. The other bomb vessel, *Devastation*, had also up-anchored without delay, and together they had headed out from the Rock's protection, both commanders expecting to be attacked within hours by the patrolling Spanish frigates which had been so much in evidence.

As he told his story Bolitho had been reminded of his own words to Draffen at Gibraltar about Inch's luck. That luck had certainly held, for they had not sighted a single ship. Until that very morning, when out of a sea mist Inch's lookout had reported a fast-moving Spanish frigate. There was little doubt in Bolitho's mind that it was the one sighted by *Coquette* turning to dash back to Spain with the news of Broughton's attack on Djafou. Perhaps her captain had imagined the two small and ungainly bombs were part of a trap being sprung to catch him

212

before he could escape. Otherwise, he would hardly have been likely to have engaged them.

Inch had sent his small company to quarters, and with his consort some half mile abeam had prepared to give battle.

With all sail set the thirty-two-gun frigate had gone about to take advantage of the wind, her first broadside dismasting the *Devastation* and raking her decks with grape and chain shot. But the little bomb was sturdily built, and her guns had replied with equal vigour. Inch had seen several balls hitting the enemy's hull on the waterline before a second savage broadside had smashed the *Devastation* into silence.

Inch had expected the same treatment, but had put his ship between the frigate and the other bomb and had opened fire. Maybe the Spanish captain had counted upon Inch to turn and run after witnessing the fate of his companions, or perhaps he still expected to see the *Coquette*'s topgallants above the horizon in hot pursuit. But the challenge was enough. The frigate had gone about again, leaving Inch to lower boats and pick up the survivors from the other bomb, which had turned turtle and started to sink.

It was obvious to Bolitho that Inch was torn between two real emotions. He was brooding over the loss of the *Devastation* and most of her company. But for his own eagerness she would still be anchored at Gibraltar, safe and unharmed.

Yet when Bolitho had outlined what he intended to do this same night he had seen something of the old Inch, too. Pride and a light of complete trust which had made him so very important in Bolitho's memory.

Now, in *Hekla*, his first and only command, Inch was anchored beyond the opposite headland, and within a very short while would be attempting something untried in naval history. With Bolitho and his own gunner he had climbed to the top of the beaked headland where the marines lolled like corpses in the scalding glare, and had carefully constructed a map of the fortress. Bolitho had said nothing which might have broken Inch's concentration, and had been very aware of the deftness with which he went about his work. Ranges, bearings and measurements were added to the map, while the gunner had murmured occasional hints about charges, amounts of powder and fuses, most of which had been a foreign language to Bolitho.

Whatever Inch might say or think about his strange com-

213

mand, he certainly appeared to have found his right niche. It was to be hoped his zeal was matched by his aim. Otherwise these boats and their armed seamen would all be blown to oblivion.

If Inch could have fired his mortars in daylight he would have been quite sure his calculations were accurate. But Bolitho knew the defenders would have that much warning and make their own preparations. More time, to say nothing of lives, would be wasted, so Bolitho's idea of a night attack was accepted without dissension, even by Broughton. Bolitho knew from experience that night attacks on shore defences were to be preferred. Sentries became tired, and there were usually so many strange noises abroad at night that one more shadow or additional squeak would excite little attention.

And why should it? The fortress had withstood siege after siege. Had seen the British squadron made to withdraw, leaving only a landing force of marines to fend for themselves amidst the rocks and scrub above the bay. They had very little to fear.

Allday hissed, 'There's the headland, Captain! Fine on the starboard bow!'

Bolitho nodded. He could see the vague necklace of white spray at the foot of the rocks, the darker blur of shadows where the land piled up into a craggy cliff beyond. Soon now.

He tried to picture his little flotilla in his mind. His barge and Bickford's cutter would enter the bay first. Then four more boats would follow at regular intervals. One, under the command of Lieutenant Sawle, contained a large pouch of gunpowder, and once laid between the apprehensive oarsmen had all the appearances of a giant corpse being taken for burial. Sewn in greased leather, with a handmade fuse lovingly constructed by Fittock, the *Euryalus*'s gunner, it was to be in position just minutes before Inch's mortars started to fire.

Bolitho wished he had Keverne with him. But he was better used in handling the ship during his absence. Meheux was too valuable a gunnery officer, and Weigall too deaf for night action, so that left only the more junior lieutenants for the boat attack. He frowned. What was the matter with him? A lieutenant, *any* lieutenant, should be capable if he was worth his commission. He smiled in spite of taut nerves, thankful the darkness was hiding his face. He was beginning to reason like Broughton, and that would never do.

He thought too of Lieutenant Lucey, the young officer who had been so frightened before the first attack on the fort. He was astern somewhere in another cutter, waiting to lead his men into the breached wall with only the haziest idea of what was awaiting him.

And Calvert, he wondered how he was managing, out there on the hillside. When Bolitho had explained how he wanted the marines under Giffard to play their part in the final assault across the causeway, Broughton had snapped, 'Calvert can convey the instructions to Captain Giffard.' He had studied the flag lieutenant without pity. 'Do him good!'

Poor Calvert had been terrified. With a midshipman and three armed seamen for protection he had been taken ashore at dusk to face a dangerous and painful march across the hills to carry the orders to the marines, who should by now be ready and waiting to move. Giffard must be thankful, Bolitho thought. After sweating and panting in the sun's glare all day, with only their pack rations and water flasks to sustain them, they would be in no mood for half measures.

The tiller squeaked and he felt the hull lift sluggishly across a fast ripple of water. They were rounding the headland now, the bay opening up beyond the bargemen's heads in a pitch-black curtain.

He held his breath. And there it was. The fortress, like a pale rock, unlit but for a solitary window high up in the nearest wall, and strangely threatening against the other darkness.

'Very quietly, lads!' He stood to peer above the oarsmen, very conscious of the noises of boat and water, of heavy breathing and his own heart.

The current was carrying them to the left of the fort, and he was thankful that one calculation at least was proving correct. He saw another pin-prick of light far beyond the fortress, and guessed it was the anchored brig's riding lantern. With any luck Broughton would have a small addition to his squadron before dawn.

He dropped on one knee and very gently opened the shutter of a lantern. Just a fraction of an inch, yet for those brief seconds as it played across his watch it seemed like a mighty beacon.

He stood up again. In spite of the deep swell outside the bay, the distance the men had pulled their great oars and all the other nagging delays, they were arriving at the prescribed moment.

The fortress was much nearer now, not more than a cable away. He imagined he could see the darker shadow below the north-west corner where the sea entrance lay, protected it was said by a rusting but massive portcullis. Where Fittock's explosive charge would soon be laid and a way blasted for their attack.

He gritted his teeth as somewhere astern a metallic click came from one of the boats. A careless seaman must have kicked against his cutlass. But nothing happened, nor any shout of alarm from those high, forbidding walls.

Which was just as well, he thought grimly. Broughton's ships would be well clear of the land by now, and without any real wind to fill their sails they would be in no position to send aid.

Something white flashed in the darkness, and for an instant he thought it was an oar blade cutting through the water. But it was a fish jumping, falling with a flat slap within feet of the boat.

When he looked for the fort again he saw it was very close. He could distinguish the individual slits cut in the walls for the guns, the paler patches to show where some of the squadron's guns had made their mark.

'Easy all!' He saw Bickford's boat gliding slowly abeam and the others fanning out within easy hailing distance. It was time.

The one boat which was still moving under oars pulled steadily past, and he saw Lieutenant Sawle's figure upright in the stern, and another, probably Mr Fittock the gunner, stooping below him. This was the vital part of the whole attack, and it was also Sawle's chance to distinguish himself to such a degree that, bully or not, his future in the Navy would be assured and profitable. He had an equally good chance of being blown to pieces if the fuse was mishandled. He was a competent officer, but if he were to die tonight, Bolitho was aware he would not be mourned aboard the *Euryalus*.

Allday muttered, 'We've seen a few, eh, Captain?'

Bolitho did not know if he was speaking of the lieutenant or the actual attack. Either could be true, but he had other things on his mind.

He snapped, 'We have five minutes or thereabouts.'

Oars moved restlessly abeam and he saw Bickford's men back-paddling to stop their boat from being broached sideways on the swirling current.

He thought of Inch again and pictured him aboard the *Hekla* making final preparations for firing his squat mortars high over the beaked headland. He would have no problems with secrecy now. He could use all the lights he required, knowing there were marines on the hillside above his ship waiting to signal the fall of shot as well as to protect him from unwanted intruders.

A strange craft, Keverne had said. *Hekla* was little more than a floating battery, with just enough sail power to carry her from one theatre of operations to another. Once in position she was anchored firmly at bow and stern. By slackening or hauling on either cable Inch could move the hull and therefore the twin mortars to the desired bearing with very little effort.

'Mr Sawle's boat is below the wall, Captain.' Allday sounded tense.

'Good.' He accepted Allday's word, for there was nothing but the slash of black shadow at the foot of the fortress to distinguish boat from entrance.

A midshipman squatting by his feet yawned silently, and Bolitho guessed he was probably fighting his own sort of fear. Yawning was one of the signs.

He said quietly, 'Not long now, Mr Margery. You will take charge of the boat once the attack is begun.'

The midshipman nodded, not trusting himself to reply.

Allday stiffened. 'Look, Captain! There's a boat to the left of the wall!'

Bolitho saw the telltale froth of oars and guessed the garrison had taken the precaution of having a guardboat patrolling around the bay. Probably it was intended to prevent any attempt at cutting out the anchored brig, but it was just as deadly as an army of sentries.

Up and down, the oars dipped and rose with tired regularity, the green phosphorescence around the stem marking the boat's progress better than daylight.

The movements halted, and he guessed they were resting on their oars, letting the current carry them along before starting on the next leg of the patrol.

Allday muttered between his teeth, 'Mr Sawle should have the charge laid by now.'

As if in response to his words there was a brief, spurting gleam of light like a bright red eye below the wall, and Bolitho knew Fittock had fired the fuse. The light would be hidden from the guardboat by the wall's curve, but once Sawle's men pulled clear the alarm would be sounded.

Bolitho bit his lip, imagining Sawle and his men clinging against the great iron portcullis, listening for the guardboat moving again and hearing the steady hiss of the lighted fuse.

Almost to himself he said, 'Come on, man, get away from it!' But nothing happened to break the dark patch beneath the wall.

There was a sudden jarring thud and he saw the eyes of the nearest oarsman light up with an orange glow, as if the sailor was staring directly at a freak sunrise. He knew it was the reflected glow from one of Inch's mortars beyond the opposite headland, and as he swung round in the boat he heard a sharp, abbreviated whistle, like a marsh-bird disturbed suddenly by a wildfowler. The crash of the explosion was deafening. He saw the far side of the fort light up violently, the billowing smoke very pale before darkness closed in again, leaving him moment-arily blinded.

But it had been long enough to tell him Inch's first shot had been near perfect. It had hit the fortress on the opposite rampart, or perhaps below the wall itself. He could hear the grinding sounds of falling masonry, the splash of larger pieces hitting the water.

Another thud, and the next shot fell in much the same place as the first. More crashes and rumbles, and he saw the smoke drifting in a thick bank low above the bay like a dust cloud.

The guardboat had been hidden by the smoke, but he could hear voices yelling in the darkness and then the sudden blare of a trumpet from the direction of the fortress.

The *Hekla*'s third shot overreached, and he heard the splintering crash of stonework and guessed it had hit the causeway or part of the islet below the walls. The marines would be using their shuttered lanterns to signal the news to Inch, and fresh adjustments would have to be made to the charges or elevation before another attempt.

Allday said, 'Mr Sawle is pulling away now.' He sounded relieved. 'He cut it fine, an' no mistake.'

Bolitho called, 'Pass the word, Mr Bickford! We are about to attack!'

No need to be quiet now. There was enough clamour from the fortress walls to awaken the dead as the dazed Spaniards ran to their defences. Some might have guessed what was being used against them, others would be too terrified to think as the fortress shook to the battering from Inch's mortars.

It was at that moment Sawle's charge exploded. Bolitho saw the low entrance erupt in a great gushing tongue of fire, watched with fixed fascination as a small tidal wave surged out from below the wall to hurl Sawle's cutter on to its beam ends, spilling men and oars into the sea in a kicking tumult, like a whaleboat before a wounded narwhal.

As he drew his sword and waved it towards Bickford he saw part of the upper rampart fall slowly across the belching flames, taking with it an iron-wheeled cannon and a length of heavy chain, which he guessed was part of the portcullis hoisting gear.

'Right, lads! Give way together!' He almost fell as the boat surged forward beneath him, feeling the hot smoke fanning above his head to mark the power of the last detonation.

The upended cutter passed in the gloom, and here and there he saw a pale face, thrashing arms and legs, to show that some at least had survived the explosion.

Then he forgot everything but what he had to do, as like a gaping mouth, the blasted portcullis protruding from the breached wall like rotten teeth, the opening was right ahead and then over the bows.

A musket ball slammed against the gunwale, and somewhere a man screamed in sudden agony.

He waved his sword above his head and yelled, '*Pull*, lads!'

The barge seemed to be hurling itself through the smoke at a tremendous speed. He saw pieces of scorched woodwork floating on the surface, and then two grotesque sternposts of what must be old galliasses which the fortress had once used to defend the coast against pirates. Oars crashed against wood and stone alike, and he saw Bickford's boat following dangerously close astern, the oarsmen momentarily illuminated as someone fired a pistol from the wall above.

'Easy!' Allday's voice was almost lost as an explosion shook the air to announce the arrival of another of Inch's bombshells. 'Toss your oars!'

Grinding savagely against a low jetty, the barge lurched to a halt. A figure charged from the darkness, but reeled and fell without a sound as a seaman fired his musket at point-blank range over the edge of the jetty.

Bolitho clawed his way on to the wet stone, feeling the wildness all about him and trying to recall the layout of this alien place as he had seen it on the plan.

Too late to change anything now. Too late for second thoughts.

He pointed with his sword towards some stone steps, and yelling like fiends the seamen charged across the jetty. They were inside. What happened now could only be decided one way.

With Allday at his side he ran up the steps towards the smoke, his mind empty of everything but the madness of battle.

14. 'A Fearsome Place . . .'

THE CURVING FLIGHT of stone steps to the top of the ramparts seemed endless. As Bolitho dashed breathlessly towards the open ledge where smoke still drifted across the stars he was aware of a rising chorus of shouts and cries, the occasional bang of muskets, and above all the urgent blare of a trumpet. Inch's mortars had fallen silent right on the arranged minute, and but for the careful planning and timing of the attack a further shot from *Hekla* might well have killed the yelling seamen before they could even reach their first objective.

Below, where the barge had grounded alongside the jetty, Bolitho heard more shouts and bellowed orders as one by one the boats surged through the broken entrance, their crews spilling out into the smoke even before the craft were made fast.

He felt the cooler air on his face as with Allday beside him he found himself on the broad expanse of the main battery. He could see the smaller central tower, the regular crouching shapes of the heavy guns, and darting figures which seemed to come and go from every direction at once.

The Spanish soldiers had at last realized that one deafening explosion which had torn them so violently from their sleep had not been from a mortar. Now, as they hurried from the central tower, they were already firing and reloading as they ran, some of the balls shrieking impotently into the night, while others brought down a running seaman or raised a scream of pain in the deeper shadows by the ramparts.

He shook his sword at Bickford, as with his own party of men he blundered up the steps and almost fell across two interlocked corpses.

'The tower! Fast as you can!'

Bickford did not answer, but ran desperately across the open space, his mouth like a black hole in his face as he yelled at his men to follow.

Bolitho halted and peered towards the steps. Where was Lucey? He should be here by now to help attack and seize the deep courtyard on the opposite side of the lower fortress. Shots cracked and flashed against the inner wall, and he heard steel clashing on steel, interspersed with short, desperate cries and curses.

Allday shouted, 'The guardboat's followed them in, Captain!' He gestured with his cutlass through a deep embrasure. 'Mr Lucey's lads are closing with them!'

Some of Lucey's men were already running up the steps, while others were still locked in close combat with the guardboat's crew across the jetty and out of sight below the wall.

Someone gave a hoarse cheer, and Bolitho saw another low shape edging through the breach, and heard Allday say fervently, ' 'Tis the gig, and not a blasted moment too soon!'

The additional weight of attackers was enough for the guardboat, and caught between two prongs of the attack they started to throw down their arms, their voices almost drowned by the jubilant cheers from the seamen.

But that one delay caused by the guardboat's unexpected appearance had cost Bolitho the precious minutes needed to reach the other stairway which led to the courtyard. Even as he waved his men forward he saw a serried line of musket flashes, heard the thud of a ball smashing into muscle and bone and screams on both sides of him.

The seamen hesitated, some pausing on the steps even though pushed forward by those from the boats behind them.

Bolitho rasped, 'Come on, Allday! Now or never!'

Allday brandished his cutlass and bellowed, 'Right, lads! Let's open the door to the bloody bullocks!'

Once again they lunged forward. Beside Bolitho a man shrieked and toppled to the ground, his neck impaled by a musket ramrod. The soldier must have been so confused by the swiftness of the attack that he had failed to withdraw it after reloading.

All at once there seemed to be figures striking forward from every angle. The next instant they were locked steel on steel. As men reeled and kicked in the darkness, or fell on the blood of their comrades, Bolitho saw a Spanish officer hack down a screaming sailor and run towards him. Bolitho tugged a pistol from his belt and fired. In the bright flash he saw the top of the officer's skull blasted away to spatter the wall behind him with bloody fragments.

Lucey ran past him, sobbing violently, his jaw clenched as he was carried forward by the wild mob of seamen.

Allday shouted, 'There are the steps!' He swung his cutlass at a man kneeling by the wall. He could have been reloading his musket or using it as a crutch because of a wound. He dropped dead without even a whimper.

There was a lantern burning in the lower courtyard, and as they ran or fell down the steep steps Bolitho saw another force of soldiers already forming into line to resist them. Some of them were only partly dressed, others were covered with dust and chippings from the mortar's bombardment, like workers in a flour mill.

An officer dropped his sword and a loud volley banged out from the wavering muskets. A few seamen fell dead or wounded, but the enemy's aim had been bad, and they had no time for a further attempt.

Again it was hand to hand, with blood splashing victor and vanquished alike, with no thought or hope but that of killing and staying alive.

From a corner of his eye Bolitho saw Midshipman Dunstan, who had commanded the gig, leading his party round the curve of the wall towards the massive double gates. A soldier darted towards him and aimed a pistol at point-blank range. But it was a misfire, and before the luckless Spaniard could fall back again he was hacked down by a burly gunner's mate, and received several more cuts from the other yelling seamen as they scurried past.

Allday said between breaths, 'Look, Captain! Mr Bickford's taken the inner tower!' His teeth were white in his face as he pointed upward, and Bolitho saw someone waving a lantern from side to side from the upper rampart where only hours before the Spanish flag had appeared to mock them.

At that moment the gates were flung open, and as Bolitho ran across the uneven courtyard he realized with sudden shock there was nothing beyond them.

Allday said, 'Jesus, where are the bloody bullocks?'

More soldiers were running from another gate at the foot of the inner wall, and at a shouted command opened fire across the front of their scattered comrades. Then, fixing bayonets they doubled forward towards the invaders.

Bolitho held his sword in the air. 'Stand fast, my lads!' His voice brought the men round to face the new threat, and he was amazed how steady he sounded. Yet his mind was reeling and grappling with the realization that Giffard's marines had not arrived, that already his limited force of seamen had been split in two. Bickford held the inner tower, but without the lower garrison and courtyard being seized also he was more prisoner than conqueror.

Snarling and yelling like enraged demons the lines of shadowy figures came together. The seamen with boarding pikes were able to meet the bayonets as equals, but those armed only with cutlasses were already dying, their bloodied corpses held upright in the press of combat.

Bolitho slashed down a soldier's neck, saw his face change to a grotesque mask of agony before he was carried past in the swaying, hacking mass of men. Another was trying to reach him with a bayonet across the shoulder of a comrade, but disappeared as a pike found its mark.

But the line was breaking. Even as he pushed his way to the opposite end of the wavering pattern of seamen he heard a terrible scream and saw Lieutenant Lucey rolling over on his stomach, while a tall trooper stood astride his body with an upraised musket. In the glare from the lantern Bolitho saw the blood gleaming on the bayonet before it went down again with all the force of the man's arms. Another scream, and even though the soldier had one foot on the lieutenant's spine he was unable to tear the bayonet free. And Lucey was still alive, his screams like those of a woman in agony.

Allday gasped, 'In God's name!' Then he was across the small strip of cobbles, his cutlass swinging in a tight arc before the soldier realized what was happening. The heavy blade hit him across the mouth, and Bolitho heard the man's bubbling cry even above the sound of the cutlass biting through flesh and bone.

But it was no use, any of it. Bolitho dragged his sleeve across his eyes and parried a soldier's sword away, swinging him around and then driving the blade beneath his armpit. His sword arm was so weighty he could hardly raise it, and with sick despair he saw two pigtailed seamen beyond the gate waving their hands in surrender.

In those brief seconds he saw everything which had brought them here. His own pride, or was it only conceit? All the men who had depended upon him were dead or dying. At best they would end their lives in misery in the Spanish galleys or some rotting prison.

The soldiers paused and then retired to a further shouted command. Leaving the corpses and writhing wounded in the centre of the courtyard they fell back and formed into their original lines, only this time they were reinforced by more Spaniards from the lower fortress.

Bolitho let his sword fall to his side and looked at the remainder of his men. Gasping for breath, clinging to each other for support, they were standing dull-eyed to watch their own execution. And that is what it would be unless he surrendered at once.

As if from another world he heard a harsh voice bellow, 'Front rank kneel!' And for a moment he imagined the Spanish officer was giving his commands in English to add to his misery.

The voice continued, 'Take aim!' The order to fire was lost in the blast of muskets, and Bolitho could only stare as the ranks of Spanish soldiers reeled about in disorder under the deadly volley.

Of course, it was Giffard's voice. He had heard it countless times on the quarterdeck at drills and ceremonial occasions. Giffard, plump, bombastic and pompous. A man who liked nothing better than to show off his marines. As he was doing now.

His voice was like a trumpet, and although hidden by the arched gateway, Bolitho could picture him exactly.

'The marines will advance! By the centre, quick *march*!'

And then it was all over. Like the passing of a cruel nightmare.

The marines entered, perfectly dressed as if on parade, their bayonets making a lethal glitter in the lantern light, their crossbelts very bright against the surrounding shadows.

Behind them the next rank followed in stiff precision, reloading from their first volley, while Boutwood, the colour-sergeant, beat out the time with his half-pike.

Muskets clattered on the cobbles, and almost gratefully the Spaniards clustered together by the steps, the fight gone out of them.

Giffard stamped his boots together. 'Halt!' Then he wheeled round and brought his sword hilt to his nose with a flourish which would have turned the head of King George himself.

It was suddenly very quiet, and once again Bolitho was aware of several vivid details, like parts of a pattern. Giffard's boots squeaking. The smell of rum on his breath. And a wounded seaman crawling into the circle of lantern light, very slowly, like a broken bird.

Giffard barked, 'Beg to report the arrival of my marines, *sir*! All present and correct.' The sword came down with a swish. 'Request instructions, *sir*!'

Bolitho looked at him for several seconds. 'Thank you, Captain Giffard. But had you left your attack any longer, I am afraid you would have found the gates shut in your face again.'

Giffard turned to watch his lieutenant supervising the prisoners. 'Heard the explosions, sir. Saw the musket fire on the ramparts an' put two an' two together.' His voice took on a hurt note. 'Couldn't have you taking the fort without my marines, sir. Not after being out in the bloody sun all day, what?'

'You received no message, then?'

He shook his head. 'None. We did hear musket fire towards the beach, but the whole place is full of skirmishers and damned felons. I had cause to hang one meself in the afternoon. Tiresome fellow was trying to steal our rations!'

Bolitho said quietly, 'Lieutenant Calvert should have reached you with news of the attack.'

Giffard shrugged. 'Probably ambushed.'

'Probably.' Bolitho tried not to recall Calvert's fear.

Giffard looked around at the weary, gasping seamen. 'But you did very well without our help, it seems, sir.' He grinned. 'But you can't beat a bit o' discipline and cold steel when it comes to real fighting!'

When Bolitho looked up at the towering wall again he saw

that almost every window and slit was alight. There was such a lot to arrange before dawn. He rubbed his eyes and realized the sword was still firmly grasped in his hand. His fingers ached as he slid the blade into the scabbard. Ached as if they would never come free from it.

He said, 'Secure the prisoners and have the wounded taken into the lower fortress. *Coquette* and *Hekla* will enter the bay at first light, and there is a world of work to do before then.'

Bickford clattered down the steps and touched his hat. 'All resistance finished, sir.' His eyes fell on Lucey's corpse, the bayonet still upright in his back, as if pinning him to the ground. 'God,' he muttered shakily.

'You did well, Mr Bickford.' He walked slowly towards the steps, the tension still within him like the spring of a pistol. 'As you are the only lieutenant left . . .'

Bickford shook his head. 'No, sir. Mr Sawle is safe. Your barge picked him up. And Mr Fittock.'

Bolitho turned and looked back at Lucey's body. It was strange how the Sawles of this world always seemed to survive, when others . . . He pulled himself from his brooding thoughts and snapped, 'See to our wounded and then recall all the boats. I want a close watch kept on the anchored brig in case she tries to escape before daylight.'

'She might be scuttled, sir.'

Bolitho looked at him. 'I think not. This is Djafou, Mr Bickford. They have nowhere else to go.'

Something was still keeping him here on the blood-spattered steps when he should be inside the fortress. Meeting the garrison's commander and attending to countless other details before the squadron returned.

Giffard seemed to have been reading his thoughts. And that was strange, too, for Bolitho had never given him credit for having any imagination. He asked, 'Would you like me to send some of my men to search for the flag-lieutenant, sir?' He waited, squeaking back on his heels. 'I can spare a platoon long enough for that.'

Bolitho imagined Calvert and his four companions out there somewhere in the darkness, terrified and helpless. Better they were dead than to fall into the hands of some of the marauding tribesmen described by Draffen.

He replied, 'I would be grateful.' He made himself add, 'But do not risk their lives to no purpose, Captain Giffard.'

The marine said, 'They will obey orders, sir.' Then he grinned, as if more at ease with his usual pomposity. 'But I will pass your order to them immediately.'

The central tower was divided up mainly into living quarters for the garrison officers, three of whom were accompanied by their wives. As Bolitho trod carefully over scattered stone chippings and various items of personal clothing and equipment he wondered briefly what sort of a life a woman could expect in a furnace like Djafou.

The commandant's quarters were at the top of the tower and looked out across the bay towards the beaked headland.

He was sitting in a huge, high-backed chair, and made to rise as Bolitho, followed by Bickford and Allday, entered the room. He had a neat grey beard, but his face was the colour of faded parchment, and Bolitho guessed he had been the victim of a severe fever on more than one occasion. He was an old man, with wrinkled hands which hung as if lifeless on the arms of the big chair, and had probably been given the post of commandant because nobody else wanted it, or him.

Fortunately, he spoke good English, and had a gentle, courteous voice which seemed so out of place in the fortress's grim and uncompromising surroundings.

Bolitho had already been told by Bickford that his name was Francisco Alava, once a colonel in the dragoons of His Most Catholic Majesty's household. Now, and until the day he died, he was designated commandant of the most dismal place in the Spanish chain of possessions in the Mediterranean. He had probably committed some petty breach of etiquette or misdemeanour to receive such a post, Bolitho thought.

He said, 'I would be pleased if you would make your quarters available to me for the present, Colonel Alava.'

The two hands lifted shakily and then fell back on the chair again. Sickness, old age and the awful explosions of Inch's mortars had taken a hard cost of his frail resources.

Alava said, 'Thank you for your humanity, Captain. When your soldiers arrived I feared they would slaughter all of my people here.'

Bolitho smiled grimly. Giffard would certainly take exception to hearing his marines called soldiers.

He said, 'At daylight we will see what can be done to restore the defences here.' He walked to an open window and looked across the dark, swirling currents below the fortress. 'I will be expecting other ships soon. Also a vessel which will need to be beached so that repairs can be made to her hull.' He paused and then swung round from the window so that even Allday started. 'You may know her, Colonel. The *Navarra*?'

Just for a fraction of a moment he saw a spark of alarm in the old man's eyes.

Then the hands twitched again, dismissing it.

'No, Captain.'

Bolitho turned back to the window. He was lying, and that was as good as proof Witrand had indeed been intended for this desolate place. Probably the brig was the vessel which had been waiting to make the transfer at sea.

But there would be time for that later. Time to allow the commandant to reconsider, to decide where his own safety lay now his defences had fallen.

He nodded to Bickford. 'Escort him to the other room and have the officers kept apart.'

As the commandant hobbled through a door, Sawle entered on the opposite side, his shirt sodden and torn, and carrying his coat casually over one arm.

'You did the task very well.' Bolitho watched the new light in the lieutenant's eyes. A kind of contained wildness, a confidence born of a single dangerous act. He had been more afraid of showing fear than of fear itself, and now that he had survived he would expect his reward and more.

Sawle said, 'Thank you, sir.' He did not attempt to hide the new arrogance which his triumph had roused in him. 'It was easy.'

You only think it was easy, my friend, now the danger is past. Aloud Bolitho said, 'Report to Mr Bickford and he will give you your orders.'

Allday watched him leave and murmured, 'Weasel!'

Bolitho looked past him. 'Go and take care of Mr Lucey.' He sat down suddenly in the commandant's great chair. It was just as if his legs had given way under him. He added, 'See if you can find something to drink. I am like a kiln.'

Alone, he stared round the gloomy, barren room. Perhaps one day, because of a bad wound or disability, he would be given a task like Alava's. An outpost with the grand name of governorship where he would spend the days trying to hide his bitterness, and the ache for a ship from home, from his subordinates.

He realized his eyelids had started to droop and that Giffard had entered the room without his hearing.

Giffard said, 'My men found Mr Calvert, sir.' He looked uneasy. 'He was wandering around lost, and near out of his mind to all accounts.

'And the others?'

'No sign of the three seamen, but he was carrying the midshipman on his back.' He shrugged wearily. 'But he was already dead.'

'Who was it?'

'Mr Lelean, sir.'

Bolitho rubbed his eyes to hold the dragging tiredness and strain away. Lelean? Lelean? Which one was he?

Then he remembered. Keverne leaning over the quarterdeck rail to relay his instructions to the gundecks. Three apprehensive midshipmen. One upturned face had been covered with pimples. Lelean. He had been fifteen years old.

'Ask Mr Calvert to report to me.' He looked at Giffard's red face. 'I will see him alone.'

Allday arrived with a large glass jug filled to the brim with dark red wine. It was very bitter, but at that moment tasted better than any admiral's claret.

Allday said, 'Mr Calvert's here, Captain.'

'Show him in, then wait outside.' He watched Allday leave, his shoulders set in stiff disapproval.

Calvert was swaying from exhaustion, and as he stood staring listlessly at Bolitho he looked almost ready to fall.

'Easy, Mr Calvert. Take some of this wine. It will refresh you.'

Calvert shook his head. 'I would rather speak, sir.' He shuddered. 'I cannot think of anything else.'

In a strange flat voice, broken only occasionally by deep shudders, he told his story.

From the moment he had been landed from a boat things had started to go wrong. The three seamen had deliberately misunderstood his every order, probably testing for themselves the lieutenant's incompetence which was common gossip throughout the ship.

Lelean, the midshipman, had attempted to restore discipline, but had been unnerved by Calvert's inability to take charge of three ordinary seamen.

They had made their way inland, pausing frequently while

one seaman or the other complained of sore feet, exhaustion and other trivial excuses to rest. Calvert had grappled with the vague map and had tried to gauge their distance from Giffard's pickets.

He said brokenly, 'I got lost. Lelean was trying to help me, but he was just a boy. When I told him I did not know where we were he stood up to me and said that I *ought* to know.' He moved his hands vaguely. 'Then there was the attack. Lelean was hit by a musket ball and two of the seamen killed outright. The third ran off and I never saw him again.'

Bolitho watched his agonized face, seeing the sudden terror in the darkness, the swiftness of death. Probably tribesmen, lurking like jackals for pickings after the fight between Spaniard and Englishman.

Calvert was saying, 'I carried Lelean for miles. Sometimes we hid in the scrub, listening to the others talking. Laughing.' His voice broke in a sob. 'And all the time Lelean kept repeating how he trusted me to get him to safety.' He looked at Bolitho, his eyes blurred and unseeing. 'He actually *relied* on me!'

Bolitho stood up and poured a goblet of wine. As he thrust it into Calvert's hand he asked quietly, 'Where were you when the marines found you?'

'In a gully.' Some of the wine ran down his chin and across his soiled shirt. Like blood. 'Lelean was dead. The wound must have been worse than I realized. I didn't want to leave him there like that. He was the first one who ever trusted me to do anything. I knew . . .' He faltered. 'I thought no one would come to search. There was the attack. All this.'

Bolitho took the empty glass from his nerveless fingers. 'Go and rest, Mr Calvert. Tomorrow things may seem different.' He watched the other man's eyes. Tomorrow? It was already here.

Calvert stared at him with sudden determination. 'I will never forget that you sent men to look for me.' The determination faded. 'But I couldn't leave him there like that. He was just a boy.'

Bolitho recalled Broughton's scathing comment, as if it had been spoken aloud in the room. *Do him good!* Well, perhaps after all he had been right.

He said gravely, 'Many good men have died today, Mr Calvert. It is up to us to see their efforts are not wasted.' He paused before adding, 'And to ensure that young Lelean's trust is not betrayed.'

Long after Calvert had gone Bolitho sat slumped in the chair. What was the matter with him to offer Calvert such comfort?

Calvert was useless, and probably always would be. He came of a background and social climate which Bolitho had always mistrusted and often despised.

Was it because of that one spark which had been given him by the dead midshipman? Could he really hold on to such ideas in a war which had passed all reason and outwitted traditional sentiment?

Or was it that he had replaced Lelean with his own nephew? Would it have been fair to add to Calvert's misery when inwardly he knew he would have acted the same had it been Adam out there in an unknown gully?

When the first grey fingers of dawn explored the wall of the commandant's room Bolitho was still in the chair, dozing in exhausted sleep, and awakening at intervals to new doubts and problems.

On the top of the central tower Bickford was already awake and watching the probing light. After a while he could wait no longer and beckoned to a seaman standing near by.

'Good enough, eh?' He could not stop grinning. His part of the action was done, and he was *alive*. 'Run up the colours! That'll make *Coquette* sit up and beg!'

At noon Bolitho climbed to the top of the central tower and leaned over the battlements to study the activity in the bay. Just after dawn the frigate *Coquette*, followed by Inch's *Hekla*, had passed through the narrow channel below the fortress, and within an hour had been joined by the battered and listing *Navarra*. Now, as he watched the boats pulling busily back and forth from the shore to the ships, from the marine outpost on the beaked headland to the pickets on the causeway, it was hard to remember it as the empty place it had once been.

He raised a telescope and trained it across the anchored bomb vessel until he had discovered Lieutenant Bickford and his landing party searching amongst the low-roofed buildings at the top of the bay. Giffard had already reported the village —for it was little more than that—to be quite deserted. The fishing boats which they had sighted before the first attack proved to be derelict and had not been used for many months.

Like the village, they were part of some ghost habitation from the past. The one good capture had been the little brig, *Turquoise*. She was a merchant vessel, armed only with a few outdated four-pounders and some swivels, but refitted and properly equipped would make a very useful addition to the Navy List. She also represented a command for a junior officer. Bolitho had promised himself that Keverne should get her as his just reward.

He moved the glass slightly to watch the *Navarra* being warped closer and closer to the beach. The master's mate sent to command her had made sail as fast as he had been able, just as soon as he had sighted the British ensign flying over the fortress. The makeshift repairs had begun to give way, and it had been all he could do to reach Djafou before the sea overtook the pumps for the final plunge.

Bolitho was glad Keverne had selected the master's mate in question. A less intelligent seaman might have obeyed his last order to stand clear of the land until the squadron's entrance, for fear of incurring the displeasure of his superiors. Had he done so, the prize ship would indeed have been lost, for within thirty minutes of her arrival the wind had died completely, and the sea, from the headlands to the burnished horizon, was like a sheet of dark blue glass.

Boats were all around the listing vessel, and he could see parties of men from the other ships busily unloading stores and heavy spars, swaying out guns and anchors to lighten the hull as much as possible in readiness for beaching.

Like the crew of the little brig, who had surrendered without a murmur of protest, the arrival of the *Navarra*'s company and passengers posed another real problem. He saw many of them being gathered in lines on the beach, the women's clothing contrasting vividly with the silver-coloured sand and the hazy hills beyond the village. They had to be fed and quartered, as well as protected from any marauding tribesmen who might still be near. It was not going to be easy, and he doubted if Broughton would view their presence as anything but an unwanted nuisance.

The squadron was probably just below the horizon, and he could picture the admiral fretting and fuming at being becalmed, and still in ignorance of the success or failure of the attack. But the lack of wind was an ally too. For if Broughton could not reach Djafou, then neither could an attacker.

Metal groaned and clattered on the lower rampart, and he saw Fittock, the gunner, supervising the removal of one of the iron-mounted cannon so that the damaged wall could be partially repaired. The guns had already shown they could hold the entrance against powerful ships of war. And with the innocent-looking *Hekla* anchored in the centre of the bay, even a heavy attack along the coast by troops was a bad risk.

He lowered the glass and tugged at his shirt which was clinging to his skin like a hot towel. The more he mulled over what they had found at Djafou, the more convinced he became that it was useless as a base. Automatically he thrust his hands behind him and started to pace slowly back and forth on the heated flagstones, his feet measuring almost exactly the span of the *Euryalus*'s quarterdeck.

If he had held the final responsibility, would he have acted differently from Broughton? Return to Gibraltar and admit failure, or go further east in the hope of discovering a suitable bay or inlet without informing the Commander-in-Chief?

He felt his scabbard slapping against his thigh as he paced, and let his mind stray back to the grisly hand-to-hand fighting during the night. Every time he allowed himself to be drawn into these reckless raids he was narrowing his own chances of survival. He knew it, but could not help himself. He guessed that Furneaux and some of the others imagined it was conceit, a desperate yearning for glory which made him leave his proper role of flag captain to take part in such dangerous forays. How could he explain his true feelings when he did not understand them himself? But he knew he would never allow his men to risk their lives because of some hazy plan from his own mind without his being there with them to share its reward or failure.

He smiled grimly to himself. Which was why he would never attain flag rank. He would go on facing battle after battle, passing experience to the barely trained officers who were being promoted to fill the growing gaps left by the war's harvest. And then one day, in a place like this, or on the deck of some ship, he would pay the price. As always, he found himself praying fervently it would be instant, like the closing of a door. Yet at the same time he knew it was unlikely. He thought of Lucey, and those others who were down below in the great cool storerooms which were being used as a hospital. *Coquette*'s surgeon would do his best, but many of them would die slowly, with no relief from pain but the fortress's supply of wine, which was mercifully plentiful.

Bolitho paused by the battlements and saw a boat shoving off from the *Coquette* and turning towards the fortress. Another was leaving the bomb vessel, and he realized he had been so busy with his thoughts he had almost forgotten he had invited Inch and Captain Gillmor to dine with him. One of them might think of some idea, no matter how vague, which would throw light on Djafou's total lack of strategic value.

Later as he stood in the commandant's cool room sharing a jug of wine with the two captains, he marvelled at the way in which they could discuss and compare their experiences and viewpoints of the brief, fierce battle. It was hard to realize none of them had slept for more than an hour or so at a time, nor did there seem much likelihood of rest in the near future. The Navy was a good school for such stamina, he thought. Years of watchkeeping and snatching catnaps between all the endless necessities of making and shortening sail, going to quarters or having to repair storm damage under the most severe conditions hardened even the laziest man to going without proper rest almost indefinitely.

Inch was describing the excitement aboard *Hekla* as the marine spotters had recorded his first fall of shot when Allday entered to announce that Lieutenant Bickford had returned from his expedition to the village.

Bickford looked weary, his uniform covered with sand and dust, and he downed the wine with obvious relish before saying, 'I am afraid it is a fearsome place, sir.' He shook his head as he recalled his grim discovery. 'It has not been lived in for years. Not by villagers, that is.'

Gillmor said chidingly, 'Come now, Mr Bickford, surely it is not the home of goblins!'

'No, sir.' Bickford's serious face was strained. 'We found a great pit behind the dwellings. Full of human bones. Many hundreds must have been thrown there to be picked clean by all the vermin from the rocks.'

Bolitho watched him, and was aware of a coldness growing in his heart. It had been here all the time, and he had not seen it. The next part of the puzzle.

Bickford was saying, 'Most of the dwellings are mere shells. But there are chains . . .'

They all stared at Bolitho as he said quietly, 'Slaves.' It

was incredible it had taken him so long to accept the obvious. Or maybe his mind had rebelled against it. Why else would Draffen have had business here in the past? A business which had taken him as far as the West Indies and Caribbean where he had met Hugh during the American Revolution. The Moors had built the fortress to protect and further this obscene trade in human lives, and after them had come others. Barbary pirates, and Arab slavers, who could sweep far and wide to bring their helpless victims here, the fountainhead of their rich trade.

How easy it had been made for Draffen. Disguised by an apparent genuine offer to help further British naval activities in the Mediterranean, he had been ensuring his future profits, and by having Broughton destroy the Spanish garrison had paved the way for the continuance of his supply.

He added, 'They must have been brought here from many parts of the country. There are caravan trails to the mountains, which have probably been there for centuries.' He could not hide the bitterness of his thoughts. 'I have no doubt that in the Indies and Americas there are many growing rich at the expense of these poor wretches.'

Gillmor said uneasily, 'Well, there has always been a trade in slaves. . . .'

Bolitho eyed him calmly, 'There has always been scurvy, but that does not mean anyone but a fool would allow it to continue!'

Gillmor swung away, his voice suddenly angry. 'God, how I loathe the land! As soon as you touch it you feel infected, unclean!'

Inch said, 'Sir Hugo Draffen will not be pleased, sir.'

'As you say.' Bolitho refilled the glasses, feeling the jug quivering in his grasp. Speaking with his own kind it all seemed so clear and very simple. But he knew from past experience that nothing ever appeared quite so neat and clean-cut in the austere surroundings of a court-martial, many miles from the occurrence, and maybe many months after it had happened. Draffen was an influential man, his very scope of operations had shown that. Even Broughton was afraid of him, and there would be many in England who would be quick to take his side. He had, after all, discovered a base for the squadron's first probe into the Mediterranean. In war you must make do with what you had. His glib promise of a new ally to harass the enemy's coastal movements might well cover his other, more personal ambitions.

He crossed slowly to the window, feeling their eyes on his back. He could turn his back on Draffen's action just as easily as he was on them. He was the flag captain, and had little say in wider decisions. No one could hurt him for it, and few would blame him. While Broughton's flag flew over the squadron's affairs, so too was it his responsibility.

As he tortured himself a few moments longer he thought suddenly of Lucey and Lelean, of all the others who had died and would die before they were rid of this hateful place.

Draffen must have been trying to prepare him for it, he thought bitterly. When he had described how the squadron would soon quit Djafou for good he had not been thinking of the local people, for there were none. None but a regular stream of slaves and those who guarded them for the traders like Draffen. He was probably somewhere along the coast right at this minute, explaining to his agent what he required to make his own victory complete and lasting.

He asked sharply, 'How long did *Restless* take to make contact before?'

Bickford shrugged. 'No more than a day or so, sir. She'll be becalmed too, if I'm any judge.'

Bolitho faced them. 'Then the meeting place cannot be far.' He crossed quickly to the door. 'I must see the commandant. So take your ease, my friends.'

As the door closed, Gillmor remarked, 'I have never seen him like that before.'

Inch swallowed his wine. 'I have.' The others waited. 'When I was serving under him in the old *Hyperion*.'

Gillmor said testily, 'Bring it out of the oven and on to the table, man!'

Inch replied simply, 'He has a hatred of treachery. I doubt that he will sit quietly with this burr under his saddle!'

Bolitho found the commandant sitting beside a window, his tired face relaxed in thought, so that he looked like a piece of church carving in the filtered sunlight.

He waited until the man's shadowed eyes turned towards him. 'Time is now in much demand for there is little of it. There are certain things I must know, and I believe you are the only one who can tell me.'

The withered hands lifted slowly. 'You know that my oath

forbids me to speak, Captain.' There was no anger, nothing in his tone but resignation. 'As commandant I have . . .'

Bolitho interrupted harshly, 'As commandant you have a duty to your people here. Also the crew and passengers of the *Navarra* who are citizens of Spain.'

'When you seized Djafou, you also took that responsibility.'

Bolitho walked to a window and leaned on the warm sill. 'I know of a French officer called Witrand. I believe you know him also, and that he has perhaps been here before.'

'*Before?*'

One word, but Bolitho heard a catch in the man's breath.

'He is a prisoner of war, Colonel. But I wish you to tell me now what he has been doing and the reason for his interest in Djafou. Otherwise . . .'

This time Alava interrupted. 'Otherwise? I am too old to be threatened.'

Bolitho turned and regarded him impassively. 'If you refuse I will have to destroy the fortress.'

Alava smiled gently. 'That of course is your privilege.'

'Unfortunately,' Bolitho spoke harshly to cover the nagging uncertainty of his thoughts, 'I do not have the ships available to remove all these extra people and your garrison to safety.' He relaxed slightly, seeing his words strike home, the sudden quivering in the withered hands. 'So although the necessities of war dictate that I destroy the fortress and remove any future threat from it, I cannot leave you any protection.'

He looked down from the window again, hating what he was doing to the old man. He saw Sawle leaning against the parapet, his head within inches of a black-haired Spanish woman's, one of the garrison officers' wives. She was moving her body closer, and he could see Sawle's hand resting on her arm.

He turned his back on them and asked, 'You have heard of one Habib Messadi?' He nodded slowly. 'Yes, I see from your face you have.'

Bolitho swung round angrily as the door banged open and Captain Giffard marched into the room. Behind him was a young marine carrying a small basket.

'What in hell's name do you mean by bursting in here?'

Giffard remained rigidly at attention, his eyes on some point above Bolitho's epaulette.

'A horseman came riding hard towards the causeway, sir.

Arab of some sort. My men challenged him, and when he galloped off they took a shot but missed him.' He gestured with his hand towards the marine by the door. 'He left the basket, sir.'

Bolitho tensed. 'What is in it?'

Giffard dropped his eyes. 'That Frog prisoner, sir. It's his head.'

Bolitho gripped his fists so tightly he could feel the bones throbbing. Somehow he managed to withstand the rising nausea and horror as he faced Alava's shocked eyes and said, 'It seems that Messadi is closer than we thought, Colonel.' Behind him he heard the young marine retching uncontrollably. 'So let us begin at once.'

15. Retribution and Darkness

BOLITHO was standing beside an open window in the commandant's gloomy quarters when Allday entered to announce that *Hekla*'s gig had arrived to collect him. It was amazing to see the change in the weather which had come about in the last few hours. It was early evening, and should have been bright sunlight. Instead, the sky was concealed by low, threatening cloud, and the flag on the upper tower was standing out stiffly to a westerly wind which showed every sign of strengthening.

He had just been leaving the elderly commandant when a sentry on the ramparts had reported the change. When he had gone to the tower to see for himself he had watched the western headland slowly disappear beneath a great bank of rolling sand and dust, so that it had appeared as if the causeway was ended abruptly and pointing into a swirling void. Even within the bay the ships had begun to pitch, and Gillmor had sighed with relief when he had seen his first lieutenant laying out a second anchor for safety's sake.

But safety, doubt and even the horror of Witrand's hideous death had given way to an attentive excitement as Bolitho had told them of his discovery.

Once Alava had begun to talk he had seemed unable to desist or stem his flow of intelligence. It had appeared as if the burden of his knowledge had been too much for his bent shoulders, and with the additional shock of what lay in the small basket he wanted to rid himself of every link with his responsibilities.

Bolitho had listened to his low, cultivated voice with fixed attention, using it as a barrier against his pity for Witrand, his disgust at those who had thought the manner of his death a necessary gesture.

Now, as he heard the wind moaning against the thick walls and along the unsheltered ramparts, he still found it difficult to accept that so much of his earlier beliefs had been proved right. Witrand had been in Djafou once before, with strict orders to pave the way for further developments. How much of Alava's information was fact and how much guesswork was hard to tell. One thing was certain, Witrand's visits were not to merely examine the possibilities of a new French base to forestall any future British naval moves in the Mediterranean. Djafou was to be the first of several such footholds on the North African shores, a gateway to the east and the south. Troops, guns and the ships to carry and protect them would lead the enemy's new and powerful thrust into a continent hitherto denied them, at a time when England could least afford to stop them.

Yet Alava must have known Bolitho was bluffing when he had threatened to leave the garrison and passengers to the mercies of the Barbary pirates. Must have toyed with the idea of standing his ground until that moment when Giffard had burst in with his grisly discovery. If he had planned it himself, he could not have timed it better.

As he had spoken with Gillmor and Inch he had recalled Broughton's warning, his lack of trust in Draffen. What would he say when he discovered the full extent of Draffen's treachery, if such it was? Draffen might also be dead, or screaming out his life under an agony of torture.

The wind had arisen like a last touch of hope. It was obvious from the moment the horseman had hurled the basket at Giffard's pickets that the seizure of the fortress was common knowledge along the coast. With the squadron still absent, and heaven alone knew how far they had been carried in a mounting wind, an all-out attack on the fortress was very possible. Alava had spoken of vast arcas of coastline being terrorized and controlled by the pirates under their leader Habib Messadi. Chebecks, such as those which had mauled the *Navarra*, could work close inshore if need be, without fear of attack by heavier and more ponderous ships of war.

Messadi's information must be as good as Draffen's, he thought. For it was obvious the attack on the *Navarra* had been no accidental meeting at sea. The chebecks had been too far from land, and but for the unexpected storm would no doubt have been far greater in numbers. In which case they would not have been able to repel their attack, and Witrand would have died there and then with all the others, and the occupation of Djafou perhaps delayed long enough for the fortress to be taken and occupied by its original inhabitants. Or for Broughton to make the capture and see for himself the uselessness of the bay for a British base.

Gillmor had said heavily, 'So the Frogs intend to take Malta, eh? And then on and on, with not a British ship to stand against them!'

Inch had added, 'There is nothing we can do without help.'

It had been like speaking his thoughts aloud. Bolitho had watched the doubt in their faces changing to caution and then to excitement as he had said, 'I have always maintained, the fortress *is* Djafou. Without it the bay is unsafe for Frenchman, pirate, or for that matter ourselves. We must destroy it, blast it down so that it will take months, perhaps a year, to replace. Given that time we can return to these waters in strength, and meet the Frenchman where it hurts him most. At sea.'

Gillmor had put in a note of caution. 'Sir Lucius Broughton must surely be consulted?'

Bolitho had pointed at the bay, the sea's face ruffling in whitecaps to the rising wind. 'First we must strike at those who need this fortress so desperately for their own foul uses. The wind may hold, and if so, will give us an unexpected edge on them.'

That had been merely hours ago. Now it was time to act, otherwise the *Hekla* would have real difficulty in clawing past the fortress and to the open sea beyond. *Coquette* would remain at anchor, and should Bolitho's attack fail, be prepared to act on his written orders. To demolish the fortress and remove every Spaniard, marine and other living soul with whatever resources at his disposal.

Gillmor had not let his disappointment at being left behind override his concern for Bolitho. 'Supposing Alava's information is false, sir, and you cannot find these Barbary pirates?

Or you might be overwhelmed, in which case I will have to obey the orders you are leaving behind for me. It could well mean your ruin, when we all know you are only acting for the best.'

'If that occurs, Captain Gillmor, you will be spared from watching my final downfall.' He had smiled at Gillmor's uncertainty. 'For I will no doubt be dead.'

But as he picked up his hat from the commandant's great chair Gillmor's warning returned to him. With luck they should meet with *Restless* somewhere along the coast, and she, unlike the heavier frigate, would be able to give them support. With *luck*. It never did to rely on it too much.

He looked at Allday. 'Ready?'

'Aye, Captain.'

Below on the jetty, the stonework of which still bore the scars of musket balls and Sawle's explosive charge, the wind felt stronger. But it was clinging and oppressive and left grit or sand between the teeth. Bolitho saw several boats coming through the breached wall crammed with passengers from the *Navarra* and some of Giffard's marines. Bolitho had ordered that everyone but the pickets were to be withdrawn to the safety of the fortress, and he found time to wonder what they were thinking as they stared up at the grim walls like trapped animals.

Giffard and Bickford were waiting by the gig, and the marine said gruffly, 'I still think we should use my men to make a forced march across country, sir.'

Bolitho studied him with something like affection. 'Given more time I might agree. But you have said yourself that a few carefully placed sharpshooters could delay an army in those hills and gullies. But have no fear, I think there will be plenty of work for you soon enough.'

To Bickford he said, 'Tell Mr Fittock to set about laying charges in the magazine and lower storerooms.' He smiled at the lieutenant's grim features. 'He will, I am sure, be delighted at the prospect.'

Then he saw Calvert hurrying down the stairs, his face set in a frown of unusual determination. He said, 'With permission, sir, I would like to accompany you in *Hekla*.'

Bolitho was conscious of Giffard's mouth turning down in disapproval, of some of the gig's crew watching Calvert with curiosity, if not actual contempt.

He heard himself say, 'Certainly. Get in the boat.'

Giffard said awkwardly, 'I have buried the, er, basket, sir. At the end of the causeway.'

'Thank you.' Bolitho thought suddenly of the wife who waited in Bordeaux. He wondered if he would ever write and tell her where Witrand had died. That he lay beside a British lieutenant and a pimply-faced midshipman.

Then with a nod he jumped into the boat and snapped, 'Cast off.'

Inch was waiting to greet him at the bomb's low bulwark, his hat askew as he squinted towards the wavecrests beyond the headland. He saw Calvert, opened his mouth to say something, but decided against it. He, after all, knew Bolitho better than most. And if he did something, he usually had a damn good reason.

He watched the boat being swayed inboard on its tackles and shouted, 'Stand by the capstan!' Then he looked enquiringly at Bolitho. 'When you are ready, sir?'

Their eyes held. Across the years like a conspiracy. He grinned and replied, 'Directly, Commander Inch!'

Inch bobbed with pleasure. '*Directly* it is, sir!'

After his own quarters in *Euryalus* the bomb's stern cabin was like a rabbit hutch. Even here her sturdy build was very apparent, and the massive deckhead beams gave the impression they were pressing down forcibly to further restrict movement and space.

Bolitho sat on the bench seat and watched the salt spray dashing across the thick glass, feeling the shallow hull staggering and groaning in a steep beam sea as she plunged awkwardly on the larboard tack. The deckhead lanterns were gyrating wildly, and he pitied the helmsmen on the unsheltered upper deck, and those unfortunate souls aloft at this moment trying to take in another reef.

The door banged open and Allday appeared carrying a jug of coffee. He rocked back on his heels, swayed and then hurtled towards the table, cracking his head on a low beam as the *Hekla* pitched sickeningly into a deep trough. Miraculously none of the scalding coffee was lost, and Bolitho marvelled at the cook's skill in such a sea.

Allday rubbed his skull and asked, 'Can't you sleep, Captain? 'Tis four hours before daylight.'

Bolitho let the coffee explore his stomach and was grateful for it. His mind had defied rest while the *Hekla* had clawed her way clear of the coast, but now that time was running out he knew he should try to sleep. Calvert was rolled in a blanket in one of the two boxlike cabins, but whether he was asleep or brooding over Lelean's death it was hard to say. He should have left him in Djafou, he knew it. Just as he was certain that Calvert would have gone out of his mind at being abandoned to his tortured thoughts.

He said, 'I will rest in a moment.'

Inch entered the cabin, his tarpaulin coat glistening with salt rime as he staggered towards the coffee jug. He wiped his streaming face and said, 'Wind's veered a piece, sir. Gone round to west nor' west, as far as I can tell. I'll go about in an hour.' He hesitated, suddenly aware of his authority. 'If that is suitable, sir?'

Bolitho smiled. 'You are the captain. I am sure it will be convenient for our purpose. At daylight we may sight *Restless*.' He forced his mind to stop probing and re-examining his doubts. 'But now I will sleep.'

Allday followed Inch towards the companion ladder and muttered, 'My God, sir, I thought I yearned for small ships again!'

Inch grinned. 'You are getting old.'

The sea thundered over the upper deck, and a goodly portion of it cascaded down the ladder towards them.

Allday swore and replied, 'And, with respect, I should like to get older before I die!'

'Good morning, sir.' Inch touched his hat as Bolitho appeared at the companion and stepped over the coaming.

Bolitho nodded and walked to the lee rail, the sleep already gone from his mind in the keen, damp air. The daylight was as yet only a glimmer, and now that *Hekla* had gone about to run almost parallel with the coast he guessed they were barely more than two miles offshore. The wind had veered still more and now pushed steadily across the larboard quarter, the spray leaping occasionally above the stout bulwarks to sluice noisily away into the scuppers. He could see the land, although it was little more than purple shadow, and it was strange to accept the fact that due to the slow necessity of clawing away from it to gain the wind's advantage, Djafou now lay less than thirty miles ahead of *Hekla*'s blunt bows. Inch had done well, and there was nothing in his long horseface to show he had been on deck for most of the time while his ship had tacked and beaten around one great circle to her present position.

Astern they were being followed by a thick sea mist, so that it gave a false impression of being motionless, an impression made a lie by the flying spray around the bowsprit and the bulging tan sails above the deck.

As he peered forward he saw a sheen of dull silver on the dancing wavecrests, and knew dawn was nearby, but as yet the eastern horizon was still lost in spray and shadow. A few gulls drifted and shrieked above the topmasts, and he wondered whether eyes other than theirs had seen their careful approach. Careful for reasons other than surprise. Even as he considered the treacherous coastline so close abeam he heard the leadsman chant from the chains, his cry almost lost in the crack and thunder of the sails.

'By the mark seven!'

But Inch appeared satisfied, and surely knew his shallow hull better than Bolitho did.

Shadows around the bomb's decks were already taking on strength and personality, and he saw the hands at work around the guns, while others moved restlessly on the forecastle where Mr Broome, Inch's elderly gunner, was examining his mortars.

But mortars were not the only teeth in *Hekla*'s defences. Apart from a few swivels, she mounted six massive carronades. Altogether they would certainly find any weakness in her stout construction and timbers.

'By the mark five!'

Inch called, 'Bring her up a point, Mr Wilmot!'

His first and only lieutenant walked straddle-legged up the slanting deck, and as the helm squeaked over he shouted, 'Steady, sir! East by south!'

'By the mark seven!'

Inch said to no one in particular, 'Damme, it's like a sailor's lot hereabouts. All ups and downs!'

Bolitho set his teeth against the screech and scrape of a grindstone from below the foremast where some of the seamen were busily putting new edges to their cutlasses. How over-crowded the deck appeared, mainly because in addition to her normal complement the *Hekla* carried the survivors from the

Devastation as well as the remnants of his own landing party.

Inch rubbed a hand across his wind-reddened face. 'Won't be long now sir.' He gestured aloft. 'I've a good man to watch for *Restless*.'

Bolitho said, 'There is supposed to be an inlet where this Messadi takes refuge. Shelter enough for his chebecks, and within reach of several villages for his needs.' He looked searchingly at Inch. 'You will be able to fire the mortars without anchoring, I hope?'

'Aye, sir.' Inch frowned. 'We have never done it before, of course.' He chuckled, all doubt gone. 'But then we had never fired at a fortress either!'

'Good. Once you have awakened their nest, we will engage whoever comes out.' He looked at the sky. '*Restless* will close and give ready support once we have made contact.'

Inch eyed him soberly. 'And if she is *not* available, sir?'

Bolitho shrugged. 'Then she is not available.'

Inch grinned again. 'It'll be like stirring wasps with a stick!'

Another cry from the leadsman took him away again and left Bolitho to his thoughts.

He watched the land hardening and taking on its true form, and recognized the same bleak hills and desolation as they had found in Djafou. It looked uneven but as yet unbroken by any sign of a cove or inlet, but he knew from boyhood it was deceptive. Once when a mere child he had taken out a small boat from Falmouth and had been horrified to find himself carried away on a swift coastal current. There should have been a safe cove near by, but as the light faded he could see nothing but those grim, hostile cliffs. With all hope and most of his courage gone he had suddenly found it. Almost hidden by an overlap of cliffs, beyond which the water was flat calm, and his relief had given way in a flood of tears.

His father had been away at sea. It had been his brother Hugh who had come to find him and had boxed his ears.

Thin sunlight filtered above the cruising haze and he heard the masthead lookout call, 'Oi think 'tis there on the lee bow, zur! Broken water!'

Bolitho raised a telescope and eagerly scanned the murky shoreline. Then he saw the telltale cluster of small breakers marking the inward curve of a headland. He strained his mind until he fitted it into the mental picture of Inch's chart, the place as described by Alava in his soft, gentle voice.

He heard a man slip and apologize awkwardly in the half-light, and saw Calvert feeling his way along the lee bulwark. He looked pinched and strained, and there were dark shadows under his eyes.

Inch cupped his hands. 'Masthead! Any sign of *Restless*?'

'None, zur!'

Inch said with unusual irritation, 'That damn fellow must have lost himself!'

Bolitho looked at him. Maybe Inch was more worried than he showed, to be groping his way along this treacherous coast. Or perhaps he was masking his true feelings about the task he had been given? It was not going to be easy for him. He watched Inch nodding and whispering with his gunner and first lieutenant. Or was it that he was unwilling to be the one to witness Bolitho's failure?

Slowly but surely the rounded headland was moving out to greet them, its summit already shining dully in the dawn light. Very soon now.

Inch came aft. 'With your permission, sir, I will fire the mortars as we come abeam of the point. That will give my people time to reload for the next shots as we pass the entrance. Mr Broome is confident that we will make a good deal of confusion, even if we hit nothing.'

Bolitho smiled. Inch had certainly discovered new confidence, and that in itself was infectious.

'Good. Then carry on.'

Inch shouted, 'Send the hands to quarters, Mr Wilmot! You know what we have to do today.'

The carronade crews had been up and about for several hours, and apart from dousing the galley fire there was little else to do but wait and watch Mr Broome with his men grouped like high priests around their two crouching mortars.

Allday murmured, 'They'll wake the bastards up, God rot them!'

'By the mark three!'

The headland was hard and clear against the skyline now, leaning out into the lively wavecrests as if to nudge the bowsprit.

Broome raised his hand. 'Stand clear o' they mortars, lads!'

Bolitho saw the spark of a fuse, the momentary jerk of the gunner's shoulder, and held his breath.

The mortars fired within seconds of one another, and he

was surprised the noise was negligible compared with the terrific shock of their recoil. He felt the deck bounce and vibrate beneath his feet with such force that his teeth were jarred painfully and his neck felt as if he had just been thrown bodily from a stampeding horse.

Inch was peering at him. 'Fair shots, I believe, sir.'

Bolitho nodded, not trusting his voice. Then he hurried to the rail and watched as the top of the headland glowed dull red, and seconds later the air trembled to a double, muffled explosion.

He heard Broome yelling at his crews to reload, the excited chatter from the waiting men on the main deck. What a strange, unnerving form of warfare, he thought. To be able to fire high over a solid land mass, unseen and unhampered by what lay beyond.

Inch rapped, 'Watch your helm, Mr Wilmot!' He ran to the side and stared towards the nearest line of breakers. 'We will have to wear ship if we draw much closer.'

Broome bellowed, 'Ready, sir!'

Bolitho said, 'Hold your fire!' He waited as a line of spray-dappled reefs drifted past the lee side. 'We will be across the point at any moment.'

He tore his eyes from the glistening rocks and imagined what would have happened if the hull beneath him had been any deeper.

Inch said, 'Here it comes.' Then, 'There's a fire of some sort, so we must have hit the land.'

Bolitho tried to hold his telescope steady against the jarring pitch of the swirling currents. It was very dark inside the cove, and the glowing fire which was already dying appeared to be at the far end of it, like gorse alight on a tinder-dry hillside.

'Again.' He opened his mouth and was relieved to find the shock of the next salvo was less painful to his teeth. Even so, the violent leap of the deck planking spoke much for *Hekla*'s builders.

There was a single bright flash, blossoming out into a great wall of fire, reflected on the sheltered water inside the cove so that it appeared to double and treble in power and size. In the few seconds before it wavered and died he saw the low black shapes of several motionless craft, and felt almost sick with sudden relief.

Allday said, 'They're in there all right.' He shifted impatiently against the rail. 'I'll lay odds that singed their bloody beards!'

Bolitho did not hear him. 'Close enough, Commander Inch. Put her about and we will see what happens next.'

He walked aft to the taffrail to keep clear of the hurrying seamen as they ran to braces and halliards in readiness for wearing ship. So far, so good. The next minutes would tell whether he was wasting his time. If the pirates decided to remain in their deep cove there would be nothing for it but to maintain a bombardment from the sea. The mortars had been impressive, but in fact could do little more but create panic under such conditions. They needed stability and a good anchorage, with spotting parties ashore to signal success and failure after each shot.

He held the rail firmly as with blocks and rigging banging and humming in protest the *Hekla* swung her stern across the wind, canting still further in response to rudder and canvas.

Her deck seemed very wide for her stubby length, and every foot of it appeared to be crammed with scampering men as the manœuvre was completed and the bomb laid close-hauled on the larboard tack, her stern once more towards the land.

She was a difficult ship to handle, he thought, and for the first time that he could recall in years he felt his stomach contracting with uneasy nausea.

But Inch was grinning and waving his arms, his voice quite lost in the din of wind and sea. *Hekla* was more than a command to him. She was like a new toy, still possessing secrets to excite him.

It took another half-hour to complete the manœuvre and bring the ship back again to her original position with the headland on her lee bow. By that time the light had grown to such an extent it was possible to see the next line of round hills beyond the sea's edge, the occasional small crescent of beach, as well as far more reefs than he had first imagined.

Inch said thoughtfully, 'Wind's dropping, sir.' He rubbed his chin, his palm rasping across bristles as he added, 'May be a hot day after all.'

But there was plenty of mist and spray to hide the horizon, and in spite of the mounting patterns of light there was no warmth to ease the chill from their sodden clothing.

Bolitho turned his back on the others. Inch was probably worried at the prospect of being so close to the land now the wind was falling away. He could tell from the manner in which some of the seamen were fidgeting and muttering on the main deck that they were uneasy, too.

It was unfair to keep Inch in such danger, but he must wait just a few moments longer. He kept hearing Giffard's comments, like an epitaph. Perhaps he should have ordered the marines to march across country after all, regardless of human losses. But he knew he was only groping for misgivings. He was right, he must be. Even if all the marines available had reached the cove there was nothing to prevent those chebecks from slipping out to sea unhindered by their puny muskets.

He looked round as Calvert said, 'Listen!' He dropped his eyes under their combined stares but added quickly, 'I am sure I heard something.' It was almost the first time Calvert had spoken since he had come aboard.

Then Bolitho heard the sound, and sensed the same chill he had experienced aboard the *Navarra*. The steady, resonant beat of drums, so that without difficulty he could picture those lean chebecks with their powerful banks of oars, their grace and latent cruelty as they swept in to the attack.

He saw Inch watching him anxiously and snapped, 'Stand by! They are coming out!'

A ripple of excitement transmitted itself along the deck, and he saw the gun-captains pulling their men down from the bulwarks and breaking the tension of the moment with threats and curses.

Inch murmured, 'We have them, sir. They cannot take the advantage from us.'

Bolitho crossed to him, his hand resting on his sword. 'They need no advantage. They carry their own power.'

A dozen voices shouted excitedly as the first of the chebecks thrust clear of the shadows, their long prows throwing back foam and spray as they rode over the low breakers.

The drums became clearer and more menacing as one by one they pulled away from the land, and Bolitho heard Inch counting aloud, realizing perhaps for the first time the extent of his enemy.

Allday said quietly, 'There are many more of 'em than last time, Captain.' He licked his lips. 'Twenty, maybe twenty-two.'

Bolitho watched them narrowly, his face a mask to hide his mounting concern. As soon as they were clear of the rocks the

249

chebecks began to open out in a huge fan, so that the whole area of lively water was filled with flashing oars and intermingled bow waves.

On *Hekla*'s decks was total silence, the gun crews standing like statues to watch the oncoming horde of craft. It was a veritable fleet, the like of which none of them had ever seen, nor would live to describe if they failed to destroy them.

Bolitho strode to the rail, feeling the early excited anticipation giving way to sudden anxiety. He saw their faces turn towards him as he shouted, 'Remember, they will no more have seen anything like your *Hekla* than you have laid eyes on them. I doubt they have faced a carronade before, so stand to and be ready.' He saw some of them glancing at each other and added harshly, 'Let each gun-captain select his own target. Shoot as you have never done before, lads.' He looked towards the seamen by the swivels and those who crouched along the bulwarks with loaded muskets. 'Keep firing no matter what is happening. If they board us, we will be swamped.' He let his lips turn into a smile. 'So make every ball strike home!'

He heard a scrape of steel and saw Inch drawing his curved hanger and tying it to his wrist with a gold lanyard. He looked at Bolitho and grinned almost apologetically. 'It was a present,' he said.

A sullen bang echoed back from the shore and a ball whimpered low above the deck. A gun-captain stood back from his carronade but Bolitho shouted, 'Hold your fire!' He felt the deck jerk as a chebeck's bow gun belched smoke and a ball smashed hard into the *Hekla*'s waterline. The enemy's formation had fanned out even wider now, so that the ship was almost encircled by them, the furthest ones like the extremes of the crescent flags which some of them were flying above their furled sails.

He watched the range falling away, heard the drums beating faster as the long oars drove the craft towards the slow-moving *Hekla* like cavalry charging a square of foot soldiers.

He tugged out his sword and held it above his head. 'Easy, lads!' Some of the men near him were sweating in spite of the cool wind. To them it must seem as if the chebecks would drive right through their own ship.

The sword caught the frail sunlight as he swung it down. 'Fire as you bear!'

Below the rail the nearest carronade exploded with a deafening roar, hurling its blunt barrel inboard on its slide while the crew darted towards it with their sponges and rammer. Bolitho felt the detonation in his head like some terrible pain, and watched the great sixty-eight pound ball burst into the nearest bank of oars in a blinding orange flash. As the ball exploded to discharge its scything mass of grape the oars broke and flew in all directions, and he saw the hull lurching round to drive against the next chebeck in the converging line. Another carronade belched smoke and fire, and then a third from the opposite side as a chebeck pushed too near to the *Hekla*'s larboard bow to receive the heavy ball full in the prow. Yelling figures, the raked foremast and the chebeck's unfired gun all vanished in a pall of choking brown smoke. As it fanned away Bolitho saw the boat already rolling over, the sea boiling across the submerged oars to finish the kill.

Swivels cracked and banged from both forward and aft, hurling their canister amongst the white-clad figures who still crowded the chebecks' gangways, waving their scimitars and firing muskets to add to the frightful din of battle.

The hull shivered again, and Bolitho saw a ball smash into the bulwark, scattering seamen and leaving a trail of blood and flesh in its wake.

A chebeck crashed below the taffrail, her helmsman either dead or too crazed by the roar of guns to gauge his approach. As she ground and bumped across the stern the swivels raked her from stem to stern, and as she fell away the larboard carronades put two balls into her so that she broke apart and began to founder.

But two more were already alongside, and as seamen dashed to repel boarders the first yelling figures started to claw their way up and into the nets which Inch had rigged before dawn.

Bolitho cupped his hands. 'Now, lads!' And through the hatch came the rest of the extra hands, amongst them many of his own ship's company who had already faced death in the fight for Djafou.

Yelling and cheering they charged forward, thrusting with pikes and cutlasses at the boarders who hung kicking in the slack nets, impaled by the razor-sharp steel before they could get free.

Somewhere in the smoke he could hear warning cries and knew that up forward at least some of the attackers had hacked their way through the nets.

He shouted at Inch, 'Stay here!' To Allday, 'Follow me! We must keep these carronades firing or we are done for!'

Sparks flew from the capstan and iron ricocheted overhead. More balls slammed into the lower hull, although the chebecks' gunners were probably killing as many of their own men as the *Hekla*'s as they fired their long cannon into the dense smoke.

He saw several seamen falling around the forward carronade, heard their cries as the first of the attackers loomed into view, scimitars and broadswords slashing and cutting in crazed fury.

A swivel barked from the forecastle and several of them fell kicking in their blood, but others were swarming through a great gap in the nets and locking steel with the seamen.

Bolitho seized a gun-captain's shoulder and yelled into his face, 'See if you can put a ball into this one!' He saw the man nod dazedly before turning to call to his crew to reload.

Allday swung round and cut down a boarder who had somehow fought his way through Lieutenant Wilmot's men in the bows. The man slithered along the deck, his teeth bared in another wild shriek as a seaman drove a pike into his ribs.

Bolitho waved his sword and beckoned to another group of seamen below the mainmast. He felt a pistol ball fan his cheek and turned to see Wilmot fall, blood flowing from his mouth, when seconds before he had been leading his men into the attack.

He saw Inch yelling to some of his deck party to take up sweeps and stave off a blazing chebeck which was drifting dangerously close alongside. Above the crackle and roar of flames Bolitho heard terrible screams, and realized the oarsmen must be slaves, held captive by chains to their oars to endure the most horrible death of all.

A man dropped from overhead, his face smashed away by musket fire, another rolled kicking from a carronade, his foot crushed by the slide as the heavy muzzle blasted out into the dense smoke.

Bolitho saw the gun-captain waving at him, his teeth white in his blackened face, and knew he had managed to get a ball into the chebeck below the rent in the nets.

A bearded figure ducked beneath a pike and came towards him, his heavy sword scything in line with his stomach. He struck out with his sword, saw a spark jump from the steel as the shock darted up his arm. It was enough to turn the man in his charge, and before he could recover he was beaten to the deck by a belaying pin wielded by Broome, the gunner.

Inch was suddenly beside him yelling, 'They're done for!' He was almost capering with wild excitement. 'We've sunk more'n half and the others are in a bad way!'

He waved his hat in the air, and as the smoke thinned above the sweating gun crews Bolitho saw the sea's face littered with battered hulls and wreckage, while here and there a damaged chebeck pulled hurriedly towards the land. It would be a long time before Messadi's name brought terror to these shores again, he thought dazedly.

Broome roared, 'By God, sir! There's one across the bows!'

Through the smoke Bolitho saw the dovetailed flag very near, and somehow knew this was the leader's chebeck. Messadi himself trying to get past the *Hekla*'s fury and escape to the cove once more.

He followed Inch aft to where the helmsmen stood astride two of their dead comrades and gestured with his sword, his voice suddenly loud over the silent carronades. 'A guinea for the gun-captain who can bring her down!'

The realization that they had won, the sudden understanding they had beaten an overwhelming force of a terrifying enemy, was enough. Cheering, or sobbing with exhaustion, they ran back to their tackles, while the swivels and even muskets cut the air apart in their efforts to pursue the fast-moving chebeck.

Bolitho saw a massive carronade lurch inboard, and the flash as its ball burst close under the chebeck's raked stem. He turned his head as a second slammed into her ornate poop, scattering the packed figures in bloody gruel.

Everyone was yelling and shouting, and Bolitho clung to the shrouds trying to peer over the rolling bank of smoke as the enemy's twin masts began to tilt over.

He heard Inch calling to him, but as he swung round to listen he felt something like a blow in his right shoulder. It was not much and yet he was falling, and as he dropped to his knees he stared with dulled surprise at the blood which ran down across his white breeches and covered the deck around him. But something else was happening. He was on his side, the great mainsail high above him, and beyond it a wedge of pale cloud. Voices were calling, and he saw Inch running towards him, his face frozen with dismay.

Bolitho opened his mouth to reassure him in some way, but as he did so the pain came. So great and so terrible that a merciful darkness closed over him. Then there was nothing.

16. An Affair of Honour

SLOWLY, almost fearfully, Bolitho opened his eyes. It seemed to take an age for his vision to clear, and he felt his mind bunching itself to withstand the terrible pain which must surely come. He could feel the sweat running down his face and neck like iced water, but as he waited, dreading the return of torment, he realized he could find no other sensation. He tried to move his body, straining his ears to catch the sound of sea or creaking timbers, but there was neither, and as his uncertainty changed to something like panic he realized he was surrounded by total silence, and that the light was so dim he could have been in a tomb.

As he struggled to lift himself he felt the searing thrust of red-hot agony lance through his shoulder until he thought his heart would fail under it. He gritted his teeth, shutting his eyes tightly against the pain, and felt himself slipping back again into the nightmare. How long had it lasted? Days, hours, or was it an eternity since . . . He concentrated his failing reserve of will-power to try to remember, to keep his mind from cracking under the pressure in his body.

Figures and voices, looming faces and the vague motions of a ship were all parts of the confused memories. Some episodes, although brief, stood out more than others, although they had neither order nor apparent relevance. Inch cushioning his head from the deck. And Allday's agonized face coming down at him from every angle, again and again. And he had heard himself speaking too, and tried to listen, as if he had already become completely detached, his spirit hovering to watch the dying husk with nothing more than idle curiosity.

There had been other faces too, unknown to him, yet somehow familiar. Serious and young, calm and sad. His voice had come and gone repeatedly, and once when Bolitho had heard himself crying out in the enclosing darkness the stranger had said quietly, 'I am Angus, sir. *Coquette*'s surgeon.'

Bolitho tensed, feeling the sweat flooding across him as an

extension of his own rising terror. The face and the stark memory of those quiet words brought back some of the reality like the shock of the wound.

He had been protesting, his reeling mind fighting against the pain and the unconsciousness to make the surgeon understand. To stop him from touching him.

With a desperate sob he tried to move his shoulder, to discover some feeling in his arm and fingers. Nothing.

He let himself go limp again, ignoring the heated pain, and conscious only of a stinging despair which was blinding him.

As if torn from his innermost soul he heard himself cry out, 'Oh, Cheney! Cheney, help me! They've taken off my arm!'

Instantly a chair scraped across stone and feet pattered towards him. He heard someone call, 'He's coming out of the coma! Pass the word!'

A cool cloth was laid carefully over his forehead, and as he reopened his eyes he saw Allday peering down at him, his hard hands supporting his head so that someone else could sponge away the sweat of pain and fear.

He remembered the hands now. They had held him, pressing into his head as if to shut out the first pressure of Angus's knife.

From a great distance he heard him ask, 'How is it, Captain?'

Bolitho stared up at him, so astonished at seeing tears in Allday's eyes that he momentarily forgot his own suffering.

He replied, 'Easy, Allday. Rest easy.' How hoarse his voice sounded.

More faces swayed over him and he saw Angus thrust the others aside as he removed the sheet from his chest, felt his fingers probing before the pain struck at him again, making him gasp aloud.

He managed to say, 'My arm. Tell me.'

Angus glanced at him calmly. 'Believe me, sir, it is still there.' He did not smile. 'However, these are early days. It is well to be prepared.'

He moved out of Bolitho's vision and said, 'New dressing at once. And he must eat something. Broth maybe, and a little brandy.'

Bolitho strained his eyes up to Allday's face. 'Where am I?'

'The fortress, Captain. *Hekla* brought you in two days back.'

Two days. He persisted, 'And before?'

'*Hekla* took two days to reach here, Captain. The wind went against us.' He sounded desperate. 'I thought we'd never reach this damned place.'

A total of four days then. Time enough for the wound to worsen. Why should he not face the truth as Angus was doing? God knew, he had seen it happen often enough to others.

He said quietly, 'Tell me, and no lies for my sake, is my arm to come off?'

Again he saw the wretched helplessness in Allday's eyes.

'No, Captain, I am *sure* of it.' He tried to smile, the effort only adding to his misery. 'We've been through worse than this before. So let's have no more such talk.'

'That is enough talking.' Angus's face swam above him once more. 'You will rest until the dressing is changed. Then I want you to take some food.' He held something against the light, dull-coloured and half flattened by the force of impact. 'Some of these Arab muskets have great accuracy. This ball would have certainly killed you had you not turned your body at the time of delivery.' He smiled severely. 'So we must be thankful for that at least, eh?'

A door grated and he added, 'But then you have an excellent nurse.' He nodded curtly. 'Over here, Mrs Pareja. The captain will be ready in a moment.'

Bolitho watched as she moved down the side of the bed. Perhaps after all he was still drifting in unreality, or maybe even dead.

She paused and looked down at him, her face very pale against the long black hair, grave and unsmiling. And beautiful. It was hard to picture her aboard the *Navarra*, nursing her dead husband against her bloodied dress and watching him with such anger and bitter despair.

She said, 'You look a lot better.'

'Thank you for all you have done.' He felt suddenly helpless and empty under her calm stare and could not continue.

She smiled, showing her strong white teeth. 'Now I know you are getting well. Your language has been a challenge for the past two days.'

She was still smiling as Angus cut away the dressing and replaced it methodically with a new one.

Bolitho studied her in silence. She had been here with him all the time. Seeing his fight against pain, tending to his body's wants when he could do nothing to help himself or know what he was doing. He was conscious of his nakedness under the sheet, the hair matted over his forehead in sweat, and was ashamed.

She added quietly, 'It seems you are a hard man to kill.'

As Angus removed his bowl of bloodstained rags she looked at Allday and said, 'Go and rest.' When he hesitated she added sharply, 'Away with you, man! God knows you have not rested since your return, and from what I have heard, not since our charge here fell wounded.'

Bolitho shifted his left arm beneath the sheet and said hoarsely, 'My hand!'

Allday lifted the sheet and seized Bolitho's fingers with his own. Bolitho felt the sweat running across his bared chest as he used his failing strength to grip the hand tightly.

'You do as she asks, Allday.' He tried not to watch his face. 'I'll rest easier if I know you're fit and ready when I need you.' He forced himself to smile. 'True friends are hard to come by!'

Allday moved away and Bolitho heard the door close.

'He's gone.'

When Bolitho looked at her again he saw that her eyes were gleaming with tears.

She shook her head angrily. 'Damn you, Captain, it is true what they say! You bewitch all those who come near! It must be the Cornish magic in you!'

'I fear the magic, as you call it, comes from others, Mrs Pareja.'

She sat down on the bed and stirred some broth in a bowl. 'My name is Catherine.' She smiled, and for an instant he saw some of the same boldness he had noticed aboard the *Navarra*. 'But you call me Kate. I was known by that name before I married Luis.'

She lifted his head to arrange a pillow carefully and then dipped a spoon into the bowl.

He said quietly, 'I am sorry about your husband.'

The spoon did not waver, and he allowed the thick soup to explore his throat, reviving him in spite of the pain.

She said, 'You called out several times for Cheney. Your wife?'

He looked at her. 'She is dead.'

'I know. One of your officers told me.' She wiped his lips with a clean cloth before adding, 'You talked a lot, although much of it I didn't understand. Sometimes you spoke of home and some portraits on a wall.' She studied him gravely. 'But we will not speak of such things just now. You are very weak and must rest.'

Bolitho struggled to move his arm. 'No. I do not want to be left.' Almost desperately he added, 'Tell me of yourself.'

She sat back and smiled as if recalling some event long past. 'My home was London. Do you know much of it?'

He shook his head slightly. 'I have visited there.'

Surprisingly, she lifted her chin and laughed. It was a throaty, uninhibited sound, as if he had said something hilarious.

'I can see by your face you do not like London, my dear Captain. But I suspect that your London was different from mine. Where ladies danced the quadrille and hid their blushes in bouquets while the young blades made fine postures to excite their attention.' She tossed her head, so that the hair fell loosely around her throat. 'It is a way of life I have tried to learn. But it now seems that my efforts were wasted.' For a moment her eyes became wistful, and then she said shortly, 'Life can be cruel.'

She stood up and placed the bowl on a table, and Bolitho saw that she was wearing a different gown, of yellow silk, low cut and painstakingly embroidered around the waist. She saw his eyes and remarked, 'One of the Spanish ladies here gave it to me.'

He asked, 'Did you meet your husband in London?' He did not wish to disturb her memories, but somehow he needed to know.

'The first one.' She watched his puzzled expression and gave another bubbling laugh. 'Oh yes, I have buried two husbands, in a manner of speaking.' She moved swiftly to the bed and laid a hand on his shoulder. 'Do not look so worried. It is history. The first was a real dashing person. Together we were going to set the world ablaze. He was a soldier of fortune, a mercenary, if you like. After we were wed he took me to Spain to fight against the Frogs. But all the battles he fought were in taverns, over some woman or other. One day he must have met his match, for he was discovered dead in a ditch outside Sevilla. That was where I met Luis. He was twice my age, but seemed to need me.' She sighed. 'He was a widower and had nothing but his work to sustain him.' In a quieter tone she said, 'I think he was happy.'

'Of that I am certain.'

'Thank you, Captain.' She turned her face away. 'You did not need to say that.'

Once again the door scraped open but this time it was Gillmor. He bobbed his head politely to her before crossing to the bed.

'I am sincerely glad to know you are recovering your health, sir.'

Bolitho saw the strain on his face and guessed *Coquette*'s captain had had more than his share of worry because of his own incapacity.

Gillmor hurried on, 'The lookouts have just sighted the squadron returning, sir.' He breathed out slowly. 'At last.'

'What are you hiding?' Bolitho felt a sudden touch of apprehension. 'Something is wrong.'

'*Euryalus* is under tow, sir. She appears to have lost her bowsprit and fore topgallant mast. I have sent Mr Bickford in a cutter to meet the admiral.'

'I must get up!' Bolitho tried to free himself from the sheet. 'Take me to my ship, for God's sake!'

Gillmor stood aside and allowed the woman to press Bolitho back against the bed. 'I am sorry, sir, but we have decided against it.'

Bolitho clenched his teeth against the pain. '*We* have decided?'

Gillmor swallowed but stood his ground. 'Commander Inch and I, sir. There is no sense in having you die now that the worst is past.'

'Since when do you give me my orders, *Captain* Gillmor?'

The frustration and helplessness, the realization he had thought more of his own suffering than of his duty to the squadron, filled him with an unreasoning anger.

She interrupted before Gillmor could reply. 'Now, that is being *childish*! Do not excite yourself or I will call Mr Angus to you!'

Gillmor said, 'I am sorry, sir. But I think we will need you very soon, and in good health.'

Bolitho closed his eyes. 'No. I am the one to apologize. To you both.' Then he asked, 'Is *Restless* with the squadron?'

Gillmor hesitated. 'No, sir. But maybe she is too far to seaward to be observed by Giffard's men.'

'Perhaps.'

Bolitho could feel himself getting drowsy again, the throbbing in his shoulder growing more insistent. It was difficult to concentrate on what Gillmor was saying, harder still to sort his thoughts into any semblance of order.

Gillmor said, 'I will leave you, sir. As soon as we have any news . . .' He backed out of the room before Bolitho could protest.

'A good officer.' He felt her sit down again on the bed, the cool touch of a cloth across his forehead. 'When I was his age I had a ship like *Coquette*. In the Great South Sea. That was another world.' It was growing more difficult to remember. 'Lizards three feet long, and turtles big enough to carry a man. Unspoiled by civilization . . .'

'Rest, Captain.' Her voice faded away as Bolitho sank into a deep, exhausted sleep.

Some hours later he awoke shivering violently and ice cold. Although the shutters were closed across the windows he knew it was night, and as he moved his head from side to side he heard Allday say, 'He's awake, ma'am!'

A small lantern appeared around a screen and he saw their two figures peering down at him.

Allday whispered, 'My God, I must call Mr Angus!'

'Wait.' She stooped over the bed so that he could feel her hair touching his face. Then, 'Don't fetch him yet. You know what these surgeons are like. They understand little more than the saw or the knife.' She spat out the word. 'Butchers.'

'But *look* at him!' Allday was desperate. 'We can't leave him like this!'

Bolitho could not speak. He was very weak, and yet for the first time he could feel his right hand. His arm was too painful and stiff to move, but he could feel it. The sudden excitement of the discovery only added to his sweating fever, and he could not stop his teeth from chattering.

He heard her say quietly, 'Go to the next room, Allday.' Then more firmly, 'It is all right. I know what to do.'

The door opened and closed, and Bolitho vaguely imagined Allday crouching like a dog on the other side of it. Then he heard a swift rustle of silk, and before the lantern vanished behind the screen he saw her body very white against the shadowed wall, her hair loose across her naked shoulders. The sheet was pulled down, and with hardly a sound she slid in beside him, her breast and thigh closely pressed against his

260

body while she cradled his head into her arm. As the night passed, and between moments of deep sleep and distorted dreams, he heard her speaking softly to him, like a mother to a sick child, the sounds more reassuring than actual words. The heat of her body enfolded him like a warm cloak, driving out the chill and bringing a sense of peace to his throbbing mind.

When next he opened his eyes there were chinks of bright sunlight slanting through the shutters, and for a moment longer he thought all else had been another dream. Allday was lolling in his chair, and he saw the gleam of a yellow dress beside one of the windows where she sat in a high-backed seat.

She stood up and murmured, 'You look so much better.' Then she gave a small, secret smile, and Bolitho knew it had not been any dream. 'How do you feel?'

He felt his lips giving way to her smile. 'Hungry.'

Allday was on his feet. 'A miracle.'

Feet clattered in the stone corridor beyond the door and Keverne, followed by Calvert, entered the room. Keverne's dark features relaxed slightly as he saw Bolitho smiling.

He said, 'I came as soon as I was able, sir.'

Bolitho propped himself on his elbow. 'What happened?'

The lieutenant shrugged wearily. 'We sighted two French seventy-fours and gave chase. Darkness came down, but Sir Lucius insisted we keep after 'em,' he sounded bitter, 'and in close formation.'

'Continue.' Bolitho could see it all in his mind. The ships trying to maintain Broughton's fixed formation under full sail. The wind and noise, the frantic efforts to watch the other ships' stern lights.

Keverne said, 'Just after dawn we sighted the enemy again. The admiral ordered *Zeus* to tack independently, but because of the close formation the signal was misread. *Tanais* got into difficulties and we collided with her larboard quarter. We lost the bowsprit and brought down the topgallant for good measure. By the time we got ourselves disentangled the Frogs were out of sight, heading north with every square of canvas to the wind, damn their eyes!'

'The damage?'

'It will only take a day to repair. I've already had the topgallant replaced, and they are working on the bowsprit and jib boom now.'

Bolitho looked away. If the enemy frigate which had destroyed the bomb vessel had not discovered all about the squadron, the two seventy-fours would have no such doubts.

Keverne added, 'Sir Lucius sent his compliments and says he will see you when convenient.' He looked curiously at the woman. 'You did a fine piece of work here, if I may say so, sir. I heard about Witrand. I'm sorry.'

Calvert said, 'I had best return to the ship, sir.' He did not sound happy at the prospect.

Keverne ignored him. 'What shall we *do*, sir?' He walked to the window and peered through the slats. 'To me it all seems hopeless.'

Bolitho thought of Draffen, of his lies and deceit, and felt the blood begin to pump painfully in his shoulder.

And out there aboard his flagship Broughton was imprisoned with his own doubts and apprehensions. But his pride would not allow him to ask Bolitho or anyone else for advice, so his burden must be all the greater. Bolitho could admire him for his pride, but could not accept Broughton's unfailing rigidity.

Captain Giffard appeared panting in the doorway, his face the same colour as his tunic.

'*Restless* is rounding the headland, sir!'

Bolitho struggled up on his elbow again, shutting his mind against the pain.

'Signal her captain to report to me immediately!' He held Giffard's eyes with his own. 'To *me*, you understand?'

As Giffard bustled away he added, 'Return to the ship, Mr Keverne, and give my respects to the admiral. Tell him I will be returning aboard very soon.' He saw Allday dart a quick glance at the others. 'Very soon. Just tell him that.'

To Calvert he said quietly, 'Sir Lucius suggested that you should be employed ashore. You will remain here for the present.' He saw the relief and gratitude and added, 'Now go and watch for the sloop.'

When they were alone again he said, 'I know what you are about to say, Mrs Pareja.' He smiled gently. 'Kate.'

'Then why are you being so obstinate?' Her cheeks were suddenly flushed, and he could see the quick movement of her breasts.

'Because it is now that I am needed.' He gestured to Allday. 'I must be shaved and I'll need a clean shirt.' He made himself grin at Allday's stubborn expression. '*Now.*'

With Allday out of the room he said, 'It is strange, but I am able to think more clearly than for some time.'

'It is because you have so little blood left!' She sighed. 'But if you must, then I suppose you must. Men are made for war, and you are no exception.'

She moved to the bed and supported his shoulders until he was propped in a sitting position.

He asked slowly, 'What will become of you after this affair is done?"

'I will not return to Spain. Without Luis I am a stranger there again. Perhaps I will go to London.' She smiled gravely. 'I have my jewels. Far more than I had when I left there.' The smile became a chuckle. 'You might visit me in London, eh, Captain? When you come to receive some high and mighty appointment?'

But when he looked at her he saw the smile was hiding something deeper. Pleading? It was hard to tell.

He leaned gently against her. 'I will. Believe me.'

Allday was putting finishing touches to Bolitho's shirt and stock when Commander Samuel Poate of the *Restless* strode into the room.

He was small and pink, with the aggressive eagerness of a young pig, Bolitho thought. Now, as he stood with his hat beneath his arm, his upturned nose seemed to quiver with urgency and suppressed anger so that the similarity was even greater.

Bolitho snapped, 'Your report, Commander, and be quick with it. There is a feeling within me that we may soon be called to act.'

Poate had a clipped way of speaking, like a witness at a court-martial, wasting neither words nor time.

'After I landed Sir Hugo Draffen and the prisoner I stood out to sea to await his signal, sir. I waited but nothing happened, and when the wind fell away I had to anchor lest I be driven ashore. We heard the explosions and guessed that a further attack was being made on Djafou, although I did not know by what means. There was still no sight of Sir Hugo, and when the wind got up I beat out to sea again and patrolled along the coast.'

'Why did you allow the prisoner to be taken ashore?'

'Sir Hugo's orders, sir. I had no option. He said something about his being a hostage, but I was kept too busy to fathom his reasoning.' His eyes gleamed coldly as he added, 'But we did sight a man waving from a beach, and when I put a boat down I soon discovered him to be one of your seamen, sir. The survivor of a party sent to escort Lieutenant Calvert. He was near demented with terror, and I thought him half mad. But later he admitted to leaving the flag-lieutenant and a midshipman after an attack by tribesmen, and told of how he ran and hid for hours until he found a cave in the hillside.'

Bolitho stood up very carefully, supporting himself against Allday.

Poate said, 'From the cave he said he saw Witrand tortured and then beheaded, although I do not know how much of that is true.'

'It is fact, Commander.'

'But then he went on to say that as he hid there, watching this horror below him, he also saw Sir Hugo.' He took a deep breath. 'Any seaman trying to ingratiate himself with his officers after deserting in the face of the enemy would hardly be likely to invent such a story. He said he actually saw Draffen speaking with those who were torturing the prisoner!'

'I see.' He looked up, realizing there was more to come. 'Well?'

'I have since heard of how you were wounded and others killed aboard *Hekla* because you lacked my support, sir. But I was so enraged and sickened by what I had heard that I took my ship further along the coast where eventually, and with God's good fortune, I discovered a small dhow.'

'Draffen?' Bolitho felt his blood churning in his veins like fire.

Poate nodded. 'I have him below, sir. Under guard.'

'Bring him here.' He looked towards the sunlight and heard the wind hissing gently through the shutters. 'You have done very well. Probably better than either of us can yet realize.'

He heard Poate barking orders in the corridor and said, 'Leave me, Kate. You too, Allday.' He smiled at their concern. 'I will not start to wave my arms just yet.'

Alone, he leaned against a chairback and moved his arm cautiously within a makeshift sling.

When Draffen entered with Poate, and Calvert bringing up the rear, there was little about him to betray either alarm or uncertainty.

He said calmly, 'Perhaps you would be good enough to take

me to the admiral? I am not content at being so badly handled by these *people*.'

Calvert stammered, 'You are under arrest . . .'

Draffen turned towards him, his eyes cold with contempt. 'Be silent, puppy!'

Bolitho said flatly, 'It is useless to deny that you contrived to have Djafou reoccupied for your own future gain, Sir Hugo.' How strange that he could speak so calmly when his mind was sick with disgust. 'Whatever the outcome here, you will be made to stand trial in England.'

Draffen stared at him and then laughed. 'My God, Captain, what world do you live in?'

'Our world, Sir Hugo. I think that what we have discovered at Djafou will be more than enough to break your mask of innocence.'

Draffen spread his hands. 'Slavery is a fact, Captain, no matter what the law might proclaim publicly. Where demand exists, so too must supply. There are those in the City of London who would place more value on the head of one fit slave than a whole boatload of your sailors who have died in battle, let me assure you of that! Learn your lesson well, as I have. Law and justice are for those who can afford it!'

Poate opened his mouth to interrupt as a bright spot of blood appeared suddenly on Bolitho's clean sling. But he shook his head towards him and said, 'Then I hope that those people will support you well, Sir Hugo, for I am sure the rest of England will condemn you for what you are. A liar, a cheat and . . .' he clenched his teeth against both pain and anger, 'a creature who could stand by and watch a man tortured and then murdered. A prisoner under the King's protection!'

For the first time he saw a spark of alarm in Draffen's eyes. But he answered harshly, 'Even if it were true, Witrand had no such protection. As an army officer hiding under civilian guise he must be accepted as a spy.'

His mouth tightened as Bolitho said calmly, 'No one but the admiral and I knew that, Sir Hugo. So unless you knew him already, which I believe is so, since you made no effort to see him aboard *Euryalus*, then you must have heard him give out his identity under torture. Either way you are branded!' He could feel the blood seeping down inside his bandages but could not stop himself. 'By God, I detest the naked ritual of a hanging, but I'd give a month's bounty to see you dance at Tyburn!'

Draffen watched him warily. 'Send these others from the room.'

'No bargains, Sir Hugo. You have caused enough death and suffering.'

'Very well. Then I will speak in front of them.' He placed his hands on his hips and said in a calmer tone, 'I have, as you observed, powerful friends in London. They can make your future very hard, and put a blight on what hopes you might still have for advancement.'

Bolitho looked away. 'Is that all?'

Behind him he heard Draffen catch his breath and then reply harshly, 'You have a nephew in the Navy, I believe? Your late brother's bastard?'

Bolitho stood quite motionless, hearing Poate's feet moving on the stones and Calvert's gasp of alarm.

Draffen continued, 'How will he feel when he learns that his late father turned a blind eye to my slavers when he commanded a privateer? That he grew rich from his connivance?'

Bolitho turned towards him, his voice very calm. 'That is a lie.'

'But some will believe it, and most of all, your nephew's future will be finished, am I right?'

Bolitho blinked his eyes to clear away the mist of pain. He must not faint now. *Must* not.

'Had I some pity or regard for you at all, Sir Hugo, it would now be gone. Any man who could threaten the life of a young boy, who has had *nothing* in his upbringing but misery, deserves none.' He looked at Poate. 'Take him out.'

Draffen said quietly, 'You have accused me of many things. Whatever others may say, you shall give *me* satisfaction when you have the strength!'

'As you wish. You will find me ready enough.'

He sat down heavily as Draffen was escorted from the room.

Then she was beside him again, scolding him as she guided him back to the bed.

He said, 'I cannot write, so will you do so if I dictate? I must send my report to the admiral at once.'

She studied him curiously. 'Was that true about your brother?'

266

'Some, but not all.'

The door swung open again and Poate burst into the room. 'Sir! Lieutenant Calvert must have gone mad!'

Bolitho gripped the chair. 'What's happened?'

'He has taken Draffen to the top of the tower and locked the hatch on us. When I demanded that it be opened he said nothing.' Poate sounded incredulous.

'*Listen!*' They all looked at Allday who was leaning from a window. Above the sigh of sea and wind Bolitho heard the sudden clash of steel, and felt moved.

It did not last long. Calvert appeared in the doorway, two swords beneath his arm, his face extremely composed, even sad.

He said, 'I am placing myself under arrest, sir. Sir Hugo is dead.'

Bolitho replied quietly, 'I was the one he challenged, Calvert.'

He shook his head. 'You forget, sir. He called me *puppy* before that.' He turned away, not even seeing Poate and the others who crowded outside the door.

'Anyway, sir, you'd never match him in a duel. Not with a sword in your left hand.' He shrugged wearily. 'You are a fighter, sir, but, I suspect, not used to the more precise art of duelling.' He swung round, his eyes flashing. 'You saved me, and more than that, you gave me back my honour. I'll not stand back and see you destroyed when I can help, perhaps better than anyone else.'

Angus, the surgeon, pushed through the crowd and shouted, 'What madness is this? Cannot you see the state the captain is in?'

Bolitho eyed him coldly. 'Go to the top of the tower. You will find a body there.'

Then he said to Calvert, 'You mean well, but . . .'

Calvert shrugged. '*But*. What a great span that word can cover. I know what may become of me, but I do not care. Perhaps I did it to avenge Lelean, I am not certain of that either.' He met Bolitho's eyes with sudden determination. 'Lelean needed me, just as the squadron needs you at this moment. Maybe that is the best reason for killing Draffen.'

He unbuckled his swordbelt and handed it to Captain Giffard.

The faces at the door melted away as Broughton's voice rasped, 'Give him back his sword, Giffard!'

He strode into the room, nodding curtly to Bolitho before saying, 'Once I wronged you, Calvert. I cannot spare you the trial for your act.' He studied the lieutenant's face with obvious interest. 'But if and when we return to England, I will see to it that you are ably defended.'

Calvert looked at the floor. 'Thank you, Sir Lucius.'

Broughton turned to Bolitho. 'Now, seeing that *you* seem able and strong enough to conduct my affairs, it appears I must come to you, eh?' He glared round the room. 'Get these people out of my sight.' He relented slightly. 'Except you of course, dear lady, for I have learned that but for your, er, ministrations I would now be without my flag captain.' He smiled coolly as he ran his eye over her. 'Which would never do.'

She met his eyes unflinchingly. 'I agree, Sir Lucius. It would appear you have *great* need of him.'

Broughton frowned and then gave a small shrug. 'That was a fair match of words, ma'am.'

To Bolitho he said, 'This is what I intend.'

There was no hint of shock or anger at the manner of Draffen's death. As in the past, Broughton had already discarded him. A memory, and nothing more. Later, in England, he might find it less easy to ignore.

He said, 'It seems almost certain the French will try and drive us from here.' He paused as if expecting an argument. 'Sighting those ships and then losing them because of Rattray's stupidity over my signal makes me more inclined to accept your earlier remarks.' He nodded. 'You certainly left Gillmor a good report before you sailed on that fool errand against the pirates.' He sighed. 'Really, Bolitho, you must learn to accept that you are already out of reach of those more lighthearted events!'

'It seemed advisable to remove one threat before we took on another, sir.'

'Maybe.' He sounded cautious. 'But by now the Franco/Spanish alliance will know that the squadron which left Gibraltar is here on their porchway. Urgency to complete their plan will become even more apparent.' He nodded as if to confirm his thoughts. 'I am not waiting for *them*. I propose to take the squadron towards Cartagena. For if only half the reports are true, that is where the enemy has been concentrating his transports and war vessels. What could be more likely? A further attempt to strengthen the relationship between the two countries after their defeat at St Vincent.'

Bolitho nodded. It was obvious the admiral had given the matter a great deal of thought during the past day or so. As well he might. For to return to Gibraltar and report that Djafou had been found useless, and Draffen had been killed by one of his own officers, would be asking for certain retribution. Broughton had already incurred the Admiralty's displeasure over his part in the Spithead mutiny and the loss of the *Auriga*, and he more than anyone needed to obtain some credit, which the capture of the *Navarra* and a small brig hardly represented.

He replied, 'It is very likely, sir. It is equally possible we may meet with the enemy in open water.'

'That is what I pray for.' Broughton paced to the window, showing some signs of agitation. 'If we can bring them to grips we will have shown them that we are not merely a cat's-paw. And that others will follow us in even greater strength.'

'And if we discover nothing at Cartagena, sir, what then?'

Broughton turned and looked at him calmly. '*Then*, Bolitho, I am a ruined man.' He seemed to realize he had shown too much of a confidence and added abruptly, 'We will weigh tomorrow morning. Commander Inch will return to Gibraltar with the brig and *Navarra*. He will also carry all the garrison and other, er, people we have gathered. I have no doubt the governor there will be pleased to use them for exchange with British prisoners of war.'

'I have ordered charges to be laid in the fortress magazine, sir.'

'Good. We will fire them as we leave.' He sighed. 'So be it.'

As he made as if to depart Bolitho asked quickly, 'I am hoping you may recommend Mr Keverne for command of the brig, sir?'

The admiral turned his eyes instead on the woman. 'I am afraid not. You already have shortages, and we will need every experienced officer. I will tell Furneaux to supply a prize officer.'

He nodded to Angus as he came into the room wiping his hands.

The surgeon said, 'He was dead, sir.'

The admiral said indifferently, 'As I expected. Now, Mr Angus, Captain Bolitho will remain here until half an hour before sailing tomorrow. Make all arrangements. Then send someone to find Calvert and tell him I wish some orders to be drafted for the squadron immediately.' He smiled suddenly, so that he looked years younger.

'Do you know, Bolitho, I was once tempted to match rapiers with Calvert, just to teach him a lesson! If I had, you would now be in command here, and your head instead of mine would be on the block!' It seemed to amuse him, for he was still smiling as he strode out of the room.

Bolitho leaned back in the chair and closed his eyes, feeling the energy and tension draining from him, leaving him spent.

Half to himself he said, 'One more night.'

She touched his hair with her hand, her voice husky. 'Yes. One more night.' She hesitated. 'Together.'

17. Reunion

LIEUTENANT CHARLES KEVERNE stood by the quarterdeck rail with his arms folded while he watched the busy activity around and above him. The *Euryalus* had not re-entered the bay, but instead had anchored with her consorts off the beaked headland. Now, in the pale morning light, even the barren hills and skyline appeared less hostile, the fortress quiet and harmless.

He took a telescope from the midshipman of the watch and trained it towards the *Tanais* which was tugging at her cable in the freshening wind, her yards and decks also alive with seamen. He could see the scars on her quarter where *Euryalus*'s massive bulk had left evidence of the collision, and was thankful he had managed to complete repairs to spars and rigging before the captain's return.

Like the rest of the watching officers and seamen, he had studied Bolitho's appearance through the entry port with both relief and anxiety. The smile had been genuine, and there had been no doubting his pleasure at being back on board his own command. But the arm held stiffly in a sling, the twist of pain on his mouth as he had been assisted through the port, made Keverne wonder if Bolitho was yet fit enough for his work.

The ship had been fairly buzzing with speculation since their unhappy return after the fruitless chase, and collision with *Tanais*. Broughton's temper had matched the occasion, and for that reason too he hoped Bolitho would be able to advise his superior as well as control the teeming affairs of his own ship.

Keverne thought back over what he had done so far. The task of replacing some of the men killed and injured in the attacks on Djafou, the re-embarkation of the marines, and all the business of preparing to get under way once more. But he would have to speak with Bolitho about the officers. With Lucey and Lelean dead, and Bolitho far from fit, it left them very shorthanded when they were most needed.

Lieutenant Meheux strode aft along the larboard gangway and touched his hat.

'Anchor's hove short, sir!' He seemed cheerful enough. 'I'll not weep to quit this hole for all time!'

Partridge said, 'Flag's comin' down on th' fortress, sir.'

Keverne raised the glass again. 'So I see.' He watched the ensign as it disappeared below the ramparts and wondered how it would feel to be the last man to leave after the fuses had been lit.

He beckoned to a midshipman. 'My respects to the captain, Mr Sandoe. Inform him that the anchor is hove short and the wind has backed to the sou' west.'

Partridge watched him scurry away. 'Bit o' luck that. 'Twill save all the damn sweat to clear the 'eadland.'

Keverne tensed as a set of tan sails glided clear of the fortress. It was the brig, *Turquoise*, and in the clear morning light she looked lively and beautiful. Another chance gone. She could have been his. Momentarily he wondered if Bolitho had decided to retain him as first lieutenant merely because of his own disability. He turned his mind away just as quickly. Neither Bickford, who had been with the captain, nor even Sawle, whom he heartily disliked, had been offered the command. So it was obviously Broughton's hand which had written the order to make a mere lieutenant from *Valorous* rise like a shooting star towards the first real step of promotion.

He stamped his feet with sudden irritation. What a waste it had all been. And no doubt when they reached the enemy coast they would discover some new frustration for the admiral to complain about.

'*Navarra*'s clear, sir!'

Keverne watched the prize ship setting her topsails as she

tacked heavily below the fortress walls. Like all of the little convoy destined for Gibraltar, she was crammed with people, prisoners and civilians alike. It would be an uncomfortable passage, he decided glumly.

There was a step beside him and Bolitho said, 'It looks like a good wind.' He glanced searchingly along the upper deck. 'Make a signal to the squadron. Up anchor. Then get the ship under way, if you please. We will lay a course nor' west by north as Sir Lucius has instructed.'

Keverne shouted, 'Stand by the capstan!'

A midshipman was scribbling on his slate watched by the signal party who had already bent on the required flags.

Midshipman Tothill said, '*Hekla*'s clearing the fortress now, sir.'

Bolitho took a telescope and trained it towards the little bomb vessel. But for a cutter to retrieve the demolition party at the last possible moment, *Hekla* was the last to leave the bay. Leaving it with its relics of suffering and death, its memories of conquest and surrender. Perhaps one day someone else would try to reoccupy the place, to repair the fortress and install once more the means of slavery and oppression. But maybe by then the world would have turned once and for all against such methods, he thought.

The *Hekla*'s topsails filled to the wind as she ploughed into the first inshore troughs. Holding the telescope with one hand was not easy, and he was dismayed to discover that he was already breathless from exhaustion. But just a moment longer. He edged the glass slowly across *Hekla*'s forecastle where the seamen in their checked shirts ran in orderly confusion to complete the new tack, and then saw Inch clinging to the low rail, his thin body leaning against the steep tilt as he waved his hat in the air. It was not hard to recall him on the exposed deck as the carronades kept up their savage bombardment, or his shock and grief at seeing him fall to that unknown marksman. Now, with his mixed flotilla and chattering passengers, he was taking another turn in his life, and it was to be hoped he reached Gibraltar without meeting an enemy.

He stiffened as he saw another figure moving carefully across the deck to Inch's side. Even although the *Hekla* was now a good half-mile distant he could see her hair whipping out to the wind, the yellow dress very bright in the glare. She too was waving, her teeth white in her tanned face, and he imagined he could hear her voice once more, as he had listened to it in the night when all else was still and silent.

'Take the glass, Mr Tothill.'

Then, stiffly, he braced his legs and waved his own hat slowly back and forth. Some of the others watched him with surprise, but by the ladder Allday saw Bolitho's face and gave a grateful smile.

It had been a close-run thing. And but for her . . . he shuddered involuntarily and turned to watch as Calvert walked moodily along the gangway and leaned against the nettings. He seemed to be more inside himself than ever, and hardly spoke, even to the other officers. That was a rare pity, Allday decided, for the flag-lieutenant was unaware how he was admiringly discussed on the crowded messdecks since his return. Allday shook his head. No doubt Calvert had a rich father who would save his neck, but maybe he no longer cared. As he stared down into the lively water alongside, his face registered nothing at all.

'Ah, Calvert!' Everyone looked round as Broughton strode briskly from the poop. He raised his voice. 'Come here!'

Calvert wandered aft and touched his hat, his eyes guarded. 'Sir?'

'There is a lot I want done today.' Broughton watched idly as the *Hekla* butted her blunt bows into a lazy roller. Then he looked at Bolitho and pursed his lips into the shadow of a smile. 'So perhaps you would dine with me after we have done with the writing, eh?'

Allday saw Calvert's jaw dropping open and felt more amazed than ever. Even Broughton, it appeared, had changed towards him.

Bolitho turned, caught unaware by the admiral's voice. 'I beg your pardon, sir. I did not see you.'

Broughton nodded. 'Ah.'

'The squadron has acknowledged, sir!' Tothill was oblivious to the brief exchange. 'At the dip!'

Bolitho turned and shouted, 'Carry on, Mr Keverne!'

As the flagship's signal vanished from her yards the deck became alive to the turmoil of making sail. Bolitho gripped the rail and looked up as the topmen swarmed along the yards, and with a bang and thunder of canvas the released sails exploded to the wind.

'Anchor's aweigh, sir!' Meheux looked very small, outlined against the opposite headland as he waved his hand in the air.

With a deep surge the *Euryalus* sidled heavily above her reflection, her lower gunports awash as with her seamen heaving on the braces and the wheel hard over she came ponderously but with dignified obedience under control of wind and rudder.

Keverne was yelling through his trumpet, 'Lee braces, there! Put those laggards to work, Mr Tebbutt! *Valorous* has the edge on *you* today!'

Bolitho leaned over the stout rail and watched the anchor, streaming yellow weed from its massive flukes as it was catted home by Meheux's frantic seamen.

He shifted his gaze across the opposite side and saw *Coquette* and *Restless* already spreading their topgallants and bounding through fountains of spray as they drew rapidly away from the heavier ships.

Partridge called, 'Nor' west by north, sir!' He wiped his watering eyes as he peered up at the braced yards, the hardening quiver of the main topsail as it forced the ship over. 'Full an' bye, sir!'

Broughton snatched a glass and then said irritably, 'General signal. Maintain proper station.' He turned easily to study the *Valorous*, as with her jib flapping in momentary confusion she wallowed round to follow in her admiral's wake.

Keverne asked, 'May I set the topgallants, sir?'

Bolitho nodded. 'Make the most of the wind.'

Even as Keverne hurried back to the rail there was a low, menacing rumble. Every spare glass flashed in the sunlight as they turned to watch the distant fortress. The rumble erupted with terrible suddenness into several towering walls of flame and black smoke. They seemed endless and indestructible, hiding completely what was happening beneath.

Then as the wind pushed the smoke reluctantly across the headland Bolitho saw the ruins of the fortress. The inner tower had fallen completely like the shattered chimney of an old kiln, and the rest of the walls and ramparts were blasted into rubble. More inner explosions followed in slow succession, like a controlled broadside, and he imagined Inch's gunner, Mr Broome, lovingly placing his charges of destruction. He caught his breath as a tiny dark sliver edged out through the smoke, the boat carrying Broome and his men to a hairbreadth safety.

Giffard said, 'A lot has happened in that place, by God.'

Broughton watched the set of Bolitho's shoulders and smiled briefly. 'There is certainly no denying *that*, Captain Giffard!'

When eight bells chimed out, and the forenoon watch started to go about its affairs above and below decks, the small squadron was already seven miles from the land.

In his stern cabin Bolitho rested on the bench seat and watched the *Valorous* outlined against the fading shoreline. It was little more than a blur, a rolling bank of purple, above which the darker smoke of Djafou stained the blue sky in one great sprawling pall.

He thought of Lucey and Lelean, of Witrand and so many others who had been left there forever. Only Draffen had sailed with the squadron, his corpse carefully sealed in a cask of spirits for a more fitting burial whenever the ship might touch England again.

He leaned against the sill, his ears catching the familiar strains of rigging and shrouds, his aching shoulder positioned to avoid the slow plunge and quiver of the hull around him.

Once again he had avoided the fate of others. He touched his shoulder and winced. It would soon be time to have the dressing changed, when he would again hold his breath for fear the wound had worsened.

Then he thought of Catherine Pareja and that last night together in the tower. The simplicity and desperate need as they had lain quite still listening to the murmur of waves on the rocks below the walls. Had he not been so badly wounded would he still have behaved like that? Would he have allowed it to happen? Even as he remembered their quiet embrace, he knew the answer, and was ashamed.

Spargo, the *Euryalus*'s surgeon, proffered one of his square, hairy hands and said, 'Here, sir, take a good grip.'

Bolitho stood up from his desk and glanced at Keverne. 'He is a hard taskmaster.' He smiled to hide his anxiety. 'I fear we are not giving him enough to do.'

Then he took Spargo's hand in his own, feeling the cramp tugging at his arm as he exerted all the grip he could muster.

It had been three days since the squadron had left Djafou, and every few hours during that time Spargo had come to attend to the dressings, to probe and examine the wound until Bolitho had imagined he would never be free of its torment.

275

Spargo released his fingers. 'Not too bad, sir.' He spoke with grudging satisfaction, which Bolitho had discovered earlier to be true praise for another man's work. 'But we shall have to see.' As ever, his sheet anchor was a warning. Just in case.

Keverne relaxed slightly. 'I will leave you now, sir. That concludes the ship's affairs for today.'

Bolitho eased his arm back into the sling and walked to the windows. A good half-mile astern he watched *Valorous* taking in her royals, the seamen like black dots on her yards as they fought with the salt-hardened canvas. It was nearly noon. Three days of battling with unusually perverse winds and every eye watching the dazzling horizon for a sail. Any sail.

The squadron's position was now about forty miles south-south-west of Cartagena, and had there been an enemy of any sort in view, Broughton's ships would have been ready and well placed to intercept. As he glanced briefly across the papers on his desk which Keverne had been discussing, he heard the crisp tap of shoes overhead where Broughton paced the poop in solitary detachment, fretting over the failure to find an enemy, or to throw any light on his movements. Bolitho could pity him, for he knew there were already other pressures mounting which could not be postponed much longer.

Buddle, the purser, had been to see him this forenoon; his face gloomy as he had told of falling water supplies and several rancid casks of meat. Throughout the squadron it was the same. You could not expect this many men to be without replenishment for so long, especially as there was still no certainty of obtaining more water and provisions.

He sighed and looked at the door as it closed behind the surgeon.

'So we have Sawle promoted to fifth lieutenant to replace Lucey. That still leaves a vacancy in the wardroom.' He was thinking aloud. 'Midshipman Tothill might be able to take it, but . . .'

Keverne said shortly, 'He is only seventeen and has had little experience of gunnery. In any case, he is too useful with his signals to be spared as yet.' He grinned. 'In my opinion, sir.'

'I am afraid I agree.' He listened to the shoes pacing back and forth. 'We will have to see what we can do.'

Keverne gathered up the papers and asked, 'What are our chances of finding the enemy, sir?'

He shrugged. 'In all truth, I do not know.' He wanted Keverne to leave so that he could try to exercise his arm and shoulder. '*Coquette* and *Restless* should be cruising off Cartagena by now. Maybe they will return soon with new intelligence.'

There was a rap on the door and Midshipman Ashton stepped into the cabin. He no longer wore a bandage around his head and seemed to have recovered from his rough handling better than anyone had expected.

'Sir. Mr Weigall's respects, and a sail has been sighted to the nor' east.'

Bolitho looked at Keverne and smiled. 'Sooner than I thought. I will go on deck.'

On the quarterdeck it was blazing hot, and although the sails were drawing well to a steady north-westerly, there was little freshness to ease the demands of watchkeeping.

Weigall was watching the poop, as if afraid he would not hear Bolitho's approach.

'Masthead reports that she looks like a frigate, sir.'

To confirm his words the voice pealed down again, 'Deck there! She's *Coquette*!'

Broughton came down from the poop with unusual haste. 'Well?'

Ashton was already swarming into the shrouds with a big telescope, and Bolitho said quietly, 'What would we do without frigates?'

Minutes ticked past, and by the compass a ship's boy upended the half-hour glass under Partridge's watchful eye.

Then Ashton yelled, 'From *Coquette*, sir!' The merest pause. '*Negative*.'

Broughton swung away, his voice harsh, 'Nothing there. The ships have sailed.' He turned to Bolitho, his eyes squinting against the glare. 'We must have missed them! God, we'll not see them again!'

Bolitho watched the frigate swinging round on her new tack, the big black and white flag still streaming from her yard. One flag, yet to Broughton and perhaps many more it meant so much. The enemy ships had quit the harbour and by now could be almost anywhere. While the squadron had floundered around Djafou, and had exhausted their resources in the fruitless business of capture and demolition, the enemy had vanished.

Broughton murmured in a tired voice, 'Damn them all to hell!'

Bolitho looked up sharply as the masthead lookout shouted, '*Valorous* is signalling, sir!'

The admiral said bitterly, 'Furneaux will be dreaming of his own future already!'

They all turned as Tothill shouted, 'From *Valorous*, sir! Strange sail bearing west!'

'Must be almost astern of us, sir.' Bolitho looked at Keverne. 'Inform the squadron.'

Broughton was almost beside himself with impatience. 'She'll put about the moment she sights us!' He peered towards *Coquette*. 'But it's useless to send Gillmor. He'd never be able to beat into the wind in time to engage her.'

Bolitho felt his arm throbbing, perhaps from his own excitement. The stranger could be another lone merchantman, or an enemy scout. She might even be the van of some great force of ships. He dismissed the latter idea. If the newcomer was part of the force from Cartagena he was well out of station, and the enemy would have no wish to waste any time if they were after Broughton.

He took a telescope and climbed swiftly on to the poop. It was getting less painful to manage the glass with one hand, and as he trained it past *Valorous* he saw a small square of sail, seemingly resting on the horizon line.

But far above the deck Ashton with his powerful telescope already had a much better view.

'Two-decker, sir!' His voice was shrill against the sounds of rigging and canvas. 'Still closing!'

Bolitho hurried back to the quarterdeck. 'It would be better if we shorten sail, sir. At least we will know for sure then.'

Broughton nodded. 'Very well. Make the signal.'

Time dragged by, with the hands going for their midday meal, and the air becoming heavy with the odour of rum. There was, after all, no point in disrupting the daily routine when there was plenty of time to decide on a course of action.

The other ship was coming up very fast, especially for a two-decker. It was easy to see her great spread of canvas as she plunged in pursuit. Her captain had even set her studding sails, so that the hull seemed weighed down by the towering pyramid of hard-bellied canvas.

Ashton yelled excitedly, 'She's signalling, sir!'

'For God's sake!' Broughton was gnawing at his lip as he stared up at the midshipman on the crosstrees.

Tothill had swarmed aloft to join Ashton, and together they were already peering at their signal book, seemingly indifferent to the deck so far below their dangling legs.

Bolitho said, 'A friend, sir. A reinforcement perhaps. But at least we might glean some news.'

He stared up at the masthead, unable to believe his ears as Tothill yelled, 'She's *Impulsive*, sir, sixty-four! Cap'n Herrick!'

Broughton turned sharply and looked at Bolitho. 'Know him?'

He did not know how to answer. Thomas Herrick. How often he had thought of him and Adam, had wondered at their destinations and experiences. Now he was here. *Here.*

He replied, 'For years, sir. He was my first lieutenant. He is my friend also.'

Broughton eyed him warily and then snapped, 'Signal the squadron to heave to. Make to *Impulsive*. Captain, repair on board.' He watched the flags breaking into the wind and added, 'I hope he'll be of some use.'

Bolitho smiled and said simply, 'Without him, sir, this ship would still be under French colours.'

The admiral grunted. 'Well, we shall see. I will be aft when he comes aboard.'

Keverne waited until Broughton had gone and then asked, 'Did he really help take this ship, sir? In a small fourth-rate like that?'

Bolitho eyed him pensively. 'My own ship was almost done for. Captain Herrick in his little sixty-four, which is a good deal older than you are, came to grips without hesitation.' He waved his hand across the busy quarterdeck. 'Just there it was, by Mr Partridge. The French admiral surrendered.'

Keverne smiled. 'I never knew.' He stared at the orderly deck as if expecting to see some sign of the bloody battle which had swayed back and forth across it.

Tothill slid down a backstay shouting, 'All acknowledgements hoisted, sir! Close up!'

Bolitho looked at Keverne. 'Execute. And have the side manned to receive our guest.'

Bolitho guided his friend below the poop, out of the glare and the din of flapping canvas, and then faced him by the companionway.

'Oh, Thomas, it is *good* to see you!'

Herrick's face, which had been tight with concern at seeing Bolitho's wounded arm, split into a wide grin.

'I don't have to say how I felt when I heard my orders to join your squadron.'

Bolitho steadied himself against the sickening motion as *Euryalus* floundered in a beam sea and studied him eagerly. Rounder in the face, with a few grey hairs showing beneath his gold-laced hat, but still the same. The same eyes, of the brightest blue Bolitho had ever seen.

'Tell me about Adam. Is he with you?'

'Aye.' Herrick looked at the marines below the ladder which led to Broughton's quarters. 'Burning himself to ashes in eagerness to see you again.'

Bolitho smiled. 'After you have spoken with Sir Lucius we will talk.'

Herrick gripped his good arm. 'We will that!'

As he stood aside to allow Herrick on to the ladder he saw the twin gold epaulettes on his shoulders. A post-captain now. In spite of everything, Herrick, like himself, had endured.

Broughton half rose from his desk as they entered the spacious cabin. 'You have despatches for me, Captain?' He was very formal. 'I was not expecting another ship.'

Herrick laid a sealed envelope on the desk. 'From Sir John Jervis, sir.' He grimaced. 'I beg pardon, I meant Lord St Vincent, as he is now titled.'

Broughton tossed the envelope to Calvert who was hovering nearby and snapped, 'Tell me the news. What of the damned mutiny?'

Herrick watched him guardedly. 'There was some bloodshed, and more than a few tears, but after their lordships made certain concessions the people agreed to return to duty.'

'*Agreed?*' Broughton glared at him. 'Is that all that happened?'

Herrick looked past him, his eyes suddenly sad. 'They hanged the ringleaders, sir, but not before some of the officers were removed from the ships as unsuitable to hold authority.'

Broughton stood up violently. 'How did you hear all this?'

'My ship was in the mutiny at the Nore, sir.'

The admiral stared at him as if he had misheard. '*Your* ship? Do you mean you just stood by and let them seize her from you?'

Herrick replied evenly, 'There was no choice, sir.' Bolitho

saw a gleam of the same old stubbornness in his eyes as he continued, 'Anyway, I agreed with most of their demands. I was allowed to remain aboard because they knew I understood, like many other captains.'

Bolitho interrupted swiftly, 'That is interesting, Captain Herrick.' He hoped Herrick would feel the warning in his voice. 'Sir Lucius too had much the same experience at Spithead.' He smiled at Broughton. 'Is that not so, sir?'

Broughton opened his mouth and then said, 'Ah. Up to a point.'

Herrick stepped forward. 'But, sir, I have not yet told you my own news.' He glanced at Bolitho. 'I met with St Vincent at Cadiz and was ordered to find your squadron. He requires the bomb vessels for an attack on Teneriffe, I believe. Rear-Admiral Nelson is to lead it.'

Broughton commented harshly, '*Rear-Admiral* now, is he?'

Herrick hid a smile. 'But two days back we sighted a strange sail off Malaga. I laid my ship between it and the shore and gave chase. It was a frigate, sir, and although my sixty-four is fast, she's no match for that. But I kept up the pursuit, and only lost her this very morning. I imagined it was her when I sighted your rearmost ship.'

Broughton said dryly, '*Very* exciting. Well, you lost her, so where's the cause for glee?'

Herrick watched him calmly. 'I heard of what happened, sir. I'd know that ship anywhere. She was *Auriga.*'

Bolitho said, 'Are you certain, Thomas?'

He nodded firmly. 'No doubt about it. Served with her for some months. *Auriga*, quite certain.'

Calvert laid the opened despatches on the desk but Broughton swept them aside as he groped for his chart.

'Here! Show me, Herrick. Mark it on the chart!'

Herrick glanced enquiringly at Bolitho and then stooped over the desk.

'She was heading almost due east, sir.'

'And you nearly overhauled her? In a two-decker?' Broughton sounded desperate.

'Aye, sir. *Impulsive* may be old, and her hull is so ripe that I fear it would fall apart but for the copper, but she's the fastest ship in the fleet.' There was real pride in his voice. '*Auriga* might have gone into Cartagena, sir. In which case . . .'

Broughton shook his head. 'Never. My patrols would have

seen and engaged her.' He rubbed his chin vigorously. 'Due east, you say? By heaven, we might still run her to earth!' He looked at Herrick. 'And by God I'd not have hung a few miserable mutineers! I would have hanged the lot of them!'

Herrick said respectfully, 'I can well believe it, Sir Lucius.'

Broughton did not seem to hear. 'Signal Gillmor to give chase at once. He can do anything he likes to hold or delay *Auriga. Restless* can maintain watch to the windward of us.' He glanced at Herrick. 'You will close to visual distance with *Restless*,' he gave a short smile, 'as your ship is so swift, and relay my instructions to her without delay.' He nodded curtly. 'Carry on.'

Outside the cabin Herrick asked, 'Is he always like that?'

'Usually.' Bolitho paused by the quarterdeck ladder. 'Is Adam doing well? I mean, could you . . .'

Herrick grinned. 'He is ready to sit his exam for lieutenant, if that is what you mean.' He watched Bolitho and then added, 'Shall I send him across to you?'

'Thank you. I am short of officers.' He smiled, unable to hide his eagerness. 'I would appreciate it.'

Herrick touched his arm. 'I have taught him all I know.'

'Then he will be ready.'

Herrick's grin was huge. 'I had a good teacher, remember?'

Almost before Herrick's boat had cast off from the chains the *Euryalus*'s yards were alive with flags. *Coquette* went about with the ease of a thoroughbred, as if a string had been severed to free her from the other ships, and as the seamen poured up from the gangways Bolitho felt as if he was being given a new strength.

Partridge muttered, 'Cap'n seems 'appy 'bout somethin'!'

Keverne nodded. 'So it would appear.' Then he snatched his speaking trumpet and hurried towards the rail.

18. The Trap

ALLDAY opened the cabin door and announced, 'Mr Midshipman Pascoe, Captain!' In spite of the attempted formality his face was breaking into a great grin of pleasure.

It was late evening, and but for a brief encounter when the boy had clambered hurriedly from the boat, he had not been able to speak with him. It had been a strange meeting. He had seen Pascoe's face changing from excitement to caution, a sort of reserved shyness, as he had removed his hat and said, 'Coming aboard to join, sir.'

Bolitho had been equally formal, aware of Keverne and the others nearby watching the unexpected reunion.

He had said awkwardly, 'Mr Keverne will give you your duties. You are to take the position of acting sixth lieutenant. I am sure Mr Keverne will be able to equip you with the necessary clothing and anything else you might need . . .' He had broken off as a battered midshipman's chest had been hauled unceremoniously from the boat alongside. It was then that he had fully realized the importance of that moment.

Pascoe had said quietly, 'I thought you might wish me to transfer to your ship, sir.' He had paused. 'I *hoped*. So I was ready . . .'

Now, as Allday closed the door to leave them together for the first time, he felt the warmth flooding through him, yet was aware of the change which had grown between them.

'Here, Adam, sit down by me.' He gestured to the table which Trute had laid with unusual care. 'The food is not too exciting, but doubtless no worse than you've been accustomed to.'

He fumbled with a decanter, aware the whole time of the boy's eyes watching him. How he had changed. He was taller and looked more confident, more sure of himself. And yet, there was the same dark restlessness, like that of a young colt, which he had remembered since their parting two years ago.

The boy took the glass and said simply, 'I have been waiting for this moment.' Then he smiled, and Bolitho was again reminded of those other faces in the portraits at Falmouth. 'When Captain Herrick told me you were wounded . . .'

Bolitho raised his glass. 'Let us forget about that. How have you been?' He ushered him to the table, vaguely conscious as always of the deck's steady vibration and the regular rolls of the hull as the ship plunged in pursuit of *Coquette* in accordance with Broughton's orders.

He pulled a steaming dish of beef towards him. It was recently from the cask and was probably already going bad. But in the warm lantern light, and served as it was on the best cabin pewter, it looked almost luxurious. He hesitated, suddenly confused by his inability to use the knife. The realization both angered and embarrassed him. This was to have been a perfect moment, spared of duties on deck, and for once almost free of pain.

Pascoe reached across the table and took the knife from his hand. For a moment their eyes met and then he said softly, 'Let me, Uncle.' He smiled again. 'Captain Herrick has trained me to do all manner of things.'

Bolitho watched him as he bent over the plate, the hair, as black as his own, falling rebelliously over his eyes as he sawed busily through the tough meat.

'Thank you, Adam.' He smiled to himself. Seventeen. It was so easy to remember what it had been like as a young midshipman. And Adam was actually enjoying himself. There was neither pity nor deception in his voice as he chatted excitedly about the *Impulsive*'s part in the mutiny, of Herrick and all the dozens of things which had changed him from a young boy to a confident replica of his father, and himself.

Bolitho had difficulty in eating the meat even after it had been cut into small pieces for him. But Adam had no such qualms and helped himself again and again from the platter.

Bolitho asked, 'How can you keep stuffing yourself and be as thin as a stick?'

Adam eyed him gravely. 'A midshipman's lot is a hard one.'

They both laughed and Bolitho said, 'Well, maybe your days in the gunroom are numbered. Once an examination can be arranged, I see no reason why you should not sit for lieutenant.'

The boy dropped his eyes. 'I will try not to betray that trust.'

Bolitho watched him for several seconds. This boy could never betray anyone. He was the one who had been wronged. Again he had the pressing feeling that he wanted to do something about it and without more delay. The wound in his shoulder was a warning. The next time might be final.

He said clumsily, 'There is a lawyer in Falmouth named Quince.' He hesitated, trying to make his voice sound matter-of-fact. 'When we return home I would like you to come with me and see him.'

Pascoe pushed the plate away and wiped his mouth. 'Why, Uncle?'

Why? How could so great a question be crammed into one tiny word?

284

He stood up and walked along the swaying deck towards the windows. Below he could see the frothing wake gleaming like snow in the light of a stern lantern and imagined he could see *Valorous* following at a discreet distance through the darkness. In the thick glass he saw Pascoe's reflection as he sat at the table, his chin in his hands. Like a child for these moments of privacy and value which might soon pass.

He said, 'I want to be sure that you have the house and property when I am dead, Adam.' He heard the boy gasp and cursed himself for the crudity of his words. 'I know that with luck I will be bothering you for years to come.' He turned and smiled at him. 'However, I want to be *certain* about this thing!'

Pascoe made to rise but Bolitho crossed to the table and laid one hand on his shoulder.

'It would have been yours one day had life been kinder. I intend to see that right is not ignored by others.' He hurried on, unable to stop himself. 'You do not bear our family name, but you are as much a part of it and of me as would otherwise be possible.' He squeezed his shoulder, seeing the boy wipe his eyes with his hand. 'Now away with you to your watch. I'll not have my officers saying behind my back that I show favour to some upstart nephew!'

Pascoe stood up very slowly and then said quietly, 'Captain Herrick was right about you.' He walked from the table, his face hidden until he turned again by the door. 'He said you were the finest man he ever met. He also said . . .' But he could not finish it and almost ran from the cabin.

Bolitho walked to the stern windows and stared unseeingly at the leaping spray. He felt at peace for the first time since . . . he could not remember when that had been. Perhaps at last he would be able to help the boy. To right some of the wrong which had been done to him. At least he had been spared meeting with Draffen. To hear his hints about Hugh's implication with slavery would turn the knife in his heart yet again and might damage him to an extent beyond repair.

There was a tap at the door. It was Ashton. 'Mr Meheux's respects, sir.' His eyes wandered to the greasy plates. 'He would like to take in another reef. The wind is rising from the nor' west.'

Bolitho nodded and picked up his hat. The moment of peace was to be laid aside again.

'I will go up directly.' He walked to the door adding, 'When I return, I will not think it amiss if the rest of that meat has vanished.' He smiled as he closed the door behind him. It was the same frugal food as was served to the ship's company. But seated in the undreamed-of splendour of his captain's cabin, Ashton would think it a banquet, although what Trute would say was hard to imagine.

The morning watch still had an hour to run when Bolitho strode on to the quarterdeck. Although he had been up and about several times during the night, he felt remarkably fresh, and his shoulder was sore rather than painful. He paused to peer at the swinging compass card. North-east, as it had remained since his last inspection before dawn.

The sky was very clear, with a washed-out look, and in a fresh north-westerly wind the sea stretched in an endless display of small white-horses from horizon to horizon.

As he had sat toying with his breakfast and lingering over his last supply of good coffee he had waited for the call from a lookout or the scamper of feet as someone came to bring a message that *Coquette* had been sighted. But as daylight strengthened and the deck above his head had echoed to the sluice of water and swabs, with all the usual chatter between the seamen, he had known there was no ship to see.

Now, as he walked towards the quarterdeck rail, his face impassive to shield his sudden uncertainty, he knew too that he must dissuade Broughton from continuing the chase.

For over seventeen hours since Broughton had sent *Coquette* in hot pursuit of the captured frigate the squadron had pressed on with every sail set to maximum advantage. During the night when they had altered course to this present tack there had been several breath-stopping moments as *Valorous* had surged out of the gloom like a phantom ship bent on smashing into *Euryalus*'s stern.

He had examined his chart while he had finished the coffee in the private world beyond his cabin bulkhead. They were now some sixty miles due south of Ibiza and still pushing further and further into the Mediterranean. Ironically, Broughton's determination to recapture the *Auriga* had taken them back across the same waters as before, and the ships were now less than eighty miles north by east from Djafou.

Keverne gauged it was time to speak. 'Good morning, sir.'

Bolitho looked past him and saw the *Impulsive*'s bulging top-gallants far out on the lee quarter, pale yellow in the sunlight. Broughton had decreed that she should play a lone role on the squadron's flank. She was faster than the others, and without a frigate at his disposal, and only the *Restless* away on the horizon, Broughton had little choice in his deployment.

He said, 'Signal *Tanais* to make more sail, if you please. She is out of station again.'

Keverne frowned and touched his hat. 'Aye, aye, sir.'

Bolitho walked to the weather side and commenced his morning pacing. *Tanais* was a little to leeward of the line, but hardly sufficient to warrant a signal under their peculiar circumstances. Every ship was doing her best, and the squadron had logged an almost regular seven knots since the last alteration of course. Keverne was probably thinking he had mentioned it merely to remind him of the earlier collision with the two-decker. Imagined perhaps that Bolitho was making an offhand criticism.

His feet moved faster in time with his thoughts. Keverne could think what he liked. There was more than his comfort at stake this morning. On the face of it Broughton's insistence was fair enough. *Coquette* and *Restless* had been off the Spanish coast when the captured frigate had somehow passed between the separated groups of vessels. It was equally possible that *Auriga* could not regain the Spanish coast without losing her lead and exposing herself to a clash with the pursuers. The prevailing north-west wind, which was so favourable to Broughton's ships, would soon make short work of *Auriga*'s advantage. He frowned. It was getting him nowhere. Anyway, that was yesterday, when there had still been some real hope of a capture. But *Auriga*'s captain may have had no intention of turning towards Spain or France. Majorca or Port Mahon, further east even to some secret mission all of her own, she might be heading on and on with all the speed her sails could muster.

Perhaps if he had not been so concerned with his own personal affairs, his pleasure at seeing the boy again, he might have confronted Broughton earlier. He frowned angrily. Always the *perhaps* and the *maybe*.

'Good morning, sir.'

He halted and saw Pascoe watching him from the top of the starboard gangway.

Bolitho relaxed slightly. 'How are you settling in?'

The boy nodded. 'I have been all over the ship, sir.' He looked suddenly grave. 'It is hard to realize that it was here where the French surrendered.' He walked a few paces aft and stared at the damp planking. 'I was thinking of Mr Selby, the master's mate, who died to save me. I often think about him.'

Bolitho clenched his hand behind him. Would it never end? Always Hugh seemed to be at his shoulder, making mock of his efforts to forget. What would Adam say now, this second, if he knew Selby had been his own father? Perhaps their blood had been so strong that even the deception had been only temporary.

He knew too that the boy's words had made him realize something else. He was jealous. Jealous because he still remembered a father he had not knowingly seen, and because it was something which could not be shared. Suppose he did discover the truth about Hugh and learn that his identity even at the moment of death had been denied him? At the time it had been vital for his own safety, as it was now for the boy's future. But would those things seem important to him if he found the truth?

He realized Adam was studying him anxiously. 'Is something wrong, sir? Your shoulder?'

Bolitho shook his head. 'I am bad company today.' He smiled. 'I am glad you still remember Mr Selby.' A lie, or was he being genuine? 'I often find it hard to accept that this is the same ship which cost us so dearly to win.'

Pascoe said quickly, 'The admiral is coming, sir.' He walked away as Broughton crossed the deck and gazed bleakly at the horizon.

Bolitho made his customary report and then said, 'I think we should put about, sir.' There seemed to be no reaction. 'Maybe Gillmor will call her to give battle, but I think *we* have little to gain by continuing.'

Broughton's eyes swivelled towards him. '*Do* you?'

'Yes, sir. *Coquette* should be able to take the enemy well enough, for all the French company will be new to their ship. Gillmor has already proved himself very capable in ship-to-ship actions.'

'We will continue.' Broughton's jaw tightened. '*Auriga* may try and retrace her course soon, and *I want her*!'

Bolitho said quietly, 'It is like taking a hammer to crack an egg, sir.'

Broughton swung on him violently, his face suddenly livid. 'My new orders state that unless I have secured a base to my satisfaction I am to return to the fleet off Cadiz! Do you know what will be said?' He raised his voice. 'Do you?' He did not wait for a reply. 'It will be put to me that I failed to complete any part of my mission. That I lost contact with the enemy because I allowed *Auriga* to be taken. *My* fault, *my* damned ruin, it is as simple as that!' He saw Meheux watching from the opposite side of the deck and barked, 'Tell that officer to find himself some work, or I'll make him sorry he was born!'

Bolitho said evenly, '*Impulsive*'s first report of sighting the frigate . . .'

The admiral interrupted, '*Impulsive*? In God's name how do we even know she tried to catch that bloody ship? She was in the Nore mutiny, her captain seems almost proud of the experience, so is it not likely his company hindered the chase? Maybe they saw *Auriga* as a symbol of their own damn treachery at the Nore!'

'That is unfair, sir!'

'Unfair, is it?' Broughton's reserve had completely gone and he was oblivious to the seamen working at the guns near by, their faces screwed tight with expectancy. 'I'll tell you what I think.' He stuck out his chin, his face barely inches from Bolitho's. 'I believe that you have not learned even the first thing about senior command. I know you are popular! Oh yes, I've seen the way people like you.' He stared suddenly across the nettings, his eyes empty. 'Do you imagine that I never wanted to be admired as well as obeyed? By God, if you ever attain flag rank you will learn there is no middle road to follow!'

Bolitho watched him in silence. He was still angry at Broughton's slanderous attack on Herrick, but at the same time he could guess the full extent of his disappointment and despair. *Auriga* was indeed a symbol, but not as described by Broughton. To the admiral she represented the very beginning of his misfortune, almost from the moment he had hoisted his flag at the foremast.

He said, 'I believe that Captain Herrick's discovery of the *Auriga* was a pure accident, sir. Just as his arrival here was totally unexpected, so too the enemy would have been surprised.'

Broughton tore his mind from some inner thought. '*So?*'

'Our departure from Gibraltar was seen, and we have been sighted by other enemy ships, and some which we might not even have known were there.' He persisted, seeing the returning hostility in Broughton's eyes. 'After all, sir, why *should Auriga* come here?'

'I have no more idea of that than you, Bolitho.' His voice was icy. 'But I am going to find and take her. When we return to the fleet it will be as a complete squadron. One which will be ready to re-enter the Mediterranean and act with the full authority at *my* disposal!'

He made as if to walk away and then added, 'Inform me the moment you sight *Coquette*!' Then he strode beneath the poop.

Bolitho walked to the rail and stood looking down at the sailmaker and his mates squatting on every square foot of deck, needles flashing while they carried out their endless repairs to some of the canvas. Everywhere around and above him there were men at work. Splicing and greasing, reeving new lines or merely putting a touch of paint where it was most needed. A squad of marines was climbing heavily to the foretop to do their drill at a swivel gun, and on the larboard gangway he saw Pascoe in close conversation with Meheux.

All this was what Broughton had *failed* to see. He saw all these men as some sort of threat, or a form of weakness which might imperil his own set plans. Yet here was the true strength without which any ship was just timber and cordage. Broughton spoke often enough of loyalty, but he had failed to realize that it was merely another word for trust. And trust was two-sided, not the personal possession of one man.

He looked up sharply as Tothill called, 'Gunfire, sir!'

Bolitho pressed his hand on the rail and leaned forward, straining his ears above the constant shipboard sounds. There it was, very faint, like surf booming in a deep cave. But it would be faint, with the wind so strong across the larboard quarter.

Trute, who was carrying a tray of empty mugs, was almost knocked from his feet as Broughton burst from beneath the poop, his face contorted with sudden agitation. He was hatless, and still carrying a pen in his hand like a baton.

'Did you hear that?' He peered round at the swaying figures of the watchkeepers. 'Well, *did* you?' He crossed to Bolitho's side, his eyes slitted in the sunlight. 'What price your damn caution now?'

Bolitho watched him impassively. He was more relieved than angered by Broughton's tirade. With luck, Gillmor could disable the *Auriga* or even take her completely within the hour, and then this escapade would be over.

He said to Keverne, 'Tell the masthead to report the instant he sights them.'

Tothill said, 'Sir, *Impulsive* is signalling.'

Broughton glared at him. 'I suppose your *friend* Herrick will expect all the credit for it!'

Bolitho took a glass and levelled it towards the distant two-decker. She had turned slightly, and he could see her leaning heavily to the wind, her masthead pendant as straight as a pike.

Tothill scrambled into the shrouds, his large telescope swaying about like an unruly cannon. His lips moved soundlessly, and when he looked down at the quarterdeck his face seemed very pale.

'*Impulsive* to *Flag*, sir. Strange sail bearing west by north.'

'Acknowledge!'

Bolitho turned to the admiral who was still bending his head to catch the far-off sounds of gunfire.

He said, 'Did you hear that, sir?'

Broughton stared at him. 'Of course I did! I'm not bloody deaf!'

The masthead lookout's voice made him start. 'Deck there! Sail fine on the larboard bow, sir! I kin see flashes!'

Broughton rubbed his hands. 'We'll have *Auriga* to heel any minute now!'

'I think we should detach *Impulsive* to investigate the other sighting, sir.' It was like speaking to a deaf man. It was obvious Broughton could think of nothing but the two frigates fighting it out on the sea's edge.

Tothill again. 'From *Impulsive*, sir. Estimate four strange sail.'

For the first time Broughton seemed to tear himself away from his anxiety over the *Auriga*.

'*Four?* Where the hell are they coming from?'

Impulsive had shortened sail and was growing smaller as she fell astern of the squadron's line. Bolitho bit his lip hard and was thankful for Herrick's initiative. To proceed like this was

291

sheer madness. The newcomers, and they could only be hostile, were coming down towards the squadron's flank with full advantage of the wind. If Herrick could ascertain exactly what they were about, there might still be time to put Broughton's ships into some sort of order.

Keverne said, 'Gunfire seems to have stopped, sir.'

'Good.' Broughton was frowning. 'Now we shall see.'

Captain Giffard remarked, 'Pity *Coquette* is so far ahead. We could use her now to spy out the land, eh, sir?' Bolitho saw the marine recoil as Broughton snapped, 'What did you say?'

Before he could repeat it Bolitho swung on Broughton, his eyes suddenly angry. 'Damn them, they *must* have known! I daresay that Brice told what he knew when he was taken, and the rest they guessed.' He knew Broughton was staring at him as if he had gone mad, but continued bitterly, 'They sent *Auriga* to us, knowing what you would do!' He gestured with his good arm across the nettings. 'And you *did* it, sir!'

'What in hell's name are you babbling about, man?'

Bolitho said flatly, '*Auriga* was the bait. One which you were unable to ignore because of your own outraged dignity!'

Broughton flushed. 'How *dare* you speak like that? I'll have you put under arrest, I'll . . .'

Tothill's voice was hushed. '*Impulsive* to *Flag*, sir. Strange fleet bearing west by north.'

Bolitho walked slowly to the rail. 'Not ships, Sir Lucius, but a fleet.' He turned and looked at him, suddenly very calm. 'And now these men whom you despise and have accused of every vice from mutiny to sloth will have to fight and die.' He let the words sink deeply. 'For *you*, sir.'

Tothill said shakily, '*Impulsive* requests instructions, sir.'

Broughton stared at the pen which he was still gripping in his hand. In a strange tone he murmured, 'It was a trap.'

Bolitho kept his eyes on Broughton's face. 'Yes. Colonel Alava was right after all. And the French motives towards Egypt and Africa are every bit as true as he described.' He jerked his head towards the cruising patterns of white-horses. 'This battle is important to the enemy. So important because they know that this one crushing victory, the complete failure on our part to return our presence in the Mediterranean, will be more than enough to pave their way to success.'

Tothill seemed almost fearful to intrude. 'From *Impulsive*, sir. Estimate *ten* sail of the line.'

Broughton appeared unable to move or react.

Eventually he said thickly, 'And fight them we will.' But there was no conviction in his voice.

Bolitho pushed the pity from his mind. 'We have no choice in that, sir. They have the advantage, and if we run, can hunt us at leisure until they pin us against the land like moths.' He added bitterly, 'No doubt there are other ships already sailing from Toulon or Marseilles to ensure the trap is not short of teeth!'

The admiral took a grip on himself. It was almost a physical thing to watch as he screwed up his eyes and spoke in short, staccato sentences.

'Make a general signal. We will put the squadron about and approach the enemy on an opposite tack. Ship to ship we can . . .' He saw Bolitho's expression and said desperately, 'For God's sake, it will be two against one!'

Bolitho turned away, unable to watch Broughton's apparent helplessness.

'Deck there! Sail in sight to wind'rd!'

Bolitho nodded. So they were already visible, and coming in fast for the kill.

Ten ships-of-the-line. He gripped his hand against his side, willing himself to think instead of allowing his mind to grow numb before such odds. Two to one, Broughton had said, but *Impulsive* was not much more than a large frigate. Old too, her hull rotten from rough usage over the years. He smiled sadly. *Ripe*, as Herrick had described it.

He swung round, his mind suddenly steady again.

'With your permission, sir, I believe we should re-form in two divisions.' He spoke fast, seeing the plan of battle like counters on a map. 'The French have a liking for fighting in a set line of battle. Too much time in port has left them little scope to exercise much else.' Like you, he thought, as he watched Broughton's uncertainty. 'We can take the weather division, with just *Impulsive* astern of us. Rattray can lead the lee division with the same order as before. If we can break the enemy's line in two places we might still give a good account of ourselves.' Broughton was still wavering, so he added harshly, 'But ship to ship and line to line you will witness your squadron dismasted within one half-hour of close action!'

Lieutenant Bickford said quietly, 'I can see *Auriga*, sir.' He lowered a big signal telescope. 'She has struck to *Coquette*.'

It was like a final taunt at Broughton's unbending determination to recover her.

Broughton looked at Bolitho and said, 'I am going below for a moment. You have my authority to put your plan to the test.' He seemed about to add a rider but said savagely, 'I wish Draffen was up here to see for himself what his deceit has cost us.'

Bolitho watched him go and then beckoned to Keverne and Tothill. 'General signal. Squadron will tack in succession and steer due west.'

Keverne hurried to the rail yelling at the watching seamen.

As pipes shrilled and the men ran to their stations Bolitho watched the signal flags soaring aloft, the colours very bright against the pale sky.

As one acknowledgement after another was reported he said, 'Another general, Mr Tothill. Prepare for battle.' He made himself smile at the midshipman's intent expression. 'Yes, it seems we will fight this fine morning, so keep a good eye on your people.'

Order had settled over the decks as petty officers checked their watch-bills, and Partridge stood close to the helmsmen in readiness to follow the *Tanais* round and across the wind.

Tothill called, 'Acknowledgements close up, sir!'

They were ready. '*Execute!*'

As Keverne waited, balanced on his toes to watch first *Zeus* and then *Tanais* labouring round with all their sails in confusion, Bolitho said to him, 'Lay her on the starboard tack while I prepare instructions for the other captains.'

'And then, sir?' Keverne kept his eyes on *Tanais*.

'You may beat to quarters and clear for action.' He smiled. 'And this time you will do it in *eight* minutes!'

Keverne yelled, 'Stand by on the quarterdeck! Man the braces there!'

'Ready aft, sir!'

Bolitho turned at the sound of that voice and saw Pascoe standing by the afterguard at the mizzen braces, his hat pulled over his unruly hair as he squinted into the bright sunlight.

For an instant their eyes met, and Bolitho made to lift his hand to him. But the sudden stab of pain reminded him of his wound and he saw the dismay on the boy's face, as if he too was sharing it with him.

'Helm a'lee! Let go and haul!'

Figures darted in every direction, and groaning under the thrust of wind and tiller the *Euryalus* began to turn, until like a giant tusk her jib boom pointed once again at an enemy.

19. A Ship of War

ALTER COURSE a point to larboard, Mr Partridge.'

Bolitho walked to the lee side to watch the *Zeus* which was almost directly abeam at the head of the other seventy-fours. It had taken less than an hour to put the squadron about and for individual captains to form up in their present divisions, and he was grateful they had had sufficient time for getting to know each other's ways.

'West by south, sir!' Partridge sounded grim.

'Steady as you go.'

Bolitho walked forward to the quarterdeck rail and ran his eye along his command. How much more space and vision to see and think now that *Euryalus* was in the van. With her great courses clewed up and topsails braced round to hold her on a steady starboard tack he could see the enemy like some painted panorama of battle. The ten ships were sailing in an almost perfect line, their approach diagonal to that of the British squadron. To an untrained eye it would appear as if the way ahead was completely sealed by this great line of ships, and even to the experienced onlooker the sight was enough to chill the imagination.

He made himself walk a few paces athwart the silent quarterdeck, darting an occasional glance towards *Zeus* to ensure she was still keeping on station to leeward. Astern of her, *Tanais* and *Valorous* followed at regular intervals, their double lines of guns glinting in the hard sunlight like rows of black teeth.

The *Euryalus*'s high poop hid most of the *Impulsive* from view, but he could see her furled topgallants and whipping masthead pendant, and just as easily picture Herrick standing stolidly on his deck, feet apart, with those bright blue eyes watching the flagship.

Keverne asked quietly, 'Do you think the Frogs have guessed what we are about, sir?'

Bolitho gauged the distance for the tenth time between the two small divisions. Captain Rattray's *Zeus* was about three cables distant, and he saw a gleam of scarlet as her marines began to climb up to the fighting tops. The best marksmen would be in dire need today.

He replied, 'Our divisions are so ill-matched that I hope the French admiral imagines us to be unprepared.'

As well he might, he thought grimly. Five ships in two unequal divisions approaching that unwavering line like huntsmen trotting towards some unbreakable barrier.

He looked once more at his own ship. Keverne had cleared for action in eight minutes in spite of everything else. From the moment the drummer boys had started their nerve-jarring tattoo the seamen and marines had gone to quarters with the intentness of men under sentence of death. Now there was only silence. Only here and there was there any movement. A ship's boy scampering with sand to give the gun crews better grip on the deck. Fittock, the gunner, in his felt slippers making his way once again down to the threatening gloom of the magazine.

Nets were rigged above the decks and chain slings on each yard, and at every hatch an armed marine had been posted to prevent those terrified by the sights of battle from fleeing below to illusionary safety.

How clean and open it all seemed. The boats were either cast adrift or being towed astern, and below the gangways he could see the gun crews, naked to the waist, as they stared at their open ports and waited for bedlam to begin.

And it would not be long. He raised a glass and steadied it upon the leading enemy ship. She was less than two miles away on the larboard bow and therefore almost directly across *Zeus*'s line of advance.

She was strangely familiar, but it had taken Partridge to explain the reason. He had said with professional interest, 'I knows 'er, sir. *Le Glorieux*, Vice-Admiral Duplay's flagship. Met up with 'er once off Toulon.'

Of course he should have seen it. It was like the one additional twist of fate, for *Le Glorieux* came from the same yard as *Euryalus*, to the same specifications down to the last keel bolt. But for her colouring, the broad scarlet stripes between her gunports, she was an exact twin of his own command.

He shifted the glass slowly to starboard and then held it on the two vessels in the middle of the line. Unlike the rest, they wore the red and yellow colours of Spain, placed for security's sake in the centre where they could follow their admiral without having to display too much initiative. Initiative which had already cost their French allies dearly at St Vincent.

He heard Calvert murmuring to Midshipman Tothill, and when he lowered the glass saw him poring over the signal book, as if giving one last effort to make himself useful. Poor Calvert. If he survived this day, arrest and trial awaited him in England. Draffen's friends would see to that.

Bolitho turned and saw Pascoe standing by the quarterdeck nine-pounders, a hand resting on his hip, and one foot on a bollard. The boy did not see him and was staring towards the enemy line.

He said to Keverne, 'If possible we will break through by the Spanish ships. It will be the weakest point, if I am any judge.'

Keverne was watching *Zeus*. 'And Captain Rattray, sir?'

Bolitho looked at him gravely. 'He will act as he sees fit.' He thought of Rattray's heavy, bulldog face and guessed he would need no urging to close with the enemy. Only one thing counted now, that they could separate the French flagship from her consorts long enough to break the line and obtain the advantage of the wind. After that it would be every man for himself.

Vice-Admiral Broughton strode out into the sunlight and nodded curtly to the officers on the quarterdeck.

For a moment longer he looked at the lee division of ships, his eyes clouded with doubt and anxiety. Then he said, 'The din of battle I can endure. But the waiting is torture.'

Bolitho watched him thoughtfully. He appeared calmer again. Or was it resignation? The admiral was wearing his beautiful sword, and beneath his coat the scarlet ribbon of the Bath. Was he so despairing that he was even offering himself as target to some French marksman? All at once he felt sorry for Broughton. Recriminations and accusations were pointless now. He was watching his squadron and his proud hopes sailing towards what must seem certain destruction.

He asked, 'Will you walk a while, Sir Lucius? I find it helps ease the tension.'

Broughton fell in step beside him without protest, and as they strode slowly up and down Bolitho added quietly, 'The centre of the line is the best choice, sir. Two Spanish seventy-fours.'

Broughton nodded. 'Yes, I saw them. Astern of them is the

second-in-command.' He halted suddenly and snapped. 'Where the hell is *Coquette*?'

'She is making good some repairs, sir. *Auriga* too has suffered damage to foremast and mizzen.' He added quietly, 'They will not be of much use yet.'

Broughton looked at him for several seconds, his eyes very still. Then he asked, 'Will our people fight?' He held up his hand urgently. 'I mean *really* fight?'

Bolitho turned away. 'Have no fear on that score. I know them, and . . .'

Broughton interrupted, 'And they know *you*.'

'Yes, sir.'

When he looked forward again the enemy line had extended itself across either bow, so that it seemed to hide all of the horizon with a wall of sails. At any moment now the French admiral might guess what was happening, in which case they were beaten before they had made even the smallest impression on him. Had they been given more time, or better still the fluidity and independence denied to them by Broughton's rigid demands, they could have sent some meaningless signal to Rattray and the others. It would have made the enemy believe that at any moment now they would tack and engage his line in the same hidebound traditional style still approved by so many. But without previous experiments of that sort, any false signal would throw their meagre resources into terrible and fatal confusion.

Unless . . . He looked at Broughton's strained profile.

'May I suggest a general signal before the one to engage, sir?' He saw a nerve jumping in Broughton's throat, but his eyes were unblinking as he stared at the oncoming ships. He persisted. 'From you, sir.'

'Me?' Broughton turned and looked at him with surprise.

'You said earlier that our people know *me*, sir. But this is my ship, and they understand my ways, as I have tried to appreciate theirs.' He gestured towards *Zeus*. 'But all these ships are *yours*, and they are depending on you today.'

Broughton shook his head. 'I cannot do it.'

'May I speak, sir?' It was Calvert. 'The signal should read "My trust is in you"' He flushed as Keverne strode towards him and clapped him on the shoulder.

'By God, Mr Calvert, I never thought you had the imagination!'

Broughton licked his lips. 'If you really believe . . .'

Bolitho nodded to Tothill. 'I do, sir. Now get that bent on and hoisted immediately. We have little time left.'

He saw the sunlight flashing on glass as several officers on *Zeus*'s poop watched the sudden array of flags streaming from *Euryalus*'s yards.

But he turned swiftly as the air quaked and shook to a sudden roar of gunfire. The French flagship had fired, the orange flame spurting from gun after gun as she discharged a slow broadside towards the oncoming squadron. With the approach being diagonal, most of the balls were blind, and he saw them ripping through the short wave crests and throwing up waterspouts far beyond the lee division. The smoke rolled down from the enemy in a steep brown fog, until only *Zeus*'s topmasts were visible.

Broughton was gripping his sword-hilt, his face tight with fixed concentration as another French ship fired and a ball slapped through the fore topsail and shrieked away over the water.

Bolitho said tersely, '*Listen*, sir!' He strode to the admiral's side. 'Hear them?'

Faintly above the wind and the dying echo of cannon fire came the sound of cheering, distorted and vague, as if the ships themselves were calling the tune. As word was shouted from gun to gun and deck to deck the *Euryalus*'s seamen joined in, their voices suddenly loud and engulfing. Some stood back from the main deck twelve-pounders and waved to Broughton, who still stood like a statue, his face as stiff as his shoulders.

Bolitho said quietly, 'You see, sir? They don't ask for much.'

He turned away as Broughton muttered, 'God help me!'

More ships were firing now, and some of the balls were flicking across the water close by, and he saw several holes in the *Zeus*'s sails as she continued purposefully into the smoke.

He turned as Broughton said firmly, 'I am ready. Signal the squadron to engage.' Before he hurried back to the rail he saw that Broughton's eyes were bright with shock or surprise at hearing the cheers. Cheers for a short, trite signal which at the threshold of death could mean so much.

Bolitho shouted, 'Make the signal, Mr Tothill!' To Keverne, 'Man the braces. We will endeavour to keep station on *Zeus* until the last moment.'

More crashes echoed across the shrinking arrowhead of

water, and he felt the deck shudder as some hit home. He saw Meheux walking behind the forward guns, his sword bared as he spoke to some of the crews, his round face completely absorbed.

'Ready, sir!'

Bolitho raised his hand very slowly. '*Steady*, Mr Partridge!' He felt the pain throbbing in his shoulder to mark the rising tension in his blood. His hand sliced down. '*Now!*'

The flags vanished from *Euryalus*'s yards, and while men threw themselves on the braces and the wheel squealed against the rudder lines he saw the French line changing as if on a great gate, swinging across the bowsprit until *Euryalus* was pointing directly towards it at right-angles.

A quick glance told him *Zeus* was leading her own division in obedience to the signal, her sails flapping violently as more balls screamed through them from the enemy guns. But instead of a converging bunch of ships, the French gunners now had the more slender targets to compete with. End on, their gun-decks still silent, the two British lines moved steadily towards them, although because of the gentle turn to starboard *Euryalus* was a good ship's length ahead of *Zeus*.

Bolitho gripped the rail as smoke rolled down from the flashing guns. Iron shrieked above the quarterdeck, and here and there a severed line or block fell unheeded on the taut nets.

'Steady!'

He wiped his eyes as more smoke swirled above the deck and watched the nearest set of topmasts standing, as if detached, fine on the larboard bow. He felt the deck jerk again as more shots smashed into the hull, and recalled suddenly the time he had described the superiority of her French build to Draffen. It was macabre to think of him down in the undisturbed darkness of a lower hold in his cask of spirits while the rest of them waited to fight and die.

He strode to the nettings as a small patch of colour showed itself above the smoke. The Spanish flag was flapping from her gaff, and he knew he had not mistimed his approach.

'Stand by on the gundecks!'

He saw the midshipmen scamper to the hatchways and imagined Weigall and Sawle down there in their world of semi-darkness, the great muzzles glinting perhaps in the open ports.

Meheux was facing aft, his eyes fixed on the quarterdeck,

and Bolitho noticed that he had his sword sloped across his shoulder as if on parade.

With sudden alarm he clapped his hand to his hip and said, 'My sword!'

Allday ran forward. 'But, Captain, you can't use it yet!'

'Get it!' Bolitho touched his side and marvelled at the stupid value he had given to wearing the sword. And yet it *was* important to him, although he could not put words to it.

He waited as Allday slipped the belt around his waist and said, 'Left-handed or not, I may need it today.'

The coxswain took up his position by the nettings and watched him fixedly. While he had his cutlass the captain would not need his arm, he would lay an oath on that.

A new sound made several faces turn upwards. Screaming and sobbing, like some crazed spirit, it passed overhead and faded into the drifting smoke.

Bolitho said shortly, 'Chain shot.'

The French usually tried to dismast or cripple an enemy if at all possible, whereas the British gunnery was normally directed at the hulls, to do as much damage and create sufficient carnage to encourage surrender.

The smoke glowed red and orange, and he heard cries from the forecastle as more chain shot scythed past the carronades to cut away shrouds and rigging like grass.

A strong down-eddy of wind thrust the smoke to one side, and while gunfire continued up and down the enemy line Bolitho saw the nearest Spanish seventy-four less than half a cable from the larboard bow. Just before the smoke billowed down again she stood there on the glittering water, clear and bright, her gold scrollwork and elegant counter throwing back reflections, while on her tall poop there were already flashes of musket fire.

To starboard the second Spanish ship was wallowing slightly out of line, her jib and fore topsail in torment as her captain tried to avoid the oncoming three-decker.

When he looked at Broughton he found him as before. Standing motionless with his hands hanging at his sides as if too stricken to move.

'Sir! Walk about!' He pointed at the nearest ship. 'There are sharpshooters there this morning!'

As if to verify his warning several splinters rose like feathers from the planking, and a man beside a gun screamed in agony as a ball smashed into his breast. He was dragged away gasping and protesting, knowing in spite of his pain what awaited him on the orlop.

Broughton came out of his trance and began to pace up and down. He did not even flinch as a corpse bounced down from the main yard and rolled across the nets before pitching overboard. He seemed beyond fear or feeling. A man already dead.

More crashes and thuds against the hull, and then as the smoke cleared once again Bolitho saw the Spanish ship's stern swinging level with the foremast. They were passing through the line, and the realization almost unnerved him. He gripped the rail and tried to make himself heard above the din.

'Both batteries, Mr Meheux! Pass the word!' Fumbling and cursing, he tried to draw his sword with his left hand. It was hopeless.

A voice said, 'Here, let me, sir.' It was Pascoe.

Bolitho took the worn hilt in his hand and smiled at him. 'Thank you, Adam.' Was he thinking the same in that small fragment of time? That this old sword would be his too one day?

He held it above his head, seeing the hazed sunlight touch the keen blade before the smoke rolled inboard again.

'As you bear!' He counted the seconds, *'Fire!'*

The ship gave a terrible lurch as deck by deck, gun by gun, the deadly broadsides flashed and bellowed from either beam. He heard the groan of falling spars, the sudden screams in the smoke, and knew that the nearest ship had been badly mauled. And it had not even begun. The lower batteries of thirty-two-pounders were roaring above all else, their recoil shaking the hull to its very keel as their double-shotted bombardment raked the two ships with merciless accuracy. The one to starboard had lost both her fore and main topmasts, and charred canvas dropped alongside like so much rubbish. The nearest two-decker was idling downwind, her steering gone and her stern gaping to the sunlight like a great black cave. What the broadside had done within her gundecks was past speculation.

A blurred shape was edging around the other Spaniard, and Bolitho guessed it must be the French second-in-command. *Euryalus*'s lower battery had already reloaded and raked the Frenchman's bows almost before she had drawn clear of her consort. He saw her guns belching fire and smoke, and knew she was shooting with little attention to accuracy.

'Stand by to tack, Mr Partridge!'

They were through. Already the disabled seventy-four was lost in smoke and there seemed an immense gap before another ship, the third in the line, could be seen.

Yards creaking and voices yelling above the thunder and crash of gunfire, *Euryalus* turned slowly to follow the enemy line. The difference was startling. With the wind's advantage on their side it was possible to watch the enemy unhindered by gunsmoke, and he breathed with relief as the deck cleared and he saw that masts and yards were still whole. The sails were pitted with holes, and there were several men lying dead and wounded. Some had been hit by marksmen in the enemy's tops, but most had been clawed down by flying wood splinters.

Somewhere astern there was a sickening crash, and when he leaned over the nettings he stared with disbelief as *Impulsive* swung drunkenly in a welter of broken spars, her passage through the enemy's line only half completed. Her foremast had gone completely, and only her mizzen topsail appeared to be intact. There were great gaps in her tumblehome, and even as he watched he saw her main topmast fall crashing into the smoke to drag alongside and pull her still further under the guns of a French two-decker. Chain shot had all but dismasted her, and he could already see another French ship tacking across her stern to rake her, as *Euryalus* had just done to the Spaniard.

He made himself turn back to his own ship, but his ears refused to block out the sounds of that terrible broadside. He saw Pascoe staring through the smoke, his eyes wide with horror.

He shouted, 'Cast the boats adrift!' The boy turned towards him, his reply lost in a sudden burst of firing from ahead. Then he ran aft, beckoning to some seamen to follow him.

Bolitho watched coldly as the wind pushed his ship steadily towards the next Frenchman's quarter. He was staring at her stern, knowing that her captain would either stay and fight or try to turn downwind. In which case he was doomed, as *Impulsive* had been. He had to grind his teeth together to stop himself from speaking Herrick's name aloud. Casting the boats adrift had been more to ease the boy's pain than with any hope of saving more than a handful of survivors.

Almost savagely he shouted, 'Stand by on the fo'c'sle, Mr Meheux! Carronade this one!'

'Fire!'

The first guns roared out from the larboard battery, and then the air shivered to the deeper bang of a carronade. Timber and pieces of bulwark flew from the enemy's poop, and the mizzen, complete with tricolour, toppled into the rolling bank of smoke.

Broughton was shouting at him. 'Look! God damn it!' He was all but jumping with excitement as like a great finger a jib boom and then a glaring figurehead thrust ahead of the nearest ship.

'*Zeus* has broken the line!' Keverne waved his hat in the air. 'God, look at her!'

Zeus came through firing from either beam, her sails in rags and most of her side pitted and blackened with holes. Thin tendrils of scarlet ran from her scuppers, as if the ship herself was bleeding, and Bolitho knew that Rattray had fought hard and at a great price to follow the flagship's example.

As far as he could tell the action had become general. Guns hammered from ahead and astern, and there were ships locked in combat on every hand. Gone was the prim French line, as were Broughton's divisions. Gone too was the French admiral's control, separated as he was downwind, blinded by smoke in a sea gone mad with battle.

Broughton shouted, 'General signal! Form line ahead and astern of admiral!'

Tothill nodded violently and ran to his men. There was not much chance of anyone complying, but it would show the others that Broughton was still in command.

And there was *Tanais*, her mizzen gone, her forecastle a splintered shambles, but most of her guns firing as she raked the enemy and pushed after *Zeus*, her ensign ripped by musket fire as she passed.

More gunfire echoed through the smoke, and Bolitho knew it must be Furneaux fighting for his life in a press of disabled but nevertheless deadly ships.

'Ship on the starboard quarter, sir!'

Bolitho hurried across the deck and saw a French two-decker, unmarked, her sails showing not a single hole, thrusting towards him, her speed gaining as she set her forecourse and topgallants, so that she leaned heavily under the pressure.

While everyone else had been engaged, her captain had

taken his ship out of the line to try to regain an advantage. As she turned slightly, shortening her silhouette until almost bows on, Bolitho saw the *Impulsive*. Dismasted, she was so settled in the water that her lower gunports were already awash. A few tiny figures moved vaguely on her listing decks and others were jumping overboard, probably too stricken by the slaughter to know what they were doing.

Keverne asked harshly, 'Do you think many of them will survive?'

'Not many.' Bolitho looked at him steadily. 'She was a good ship.'

Keverne watched him as he walked back to the rail. To Pascoe he said, 'He is taking it badly. In spite of his bluff, I know him well by now.'

Pascoe glanced astern at the sinking ship beneath her great pall of drifting smoke. 'His best friend.' He looked away, his eyes blind. 'Mine, too.'

'Deck there!' Maybe the masthead lookout had been calling before. Amidst all the noise his voice would have been unnoticed. Keverne looked up as the man yelled hoarsely, 'Ship, sir! On the larboard bow!'

Bolitho gripped his sword in his left hand until his fingers ached. Through the shrouds and stays, just a fraction to larboard of the massive foremast, he saw her. Wreathed in the endless curtain of gunsmoke she loomed like a giant, her braced yards almost fore and aft as she edged very slowly across *Euryalus*'s course.

Bolitho felt the hatred and unreasoning fury running through him like fire. *Le Glorieux*, the French admiral's flagship, was coming to greet him, to repay him for the shameful destruction done to his ships and his overwhelming confidence.

He seized the sword even tighter, blinded by his hatred and sense of loss. She, above all, would be Herrick's memorial.

'Stand by to engage!' He pointed his sword at Meheux. 'Pass the word! Double-shotted and grape for good measure!' He saw Broughton staring at him and rasped, 'Your contemporary lies yonder, sir.' He could feel his eyes stinging and knew Broughton was speaking to him. But he could see nothing but Herrick's face staring up through the smoke as his ship died under him.

Broughton swung round and then strode along the starboard gangway, his epaulettes glinting in the dim sunlight.

His feet seemed to be carrying him in spite of his wishes, and as he walked above the smoke-grimed gun crews he paused to nod to them or to wish them good luck. Some watched him pass, dull-eyed and too dazed to care. Others gave him a grin and a wave. A gun-captain spat on his heated twelve-pounder and croaked, 'Us'll give 'ee a victory, Sir Lucius, don' you fret on it!'

Broughton stopped and seized the nettings for support. Aft, above the chattering seamen and the marines who were already levelling their muskets through the smoke, he saw Bolitho. The man who had somehow given these men a faith so strong they could not weaken even if they wanted to. And in their own way they were sharing it with him.

Bolitho was quite motionless by the rail, the sling white against his coat and the sword hanging in his hand by his side. He saw too the captain's coxswain at his back, and Pascoe watching him with something like despair.

It was then that he made up his mind. Bolitho had given them, and him, all this, yet now that he was crushed by grief none of them could help.

Almost angrily he strode aft and snapped, 'By God, we'll teach that fellow a lesson, eh, lads?' He felt his tight skin cracking into a grin. 'How about it, Mr Keverne? Another three-decker for the fleet!'

Keverne swallowed hard. 'As you wish, sir.'

Bolitho lifted his head and looked at him. 'Thank you, Sir Lucius.' He sighed and rested his sword on the top of the rail. 'Thank you.'

When he looked again at the French flagship she seemed much clearer. And his mind had become empty of everything but the need to destroy her.

Broughton was on the opposite side of the quarterdeck and peering at the French two-decker.

'She's wearing!' He gestured to Bolitho. 'Look!'

Bolitho saw the enemy ship swinging heavily away to expose her full broadside to *Euryalus*'s starboard quarter. Either her captain had failed in a first intention to cross their stern, or had changed his mind about drawing too near.

Then the Frenchman fired. Being the first time she had taken part in the desperate battle the broadside was well timed and aimed, and as the thick smoke billowed along her hull Bolitho felt the deck lurch sickeningly, the air suddenly alive with splinters and that terrible screaming sound they had heard earlier.

The deck gave one more tremendous lurch, and as his hearing returned he heard Giffard yelling, 'The mizzen! The bastards have got it!'

Before he could follow Giffard's agonized stare he saw the slicing shadow sweep across the poop, as with rigging and shrouds and screaming men falling on every hand the mizzen, complete with topsail and yards, thundered amongst them.

Trailing lines and braces tore through the crouching gun crews and startled marines like deadly snakes, as with a further savage crash the mast toppled drunkenly over the side. Another blaze of gun flashes made the smoke writhe above the deck, and he felt the chain shot whirling overhead and crashing into the hull with a scream of metal.

Blackened figures pushed past him, and he saw Tebbutt, the boatswain, waving an axe, urging his men to hack away the great weight of wreckage alongside. Mast and spars, mangled corpses and a few trapped seamen from the top who were still trying to struggle free before they were carried astern, all were acting like a sea anchor, dragging the ship round in a nightmare of smoke and deafening explosions.

Where there had been a line of marines seconds earlier was a grotesque heap of ripped and pulped bodies, broken muskets and a fast-spreading pattern of blood. Giffard was already yelling orders, and other marines were stepping blindly amongst the carnage to fire their muskets into the choking smoke.

In the middle of it all Bolitho saw Broughton dragging a sobbing midshipman to the shelter of the mainmast trunk, his hat gone, but his voice as sharp as ever as he yelled, 'Reload and run out, damn you! Hit 'em, lads! *Hit 'em!*'

Bolitho climbed over a great pile of fallen blocks and cordage, almost blinded by smoke, and shouted, 'Mr Partridge! More men on the wheel! She's broaching to!'

But the master did not hear. One section of chain shot had cut his rotund body almost in half, so that Bolitho had to fight back the vomit as he saw the horror below the poop.

Part of the double wheel had been carried away, but cursing and gasping more seamen slithered and stumbled towards it, throwing themselves on the spokes.

With a long shudder the mizzen slipped clear of its lashings and plunged into the sea. Bolitho felt the ship responding almost immediately, but as he pushed past some more hurrying figures he saw the French flagship and knew it was too late. With his ears and brain cringing against the thunder of the thirty-two-pounders he tried to think of some last-minute alternative. But the pull of the heavy mizzen, the momentary loss of control by the rudder, had thrown *Euryalus* off course, so that now her bowsprit was pointing directly at the enemy's forecastle. Collision was unavoidable, and even had there been greater distance between them, the sails were too pitted, too torn to give anything but small steerage way.

He saw Keverne and yelled, 'Up forrard! Repel boarders!'

More crashes rocked the hull, and he watched the French two-decker passing slowly down the starboard side, her guns firing, her masts and sails unharmed.

He pulled himself to the rail and sought out Meheux in the confusion of smoke and yelling gun crews. He saw the shining bodies of half-naked seamen, powder-blackened and almost inhuman as they hurled themselves on the tackles and sent the gun trucks rumbling and squealing back to the ports. Up and down the line captains jerked their lanyards and the muzzles spat out tongues of flame, while the smoke came funnelling inboard to blind and torment the desperate crews.

But Meheux needed no telling. He was crouching beside one of the guns, shouting at its captain, his eyes very bright in his grimy face. More balls screamed above the deck, and a seaman who had been running with a message fell in a flounder of arms and legs, his head lopped off by the ball.

Then Meheux raised his sword, and the gun crews stooped and crouched behind their ports like athletes awaiting a signal.

'On the uproll!' Meheux glared along his line of men. '*Fire!*'

Every one fired at once, and Bolitho saw the Frenchman's foremast and main topmast vanish into the smoke together. The lower batteries were firing again, and hampered by her trailing spars the French two-decker took the broadsides again and again. When the smoke drifted above the *Euryalus* there was no more firing from the enemy.

Bolitho almost fell as the bowsprit and jib boom ploughed into the French flagship's shrouds and with a further grinding convulsion both hulls came together.

The smoke was bright with darting flashes of muskets and

swivels, and Bolitho watched Lieutenant Cox of the marines leading his men across the forecastle to close with the enemy.

Below decks the larboard guns recommenced firing, as swinging like parts of a mammoth hinge the two ships angled towards each other. Right forward the gun muzzles were almost touching, and Bolitho felt the enemy's shots crashing through the hull, upending guns and turning the lower batteries into places of slaughter and stark horror.

Musket balls ricocheted and whined around the exposed quarterdeck, and Meheux peered at the maintop where the swivel gunners were firing towards the enemy's poop.

He yelled, 'Shoot down those marksmen!' But the noise was so great they did not hear. Desperately he climbed on to the gangway and cupped his hands to try again. A marine, wild-eyed and grinning, peered down at him and then swung the swivel towards the other ship's maintop. Even as he jerked the lanyard Meheux took a ball full in the stomach, and with his eyes already glazing in stunned surprise he rolled over the rail and fell unseen beside one of his beloved twelve-pounders.

Broughton watched the French marksmen as they fell to the vicious canister. Some hung kicking across the enemy's main yard and others, more fortunate, fell to the deck below and died instantly.

Then he said calmly, 'Our people are not holding them off.'

Bolitho looked along the larboard gangway and saw the enemy boarders already overflowing on to the forecastle, while others swayed back and forth between the two hulls, steel against steel, pike against musket.

Here and there a man would fall out of sight to be ground between the two massive bilges, or a solitary figure would find himself isolated on his enemy's deck to be hacked down with neither thought nor mercy.

A marine officer dropped screaming, his white crossbelt already soaked in blood, and Giffard snarled, 'Cox is gone!' Then with an oath he was charging along the gangway, soon to be lost in the packed mass of figures.

The two hulls were grinding closer and closer, and with a violent jerk *Euryalus*'s bowsprit splintered and tore free, the jib flapping uselessly above the confusion like a banner.

More men were clambering across from the other ship, and Bolitho saw some of them fighting their way steadily aft towards the quarterdeck. A young lieutenant appeared as if by magic on the ladder, his sword swinging as he hurled himself across the deck. Bolitho tried to parry him to one side, but saw the French officer's eyes wild with triumph as he knocked the blade away and turned on his heels for the fatal blow.

Calvert thrust Bolitho aside, his face calm as he snapped, 'This one is mine sir, sir!' His blade moved so fast that Bolitho did not see it. Only the Frenchman's face slashed from eye to chin as he reeled gasping against the rail. Calvert's wrist turned deftly and then he lunged, taking the Frenchman in the heart.

He said, '*Amateur!*' Then he was down amongst more of the attackers, his hair flying as he sought out another officer and fought him back against the ladder.

Keverne staggered through the smoke, blood dripping from his forehead. 'Sir!' He ducked beneath a swinging cutlass and fired his pistol into the man's groin, the force of the shot hurling him bodily amongst the others. 'We must get clear!'

His voice was very loud, and Bolitho realized dazedly that the guns had ceased firing. Through open ports on both ships men jabbed at one another with pikes or fired pistols in a madness of hatred and despair.

Bolitho gripped Keverne's arm, his sword hanging from his wrist on its lanyard. 'What is it, man?'

'I—I'm not sure, but . . .'

Keverne pulled Bolitho against him and thrust at a yelling seaman with his sword. The man faltered, and Bolitho saw Allday run from aft, his cutlass driving forward and down with such force that the cutlass's point appeared through his stomach.

Keverne retched and gasped, 'The Frenchman's afire, sir!'

Bolitho saw the admiral slip to his knees, groping for his sword, and watched helplessly as a French petty officer charged towards him with a bayoneted musket.

A slim figure blocked his path and Bolitho heard himself yell, 'Adam! *Get back!*'

But Pascoe stood his ground, armed only with a dirk, his face a mask of stricken determination.

The bayonet lunged, but at the last second another figure jumped through the smoke, his sword dark with blood as he parried the blade up and clear of the boy's chest. The musket exploded, and Pascoe stood back, horrified as Calvert crumpled at his feet, his face blown away. With a sob he struck at the

petty officer with his dirk, hurting him sufficiently to make him recoil. Allday's cutlass finished it.

Bolitho tore his eyes away and hurried to the side. Beyond the enemy's mainmast he could see a steady plume of black smoke. Figures darted down the hatchway, and he heard sudden cries of alarm, the urgent clatter of pumps.

Perhaps in the confusion a lantern had been upended, or a blazing wad from one of the guns had found its way through an open port. But there was no mistaking the signs of fire, nor the desperate urgency now needed to get clear.

He shouted, 'Pass the word. Lower battery reload. Fire on the order!'

He stared round at the shattered planking, the sprawled corpses and sobbing wounded. It was a faint hope, but it was all he had. Unless they got away from *Le Glorieux's* embrace they would become one inferno together.

A midshipman yelled, 'Ready, sir!' It was Ashton.

'Fire!'

Seconds later the lower battery erupted in a great, blasting roar. It felt as if the ship would fall apart, and as smoke and pieces of wreckage flew high above the nettings Bolitho saw the other ship reel drunkenly under the full weight of the lower battery's broadside.

The French flagship's sails were still drawing and quivering in the wind, and as she idled clear she began to move slowly towards the *Euryalus's* bows. The smoke was rising thickly from her main hatch, and Bolitho felt himself shaking uncontrollably as the first tip of flame licked above the coaming like a forked tongue.

All resistance had ceased on *Euryalus's* deck, and the French boarders left behind by their ship watched in silence, their hands in the air, as *Le Glorieux* continued to draw away.

Broughton said hoarsely, 'They're finished!' There was neither pride nor satisfaction in his voice. Like the others, he sounded completely crushed by the ferocity of the battle.

Tothill limped to the rail. '*Zeus* is signalling, sir.'

When Bolitho looked down at him he saw the midshipman was grinning even though uncontrollable tears were cutting sharp lines through the grime on his face.

He asked quietly, 'Well, Mr Tothill?'

'Two of the enemy have struck to us, sir. One has sunk, and the rest are breaking off the action.'

Bolitho sighed and watched with silent relief as the enemy flagship began to drift more swiftly downwind. As the smoke of battle faded reluctantly away he saw the other ships scattered across the sea's face, scarred and blackened from conflict. Of *Impulsive* there was no sign, and he saw the sloop *Restless*, which must have arrived unseen in the battle, drifting above her shadow, her boats in the water searching for survivors.

He felt a sudden heat on his cheek, and when he turned saw the French three-decker's sails and rigging ablaze like torches. The lower gunports were also glowing bright red, and before a man could speak the air was torn apart with one deafening explosion.

The smoke surrounded the destruction, changing to steam as with a jubilant roar the sea surged into the shattered hull, dragging it down in a welter of bubbles and terrible sounds. Guns crashed from their tackles, and men trapped below in total darkness ran in madness until caught by either sea or fire.

When the smoke finally cleared there was only a great, slow-moving whirlpool, around which the flotsam and human fragments joined in one last horrible dance. Then there was nothing.

Broughton cleared his throat. 'A victory.' He watched the wounded being carried or dragged below. Then he looked at Calvert and added, 'But the bill is greater.'

Bolitho said dully, 'We will commence repairs, sir. The wind has eased slightly . . .' He paused and rubbed his knuckles into his eyes, trying to think. '*Valorous* looks in a bad way. I think *Tanais* can take her in tow.'

He heard distant cheering and saw the men on the *Zeus*'s battered forecastle waving and yelling as they edged past. They could still cheer after all that. He turned to watch as some of his own company scrambled into the shrouds to return the cheers.

He said quietly, 'With men like these, Sir Lucius, you never need fear again.'

But Broughton had not heard him. He was unbuckling his beautiful sword, and with a small hesitation handed it to Pascoe.

'Here, take it. When I needed it, I dropped it.' He added gruffly, 'Any damn midshipman who tackles the enemy with a dirk deserves it!' He watched the astonishment on the boy's dark features. 'Besides, a *lieutenant* must look the part, eh?'

Pascoe held the sword and turned it over in his hands. Then he looked at Bolitho, but he was standing rigidly by the rail, his fingers gripping it so tightly that they were white.

'Sir?' He hurried to his side, suddenly fearful that Bolitho had been wounded again. 'Look, sir!'

Bolitho released the rail and put his arm round the boy's thin shoulders. He was desperately tired, and the pain in his wound was like a branding iron. But just a little longer.

Very slowly he said, 'Adam. Tell me.' He swallowed hard. He could barely risk speaking. 'That boat.'

Pascoe stared at his face, then down into the sea near by. A longboat was pulling towards the *Euryalus*'s shot-scarred side, crammed to the gunwales with dripping, exhausted men.

He replied hesitantly, 'Yes, Uncle. I see him, too.'

Bolitho gripped his shoulder more tightly and watched the boat's misty outline as it nudged alongside. Beside its coxswain he saw Herrick peering up at him, his strained face set in a grin while he supported a wounded marine against his chest.

Keverne came striding aft, an unspoken question on his lips, but paused as Broughton snapped, 'If you are to have *Auriga*, Mr Keverne, I would be obliged if you would take command here until such time as a transfer is possible.' He looked at Bolitho with his arm round the boy's shoulder. 'I think my flag captain has done enough.' He saw Allday hurrying down to the entry port. 'For all of us.'

313

Epilogue

THE ADMIRALTY MESSENGER ushered Bolitho and Herrick into a waiting-room and closed the door with hardly a glance. Bolitho walked to a window and looked down at the crowded highway, his mind conscious only of sudden anticlimax. It was very quiet in the waiting-room, and through the window he could feel the late September sunlight warm against his face. But down below, the people who hurried so busily about their affairs were well wrapped, and the many horses which trotted with carriages and carts in every direction gave some hint of the coming winter with their steaming breath and bright blankets.

Behind him he heard Herrick moving restlessly around the room, and wondered if like himself he was preparing for the co⁻ ing interview with resignation or anxiety.

What an unnerving place London was. No wonder the messenger had treated them with such indifference, for the entrance hall and corridors had been crammed with sea officers, few of them lowlier than captains. All intent on their own worlds of appointments, ships, or the mere necessity of appearing busy in the centre of Britain's naval power.

Nearly three months had passed since the French flagship had blasted herself apart in one terrible explosion, during which time he had been more than fully occupied getting the battered squadron to Gibraltar without further losses, and there await orders.

As the many wounded had died or made some kind of recovery, and the ships' companies had worked without respite to repair as much of the damage as possible under the Rock's limited resources, Bolitho had waited for some acknowledgement of their efforts.

Eventually a brig had arrived with despatches for Broughton. Those ships ready and able to set sail would do so immediately.

Not to join Lord St. Vincent off Cadiz, but for England. After all they had achieved and endured together it was hard to see the small squadron scattered.

Valorous was almost beyond repair, and with *Tanais*, which was in not much better state, had remained at Gibraltar. With the two French seventy-fours taken as prizes the remainder had sailed, and in due course anchored at Portsmouth. There again, the necessary business of dispersal and repair was continued. But it meant bidding farewell to many more familiar faces. Keverne, who had received his just promotion to commander, had been given *Auriga*. Captain Rattray had been carried ashore to Haslar Hospital, where with only one leg and half blinded by splinters, he would probably end his days.

Furneaux had died in battle, and Gillmor had received separate orders to take his *Coquette* and join the Channel Fleet, where as always there was a shortage of frigates.

As day had followed day in Portsmouth harbour Bolitho had found time to wonder how Broughton's report had been received at the Admiralty.

With the span of time behind him, their findings and hardships at Djafou, the last desperate battle with twice their number of the enemy seemed to fade and become less real. Broughton had appeared to feel much as he did, for most of the time he had remained aloof in his quarters or paced alone on the poop resisting every contact but the requirements of duty.

Then, just two days ago, the summons had arrived. Broughton and his flag captain were to report to the Admiralty. One unexpected addition had been for Herrick. He too was to accompany them. He had already confided that it was probably to explain more fully the loss of his *Impulsive*, but Bolitho thought otherwise. It was more likely that Herrick, being the only captain not completely involved in the squadron's previous affairs, was being called as an impartial witness and to give his own assessment. It was to be hoped he would not allow blind loyalty to damage his own position with his superiors.

But whatever happened, Adam's step on the first real rung of the ladder was secure. He had received his commission with an ease which had apparently surprised him, and even now was aboard *Euryalus*, probably fretting about his uncle's future, or lack of it.

A door opened and Broughton walked through the room towards the corridor. Bolitho had not seen him since he had left the ship, and said, 'I hope all went well, Sir Lucius?'

Broughton seemed only then aware of his presence. He eyed him flatly. 'I have been appointed to New South Wales. To manage the vessels and affairs of our naval administration there.'

Bolitho tried to disguise his dismay. 'That would appear to be quite a task, sir.'

The admiral's eyes flickered to Herrick. 'Oblivion.' He turned away. 'I hope you fare better.' Then with a curt nod he was gone.

Herrick exploded, 'By God, I know little of Broughton, but that is damned cruel! He'll rot out there while some of these powdered poppinjays in London grow fat on the efforts of such men!'

Bolitho smiled sadly. 'Easy, Thomas. I think Sir Lucius expected it.'

He turned back to the window. Oblivion. How well it described such an appointment. Yet Broughton had a name and power. A man of influence.

He thought with sudden bitterness of the *Auriga*'s chief mutineer, Tom Gates. He could see him sitting across the table in the little inn at Veryan Bay, and again confronting Captain Brice in his cabin.

Almost the first sight he had witnessed at Portsmouth Point had been the weathered remains of Gates swinging from a gibbet as a grisly reminder of the price of revolt. How strange was fate. *Auriga*'s second lieutenant had been released by the French in exchange for one of their own officers. His appointment had taken him to another frigate, where hiding under a false name he had discovered Gates. All hopes and ambition gone, and left only with the need to hide amongst his own sort, Gates had ended on a halter like so many others after the mutiny.

The door opened again and a lieutenant said, 'Sir George will see you now.' When Herrick hung back he added, 'Both of you, please.'

It was a fine room, with many pictures and a large bust of Raleigh above a lively log fire.

Admiral Sir George Beauchamp did not rise from his desk but gestured briefly to two chairs.

Bolitho watched him as he leafed through some papers. Beauchamp, distinguished for his work on reorganization at the Admiralty since the outbreak of war. A man noted for his wisdom and humour. And his severity.

He was thin and rather stooped, as if bowed down by the weight of his resplendent gold-laced coat.

'Ah, Bolitho.' He looked up, his eyes very cold and steady. 'I have been studying the reports and your findings. It makes interesting reading.'

Bolitho heard Herrick breathing heavily beside him and wondered what Beauchamp would say next.

'I knew Sir Charles Thelwall, your previous admiral.' Beauchamp eyed him calmly. 'A fine man.' He turned back to the papers again.

Still no mention of Broughton. It was almost unnerving.

The admiral asked, 'Do you still believe what you did and that which you discovered was worthwhile?'

Bolitho replied quietly, 'Yes, sir.' The question had been casually put, yet he believed it summed up all that had gone before. He added, 'The French will keep trying. They must be held. And stopped.'

'Your action at Djafou and handling of what must have appeared a hopeless situation was good. Sir Lucius said as much in his report.' He frowned. 'As well he might.'

'Thank you, sir.'

The admiral ignored him. 'New tactics and ideas, fresh objectives, all are necessary if we are to survive, let alone win this war. But the knowledge and understanding of the people who have to fight and die for our cause is *vital*!' He shrugged wearily. 'You have that understanding. Whereas . . .' He left the rest unsaid, but in Bolitho's brain the word returned. Oblivion.

Beauchamp peered at a gilt clock. 'You will remain in London for a day or so while I arrange your new orders. Understood?'

Bolitho nodded, 'Yes, sir.'

The admiral walked to a window and studied the passing carriages and townspeople with apparent disdain. 'Captain Herrick will leave for Portsmouth immediately.'

Herrick asked thickly, 'May I ask the reason, sir?'

Beauchamp faced them again, his mouth set in a thin smile. '*Commodore* Bolitho will be hoisting his broad pendant in

Euryalus as soon as he returns to Portsmouth.' He looked hard at Herrick's amazed face. 'I knew he would ask for you as his flag captain, so I thought we would try and waste less time than is customary under this roof!'

He stepped forward, his hand outstretched. Seeing Bolitho's arm strapped inside his coat he offered the other hand, saying sharply, 'Our bodies too often become charts of our misfortunes, eh?' He smiled. 'I am giving you a squadron, Bolitho. Just a small one, but enough for you to put your ideas to best advantage.' His grip was firm. 'Good luck to you. I hope I've not made a mistake.'

Bolitho looked away. 'Thank you, sir.' The room seemed to be spinning. 'And for giving me Captain Herrick.'

The admiral was back at his desk. 'Oh, nonsense.' But as they left the room together he was smiling with quiet enjoyment.

Out on the highway, amidst the hurrying figures and blowing leaves, Bolitho said, 'I think maybe I am dreaming, Thomas.'

Herrick was grinning hugely, 'I can't wait to see your nephew's face when I tell him!' He shook his head. 'A broad pendant. God damn them, I thought they would *never* give you your proper reward!'

Bolitho smiled, his emotions pulling in two directions. Broughton had warned him what it would be like if he ever attained flag rank. A superior being, unreachable and beyond personal touch. It was a challenge, something he had always wanted. And yet, when the watch turned out on deck to shorten sail or to up anchor, how would it feel? Another in command of the same ship, while he remained an onlooker.

He said, 'You had best return to the inn, Thomas. If you catch the Portsmouth Flyer you can be aboard *Euryalus* tomorrow night.'

Herrick watched him, his face suddenly grave. 'I'll tell Allday to prepare things for you, sir.'

'Yes.' He touched his arm. 'We have come a long way, Thomas. And I would not have wished for a better companion, or friend.'

He watched Herrick's sturdy figure until he had vanished into a side street and then turned to stare at the busy scene around him.

He made to cross the road but paused to allow a fine pair

of greys drawing an emerald green carriage to pass. But the coachman was reining them back and had his brightly polished boot hard on the brake.

Bolitho waited, still dazed by all that had happened and the speed of life in this great city.

The carriage window opened and a voice said, 'I heard you were at the Admiralty, Captain.'

He looked at the elegant woman who was smiling down at him like a conspirator. It was Catherine Pareja.

He stammered, 'Kate!' He could find no other words.

She rapped on the roof. 'Robert! Help the captain in.' And as Bolitho sank on to the seat beside her she added, 'We will dine together.' Her mouth lifted in that familiar smile. 'And then . . .' Her laugh was lost in the rumble of wheels as the carriage moved rapidly into the throng of vehicles and horses.

From his lofty window Admiral Beauchamp watched them go and nodded thoughtfully. He had made a good choice, he decided. Definitely a man to be reckoned with.

S P A I N

0   50   100   150

Miles

Valencia •

Alicante •   C.S.
Antor

Cartagena •

• Granada

Malaga •

Algeciras

Gibraltar

M E D I T E

Tangier

• Oran

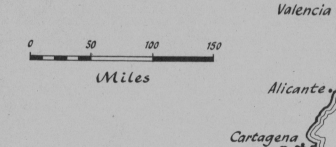